THE SHUTOUT

DIANNA ROMAN

WILD ONE PRESS

FIRST EDITION, REVISED

Published by Wild One Press
Cover design by Wild One Press

Edited by Jennifer Green
Proofread by Margaret Neal

ISBN 979-8-9853313-2-5 (ebook edition)
ISBN 979-8-9853313-3-2 (trade paperback)
ISBN 978-1-959553-12-0 (hardcover)

Visit the author at www.diannaroman.com

This book is not intended for readers under the age of 18.

SOMETIMES LOVE IS WHERE YOU LEAST EXPECT IT, AND SOMETIMES IT'S RIGHT WHERE YOU LEFT IT.

Widower, Max Hartwell, is barely keeping it together, being a single dad, managing his law firm, and navigating life's chaos. Life after loss is too difficult for surprises, which is why Max would be lost without his reliable best friend and neighbor, Jack.

Best pitcher in the MLB, Jack Spears, is at the top of his game. He has it all, except for the one thing he wants most, which happens to be the one thing he can't have if he doesn't want his private life to overshadow his career – love. When an emotional evening reveals his biggest secret, he's faced with losing everything that matters most to him.

Can Max see him for the man he truly is, or will Jack forever be doomed to live in the shadow of the image he created as America's favorite pitcher?

Heartfelt and human, *The Shutout* is a story of friendship, loss, love, and the rough road to new beginnings.

CONTENT ADVISORY

This story contains the following elements that some may find sensitive or triggering. Please read at your own discretion:

- Loss of a loved one
- Feelings of isolation and low self-worth
- A physical altercation
- Homophobic slurs by a side character
- Familial rejection
- Explicit consensual sexual content
- Adult language

*The term 'gypsies' is referenced in this story and was intended to refer to peoples who live a nomadic tradesman lifestyle, not what has become an ethnic derogatory for the Romani people

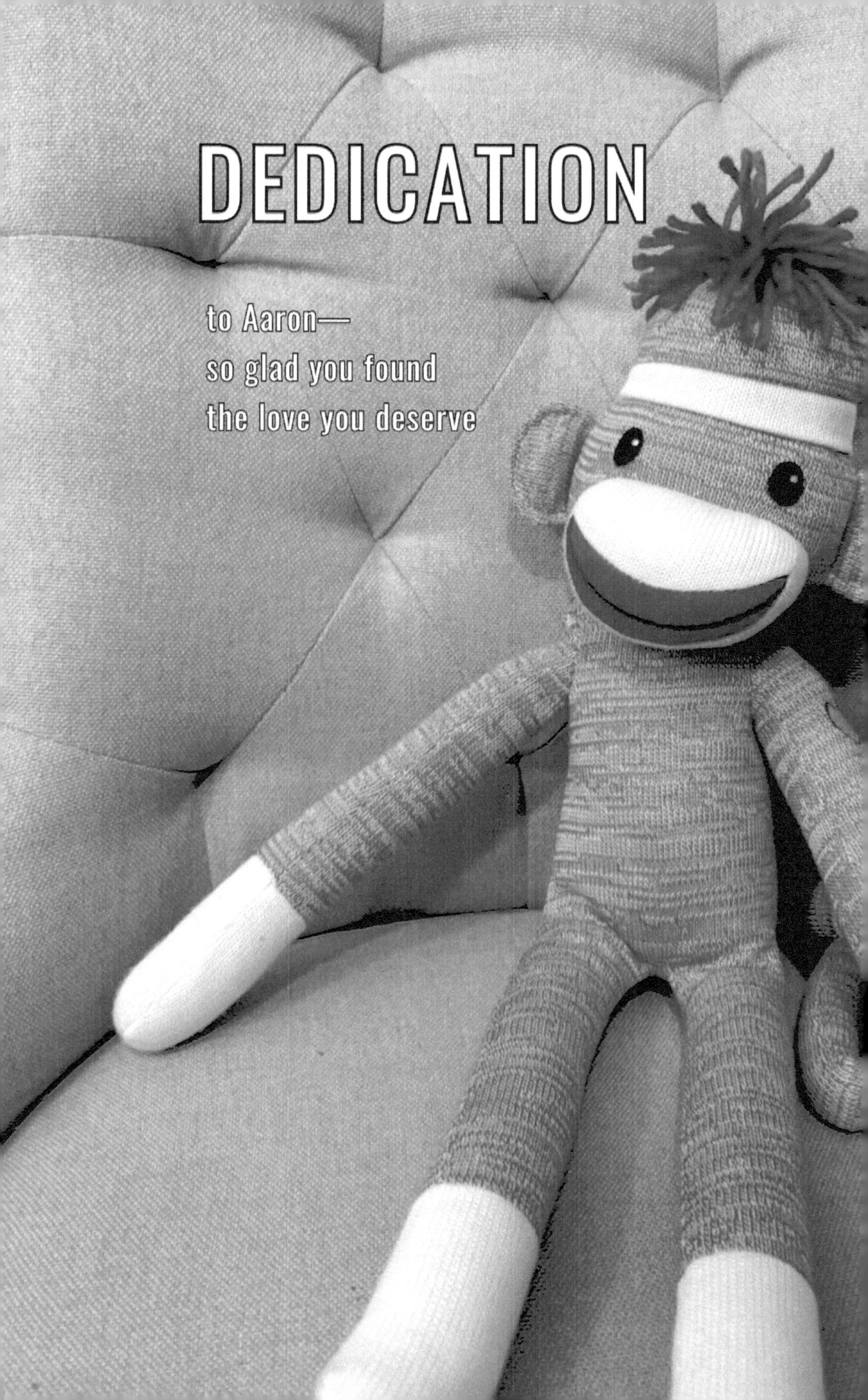

DEDICATION
to Aaron—
so glad you found
the love you deserve

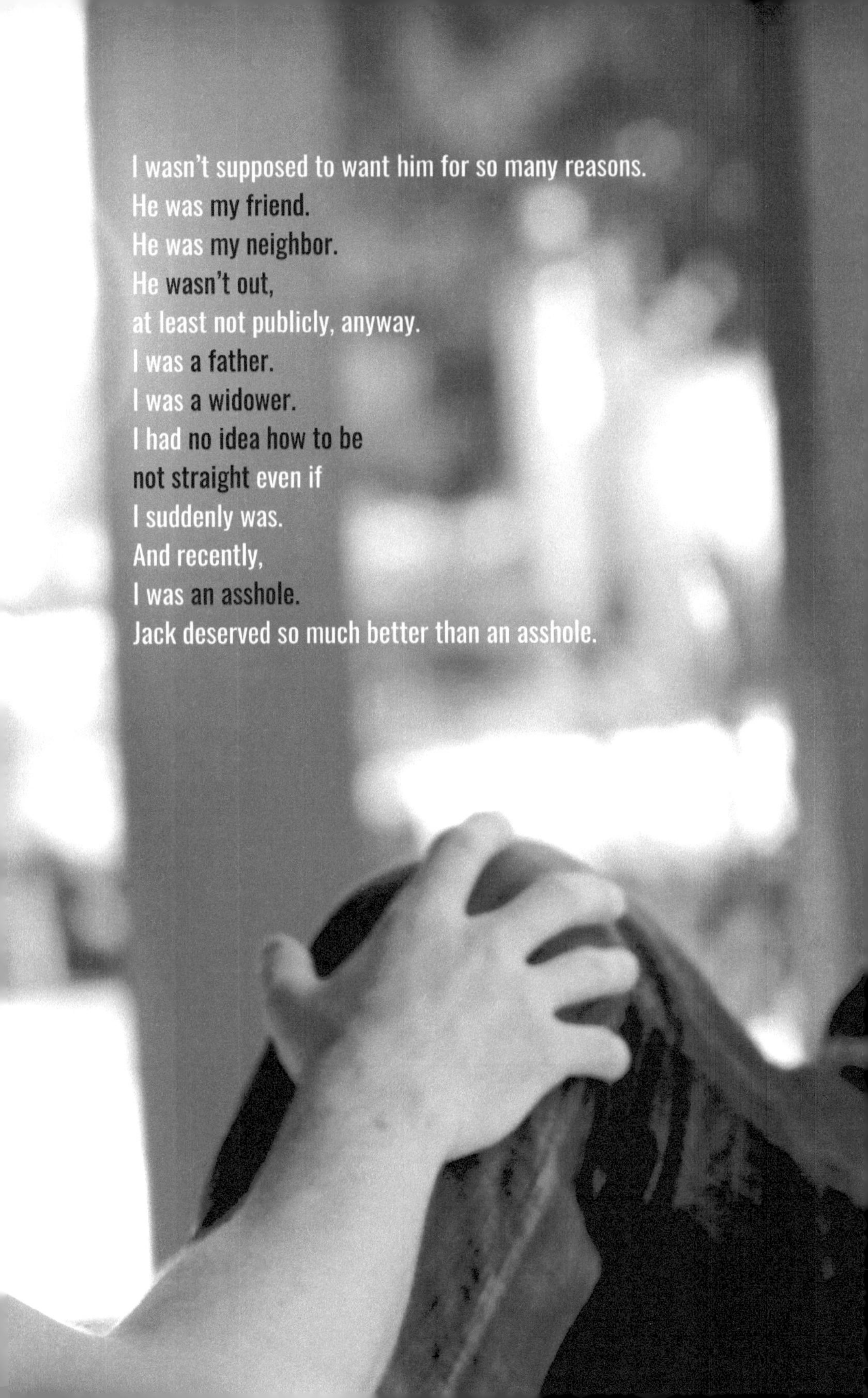

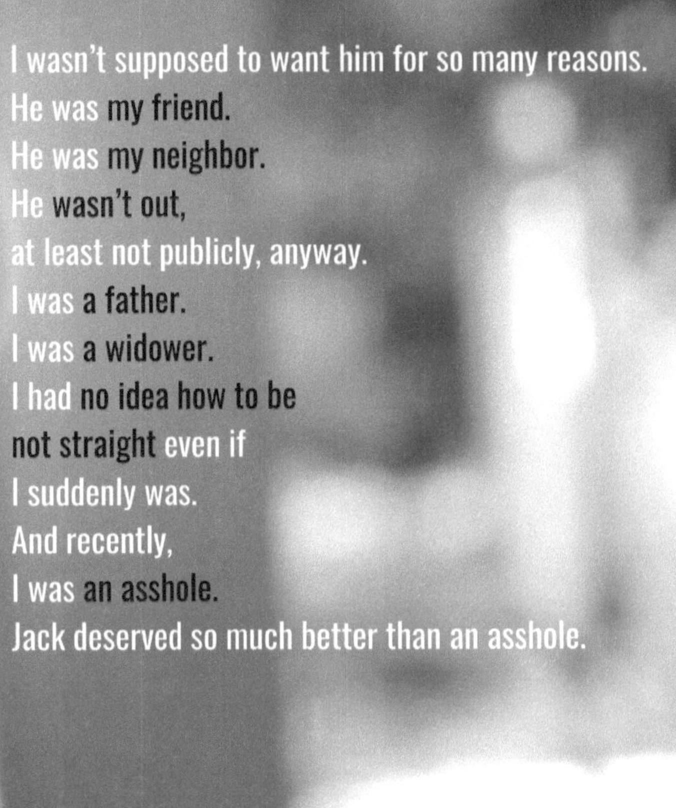

I wasn't supposed to want him for so many reasons.
He was my friend.
He was my neighbor.
He wasn't out,
at least not publicly, anyway.
I was a father.
I was a widower.
I had no idea how to be
not straight even if
I suddenly was.
And recently,
I was an asshole.
Jack deserved so much better than an asshole.

CHAPTER 1
Jack

"Mm. I can't wait to get you in my mouth. I bet you taste even better than you look."

I pulled the piping hot tray of canapés from the oven. Their yummy, bacon-y scent wafted up in a bouquet of enticing flavors, making my mouth have a mini orgasm.

Damn. I'd outdone myself. Maybe when I retired from baseball, I could start my own cooking show, *Mouth Orgasms with Jack Spears*.

Ha! No way was I running that by Ed. My agent was a good guy who looked out for my best interests, but sometimes he looked out for them a little too well.

"Jack, my man. You've got to strike while the iron's hot. Pad that retirement account while you can!"

There's a point when a person should accept they have enough money and certain exploitations would be an unnecessary sale of their dignity. Ed had roped me into doing a shampoo commercial after the playoffs—because nothing sells shampoo better than a baseball pitcher—and I attended all the post-season parties and appearances he said I shouldn't miss, but it was December now. That was almost halfway through the offseason. I had one message for the hoopla that went with being a public figure: *Behind me, Satan!*

Whenever the guys on the team asked what I did during post-season, they laughed as if to say *'Sure, Spears'* like I was trying to hide some rambunctious lifestyle by telling them my winters consisted of cooking, working out, and watching hockey. I gave up dispelling the mystery of me years ago. Maybe the thought of a single, thirty-two-year-old man spending the offseason balls-deep in cookbooks was too lackluster for some, but cooking was my serenity garden. I balanced the hobby and my restless energy with daily workouts though, hence no muffin-butt on Jack Spears. *Thank you very much.*

The syncopated beat of *'Livin' Thing'* by Electric Light Orchestra streamed from my playlist where my phone rested on the counter. My hips shifted instinctively, like a snake for a charming flute. Today had been an upper body day, so my sore abs welcomed the stretch as I shimmied around the kitchen. I was in one of those invincible moods. Was it odd that someone else's kitchen, rather than my own, was my happy place?

My friend Max's kitchen had a charming, homey vibe to it that mine, with its dark modern furnishings, lacked. His had walnut cabinets with deep drawers, a roll-out shelf just for the mixer, terra cotta countertops for days wrapped around two walls, and a roomy walk-in pantry. There was recessed lighting and the biggest island counter to ever grace the state of Illinois. It even had one of those pot-hanging racks above it that everyone in the movies hit their head on.

"Ouch! Shit."

Okay. Everyone in real life, too.

I flung my favorite oven mitt off—the one my friend Lainey got me that looked like a baseball glove—and rubbed at the stinging on my forehead. Little recognized fact: pitchers had to be good at catching, but the world didn't know I lacked the gene that alerted me when something was near my head. Case in point—the line drive I took to the face my senior year of high school that morphed my nose from Jimmy Stewart to Charlton Heston.

I let out a sigh and braced the pot rack to stop it from swinging. When I opened my affected eye, my gaze caught on a sign I'd bought for Lainey.

This kitchen is for dancing.

I chuckled. *Touché, girl. Touché.*

Remembering how she and I used to laugh our asses off in here, I busted a move in her honor as the chorus picked up its tempo. Sprinkling freshly chopped cilantro and basil on the bruschetta, I bustled around the island in time with the beat. This kitchen *was* built for dancing. It was a shame a layout of such culinary genius was now wasted on a man who couldn't cook. At all.

Seriously, the guy burned toast. Max was proof that practice did not always make perfect. He scorched everything as though it had traveled through the seventh level of hell. It was one of the reasons I nominated myself for the job of food prep for his poker game tonight.

Max's idea of being an accommodating host was to fill the spare fridge with beer and drag some potato chips out of the pantry. My best friend, God love him, knew as much about entertaining as I did about dodging face-bound projectiles. Luckily, he had an awesome neighbor like me to save his ass.

Buying the house next door six years ago was the best decision I ever made. I didn't just get to commandeer this glorious kitchen regularly or inherit great neighbors, no. I got friends, a family. I had been in the majors for six years by that time, on my second team. Baseball was everything I'd ever wanted until I realized it wasn't.

There had been a comforting permanence to my routine during the season, but my winters were filled with idleness while the rest of the guys went home to their families, or the single ones trotted the globe in search of love and adventure. I wasn't afforded the ability to do either. I had nothing outside of baseball. I was nothing without baseball. With every passing winter, it grew painfully evident there was a void the size of the Grand Canyon in my life, so much so that a nagging dread would settle in as each offseason approached.

I could have bought a penthouse downtown, could have asked for a trade to a bigger city where nightlife abounded and every necessity was a ten-minute walk or cab ride away. I'd lived like that already in my New York rental before requesting a trade to the Springfield Eagles. New York taught me that busy wasn't for me and losing myself in the crowd had done just that. I'd never felt more adrift. In a city that never slept, neither had I.

The appeal of suburbia, a backyard, cookouts, and newspapers on my lawn had beckoned me ever since I left for college. I wanted to wave to neighbors as I shoveled snow or hauled my trash cans to the street like a regular citizen, a place with the perfect balance of privacy and sense of community where someone might check on you if you didn't come out of your house for a few days. I didn't want to be lost anymore. I wanted to be found by someone or something, or maybe even myself.

When I requested the trade to Illinois and moved into the big house next door, there was a moment where I wondered if I'd be just as lonely as I had the six years prior, but that changed as soon as I met the riveting Max and

Lainey Hartwell. They welcomed me with open arms even before they even figured out who I was.

Lainey came over with a platter of brownies and within the first five minutes had me laughing so hard over her interpretation of the neighborhood's HOA rules my side hurt.

"The lawn has to be less than four inches in case a scientist shrinks his kids, and they get lost in your backyard. No burn barrels allowed, which makes it impossible to have proper cult sacrifices or get rid of incriminating evidence. Fences can't be taller than five and a half feet because apparently only short people are nosy bastards. If you have a pet and it craps on someone else's lawn, you'll be sent to a gulag in Siberia to pay for your heinous crime for all eternity. And if you see an angry guy outside, snarling and cursing like the Tasmanian devil, please don't call the police—it's probably just my husband, Max. He's crunchy on the outside, gooey on the inside. Regular feedings usually keep him from foaming at the mouth."

Lainey could not have given a more accurate description of Max unless she'd added that he was as equally hilarious as she was. He was the most intense person I'd ever met, but he applied it to all things with equal fervor. Man, he could make me and Lainey crack up. I was in heaven. For the first time, people liked me for *me*, and nothing to do with baseball.

I'd been part of the jock pack in school, but those friendships never went any deeper than the surface. I bonded with the teams I'd been on since then, but there was a sense of obligation to be cohesive because we had to work together. Lainey and Max had no obligation to be friendly toward me, and they didn't act like the awestruck fans who tried to impress or flatter me. To them, I was just... Jack.

And then there was Emma... I think my heart broke from cuteness overload when I met Max and Lainey's daughter. Six years ago, Emma was a three-year-old waddling tornado of bright, inquisitive blue eyes, and crazy blonde curls. I had never entertained the idea of having kids, but after she sized me up with the same serious face as Max and then thrust her little arms out to be picked up like I had passed an insurmountable test, I was a goner.

I hadn't spent time around children other than for brief encounters with fans toting their kids along. Watching Emma's little mind work, though, and the way she discovered emotions and new words was the most fascinating thing I'd ever witnessed. And just like her parents, she liked me for *me*. The only person in the world who liked me for me was my sister, Carrie. I couldn't fathom what was so appealing about me to a tiny human, but I was too flattered Emma let me be her buddy to question the reasons.

Life was… perfect. Year round. And then three years ago last month, the bottom dropped out.

Lainey's car accident was uncanny. One day she was here, the next she wasn't. For a while, I swear both Max and I thought she'd just come walking back through the door someday like it had never happened. She had been like another sister to me and certainly the best friend I'd ever had. As if losing her wasn't painful enough, watching Max's metamorphosis through his grief was just as heart-wrenching.

Shaking off the memories, I transferred my creations onto serving platters. Dwelling on unpleasant memories had never provided me with any benefit. As usual though, thoughts of my favorite food-incinerator stayed on my brain. He needed to have a good time tonight.

I believed happiness was a choice. Every morning when I woke up, I chose happiness. I spent enough of my formative years around negativity that I made a conscious choice years ago to be a beacon. You never knew what someone else had been through. Sometimes a smile, a helping hand, or a kind word could make a difference in someone's day or even their life. Next to baseball, my second favorite thing was being that guy.

I was determined to be that guy for Max tonight, even more so than I had since Lainey died. I had to be because Max… was not that guy.

He'd always been one step away from being admitted into an anger management program, but in a hilarious, uncontrollable cursing fit sort of way, where no children or animals were harmed in the process. For the past three years, though, his impatience had become more genuine and depressing than entertaining. When Lainey died, I think a part of him died, too.

The first few months, he was a zombie. The next few, a robot, as though he knew he had to function and was forcing himself to do so. Then he transitioned into the personality of a DMV worker, finally smiling on occasion, but the kind of smiles that never quite reach a person's eyes. It got better over the past year, but he was still a far cry from the man I knew who could be swearing at a snow blower that wouldn't start one minute and cracking jokes about it the next.

Grabbing the serving tongs, I focused on 'Operation: Shit Rainbows and Sunshine,' and clacked the tongs in time with the chorus, launching myself into a series of spins. Emma was out at the movies with a friend. It was just going to be us, Max's law firm partners, and a couple of guys from my team. Emma was securely wrapped around my heart, but this was probably only the fourth time in three years that Max had a night without her. I finally understood why parents joked about getting rid of their children.

It was just a card game, but I was more excited than a teenage girl going to the prom. I had this foreboding sense that I could be supremely evil if I wanted, like go rob a bank, do drugs, or streak naked through the street. Not that I had a desire to do any of those things, but I was totally high on the liberating freedom hanging in the air by the mere lack of Emma's presence.

Letting loose, I waved the tongs through the air, directing an invisible rock orchestra. I bobbed my head to the beat, mouthing the lyrics to the song, wiggling my hips in a way that would put Hugh Grant to shame.

The creak of the basement door caught my attention. Max cleared the top step with a folding table tucked under his arm and a mystified expression plastered on his face.

Reflex and self-preservation kicked in, heat washing up my neck. I pulled the brakes on my ass-wiggling, jabbed my arm forward, and clinked the tongs together in the air a few times with laser focus like I was wielding a sword at an invisible beast.

"Jaaack," Max drawled suspiciously. "Whatcha doing?"

"There was...a fly!" I gestured to the general area in front of me. "I was, uh, going to Mr. Miagi the shit out of it," I added with a hopeful grin, brandishing the tongs for emphasis.

"Uh-huh," Max deadpanned. "And how's that working out for you?"

I pretended to scan the room for an offending insect, not that I cared in the grand scheme of things if Max caught me acting a fool. It wouldn't have been the first time, but I'd seldom let my freak flag fly since Lainey passed.

While I had chosen to celebrate Lainey's life with the joy she had brought to the world, Max had opted for constantly remembering that it was gone. It was a strange highway where each of us said nothing about the other staying in their own lane.

"It, uh. I think it flew into the living room."

His nose twitched, and he leaned to the side to peer past me. "Mm. What's that smell?"

Thank God. Saved by *Mouth Orgasms with Jack*. I squared off with the side of the island and gestured to my newest serving platter with a proud smile.

"Bacon and Gouda canapés."

His mouth ticked up at the corner. "Canapés? Shit. Jack. It's a card game, not a banquet."

"Hey. It's offseason, man. I want to eat some carbs."

"What's wrong with the chips I bought? Those are carbs," he half-ass grumped as he shuffled over and popped an entire canapé into his mouth.

When his eyes slipped closed, pride bloomed in my chest. "Mm. Holy shit. That's good."

The deep timbre of his throaty groan sent a tingle across the skin of my arms. Damn. It just got hotter in here. If he only knew how his voice affected me.

What my cooking did to Max Hartwell, Max Hartwell did to me. It had become the biggest inconvenience of my life, but I couldn't seem to stop Julia-Childing for him every chance I got.

"Yeah?" I asked, pathetically greedy for more of his praise.

I had been awarded Rookie of the Year, MVP four times, been to the World Series three times, and been in eight all-star games. It would be a lie if I said those moments weren't highlights in my life, but I was a whore for Max-compliments. He nodded, locking a predatory gaze on the platter of canapés, and reached for another.

Shit. I knew that look. Lasagna and bacon were his greatest weaknesses, so much so that I may have had a few bizarre dreams where I was covered in either substance. I wasn't proud of it. I clacked the metal serving tongs together against his wrist.

"Hey! Don't you dare."

His eyes narrowed, pinning me. "I'm *hungry*! It's *food*!"

"Nuh-uh. You'll plow through those in five minutes. Save some for the guys."

His lips set in a straight line on that square jaw of his, as he shot me a steely glare that was absolutely fucking adorable. With that pitch-black hair set against his azure blue eyes, he looked like the definition of a dark prince. His rugged looks and commanding appearance *should* have been frightening, even though I was two years younger and had about three inches and thirty pounds on him, but it was all I could do to keep my tongue from lolling out like a dog's.

He huffed, causing his nostrils to flare. His chest puffed up underneath his snug, faded navy, U of I sweatshirt that clung to the definition of his chest and shoulders. I had to hold back a whimper.

Gah! Even his pouting did it for me.

"What the hell, man? It's my house. They can eat the damn chips."

I cast a dubious look at the three bags of potato chips he set out on the counter earlier. "Wow. Look at you. Such a gracious host."

"Oh, fuck off," he grumbled, but without much heat.

A snicker chuffed through my nostrils. He only told me to fuck off about five times a day. I'd made a game of trying to do whatever I could to earn the phrase from him. The words were Max's equivalent of laughing. I never let on I knew his secret. Sometimes I wondered if he thought he wasn't allowed to enjoy things anymore.

He gestured to the spread laid out on the island. "How come you never cook fancy stuff like this for me and Emma?"

I surveyed my work, considering the selections. A giant chive dip ball, spinach artichoke dip, hand-breaded mushrooms and onion rings, a meat and cheese tray, pico de gallo, a cold vegetable and cream cheese "pizza" on croissant crust, bruschetta, and of course, the canapés.

Shit. Maybe I had gone a little overboard. Stupid over-active but totally useless brain.

If I didn't keep my mind or body busy for a certain number of hours a day, I was more hyper than a kid snorting Fun Dip. That and I wanted Max to enjoy tonight. I wanted everything to be perfect for him. He worked too hard, stressed too much, and never got a break from Emma unless I was around. Even then, he'd spend his time on extra work for his firm in his den.

I folded my arms in a show of offense. "If you and Emma don't like what I cook for you, we can just order carry-out more."

We both knew it was a dig at his lack of culinary prowess. I made dinner for him and Emma at least four times a week during the winter. He shot me another of those murderous glares that made my blood hot.

No sexy-Max-glare! Bad! Bad!

God. What was wrong with me? I was a shameless cat in search of cream. No sane person should be attracted to a look of hostility. For that matter, no sane *gay* man should be attracted to a straight man. Things had been so much easier before I started thinking about him in ways a friend shouldn't think about a friend.

"Now you're just being an ass," he grumbled, hoisted the table under his arm, and started down the hallway toward the sunroom.

Unspoken compliment received.

Somebody liked my cooking. I smirked and *did not* stare at how good his ass looked in blue jeans.

A moment later, a ruckus echoed down the hall. There was clanking, followed by cursing. Shaking my head, I sighed, but a smile tugged at the corner of my lips, wondering what he'd gotten himself up to. I couldn't leave him alone for a minute.

Strolling down the hall, past the master bedroom and the laundry room, the noise and swearing from the sunroom grew louder and angrier. I paused in the doorway and leaned on the frame to take in the entertainment.

Max was jerking the folding table as though it were an umbrella that would spontaneously burst open if he gave it a forceful enough shake. He stopped thrashing it about to inspect the seam for an opening mechanism.

His cheeks were red. The length of his hair on top was wild, the way it got when he ran his fingers through it.

"Son of a bitch," he snarled. "What the hell is wrong with this thing? Fucking open already, or I'm going to throw you the fuck outside on the curb. You piece of shit."

That. Even that I found arousing. I needed serious help or to get laid or… probably both. Shaking my head at both of us, I cleared my throat.

"You, uh, need me to find an instruction manual, or did you want to wait and see if it complies with threats of violence?"

His steely blue eyes speared me, sending a shudder from my head to my toes.

Hello, 'smoldery Max.' Yowza.

His mouth was hard-set, but I noticed it—a minuscule uptick at one corner. It was like the moment the sun first peeked out from behind a dissipating storm cloud. Ladies and gentlemen, I cracked the iceberg. Ten points to Jack.

"Fine, fucker," he said, cracking up. "You want to try or is throwing a little white ball all you can do with those hands?"

Oh, the things I could do with my hands. He had no idea.

Swallowing the glob of lust in my throat, I ignored the delicious forbidden thoughts. Taking the table from him, I focused on the task and *not* the way his arms filled that sweatshirt, *not* the bit of dark hair at his wrists, and *not* how mouth-watering his thighs looked in those old jeans.

I had set this table up for Lainey every Christmas and for each of Emma's birthdays since she was four. I found the catch easily, released it, and pried the two halves open. Straightening, I gave Max a baffled look, as if to say *dumb luck*. We gave each other shit constantly, but gloating to this man who'd had his world torn in two was something I avoided.

He folded his arms and gave me a wry smile that made my breath catch. I wanted to freeze-frame that smile. He was so happy tonight, happier than he'd looked in a long time.

"Congratulations," he deadpanned. "You got the PhD in life that I didn't."

I shrugged to downplay my victory. "University of YouTube. Their low admission standards are popular with dumb ballplayers."

Shaking his head, he cracked up again and clapped me on the shoulder. "Whatever man. Guess I'd better enroll."

His words squeezed my heart. He knew I barely squeaked through only two years of college before I was called up to the minors. To this day, I was still never the guy saying anything enlightening. I was good with my hands, not my brains. I always appreciated that Max never made me feel as dumb as I was.

The doorbell rang, ending our time alone. When Max excused himself to let the guys in, relief washed over me. There was a saying, '*too much of a good thing could kill a man.*' Max was all the good things.

I finished setting the folding table in place against the wall for a place to serve our food, still savoring the sound of his laughter. Getting Max to laugh was a dangerous thing. I needed to remember I wasn't here for what the sound of it did to me.

I was here to keep him grounded from his misery, to keep a good day from turning into a bad one. Just like the unadulterated hope every team had that they'd win the series, I clung to the belief that one day, the old Max would come back—the one who only pretended to be crabby, the one who wouldn't need cheering up, the one who acted like he had moments ago.

My breath caught in my throat. Holy shit.

One day, Max wouldn't need me anymore. His earlier snarkiness and his chuckles were almost like old times. How much longer did I have?

A roundhouse punch couldn't have hit me as hard. What the hell was I going to do when Max didn't need me anymore?

We'd always be friends. Of course, we would. Wouldn't we?

Springfield was *it* for me. I had no plans to move. I was a free agent at the end of next year. There was no threat of me being traded, and at thirty-two I was getting old enough that retirement was a consideration. I'd already thought about coaching jobs and other careers after baseball, but my whole plan suddenly was filled with holes.

What kind of neighbors would Max and I be when he didn't need me around making breakfast in the morning, watching Emma after school, and making sure he didn't burn his kitchen down trying to cook dinner? The answers to those questions seemed way more important than retirement career choices.

My stomach cast a vote of nausea over the unknown, so much so that I had to press my hand to my gut. My brain churned out a psychological profile of myself that might as well have been written in Aramaic for how little sense it made to me.

Max *needed* me.

I loved being needed.

And now I was physically ill at the thought of him being happy enough again one day not to need me to be available on a daily basis.

Wow. What was more messed up—that I'd found some joy amid Max and Emma's misery or that I was sick over the possibility of them not needing to rely on me?

The night Lainey died, it had been like answering a blood oath. Some protective instinct told me I needed to take care of Max and Emma, since Lainey couldn't anymore. Being needed had given me purpose. It had made me the most important man in the world to be there for them, to be there for them, for Lainey.

I heard people open speeches with *'it's both an honor and a privilege.'* That defined my time with Max and Emma these last few years.

It was suddenly crystal clear why Lainey had been so infectiously happy. Being Max and Emma's person had been the greatest joy of my life. Had I really thought they would need me to be their person forever?

Christ. I really was a dumb ballplayer if it had taken me this long to realize none of it could last. As I listened to the sound of Max letting in our guests, unfiltered terror inundated my thoughts.

Emma was nine now. Weren't kids pretty self-sufficient by the time they were twelve? Like, wasn't that the age where you could leave them home without a babysitter and not worry that they'd stick metal objects in the toaster or put a cat in the dryer? *Twelve* was only three years away.

And Max? If I thought 'grumpy Max' was irresistible, how would anyone resist 'happy Max' when he came back in full force?

He hadn't dated anyone since Lainey died, but that would change. He was bound to get lonely, bound to get over Lainey enough to try dating again someday. My head went light considering it, which was stupid, and selfish, and…not a proper *friend* reaction. I couldn't date Max, and Max should date. He *should* find love again if he could.

Love.

Max in love.

Max in love with *someone else*.

My chest went tight, and my insides felt hollow. God, what kind of friend was I that the thought of him finding love again made me panic?

The sound of the guys' voices grew down the hallway. I had to pull it together.

I was gay. Max was straight. This was the most ridiculous freak out in history, and if Max noticed, I wouldn't be able to explain why.

Lainey knew my secret. The one I kept from the world. She was the coolest person I'd ever met. I could talk to her about anything, literally anything. She even asked me once if I thought Max was attractive.

I suspected she was fishing for confirmation that she'd chosen well, like if even a gay man approved of her choice of a man, it meant she'd won the husband lottery. I shared what I admired about him, which turned into both of us gushing over his appealing characteristics. Oddly enough, that conversation had seemed to strengthen my bond with her. After that, she talked about Max like he was ours.

"Jack! Oh, my gosh. Wait till I tell you what our guy did today."

We joked about him together, admired him together, and worried about him together. It was like she knew I had no one and little chance of ever having someone of my own, so she shared what she could of what she had, encouraging me to join Team Appreciate Max. That was all it was, though—just innocent appreciation. I didn't go lusting after married men, and I certainly didn't backstab friends.

The last few years, however, without Lainey as a buffer, that appreciation had grown. Had it ever grown.

Despite his grief, his crazy workload, and his responsibilities with Emma, he still pushed himself to work out regularly. I admired a man who took care of his body. Correction. Maybe I admired a man who had a great body.

Shit. That wasn't true either. I worked with an entire team of men who had great bodies.

Alright. I ardently admired Max Hartwell's body. Only Max Hartwell's. In a more than friendly way. In a more than six years ago when Lainey was around way.

There. I said it. In my head.

It wasn't just his body, though; it was all of him—the entire sexy, grumpy Max package. It was how tough he was.

Lainey told me he worked his ass off to take care of his mom and sister after his dad died when he was in high school. He had helped his mom run her florist shop and loaded trucks at the brewery where his dad had worked. He put himself through law school and worked all hours to buy himself and Lainey this fancy house.

There were other things, too. Like how he thought he was a lousy dad. Nothing was further from the truth.

Emma was his number-one concern these days. Every time he lamented his worries about not being there for her enough, it was like a vise around my heart. Maybe it was because the only time my dad gave me attention was to let me know when I disappointed him, but to me, one of Max's sexiest qualities was how much he loved Emma and the thousand little ways he showed it.

He went out of his way to take her to fun places and had quality stay-at-home nights with her. I was an easy sell. That hadn't happened in the Spears' house, which brought me to the subject of *me*.

Max didn't treat me like a famous pitcher. He treated me like a person. When I was on the road, I could call and bitch about a bad game, about an umpire, about the aggravation of travel, crazed fans, tedious publicity events, and media hassles, and he listened. Despite his grief, he didn't tell me to suck it up or to quit whining about my celebrity hardships. I needed him as much as I thought he needed me, if not more.

This was supposed to be a silly little crush. I figured it was like Stockholm Syndrome—all this extra time we'd spent together the last few years brought us closer. These feelings were going to go away like athlete's foot—air it out, dry it up. I mean, he was straight, for Christ's sake.

Footsteps at the doorway warned that my dilemma and I were no longer alone. Max led the way into the room, flanked by the two buddies from my team I'd invited, Hooper and Montez. Amid my panic, they were only background figures. I didn't even know what they just said to me. Time had stopped. All I could see was Max.

My heart flipped over. Heat spread across my face. Not the heat of dirty thoughts. I'd already shamelessly had those, trying to get this man out of my system. It was the heat of another secret rising so close to my surface that I was afraid he'd see it. It was the secret of wanting to keep belonging here, of wanting all Max's good days along with his bad ones, of wanting not just to belong in his life, but also wanting to belong to him, and him to me, no one else but me.

"Okay, Gordon Ramsey," Max quipped. "They're here. Can we bust out the goods now?"

Shit. That smirk. That toe-searing, heart-melting little smirk. It slayed me on the spot.

How had I lied to myself all this time? How had I actually believed this was a crush, a simple physical attraction? It was so much more. It had been so much more for a long time.

A hand waved through the air. Hooper, my catcher, called out, "Earth to Spears!"

Earth?

I was so far out of orbit, I didn't know how I'd ever get back into the galaxy. I tore my eyes away so no one would see the hearts in them.

I had it bad, so damn bad. An awkward laugh bubbled out of my throat. Hooper chuckled. I couldn't begrudge him. It *was* hilarious. Although, that wasn't the reaction I thought I'd have if this ever happened.

I'd never fallen in love before. Of course, the first time I did had to be with a man who could never love me back.

CHAPTER 2
Max

"Jesus, Max. You play cards like you handle cases. Fucking brutal."

"That's why we make the big bucks, Danny boy." I smirked as Dan whipped his cards onto the pile with the grace of a petulant debutante.

I raked in my winnings and the cards with a sweep of my arms. It was seldom a single dad like me got a sense of victory in life. I had to gloat over any triumph that came my way. Dan, my oldest friend and one of my law firm partners, had always been a sore loser, which made my gloating all the more enjoyable.

"What is this, Dan," I prefaced, "your *seventh* straight loss?"

Trevor Hart, our other law partner, chuckled. Dan palmed something, and the next thing I knew, a poker chip sailed across the table. My jaw fell open in the split-second it took to ding the lens of Trevor's glasses with a loud *tink*!

"Hey!" Trevor snapped, catching the chip before it could fall to the floor. "It's the holidays, Whitaker. Don't make me file a restraining order on you."

"Please," Dan dripped sarcastically. "I taught you how to file for restraining orders."

Jesus. Why did I still call this tool my friend?

Tony Montez, shortstop for the Springfield Eagles, sized Dan up. "Shit, Dan. You throw as bad as Spears."

Jack Spears, my neighbor, starting pitcher for the team, and truth be told, the best pitcher in the league, ruefully shook his head at the dig. Whatever the guy did to maintain his happy-go-lucky air, I wish I knew. Jack was so damn laid-back, just being in his presence would make you not blink an eye if your house was on fire. I think that was why I unofficially passed the best friend title from Dan to him when he moved in next door.

Maybe it was the MLB life because Montez was pretty chill, too. What was I saying? Every one of Jack's teammates I had met was *Teflon* to harassment. No-brainer—they got to play baseball for a living.

It was still surreal that I'd had half the Eagles team in my house at some point. Dan always acted like he wasn't impressed, but the smug fucker bombarded me with questions the few times a year I had a card game or cookout at my house. He always wanted to know who would be here and if Jack's teammates were bringing any celebrity guests or fan girls. Jack and I still had a running joke that Sebastian Bach had once attended one of his cookouts that Dan had missed, even though it never happened.

Garrett Hooper, the team's catcher, got up from his chair and headed toward the extra fridge I kept in the sunroom. "Anybody need another beer?"

Trevor, Montez, and Jack voiced their requests while I dealt another hand. Hooper returned and just as he sat down, Dan asked for a *Budweiser*.

God, was he this bad in college? It was like he got off having a pro-athlete who was worth millions doing his bidding.

Hooper arched an amused brow; the kind that said *you really just pull that shit*? Dan either didn't see it or pretended he hadn't. Hooper got back up, retrieved another beer, delivered it to Dan, and… wait for it…

Nope. Fucker didn't even say *thank you*.

"Appreciate it." I nodded to Hooper on Dan's behalf. I had to do that a lot, dole out the manners Dan forgot both here and at the office.

"Come on, Max," Montez growled, rubbing his palms together. "I need money for Maui."

"When are you leaving?" I chuckled.

"Right after Christmas. Staying till a few weeks before spring training."

"Shit. Maui's for tourists," Dan grumbled, scanning his cards like he was out for blood now. "You should go to the Philippines or Costa Rica."

Montez laughed. "I *am* a tourist. I've never been to Maui. Besides, got to keep the little lady happy."

His proud peacock grin both stabbed me in the chest and made me happy for him. Once upon a time, I looked like that. Just thinking of another person making me that happy now was such a foreign thought. I swept it from my mind in a blink.

"The new one?" I asked. "Is she a keeper?"

"The *new one*?" Montez parroted. "Man, that makes me sound so fickle."

Jack nudged Montez's elbow. "She must be a keeper if you're taking her to Maui for three months."

Another goofy grin split Montez's face—the kind full of secrets between people in love. I had to look away before it cut me any deeper.

Hooper let out a snort. "*Keeper*? Dude, more like a straight-up kidnapping, so you can guarantee you get laid for three months straight."

Montez shook his head. "Whatever. You're just jealous you and your cold-ass hand will be freezing your dick off up here while I'm on the beach with a beer in one hand and my girl in the other."

Hooper wrinkled his nose, his wild sandy hair flopping over one eye. "Uh. My hands *and* my dick will be plenty occupied. Thank you very much." He slapped Jack on the shoulder. "I get lonely, me and my man Spears here can just hit up the bar scene. Dude's the all-time chick magnet."

Montez busted up. "Hoop, you realize you just admitted you've got no game without him. Don't you?"

"What? The hell you say! I've got game in spades."

Montez leaned conspiratorially toward Jack. "Spears, you should start charging him for your wingman services as an offseason gig."

Jack threw a card, his eyes never leaving the table. "I only charge if he's successful."

"Yeah? How much you made off him?" Dan asked.

Jack let out a contemplative breath. "Well, you don't see me buying tickets to Maui this year, do you?"

Hooper gave Jack's shoulder a hard shove. "Ah, you bastard!"

Jack's mouth ticked up. That was it. That was his reaction.

Damn. The guy could execute a hook, line, and sinker and not even bask in the glory, while the rest of us cracked up. When I grow up, I want to be Jack Spears.

Glancing at the clock, my mood took a nosedive. I was half-eager, half-panicked that my sister, Morgan, would be back soon with Emma. I only had a few more moments of being just one of the guys, not a single dad who knew how to braid hair, read bedtime stories, and was forced to watch *Nickelodeon*. These times were rare. I loved Emma more than I knew was possible to love anything, but I would never love being an only parent.

As Jack popped open his light beer, Dan gestured. "Man, how can you drink that pussy beer?"

I felt my face heat. Could he ever stop talking shit? I was about to stop inviting him to these things. Neither Jack's crew nor Trevor ever acted like this. I guess there was always one in every crowd, and it wasn't like I could get rid of him. I still had to see him at our law firm. Every. Single. Soul-sucking day.

Jack's jaw shifted like he was contemplating the ingredients of the swig he'd downed as he studied the label. Shifting his eyes to Dan, he shrugged. "Doesn't taste like pussy."

The table's laughter echoed off the white paneled walls. Dan ground his teeth like he was trying not to admit it was funny and shook his head.

It had been a while since I contributed to the conversation. I needed to be a good host and not let the silent panic that was as constant as my pulse show its ugly head.

"You should know better, Dan," I began. "Whatever you throw at Jack bounces right off. Guy could never be a catcher."

The double dig earned me a roar of laughter, from all except Jack. His mouth ticked up again. The glint in his eye said he was impressed, even though one of his big hands covered the center of his chest as though my words were an arrow.

"Ouch, man."

My skin prickled with pride that I dented the indestructible Jack Spears with my wit. One-upping the life of the party that was Jack was like having a superpower. He got my humor, and I got his. We'd always had an unspoken acknowledgment that the rest of these guys were just amateur comedians. He knew how funny I used to be before…

Shit.

The laugh lines in his face dissipated, and I knew. He got snared by the shadows in my eyes, the shadows of the woman whose laughter used to fill this house. Just like that, the happy moment died a quick death. Some fucking host I was.

I forced my gaze to my hand, a rush of guilt pummeling me; guilt that only one man at this table could detect. He'd been here through it all. The good times, the great times, and then the barren wasteland of everything after the day we lost Lainey.

I say *we* because it's true. Me, Jack, and Emma—we all lost her that day three years ago when a semi cut her off. I didn't shudder anymore when I thought about it. I almost wished I did, so I would feel… something, but there was nothing. Just dead pockets of air around me and dead space inside my chest that manifested the first year of my grief as I cried myself to sleep almost every night for months. It was like I had nothing left to feel, like my body had expended every possible drop of agony over my loss, Emma's, and even Jack's.

I considered myself Jack's best friend, but I knew I'd only earned the title by default. It passed to me when Lainey died.

Not many men could say they'd be cool with their wives being friends with a guy, but they weren't married to my wife, and they weren't friends with Jack. I never trusted two people more. That was saying a lot since I was a criminal lawyer and got lied to on a daily basis. It's not that I had trust issues, I was just picky with whom I chose to spend my precious free time.

Growing up, my old man worked his ass off for us, so did my mom. It made me focused. When you were focused, you didn't have time for people you knew would be nothing more than a blip on the radar.

Dan was the only exception, having been my college roommate and interned at the same firm I had. We evolved professionally on the same path. Lainey and Jack, though? Who needed more friends when I had those two?

I always knew I was the third wheel in our friendship circle. My marriage? It was great. No contest. Lainey was my life force, and for some reason I never figured out, she acted like I was hers. Yet, when Jack moved in and we all hit it off over dinner one night, I knew they clicked in a way Jack and I didn't, and even in a way Lainey and I didn't. That was fine with me because clearly, Lainey and I clicked in a way she and Jack never would, and Jack and I found ground he and Lainey didn't share. We were a happy trio, everyone's dream of the perfect neighbor relationship.

It became evident Lainey, Emma, and I were the stability and family Jack didn't have, the life baseball couldn't provide. We were a home of suburban normalcy he couldn't get yet while he was still playing. Plus, Emma stole his heart the first time he met her.

You haven't seen anything until you've seen a three-year-old wrap a six-foot-four baseball player around her little finger. God, Lainey and I used to crack up watching the two of them together. It was like Emma thought he was a giant puppy we brought home for her to keep.

We used to call him to come over if we couldn't get her to sleep. She'd crawl into his arms, bury her face in his neck, and be out in two minutes. So would he. He dubbed her his little Snuggle Bug because he said she could knock him out faster than the recovery tables at the stadium.

He was such a permanent fixture in our lives that Lainey and I used to joke about who would get him in the divorce. They dished on cooking shows, music, and celebrity gossip, while he and I argued sports, yard work, jogged, and bitched to each other about our jobs. He liked to be obtuse just to piss me off, and he thought I didn't know this, but I actually got a kick out of arguing with him. Jack gave entertaining arguments like a mischievous, hyperactive kid.

Whenever Lainey and I wanted a date night during his offseason, it practically looked like we did him a favor by asking him to babysit. We would come home to coloring books and crayons spread out on the floor. He and Emma would be immersed in their artwork like a couple of kids—one tiny, one giant. There'd be stuffed animals lined up across the couches as they narrated silly voices for animals in their enchanted forest, popcorn and Disney princess movies, cookie baking lessons. If the whole *'best pitcher in the league'* thing didn't work out for him, he should open a daycare.

The guy put my fatherhood skills to shame. If he ever had kids of his own, Emma was probably going to be jealous as hell.

It was perfect for all of us. We somehow became this eccentric family unit. I never gave much thought to the life of a major leaguer before we met Jack. I had been a baseball fan since my dad took me to a game when I was eight. I appreciated the sport, but I had just assumed that pro athletes lived a pampered, trouble-free existence.

Jack wasn't one to complain, but Lainey and I figured out early on about the pressure that went with the game. The pressure of the entire world watching you through the voice of the media, critiquing your every move. The strain and isolation that went with being on the road over eighty days a year with only one day off a month.

When he was away, we video-called him during our morning routine to send him moral support. We would set the phone in front of Emma to get her to sit still and eat, as Lainey and I had coffee. After night games sometimes, when Emma was asleep, we would call to congratulate or console him.

During home games, what started as invitations for morning coffee as we got ready for work turned into Jack becoming our breakfast chef and out-the-door helper. He said home-cooked meals were important, and we could return the favor once he retired. It became another of many things. Lainey and I would be lying in bed, and wake up to delicious aromas coming from the kitchen. It was a contest to see who got up first and guessed our treat.

Mmm, pancakes.

Mmm, bacon.

Ooh, French toast.

We knew we were fucking spoiled, but something told us not to take away the joy it brought Jack to belong somewhere other than with his team. It was why we left our back patio door unlocked. Jack did the same. Still did. Our two houses became one big complex.

When Lainey died, none of us knew how to navigate the empty space at first. An empty stool at the breakfast counter. A silence the three of us couldn't quite fill without her. Our well-oiled machine was missing a vital cog. Her accident happened at the start of the offseason, so Jack was home to witness the entire nightmare. I don't know what we would have done without him.

I quickly realized all the things I took for granted, like getting Emma to and from school. Lainey used to take care of all that because her work schedule was more flexible than mine.

Jack got us through the offseason that year and had for each one since, shuttling Emma to and from school, and then watching her until I came home from work. It was fitting, the term *offseason*. Everything had been *off* since Lainey left us.

During the season, every day was an oppressive reminder of my failure. How, no matter how I tried, I would forever feel like I was drowning in the wake of a life built for two people. School schedules, dance recitals, laundry, oil changes, dentist appointments, cleaning house, making breakfast and dinner, grocery shopping, school supplies, clothes shopping with a grade school girl, bath time, bedtime, getting ready for work and school, juggling my cases, getting my suits to and from the dry cleaner, remembering and finding time to pay bills, and the obligatory visits to see family who *'just want to know how you're holding up.'*

For the last three years, when Jack was on the road, we talked at least twice a week. I could say it was so he and Emma could visit, so I could praise him for his playing, but more often than not, he was talking me off a ledge as I recounted our chaotic day—essentially a cry for help that I still hadn't mastered the single-dad thing. I was a fucking fantastic friend.

Sadly, even when he was home, I still wanted to throw a pillow over my face and yell into it. I shouldn't have to rely on my best friend to handle my responsibilities. I kept telling myself that one of these days everything would fall into place. One of these days, I would get everything right. There wouldn't be some crisis, something I forgot, or something I fucked up. I wouldn't snap at Emma. I wouldn't feel like a fucking loser who couldn't do anything right. I wouldn't have to pray for the offseason to come around just so I could get a break when a grown-ass man who wasn't Max Hartwell came home to take care of Max Hartwell's life. One of these days...

The sound of the front door opening down the hall both flooded me with relief that my child was home safe and also tightened a noose around my neck that my brief evening of not being depended upon had come to an end. Yet, the tromping of Emma's feet sprinting down the hallway brought a smile to my face. She burst into the room, her wild, long blonde curls bouncing around her shoulders. She was the spitting image of her mother.

"Hey Dad!" she called but made a beeline to Jack. The little traitor. She threw her arms around as much of his barrel of a chest as she could.

"Hey, kiddo." A smile cracked on my face, seeing her happy. That was my greatest worry—wondering if she was as happy as she would be with two parents.

"You winning, Uncle Jack?"

"It's a close tie between me and your dad," Jack replied, shooting me a smirk. The antagonizing fucker. I was up two hands! "How was the movie, Bug?" he added, dropping the *Snuggle* from her nickname, no doubt to preserve his manhood in front of our guests.

"Good. Jessica ate too many *M&M's* and popcorn and had to go to the bathroom like three times because she thought she was going to puke."

"Nice." Jack beamed.

I raised a questioning brow at my sister Morgan as she entered the room, but she gave me an innocent shrug. Emma relinquished her hold on Jack and sidled over to me with a little less gusto.

That's right. It's just me. Your dad. Chopped liver.

I squeezed her to my side, noting how cold she felt, but then thought better of giving Morgan the evil eye. I was sure Morgan bundled her up as well as I would have. It was just balls-cold in Illinois at the start of winter. No need to go all helicopter dad in front of the guys. Plus, pissing off my sister would ruin what little time I had left of her babysitting availability. She was due with her third child in two months and had informed me to take her off my call-list for the four months after the baby arrived. She was so damn selfish.

Her straight, jet-black hair, a match to mine, swished across her shoulders as she sidled up behind Jack's chair. The mischievous glint in her blue eyes made my skin prickle, having been on the receiving end of my little sister's shenanigans my entire life. She was a ballbuster personified where I was concerned. And where Jack was concerned, she was a shameless hussy. I knew deep down it was probably in part just to piss me off. She was happily married to my brother-in-law, Mike, a man who deserved an award for accepting her mentally deranged sense of humor.

My eye twitched, watching her knead the back of Jack's shoulders, and I groaned inwardly. Not now. Did she have to embarrass me the few times a year I actually had people over?

Her manicured, vixen-red nails glided down the place where Jack's neck sloped to his shoulders. Leaning her ruby lips close to his ear, I could hear her purr all the way from across the table. "Jack, when are you going to run away with me?"

Oh, God. Here we go again.

He smirked, never taking his eyes off his cards, and reached a hand around to pat her baby bulge. "Can we wait until this one comes out first?"

Her dramatic sigh and eye roll could have earned her a place in theater. "That's what you said last time."

Jack's grin belied the reddening of his cheeks as the guys laughed. "Well, that's because you were in the same condition the last time you asked."

Patting him on the back, she angled her belly around his chair and rubbed it with a mock frown. "I know. I need to stop being pregnant during offseason."

"You done yet?" I asked, shooting her a look. Couldn't she humiliate me in private? Go harass her own friends?

"Yeah. I need to get home and try to get a foot rub out of Mike before he falls asleep."

"Poor Uncle Mike," I muttered under my breath, ruffling Emma's hair. "What do you say, Emma?"

"Thanks for taking us to the movie, Aunt Morgan."

"You're welcome, honey." Morgan waddled over and planted a kiss on Emma's forehead. "Did you ask your dad about the dress?"

I had already done Emma's Christmas shopping and distinctly recalled no mention of a dress on her list. "What dress?"

Emma's little shoulders sagged with a huff. "The one I need for Jessica's Christmas party tomorrow. Remember?"

"Uh, no. And what's wrong with the dresses you have?"

Morgan stretched her mouth wide behind Emma, showing me her terrified face, and then mouthed, *'good luck.'* "Bye guys!" she hollered as she waddled-slash-abandoned me down the hallway.

I was sensing she'd just detonated a bomb. Typical freaking Morgan.

"I don't have any Christmas dresses, Dad. I only have summer dresses." Emma gestured to the window. "It's winter."

"Uh, can't you just wear pants and a sweater?"

Glancing around the table, the testosterone was oblivious to the four-foot dilemma with hostile blue eyes at my side. All except for Jack. I caught the half-sympathetic, half-amused look on his face. For a guy who didn't have kids, I would never understand how he could be so in tune with the torture I went through in this house.

Emma's lips pressed into a thin line, her nostrils flared, and her fingers curled into little fists at her sides as she gave me *the look*; that silent, *you-fucked-up-again* look. Shit.

She spun on her heel and marched into the kitchen. I heard paper rustling and a clacking noise. My breath stuck in my chest. I wasn't proud of it, but yes. At the moment, I was terrified of a nine-year-old girl.

The stomping sound of her feet preceded her before she reappeared. Like Alexander the Great, storming down a hill to raze a city, she descended upon me, wielding a...

What the hell was that? A catalog page?

Oh. Shit.

She thrust said catalog page mere inches away from my face. It was littered with five little girls, each in Christmas-themed dresses. Each one smiling the smile of children with two perfect parents who didn't forget easily fulfilled requests.

One, a curly redhead, had been circled with pink marker... four, no, five times. The scribbly writing above her head read, *'Emma's Christmas party.'* A little index finger reached around the front of the page that I was stupidly staring at, as though it were a list of my crimes. The silver glitter-painted fingernail tapped the page near the girl's feet to yet more of Emma's script.

My dignity died as I read the words, *'Don't forget!'*

It might as well have read, *'Don't forget, jackass,'* because that was what I felt like. I was the one who told her to mark the page and put it on the fridge.

We heaved twin sighs in unison. Mine said, *'yeah. I'm that guy.'* Hers, well, hers pretty much said the same thing. I was the guy who forgot one more of the few requests she made of me.

She didn't ask for much. Even at only nine years old, I think she understood that the less she required, the easier it made things for me. Sometimes I wished she was spoiled and demanding. It would have meant I gave her enough of my time and attention.

Right now, though? I just wanted to crawl underneath the table and hide. Hide from the blaring message in my brain saying she didn't have a mother, she never would, and now, thanks to me, she didn't have a damn Christmas dress for a party she'd been looking forward to for weeks.

"Dad. I circled it for you like you asked me to."

"I know. I forgot. I'm sorry." The words tasted as pathetic as they sounded, seeing the *'oh-shit-you're-busted'* looks I was getting from the guys as I was being dressed down by a child. "Just...see if the one from last year fits you. Okay?"

"I doubt it. I grew like two inches. The sleeves will probably be up to here." She indicated a spot on her arm between her elbow and wrist.

"What are you? An orangutan? Don't be so dramatic." Warily, I threw down my cards and got up from my chair.

I'd found the best practice was to put fires out immediately. It made that many fewer that could scorch me in the ass the next day. "Play without me," I told the guys. "I'll be back in a little bit."

After a twenty-minute debate over Emma's wardrobe and the discovery of garbage bags stashed in her closet—yes, full of garbage—we came to a compromise. I left her with an uplifting speech about the benefits of not being so lazy as to hide your trash bags in your closet rather than carting them downstairs. I gave her a goodnight kiss on the cheek and left orders to get ready for bed, grabbed the trash bags, a sleeveless black dress my mom got her for a spring recital, and a red cardigan. If I was lucky, I could salvage my manhood and my rights as game night host so the guys would come back the next time I invited them over.

I tossed the bags by the trashcan in the kitchen, flung the dress and cardigan I'd found crumpled on her closet floor on top of the washer in the laundry room, and just made it back into the sunroom when I saw the guys getting up.

"Taking off already?" My disappointment dissolved as soon as the words were out of my mouth. Honestly, I just wanted some fucking sleep.

"We're meeting some of the team at Sprig's for a drink," Hooper said.

"Cool. I'm down," Dan chimed.

Way to invite yourself, Dan.

I hated that he had the freedom to hang out with people I knew better than he did, even if I probably wouldn't go if I could. The thought of being in public, surrounded by laughter, left a dirty sensation on my skin these days.

"Rebecca's going to meet me there." Montez shrugged, giving me an impish smile, as though to say, '*is there really any debate*?'

I was happy for him, but damn me, did it sting, knowing those moments, those chances, those feelings were still out there happening in the world. They just didn't happen to me. Couldn't happen to me ever again.

"You coming Spears?" Hooper asked.

Jack was still in his seat, putting all the poker chips back in the case. "No. This wingman has an early morning workout planned."

Montez clapped him on the shoulder. "That's what I like to hear. Dedication. You see that, Hoop? Could be you."

"I've got a dedication for you," Hooper countered. "The Hanson Brothers set to repeat on the jukebox in your honor."

"Aw, fuck no. If I hear '*MMMBop*' one more goddamn time, your lucky batting gloves are going to disappear."

"Dad!"

The alarm in my title from Emma's shrill cry upstairs gave me a start. I shouldered past Dan, who didn't comprehend the urgency when one's child screamed your name. Racing down the hall to the base of the stairs, I found her unscathed, and in her pajamas, looking down at me from the landing with her guilty face. I let out a whoosh of relief just as Jack skidded to a stop at my side, bumping into my shoulder.

"What?" I called up to her.

In a miserable little voice, she called down, "My toilet is overflowing."

"Ah, damn it." I ran a hand down my face. "I'll be up in a minute."

"Ooh, have fun with that." Dan cackled, slapping me on the back. "And don't forget, we moved the Leopart deposition up to Monday."

"Fuck." I didn't forget. I just… yeah. I forgot. The son of a bitch could have reminded me sooner. "Thanks, dickhead."

"Anytime!"

"I've got to get this," I told Montez and Hooper, giving each of them a quick handshake.

Montez clapped my arm. "No problem, man. Thanks for having us."

"Thanks, Max," Hooper called at the front door. "If I don't see you, Merry Christmas."

"Same to you."

I bolted up the stairs, conjuring images of toilet water flowing into Emma's room and dribbling through the floor into my room below. What I found was just as bad. Of course, Morgan had loaded my kid up on pizza, popcorn, and movie theater candy, fun aunt that she was. The result—an adult-sized dump, which was now floating across the vinyl bathroom floor.

Cursing words Emma had probably heard too much of in the past three years, I waded on tiptoe into the sea of doom that had yet to crest the doorway or soggy the carpeting of her bedroom. Yanking towels off the rack and out of the closet, I created a dam at the doorway.

"I'm sorry," Emma wailed pathetically.

"Go get me a clothes basket."

Suctioning the plunger, I got the pool in the bowl to produce a *glug* and recede down the drain hole, but not before I noticed the cause of the upheaval. Little white, saturated globs of fluff. Globs of fluff with hints of silver glitter on them.

That was when I lost it. I had no patience for things that were preventable because I had no time even for the things that were.

"Emma!"

She jerked to a halt at the door with a laundry basket in her hands. "What?"

"Are these cotton balls in your toilet?"

"I had to take my nail polish off."

"How many times have I told you—the *only* thing that goes in the toilet is toilet paper?"

It was a stupid question. I had no idea how many times I'd told her, and I doubt she did either. If I was in a courtroom right now, listening to me, I'd hang my head in shame.

"I only used a few. My garbage can was full!"

Pinching my eyes shut, I tried to channel saintly thoughts but failed. There were more than a few. Almost a dozen. Almost the exact amount for ten little fingers. Apparently, the proper protocol for removing nail polish was one cotton ball per finger—something a grown-ass man didn't need to know but was finding out the hard way.

Tugging the basket from her, I started heaving the sloppy towels into it, only pausing to fling Emma-turds into the toilet with a dustpan. I would do anything for my kid, but that didn't mean I did it well. My reply came through gagging sounds from the back of my throat.

"Your garbage can…wouldn't be full, if you'd bring it downstairs…like I ask you to. And you can't throw anything but toilet paper in here or it clogs the drain! No *Kleenex*. No cotton balls. No washcloths. No toys. Nothing! You got it?"

"I wanted to paint my nails red for the party tomorrow."

That. That was her defense.

Leaning back on my haunches, I was a grenade whose pin was a millimeter from being pulled free. "Did you hear what I said?"

Her lower lip disappeared, her shoulders hitched higher, and her eyes went glassy. That was the look before the tears. I didn't see it often, but I knew the signs. We'd reached a precipice. It could go either way—tears or holding it in. Either possibility held no appeal. I didn't need a reminder that she'd grown more immune to my raised voice, and I couldn't handle a crying kid right now.

Don't make me be an asshole. Please, don't make be an asshole, I chanted in my head.

"Yes," she finally said.

The sound of the defeated word was a lead weight in my gut. Taking a breath, I doused the flames of my rant. I couldn't even handle an overflowing toilet. I was father-of-the-freaking-year. I tried. I swear I tried not to sound like a dictator, but the words came out with more edge than I intended.

"Just go to bed."

Her shuddery puff of breath rattled in my ears, stabbing my conscience. To make matters worse, a greedy bastard part of me took comfort in her reaction, knowing it meant she would be on her toes and extra obedient for a few days. It was both a reprieve and a sadistic joy. I was so fucking pathetic. I was actually looking forward to a few days of my daughter's reticence. How low had I stooped?

After I got the bathroom back in order, I carted the basket of sopping towels to her bedroom door. They were dripping down my leg and soaking the front of my sweatshirt. I was saturated in toilet water and bleach like both the jerk I was and the cleansing my miserable soul needed. I shut the light off and glanced at Emma's blonde head, buried half in her pillow, facing the opposite wall.

"Goodnight," I called through the darkness, managing a more tender tone, hoping it would redeem me, but then... she sniffled.

"Goodnight." Her voice was crushed.

My shoulders sagged under the weight of the basket. That sniffle echoed in my head all the way down the stairs.

Way to go, dickhead.

And, because I'd been blessed with the responsibility of thinking for two parents, the voice in my head sneered, *Lainey would be so proud.*

Rounding the entryway to the kitchen, I saw the platters Jack had used for the food for our game were now cleaned, and drying by the sink, along with all our glasses and plates. Bags of chips lined the counter, each held neatly closed with clips. My savior had once again helped my ass out. Jack stood at the island, snapping lids on the *Tupperware* containing the leftovers.

He threw me a nod. "All under control?"

"Yeah." I gestured with my chin. "Thanks, man. You didn't have to do all that."

"Not a problem. Sounded like you had your hands full."

Grunting, I refused to complain and made my way down the hall to the laundry room. Someday, I was going to have to find a way to repay him for the endless list of good deeds he'd done for me. Right now, though, all I wanted was to strip out of my toilet water clothes, throw this stinking heap of towels in the wash, catch a shower, and pass out.

If I got up early tomorrow, I could review my notes for the Leopart deposition after breakfast, before I had to take Emma to her party. If I was lucky, I could squeeze in a haircut, pay some bills, and get groceries before I had to pick her up later.

Her party. Her dress. Fuck.

The not-a-Christmas dress taunted me from its place on the washer lid. First thing was first. Make the kid happy. I could throw my sweatshirt and jeans in with her stuff to make a semblance of a small load.

Kudos to me for saving water. I needed all the kudos I could get. It was enough to nudge my shitty mood back in the right direction... until I opened the washer. And the smell hit me.

Mold.

"Are you fucking kidding me?"

A red haze of fury clouded my vision. The thing was, though, there was only one person to be mad at—me. Jack had asked me earlier in the week if I needed him to do some laundry. My man-pride had declined the offer. When the hell was the last time I even used the washer?

Tuesday? Wednesday?

It was Friday night. Three days of fermenting clothes were dried to the side of the washer drum, solving the riddle of why I had a shortage of undershirts this week. The musty stench invaded my nostrils, still sensitized after the toilet purge. And what the hell was that blue stuff?

Prying a half-dried T-shirt from the side of the drum, I held it up for inspection. Gray mold dots speckled the fabric, the *white* fabric, that now looked like it had been tie-dyed with Smurf diarrhea. My ink pen fell from a fold in the crusty clothing and rattled in the bottom of the drum, mocking me.

Sweet mother of mercy. That. Was. It.

"Son of a bitch!" I snarled.

And of course, there were no empty baskets in sight because that was the way the sick, twisted universe worked.

Well, fuck you, Universe. Fuuuck. You.

I hauled over the garbage can and mucked everything out of the washer, pitching it into the can harder than Jack threw at the bottom of an inning. Maybe this was the answer to one of my time-consuming chores.

Wear it once and throw it away! No more laundry! No more folding! No more hanging shit up in the closet! I was a fucking genius.

"Son of a bitch. Motherfucking bullshit laundry." The words streamed out of me like I was speaking in tongues. Whipping my sweatshirt off, I pelted it into the trash can, effectively filling it.

Jerking the weighty bag out, I hefted it against the wall. In my cranial explosion, I realized that my kid was a genius, too.

"Fuck it! Let's just throw it in the closet! Make it disappear!"

"Everything all right?" Jack's voice hedged from the doorway.

I flailed open another trash bag like I was having a seizure. Not Jack. Not now. Not Mr. Always-had-his-Shit-and-Half-of-My-Shit-Together. I couldn't face Jack when I was one *LEGO*-foot-piercing away from losing my ever-loving mind.

"Yeah! Ha! Ha!" I squawked a maniacal sound. "Everything's fucking fantastic!"

Slapping on a grin, I popped up after dumping the basket of toilet towels in the trash and started on my saturated pants. Jack's expression said I looked like the sociopath I probably was right now.

Did that stop me from kicking my jeans off and lobbing them into the can? Nope. Because if you were going to go sociopath, go full sociopath.

I grabbed a clean T-shirt off the shelf and yanked it over my head. There. Now I was a half-clothed sociopath instead of a sociopath in his underwear. Way more dignified.

"I *love* cleaning up shit," I exclaimed, "and toilet water, and moldy fucking ink pen-stained clothes, and forgetting Christmas dresses and depositions. I *love* trying to figure out when I can squeeze in haircuts and bills, and groceries, wrapping presents, and getting asked if we can get a puppy so I can have even more shit to clean up—*literally more shit* because wouldn't that be fun? And I even *love* getting asked when I'm hauling out the Christmas decorations, when I'm putting up the tree and the lights, and trying to fucking think straight at work while all this shit is in the back of my mind like a stalker from hell!"

Digging my palms into my eyes, I leaned against the dryer to catch my breath, reminding myself that my father had died of a heart attack. When I inhaled, I didn't get the sense of calm I was seeking. Instead, I caught another giant whiff of moldy, fuck-my-life washing machine.

It was the scent of a pathetic failure. I slammed the lid closed with so much force it ricocheted back up like it was as possessed as I felt.

"God, damn it. I can't fucking do this anymore," I groaned into my hands.

"Max, it'll get better," Jack said.

"When? When the fuck is it supposed to get better?" My voice broke.

Jack's arms hung dead at his sides as though I'd accomplished the impossible task of sucking all the joy out of the world's most jovial man. He didn't have the answer, and I didn't expect one. The twisted look of sympathy on his face was too much. I pinched my eyes closed, gripping my hair with two fists.

My chest was heaving like a damn bouncy house full of sugared-up kindergartners. The pressure at the back of my sinuses burst, choking me in a sputter, and... I was crying. I was standing in my underwear fucking crying over a God damned washing machine. My dignity walked out of the room, hanging its head in shame.

"Fuck!" I blubbered through my fingers.

Try as I did to rein in the onslaught of snot and phlegm at the back of my throat, it erupted with more force. All I could do was use my palm as a shield for the self-pity leaking out of my eyes.

Christ. Maybe I needed to cry the way people needed to exfoliate their pores. Maybe if I let it out, I'd wake up tomorrow with a glowing soul and youthful complexion. I imagined a sharp beep and a store clerk handing me back a declined credit card, telling me there was no way I was buying my own bullshit today.

"Ah, Max," Jack's voice soothed closer to me.

I was jostled and squeezed into an Eagles pitcher bear hug. I knew he meant well, but I was a grown-ass thirty-four-year-old man, weeping his eyes out over shit soccer moms tackled with no bravado every day. It just made this that much worse, but instead of *soccer-momming* up, my head collapsed onto Jack's shoulder.

I clung to the back of his arm out of fear my legs would give up like the rest of me. He was so freaking strong; the embrace filled me with comfort as though the same universe that told me to fuck off minutes ago was now telling me it was okay to be weak for a few moments.

"It's all right, Max. You've got this," his smooth voice murmured at the side of my face.

Feebly, I shook my head and clutched a tighter grip on his shirt and arm, so he'd understand the level of agony and desperation.

"Can't," I gasped. "Haven't been...three years. *You*...I'm not *you*."

His big hand stroked the back of my head. His chest expanded on a puff of breath, like he was sharing my pain. I was cocooned in his man-hug like a sissy, but it was my cornerstone—a big warm, fleshy security blanket. It was different from the neck hugs Emma, Mom, and Morgan gave me. I never knew being squashed could be therapeutic. It was a vise, holding my cracked pieces together. I was terrified if he let go, all those pieces would crumble to the floor.

"I don't have all my shit together either, Max, and I don't have to go through what you do. It's okay to feel overwhelmed sometimes. We all do."

Permission. The last thing I needed to keep from losing it was permission to lose it.

Three years of pent-up frustrations, abandonment, failure, worry—every soul-crushing hurt I'd been carrying inside me—flowed out in sputters and sobs. It was a full-on exorcism, and there was nothing I could do to stop it. Frankly, I didn't even want to. I needed it gone. I needed to purge. It was poison I couldn't hold in anymore.

Clutching a grip of a million-dollar shoulder and a fistful of T-shirt, I poured everything out in incomprehensible sounds. My cocoon tightened.

A warm paw of a hand rubbed my back, another my head, fulfilling a coddling need I didn't even know I possessed.

His jaw pressed into my hair, brandishing a seal of comfort on my soul. Maybe it was seconds or minutes, but the fog in my head began to clear. My awareness started returning. Warm skin grazed my temple, then my cheek.

No. Not just skin—lips. *Jack* was pressing his lips to my face the way mothers consoled distraught children.

Men didn't do that. Not to men, my brain told me in a broken signal.

I imagined all the time he'd spent with Emma, nurturing skinned knees. I scoffed in amused disbelief, drawing my head off his shoulder. Poor Jack didn't even know what to do when a grown man was blubbering in his arms. Fuck. I'd made him revert to the only gestures of comfort he probably knew for this level of desperation.

His mouth brushed near the corner of mine, snapping me fully back to the present. I sucked in a breath so I could tell him, *I'm good,* and *can we agree to never mention how I just lost my shit*? Except, I didn't get the chance.

His nose brushed against mine, and then… there were lips. On my lips. Soft and gentle. And they stayed there. Jack's lips… on my lips.

Every clock in the world stopped. I was imagining this. That was the only explanation. My best friend, *a man*, was *not* pressing his lips to mine.

My breath snagged in my throat like a hiccup as his mouth brushed against mine with feathery lightness. A zap of electricity shot down my arms and spine. It raced down my legs and shuttled right back up to my balls and cock. Warmth exploded across my lower back and stomach.

Kissing. This was *kissing*, my brain reminded me, practically shouted it.

I hadn't been kissed in years. Jesus. It had really been *years*.

My body was… celebrating with tingling flesh like I had starved it of this particular meal, but my brain pulled an emergency brake. It said, '*No.*' That was all. Just a big fat resounding, *NO*.

My God. I could feel his breath on mine, feel the wetness from his lips on mine. My fucking balls were drawn up tight. I was suddenly hungry, carnally hungry for everything that went with kissing.

No. That couldn't be right.

I pulled my head back from the fog cloud, back from this incredible mistake. Shuddering, I didn't want to but looked up a few inches into Jack's eyes. Eye contact made this real. It couldn't be real.

With his mouth parted, a look in his eyes I'd never seen stared back at me, deep and longing. His thumb rubbed across my cheek.

"Max." That was all he said—my name in tender adoration, in a husky whisper.

Jesus. He was cupping my face like we were lovers. No. I had to… was *supposed to* stop this.

I shoved at his brick wall of a chest. It felt so wrong to push him. I mean, it was *Jack*. I would never shove Jack, but a sense of fight-or-flight was making my heart hammer. I was still up against the damn dryer, so *he* needed to be the one to make room, the one to move to get us back to an acceptable friend-distance.

"What the fuck, man?"

My hand flew to my mouth, covering it like a dirty secret. His lips pressed together. When he opened his mouth, the tip of his tongue crested through, and I trembled because I knew he could taste what just happened. He could taste me on his lips. He had to because I could taste him on mine.

"I…sorry. I'm sorry." He looked as dazed as I felt.

What in the hell did you say to your best friend after he kissed you? It wasn't like that happened by accident.

"Why…w-why did you do that?"

"I…felt bad. I wanted to make you feel better."

Okay. That made sense. Sort of, but also, not fucking really.

"Yeah, but why did you do *that*?"

I waited for him to crack a joke, to tell me he did it to snap me out of my meltdown. Fuck. I would even laugh because it worked. I'd never lose my cool in front of him again out of fear of being lip-locked. Except he didn't tell me he was fucking with me. He said the last thing I ever expected.

"I… Max, I'm gay."

"What?"

"I'm gay."

I stopped. Breathing.

My brain short-circuited. His expression was the same one the doctor wore when he told me Lainey was dead.

Gay.

Gay?

Did he really just say…

"You… You're…*gay?*"

His chest, still brandished with a wet spot from my tears, heaved like he'd been holding his breath as his features sagged. Why did he look like *I* was the one who gave *him* shocking news? He was the one saying things like *gay*.

"Jack?" my voice pleaded.

His silence was agonizing, so I worked the math. We went from lips to lips and then to the word *gay*. That could only mean one thing, and I didn't know how to feel about it. I *always* knew how I felt. Feelings were instinctive. Right now, it was absolutely fucking terrifying not knowing what to feel. I didn't need terrifying. I didn't need mysteries or surprises. My life was too hectic for change. I just needed my friend to be... who he was supposed to be.

His Adam's apple bobbed. His gaze darted to his feet. I knew that look. It was the one right before people told a hard truth.

"Y-yeah, but...I'm sorry."

A thousand questions invaded my head. A thousand memory particles shifted, trying to edit the reel that contained all my knowledge of Jack Spears.

"Since when?"

"Since...always." He gave a slow shrug and had that same choked expression Emma wore when I scolded her.

Always.

Always gay, as in since the day I met him six years ago?

How? Just...*how*?

People were gay. I understood that, but *people* were—not Jack. Not my best friend—my best friend who drank beer with me, was ripped like a mother, gave me home repair advice, and made man-jokes. Not the guy who an hour ago said his beer didn't taste like pussy.

Jesus. Had he ever had pussy? Was the joke on everyone and not just Dan?

Something between betrayal and heartbreak carved out my insides. I didn't know my best friend. I didn't know the man I'd told almost all my secrets. I had no idea who this Jack was.

The man standing in front of me still looked like Jack, but also... not. His features were a cocktail of remorse and anxiousness. Gone was that vibrant Jack Spears glow that I'd always fed off of. Pod people had inhabited his body. Squatting inside was an impostor. With his own words, he had distorted all my memories of him.

Why hadn't he told me? Why had he lied?

Scouring our conversations, I couldn't recall ever asking him about his sexuality, but there had never been a need to because... he let me think otherwise. Hadn't he? That was worse than a lie. He'd been pretending. Had he pretended to be my friend? How much of it was real? Was any of it real?

Jesus.

He'd just stolen something from me with two words. I was a bigger fool than I was a few minutes ago.

And why had he kissed me? He. *Kissed.* Me. He fucking kissed me like it was the end of a first date. My freaking body had hopped off the layaway shelf and lit up like a Black Friday sale. Why did it do that from a man-kiss?

Holy shit. Another new truth slammed into me.

He kissed me *because* he's gay. I was a dessert in a bakery window, not a friend. I was fucking dessert, and our friendship was all bullshit.

"I think you should leave." My voice sounded foreign as my words launched into the air between us.

His features pinched like I delivered a slap, making my chest squeeze. I never imagined ever kicking Jack out of my house. It did not feel good at all, but I needed to think. I needed to forget. I needed to remember. Whatever I needed, I couldn't do with him two feet away, and staring at me with that mouth, like a skewed version of the man I admired most in the world.

His jaw clamped shut. It had been hanging open in this eternity like he had something to say but couldn't get it out. His cheeks were flushed. His mouth was a tight line—the mouth I could still feel on mine. Finally, he let out a shuddery breath and gave me a single nod.

I was plastered to the dryer by a sensation of wrongdoing I couldn't explain. He walked out the door, suddenly looking old and decrepit, his wide shoulders hunched. Head down. Feet dragging.

That was definitely not the Jack Spears I knew. That was the man who just kissed me and made my best friend, my rock, disappear. The loss hit me like a twenty-pound medicine ball to the gut.

Wow. And I had thought things couldn't get any worse.

CHAPTER 3
Jack

What did I do?

What. Did I. Do?

Oh my God. What *the hell* did I just do?

Crisp air stung my lungs. I was outside. I didn't even know how I got here. These were Max's patio steps.

Okay. I had made it to the patio. Why was my brain narrating my surroundings like a GPS device?

Would I ever walk up these steps again? Would Max stop leaving the door unlocked?

The answers squeezed my heart like a fist. He actually told me to leave. Max kicked me out of his house.

"Oh God, Jack. What did you do?" The gut-wrenching, disembodied sound of my own voice made me nauseous.

I was talking to myself like I was having an out-of-body experience, but that was apt. I didn't feel attached to anything right now.

My legs were jelly on autopilot. I was vaguely aware of the sound of snow crunching. Probably under my feet? I didn't even know. I didn't know anything.

No. That wasn't true.

I knew one thing. I was pretty sure I'd just ruined the best thing that ever happened to me.

He *shoved* me.

Max shoved me.

Well, of course, he did! Do you blame him? He probably thought you were coming on to him!

Oh, God! Poor Max.

I just couldn't stand it, seeing him hurting like that. It was tearing me to shreds. Those sounds. His tears. All I wanted to do was hold him and siphon his pain.

I couldn't believe I kissed him. Holy shit. *I kissed him*. Had I ever kissed him.

By the time I realized I was doing it, it had been too late to stop. A kiss wasn't like that cherry *Kool-Aid* stain Emma left on the carpet last year that I wiped up. No amount of scrubbing could undo this. No *take-backsies*. Fuck!

I couldn't even imagine what he was thinking right now. Or worse, I could, but didn't want to. He probably thought I was some kind of pervert. Holy hell. This was awful. So awful.

Would he tell Emma? What would she think? Would she understand?

The thought wrapped around me like a body bag two sizes too small, swallowing all the light from my world as I reached the gate to my yard. My hands were shaking, but not from the cold.

What if Max wouldn't let me see Emma anymore?

No.

No, no, no.

I couldn't think like that. He wouldn't do that. The sandpaper in my mouth and my runaway pulse told me how convinced I was, though.

I honestly didn't know how Max felt about queer people. We'd never discussed it for obvious reasons on my part. He had to know I was still me. I was just like everyone else. I was still Jack. Still his friend. I could still be his friend.

But that look he gave me… He looked at me like I was an alien or a traitor.

Pressing the base of my palm to my cheekbone didn't stop the burning sensation in my eyes. It was a trick I had learned long ago when my dad used to pick apart everything I did.

I was a crier. Always had been. Give me a sentimental commercial, and I teared up. Show me Emma with her feelings hurt and off went the waterworks.

Looking up at the stars set against the blackness, I sucked in a shaky breath and double-palmed my face. Tonight, it was futile, but tonight it didn't matter if I fell apart.

I wasn't in public. There were no cameras, no teammates. No one to see the most idiotic thing I'd ever done. Still, I would have done anything to go back five minutes and erase what had brought on the hot mess spilling down my face.

Positivity, my deluded, upbeat brain whispered. I had to think positive.

Maybe Max wouldn't hate me for keeping my secret from him. Maybe he wouldn't be so weirded out that we couldn't salvage our friendship.

'*And if you can't*?' the rational part of my brain sneered.

There was no way I could handle being so close to him and Emma without being able to talk to them. I could request a trade, but I liked my team. I liked Springfield. I liked my routine. More importantly, I liked Max and Emma. I loved Max and Emma. If I moved, I'd never know if I missed an opportunity for Max to accept me the way I was.

I couldn't believe I was actually pondering these things as I practically stumbled down the hallway toward my room. The chalky texture of the painted drywall was cold against my palm as I braced the wall for support, like I was drunk.

I never imagined having to move again. I was a few hours' drive from my little sister, Carrie, where she lived just outside of our hometown. I was close enough to visit in a day, but far enough away to keep a comfortable distance between me and my father—the distance he'd all but asked for.

Funny. I'd have thought by now I'd be immune to the sting of being unwanted. Yet, aside from baseball, there seemed to be nothing but a trail of rejection behind me. First, my father—my oldest, deepest wound. Then my mother followed suit. She never shamed me outright the way Dad did. It was more like she slowly faded away because no one dared question Jack Spears Sr.

I knew she loved me, but I couldn't remember the last time I heard her voice over a whisper on the phone. Imagining her hiding in the pantry or the garden just to talk to me without being overheard kind of ruined any sentiment she tried to convey. Worse were the conversations she tried to relay to me through Carrie like a spy smuggling information over enemy lines.

It made my blood boil that Carrie had been forced to play hostage negotiator all these years. She acted like it didn't bother her to live in the jagged cracks of our broken family, but that was Carrie. Her heart was big enough to make up for where the rest of us fell short. She'd been my saving grace since we were kids—my person. The thing was, though, no one should have to bear the burden of being my only confidant.

I wanted nothing more than to call her and talk this out, but I'd been selfish enough tonight, pouring my unchecked emotions into a kiss that never should have happened. I couldn't bombard Carrie with another tale of my romantic humiliations. This chapter would be called *Big brother falls for straight man.*

Yeah, no way that conversation was happening. Carrie had always been a champion consoler, but I doubted any amount of consoling would make the ache in my heart go away. Pausing between my bed and the bathroom, I contemplated vomiting or belly flopping onto my mattress.

I just needed time to think. Max needed time to think. Maybe everything would be perfectly fine. He'd slap me on the back, laughing, and say, *'Why didn't you just tell me, fucker?'*

I sputtered at the thought as I collapsed onto my bed and burrowed under my covers. That would be a perfect world. Except, there was only one thing that had ever gone right in my life—baseball.

Max and Emma weren't the game. My stupid, greedy heart latched onto more than it could have, stretching it like a rubber band. Now the rubber band had snapped.

I wished the heedless organ in my chest was a ball I could throw down the field to a batter. I could control the way it jetted through the air, the amount of spin and velocity. But there was no catcher waiting at the other end of love. Hooper wasn't crouched at home plate, guiding me with a signal, providing a target with his glove where my heart could land in the leather. I had no idea what I'd do if the obstinate ball in my chest just cost me everything that had ever mattered to me.

CHAPTER 4
Max

The roads were clear of snow and the sun was shining as I drove past leafless trees and plastic holiday figures in the yards on our way to Patti Cullen's house. Emma hummed along with the Christmas station in the passenger seat wearing the dress we'd run out and bought her this morning. The cost of easing parental guilt was apparently forty-nine ninety-five this week, but Emma looked damn impressive, so bonus points to me.

Short of the *fa-la-la-la-la'ing*, I couldn't identify a single song that had come out of the radio. My focus was programmed to the chamber of incantations in my head.

Jack kissed me. Jack kissed me. Jack is gay. Jack is gay, and he kissed me.

Late into last night, I replayed every conversation we'd ever had, trying to see how I missed it. Trying to convert memories deeply embedded in your brain was like trying to reassign meaning to words.

Up is down. Right is left. Tomato is kiwi.

For example, I remembered Jack laughing and cooking with Lainey. Converted, the memory was different, but yet, not at all. It was just Jack, *gay*, laughing and cooking with Lainey—the two of them with an inconsequential word floating in the background like a butterfly that didn't know where to land.

Was that why I couldn't fucking cook—because I wasn't gay? Was Gordon Ramsey gay?

Welcome to the new confusing land of *'Max Actually Thought That.'* In less than twelve hours, my idiotic questions had become limitless. Like did it matter who was gay?

No. Of course not.

I fucking knew that. I was not a narrow-minded prick.

Love was love. Love was beautiful. Without question, no one was ever more deserving of love than Jack, and he unequivocally deserved to love—whichever gender he preferred.

I just… couldn't get over why he never told me what he preferred. It wasn't important who he was attracted to, but the fact that he blatantly and repeatedly went out of his way to make me think otherwise made it important.

I laid in bed until the wee hours of the morning, wanting to be pissed off at him for not telling me this important thing, only to realize I wasn't. I didn't have the right to be.

He wasn't obligated to tell me things. Except, not telling me this important thing reminded me of when my favorite coffee shop sometimes forgot to toast my bagel on mornings Jack didn't fix us breakfast.

Was I allowed to feel slighted? Not about the fucking bagel, but about Super-Secret Keeper Jack. Well, okay. Also, about the fucking bagel.

I mean, come on. That was what you did to bagels. It's like, *'You had one job bagel guy!'* Kind of like how when you asked your best friend once if he was dating a woman you saw flirting with him at a cookout at his house. Instead of just saying *no*, he could have said, *'No, because I like penises. Would you like cream cheese with that?'*

Friends were supposed to tell each other things. They were supposed to talk about the important things.

Last night, it occurred to me that none of the media coverage I'd seen about Jack had ever mentioned his sexuality. They practically painted him as a sports playboy, MLB's Most Eligible Bachelor. The lack of intel would imply he wasn't out. If he was, I was sure I'd have found out in a different, less life-altering manner.

So, riddle me this. Why *did* he keep it a secret? Was he not comfortable with it, or did he just keep it from the press because they were a bag of dicks?

Shit. You see? That right there. The bane of my absurd questions.

Should I not make dick jokes anymore?

Again, something I should have learned six years ago!

The question hit me with a *Tony Stark* moment, when his *Iron Man* heart thingy malfunctioned and wracked his chest with agony, except the agony in my chest was a sense of betrayal.

I wasn't the press. *I* could keep a secret. I was a freaking lawyer. I could have written and signed an NDA for him. So, let's review again an alternate past where this could have been resolved.

Why, no, Max. I'm not dating her because I like penises, but could you write up an NDA because I don't want to talk about it? Pass the cream cheese, please.

Had I said or done something that kept him from telling me? Was I that unapproachable? Maybe *slighted* wasn't the right word for how I felt. *Inadequate?* Had I been an inadequate friend?

Shit. I fucking shoved him, and I was friends with Dan, who, in my mature years, I realized was the most bigoted man on the planet. Of course, I probably looked unapproachable. If I hadn't before, I sure as shit did now.

Fan-fucking-tastic.

Was that the message I gave off—that I was Dan's freaking minion? I never joined in on his dickery. Jack knew that. Didn't he?

As I watched Emma race up the sidewalk to her friend's house in her new dress, the thickness in my throat told me that wasn't quite true. Had I ever stopped Dan's awful jokes and crude comments? The answer was a gut-punching *no*.

I laughed them off, called him a *dick*, and either changed the subject or walked away. That was a far cry from putting my foot down and calling him out on his bullshit. I had never taken a stand because I hadn't needed to... because it hadn't applied to me. I sank lower in the seat of my car, knowing the moral was that it didn't need to apply to me. Right was right. Wrong was wrong. Tomatoes were kiwis.

Yet that made what happened last night even more of a mystery. Who would want to kiss a guy who had a friend like Dan and had, for all intents and purposes, condoned Dan's shitty behavior?

Jack would, I guess.

Emma stopped at the door to her friend's house, turned around, and waved. The smile on her face told me the fact she was wearing a dress other than the one in the catalog or the one from her closet I couldn't wash in Satan's washing machine hadn't dented her happiness. She was so damn forgiving, so understanding, so unlike how I acted last night. I waved back, the only company in my car now a secret the size of Texas.

Jack knew I was straight, and that I was friends with someone like Dan. Why would he kiss a guy like me?

To make me feel better.

Ugh. That made no sense. Again. Not gay. This guy. Right here! So why would he think kissing me would make me feel better? *Did* I feel better?

I honestly didn't feel better or worse. My brain and emotions were fried, which was the only explanation why I had just gone six blocks in the wrong direction and still had the Christmas station on. Shit. There went ten minutes of my Saturday that I could have spent browsing new washing machines.

As I turned a corner back toward the direction of sanity, I spotted two boys having a snowball fight in their yard. One hiked up his knee like he was winding up a pitch, and I mentally critiqued his poor form, and how Jack would have done it better.

The weird pulse of adrenaline zipping through my veins like a prickling charge from a battery that had been there since last night kicked up a notch. Was that how people who just learned a national secret felt?

Jack had seen me look pathetic before and never kissed me. My whole dessert theory now sounded kind of fickle by the light of day. He'd done too much good since I met him, been too kind. No one did what he'd done for my family, motivated by lust. Still, it seemed pressing to know—had he always wanted to kiss me?

Lips. A man's lips on mine.

I shouldn't have been thinking about this lying in my bed Sunday night, but it was the only place I had no distractions from Emma or the five hundred things I needed to do around the house and with my cases. I had spent the entire weekend wound like a spring, wondering if Jack would stop by or call or text and what I would say to him if he had. Every time the floor creaked, I nearly jumped out of my skin. Needless to say, clear-headed Max's photo was currently being printed on milk cartons.

Welcome to '*Restless Thoughts with Max*,' episode three. The impact of that kiss was snaked around me, tying me in a different way to the man

I thought was my best friend. This wasn't Europe. We didn't kiss people hello and goodbye. Kisses meant something here. At least, they had always meant something to me.

Many moons ago, I had a one-night stand in college after I broke up with my high school girlfriend, but before I met Lainey.

With a girl named Heather? Hannah? Herrah? H. E. Double Hockey Sticks? I didn't fucking remember, but that was my point. I couldn't kiss her. I had known what we were doing wouldn't mean anything, wouldn't be something memorable. At the time, I knew I could give away the physical part of a climax, of thrusting and moaning. But kisses? They were something I couldn't leave with a stranger.

Jack now had one of my kisses. Why had he kissed me?

The question was like a fucking chirping cricket you couldn't find. Its mission in life was to be an annoying bastard that could not be killed.

Maybe I was going about this all wrong by thinking about it from my perspective. I hadn't been the initiator Friday night.

Right. Good. I could work with this. Role reversal.

Fact: people kissed people they liked.

Shit. Not helpful. New quandary.

Did that mean Jack liked me? Like *liked me, liked me*? Christ. I sounded like I was in junior high.

Turning over, I punched my pillow like it was the reason I was still awake at midnight on a Sunday. Why the fuck was I thinking about this? And why in the hell did it still feel like his lips were on mine? Why was my heart racing? Was I having a panic attack?

Just get it out of your head, Max.

He's gay.

He kissed you.

He apologized.

Period.

Awkward accident. Move on.

But... it was a fucking cricket.

All weekend, I had pictured Jack practically every second of the day. I knew what he looked like, but it was like my brain knew I had voted him off the island and was sending me postcards on the hour with that dejected look on his face, so I wouldn't forget him or what I'd done.

Dear Max, Wish you were here.

He was now tattooed on the backs of my corneas like I was wearing glasses with his picture in place of the lenses.

CHAPTER 5
Jack

Have you ever noticed that no matter how many ferns or waterfalls or sunning rocks there are to beautify an animal enclosure at the zoo, it's still a cage? By Monday morning, my house had become a prison that grew smaller by the hour. By this time tomorrow, there wouldn't even be room for me to turn around.

Should I have gone over to Max's on Saturday? Sunday?

No. Damn it, Spears. We've been over this. Stick to the plan!

Max needed time to process. Clearly. Otherwise, he would have made contact. The fact that I had resorted to using phrases like '*made contact*,' as if our friendship was some volatile espionage operation, had not escaped me.

Gah! I realized he probably needed time, but why was time going by so slowly?

It was almost seven in the morning. I should be going over there to collect Emma for school soon. I should be there right now, cooking them breakfast. I *should*. Normally, I would. But today? After a kiss and a kick out? Did Max want me there?

My hands had sprouted about a thousand sweat glands over the weekend. They were working overtime, drenching my phone. I couldn't sit here in my kitchen like a coward.

I wanted to see Emma. I wanted to help her and Max out like I always did. He was probably feeding her sugary cereal, and himself burnt frozen waffles. No doubt he had rushed through shaving too and forgot that spot under his chin he always missed when he was in a hurry. And I wasn't even going to think about how their hair looked.

The few times I'd missed a morning and seen them after the fact, they looked like ragamuffins. It was killing me, knowing I couldn't prevent it.

Maybe Max didn't know what to say either. Maybe he was waiting to hear from me.

Were we going to pretend nothing happened? That would actually be a fantastic end to this shit show I'd created.

I stared at my phone, wondering what to say. Why were there so many variations of what I needed to ask? Was I asking for permission to watch Emma?

I didn't want him to think I didn't want to help, but I also didn't want to beg. That would be like acknowledging the reason I needed to beg. As far as I was concerned, that kiss was now unmentionable.

I didn't want him to feel like I was offering him charity by offering to drive Emma and watch her after school. After a few more crucial minutes ticked by, my fingers grew some balls, and tapped out a message in a shaky rush.

ME: Am I still taking Emma to school?

I let out a whoosh of breath and hit send. There. Simple. Direct. No groveling. No guilt. No mention of 'the unmentionable'… sweet, sweet, never should have happened, unmentionable.

I couldn't sit still. Every minute Max didn't reply was a slow torture. I paced through the living room. Then I paced around the kitchen.

Come on, Max. Don't leave me hanging.

He wouldn't go full radio silence on me. Would he?

My phone pinged, and I jumped, nearly dropping it. I felt like I had won the world series just seeing his name pop up.

I clicked open the message, and… it was like I just dropped an easy infield fly ball.

MAX: Dropping her off at my mom's. She's taking her to school. Patti's picking her up. Thanks though.

My brain erupted into a Jerry Springer show, yelling out the ironies of his plan. His mom lived twenty minutes away on the other side of town. That was the opposite direction of the school. The opposite direction of Max's firm. And Patti Cullen, Emma's friend's mom? He couldn't stand her. She hit on him every time he saw her, and her kid was a snob.

The message couldn't be any clearer. I wasn't even the last choice. I was no choice. My worst fear had come true.

The unspoken subtext hit me like a game-tying runner slamming into a catcher. I sank against the kitchen counter, almost too weak to stand. Max wasn't waiting to hear from me. He wasn't even waiting to forget me. He already had.

As I sped away from my mother's house like a getaway driver, I knew one thing for certain. I was a coward.

And probably an asshole.

Okay. No *probably* about it.

Emma bought my lame-ass excuse that Jack was busy and couldn't watch her today, but now I had lying on my conscience. I might as well have sent Jack a bullet instead of a text message because that was probably the impact it had on him for how much he adored seeing Emma.

The worst part about it? I knew that, even when I made alternate plans, even as I typed out my reply, but I still sent it like a soulless murderer.

I was grateful he still considered watching Emma, but I was just as grateful he hadn't stopped by this weekend. I had no idea what I'd have said to him if he had, and no idea what I'd say to him the next time I saw him. That itself was inconceivable—not knowing what to say to Jack.

The very definition of a friend was someone to whom you could speak without thinking of what to say. I'd never had to *think* of what to say to him.

I talked to complete strangers all day at work, but I couldn't think of anything to say to my best friend. No words of substance that would miraculously fill this space wedged between us.

As I headed toward my morning coffee stop in my SUV, the orange glow of the sunrise on the snowy horizon, my usual talk radio program was useless at drowning out my thoughts. The soundtrack in my head was on a loop at full volume.

Jack kissed me.

Jack kissed me.

Ah! Fucking crickets!

The shit I pulled this morning was going to kill him, but I wasn't ready to face him. I needed to know what he felt and thought, but sometime this weekend, I realized it was just as important to know what I felt and thought. I didn't know yet, so it was best I stayed away until I did.

I ordered my coffee and toasted-fucking-bagel, since I chased off my breakfast chef—*thanks a lot, Asshole Me*—and drove to the parking garage of my firm in a haze. Every face I passed was a featureless blur. It was like I was just going through the motions, starting my morning routine via muscle memory. I checked my messages and emails, but I didn't register their context. All I heard was the cricket.

And all I could feel was that spark, that endless trickle of electricity fluttering through my body. It had spread every day since that night in my laundry room, slowly claiming every inch of me.

When it was time to head to the conference room, I locked my computer and headed down the hall on autopilot, greeting Dan and Trevor with nods and grunts. My flesh was taut under my suit as I pretended to absorb myself in a file I had open in front of me. We kept our third-floor office fairly cool to cut down on heating costs, however, it was uncharacteristically toasty in here today. The electric pulse inside me had bloomed into a flush of warmth from my head to my toes.

Cricket. Cricket.

I didn't even know what Trevor had been saying for the last ten minutes at our morning roundtable. My body temperature and over-sensitized skin had amplified with each passing minute, with each repetitive incantation in my brain. My fucking nuts were drawn up tight like I hadn't been laid in ten years rather than only three. Christ, since when did anxiety feel like arousal?

I always thought Jack was a good-looking guy. Lainey used to joke that I had a man-crush on him because I once told her—jokingly—he was the epitome of manliness. She said it playfully, just to piss me off.

I meant that he was a top-notch athlete, famous, successful, funny, good-hearted, could get any woman he wanted, and was in the kind of physical shape any man could only hope to be in. He was the American pastime. Jack *was* baseball. He *was* man. And now… he'd fucking kissed me. The man of all men kissed me.

What did that mean? How did it change things? I mean, it *had* to change things. Right?

I'd been waiting to see if I thought of Jack as less than a man for some reason. I fucking sounded like Dan. I knew it was a dick thing to think that if a man was gay, he was defective in manliness, but that was the reaction society had predominantly had.

Like what did Jack think I looked like—the big spoon or the little spoon? And how fucking ignorant of me was it to wonder that? Why was *that* my instinctive thought? It shocked the hell out of me so hard, I couldn't swallow my fucking bagel.

How much bigotry had wormed its way into my brain cells over the years without me realizing it? And how? I didn't recall my parents ever being fuckheads about race, religion, or sexuality. What other judgmental ideas were lurking in my head that I didn't know about? Who had been controlling my brain all these years?

The thing was, though, Jack still looked and acted like a man to me. He sure as hell had more balls than I ever would to kiss a guy.

Jesus.

I was the little spoon.

CHAPTER 7
Jack

The morning light cast an ethereal glow on my black granite countertops. My hand was clammy, saturating my phone with sweat again as I stared at it like it held the answers to life's mysteries. I had never hated an inanimate object more. This thin black device was controlling my life.

When it chirped, I jolted like it was a defibrillator and imagined a heart monitor readout spiking a neon green line to a peak. It was just another message from Hooper. My heart sank, and my brain conjured the sound of a flatline, and perhaps a doctor somewhere, shaking his head, saying, *'he was so young.'*

I sighed and opened the message. *Dramatic much, Jack?*

The message was a response to an earlier text I had sent Hooper, letting him know I'd be passing on yet another workout today because I was still *under the weather.*

HOOPER: Dude. Do I need to DoorDash you some chicken noodle soup?

Normally, I might have laughed, but I seemed to have broken my funny bone, which was convenient. It made my claim of being *unwell* not a total lie. Something *was* broken, perhaps not an illusive bone, but my heart.

ME: No, man. I'll be fine. Just resting up.

HOOPER: It's been four days. Either you're dying, being a pussy and only have a man-cold, avoiding me—highly unlikely—or sick is code for doing unspeakable things with some hottie you're keeping a secret. In which case, you are forgiven if it's the last, but does she have a sister?

I tried to laugh. It was pretty bad when even Hooper's antics couldn't drag me out of my rut. Powering the phone off and chucking it in a drawer where it couldn't manipulate me was tempting, but that cruel voice in my head whispered, *then you won't know if Max calls*. The cruel voice's cousin whispered back, *Max isn't going to call, moron*.

Maybe I should take Hooper's DoorDash offer, if not for any other reason than the opportunity for in-person human contact. Our workouts weren't even in-person, and I'd still avoided them.

We used the *StreamParty* app so each of us could run on our treadmills and simultaneously watch the same YouTube music videos from our own homes while talking shit over the chat feature. I didn't have it in me to entertain Hooper for the length of a workout, though unbeknownst to him I'd run twice as long and twice as hard the last few days so I wouldn't climb the walls.

Not seeing Max and Emma was starting to remind me of being in New York—alone, empty, invisible, only interacting with people from my team because they needed to know I was alive so they could rely on my arm come February. My melodrama knew no bounds, but it was so true. I had stopped kidding myself a long time ago.

Hooper was a good guy. We shared an easy banter, but it was nothing more than all the other relationships I'd had with teammates over the years—the kind of relationships based on straight-baseball-teammate-Jack, my perfect twin. Everybody loved that guy.

The only thing that made the semblance of a friendship I shared with Hooper seem stronger was that we relied on each other more than other teammates. He was a catcher. I was a pitcher. The yin and yang of baseball. Our comradery encompassed our time on the field, working out together both in- and offseason so we could keep playing ball, playing video games while we were waiting to play ball, and occasionally hanging out where we talked mostly about—you guessed it—playing baseball.

I dug down deep and summoned the filtered version of Jack I had created years ago—cheeky, locker room humored, 'everyone's-favorite-optimistic-player-Jack.' 'Implied-straight-Jack.'

ME: Not dying. Man-colds are no joke. You are unavoidable. And the very definition of unspeakable things is that you don't speak of them. If she had a sister, I wouldn't tell you. Being related would ruin our beautiful friendship.

The typing bubbles appeared and then disappeared several times.

HOOPER: Shit. I got nothing. You're like Yoda. That was oddly profound.

ME: Thanks for the soup offer, though. Good to know you'd subject a minimum-wage earner to my contagiousness if I were dying.

HOOPER: That's what friends are for, bro. To save you from a distance.

I wished I could save Max from the distance he'd imposed between us. The only way I could think of to do that was if I kept helping out with Emma, but made myself scarce by watching her at my place after school so he wouldn't have to be uncomfortable being around me. That meant no breakfasts, no dinners, no hanging out on their couch, watching TV with them. That wasn't ideal, but it would be better than nothing.

I was so pathetic, staring at my phone, knowing I was essentially about to beg for a morsel. I didn't care, though. I would beg if that was what it took to see Emma. Somewhere in my addled brain, I knew Max had never been mine in any sense and never would be—but Emma? God. I couldn't let her go without trying everything.

ME: Need me to watch Emma today? I'd be happy to if you're okay with it.

There. Straight, but to the point. That was a laugh. I was so not straight. That was what got me into this mess.

My answer arrived faster than yesterday, like maybe he was anticipating my message. My limbs went heavy, reading my sentence.

MAX: No. Thanks. Same arrangement as yesterday.

Thanks.

The word stung. It didn't feel like gratitude. It felt like politeness disguised as gratitude. It was so un-Max.

I missed his directness. I missed his *fuck-offs*. I hated this limbo we were stuck in. It would be better if he just screamed at me and told me to get lost forever.

Except part of me knew we weren't stuck in limbo. This looked like the beginning of a complete shutout. We were stuck on goodbye, or rather… I was.

Just me.

Shit. He was really doing this. Really forgetting I existed.

A fat tear landed on my phone. I had to get out of here. I couldn't spend another day waiting to hear Max's car door, waiting to hear his and Emma's voices outside when they got home. I couldn't lie in my bed in the stifling silence of my house and my poor decisions.

If this was what Max wanted, it was what I needed to give him. He owed me nothing. I didn't need to burden him with more stress than he already had by coming off as clingy.

I tapped out a message, not wanting to write a word of it. My pulse hitched, my heart pathetically excited to have at least this minuscule connection between us. Insignificant words passed between our phones like we were having an actual conversation.

ME: Going out of town. Again, I'm sorry for what happened.

MAX: Okay.

I didn't know how I was expecting him to reply. I just wanted him to know I wouldn't be around if he and Emma needed anything. It hadn't even merited a response. I knew *Okay* was at least an acknowledgment, but the trite word killed me.

It was a harsh reminder that I needed to fall out of love with a man who had never given me any indication he'd even wanted my love. It was a soul-splitting decree—even if you chose happiness, it didn't always choose you back.

Five hours later, I knocked on the red wooden door of the only person in the world who knew me better than Max. The throbbing in my knuckles from the contact mixed with the frigid temperature was a welcome sensation after the longest wallow in self-pity, also known as the car ride from my house to Indiana.

When the hinges creaked, I sucked in a breath, hoping it would help compose me. At the sight of my little sister's big, kind brown eyes, though, and the instant concern on her face that told me I looked as pathetic as I felt, my composure turned around and ran away.

"I kissed Max," I blurted like she was deaf, and I was alerting her to a national emergency. And then, in a very manly way, I sputtered like a water-logged engine, trying to turn over, hung my head, and sobbed.

The pops and crackles from the fireplace filled the silence with ambient noise. Carrie and I lay sprawled out on the floor of her living room like two exhausted snow angels. Neither of us had moved in at least an hour. I would still be wearing the indentations of her spiral-weaved rug on my ass and back tomorrow, but I had neither the inclination nor motivation to move.

I wasn't even going to ask if she'd actually ever bought anything with the money I gave her, rather than donate it. Pretty sure this itchy monstrosity we were lying on came with the house, and belonged to the old lady who owned it before Carrie bought the place. She was definitely getting a new rug for Christmas. Something soft and comfortable, good for hashing out the life crises of hopeless big brothers.

The flickering glow of the fire made light and shadows dance across the ceiling like a warbled amber ocean. Carrie raised one lithe arm and pointed to the show above us.

"Velociraptor," she announced.

I snorted the semblance of a laugh when I realized what she was doing. We used to flop down in the grass and stare at the clouds when we were younger, often to avoid my father, mostly so *I* could avoid my father, but my misery was her misery, so she tagged along. Our most important conversations had happened under the sky. Like when I was sixteen and told her I was gay, she'd shrugged and said, '*I know.*' Eventually, when we were all talked out, we'd start calling out cloud shapes with a high amount of inaccuracy.

"Not playing?" she asked. I hadn't realized how long it had been since she spoke.

"Sorry. I'm not seeing anything."

"So? What are you going to do?"

After she'd let me snot up the shoulder of her sweater, she'd listened to my entire sordid retelling of the past few days, from my revelation the night of the card game to the kiss to the *Okay* text this morning. She already knew the part about me having a crush on him, and apparently, the part where I was hopelessly in love with him even though I hadn't. Hooper would be impressed—Carrie was the real Yoda.

"I don't know. I hadn't thought much past driving across state lines to fall apart on your doorstep."

"Well, you know you're always welcome to fall apart on my doorstep, but I wish it hadn't come to that."

"I know." I dug the heels of my palms into my puffy eyes. "I don't know how I even kissed him. One second, he was crying, and the next, we were holding each other, and I just...bleh," I finished with a word vomit sound because that was what everything that came out of my mouth sounded like at this point.

She chuckled. "You *bleh'd* all over him?".

Rolling my head, I shot her the stink-eye. She laughed harder, producing one of her signature little snorts.

"Damn it," she grumbled and shifted her glasses up to pinch the bridge of her nose. "Sorry. I'm not laughing at your pain, I swear. I was trying to cheer you up."

"Don't bother. I'm a black hole of self-pity right now. I just needed to tell someone, and as usual, you were it. Sorry, *Care Bear*. I really hate making you my love life dumpster."

She turned onto her side, propping her head up in her hand, and dug into the giant bag of peanut M&M's that sat between us. They clacked together like marbles as she rooted through them, no doubt dodging the red ones.

"Don't worry about it. It gives me good ideas for my stories, since my love life is non-existent."

"Please, God. Do *not* write about a gay ballplayer kissing his straight best friend and then crying about it to his little sister. I'm no literary agent, but... Worst. Story. Ever."

"I don't know. I think it's really sweet. I could write you a happy ending."

"No one would buy it. Newsflash: Gay man dies alone."

"Wow. You are a black hole. Here. Eat some of these. Will you?"

She extended her hand, palm up, revealing a small heap of red M&M's. I shook my head and stared in vain for more velociraptors. All I could see were Max and Emma's faces.

"No, thanks. I'm not at the eating my feelings stage yet."

Something pelted me in the cheek, something small, round, and hard. I looked over to find Carrie smirking at me as another M&M launched at me. I stared stupidly at its trajectory, flinching when it whapped me in the nose. A second later, my hand came up, batting at the air. Damn it.

Rolling onto my side, I mirrored her pose, hoping my free hand could miraculously protect me if she continued her barrage.

"You should really get that fixed." She grinned as she zinged yet another candy. This one bounced off my forehead, followed by me smacking myself in the same place. She let out another snort and then cursed herself for making the noise.

"*You* should really get *that* fixed," I countered, picking up an M&M off the floor and popping it in my mouth.

She heaved a sigh. "I know. Luke said I sounded like a wild hog, rooting in the bushes."

"Fuck Luke."

"Whoa! You f-bombed. *What has happened*?"

"Your ex deserves an f-bomb. Actually, all of them do."

"Thanks, but don't throw away your etiquette training for me."

"I save my slip ups just for you. Don't worry. I'm still America's sweetheart on camera."

She rolled me several more red candies, and I ate them like an obedient, pouting heifer. "And I was only joking. I like your snort, Care Bear. Someday you'll find a guy who likes it, too."

"Yeah. Sure. A snorting, glasses-wearing accountant who secretly self-publishes dirty books and thinks different M&M colors have mood-inspiring properties. I'm what every man wants. Newsflash: She dies alone."

"Well, you do throw a mean M&M."

She snorted again. "Damn it, Jack."

I laughed then, and the effect was like clearing a clogged drain. Carrie let out another snort, and I doubled over when she yelled at me, collapsing in her own fit of laughter.

We died down to sighs and teary eyes. Somehow, we'd managed to end up on our backs again, staring in silence at the ceiling.

"I could get you a skylight for Christmas, so we could see the clouds from inside."

"God, no. Then I'd never get anything done."

Several moments passed as I picked peanuts out of my teeth with my tongue, grateful for the distraction. Carrie must have sensed my burdened thoughts and broke the silence.

"Newsflash. Did you know *'gay man dies alone'* isn't the ending of male romances anymore? That only happened from the turn of the century through like the eighties."

"*Only*," I repeated because new-me, depressed-me, was apparently all about focusing on the negative.

"Anyway. It's a bright new future for gay literature."

"Don't say *bright*. It sounds like a glitter reference. It offends me," I half-ass joked because complaining was now my addiction.

"Your attitude toward glitter offends me." She rolled her eyes at my self-pity. "So, what I was getting at is that while I'm incredibly flattered you think of me as a dumpster fire…"

"I did *not* say that!"

"Did I say *fire*? Oh. Sorry." She waved a hand in the air. "What I meant was, while you've honored me all these years with your *non-offensive* label of *giant trash receptacle*, I'm not the only person you can talk to anymore."

It was my turn to snort. "You really are a writer. One of these days, you need to quit your shitty job and let me find you a literary agent. I'm not letting that go," I warned her with my index finger, "but who the hell am I supposed to talk to about…men? Lainey was the only other person I ever told." I sighed and rubbed my eyes again. "Which just makes this even more messed up. Do you think she'd be mad at me?"

Carrie whipped onto her stomach and propped herself up on her elbows, so she was looking down at me. "That you love Max?"

I hesitated. I'd never actually said it aloud before. "Y-yeah."

"Don't you think she'd want to know he was loved? That he was surrounded by love, if she couldn't be here?"

I said nothing. Answering would be like knowing a winning lottery number ahead of time. So, instead, very maturely, I informed her, "You have rainbow teeth."

"I wear them when I fight gay dumpster fires," she deadpanned and smacked my arm even as she drew her tongue across her candy-stained teeth. "Don't change the subject. Since you moved in next door to Max and Lainey, we don't talk as much."

Shit. Had I been so wrapped up in my own life, I'd neglected Carrie? She was kind of a recluse, but unlike me, she seemed to welcome her solitude with open arms.

"I'm sorry. I didn't know you felt like that. I always thought I pestered you too much, and you already had to do the whole speaking for Mom thing for me, so I…"

"No. No. That's not what I meant. And if Mom wants to talk to you, she can do what I tell her every time she asks me to tell you something—grow some balls and call you herself even if Dad is around."

I arched a brow. "You actually told Mom to grow some balls?"

"What do you think?" Jamming her thumb nail in between her teeth, she shot me a dubious look. "I couldn't handle the end of days *that* would cause. But quit distracting me. I was happy for you when you moved in next to the Hartwells because I saw how happy you were. I love you, Jack. I'll always get excited when you call or text or come over, and, yes, I do miss you sometimes, but it's hard to miss someone when you know they've got someone looking out for them. Someone who makes them happy. You didn't call or come to visit much the last few years because you had Max."

"I didn't *have* Max. Not really. I just…thought I did."

"He was your friend. *Is* your friend. My point is, you always talked to him, so you can talk to him now. I'm not the only one."

"Carrie, how can I talk to him if he wants nothing to do with me?"

"You go over there and talk to him just like you always have. Just ask him if he wants to talk about what happened."

"Are you forgetting the part where he told me to leave?"

"Are you forgetting the part where he didn't say *forever*? So, he got scared when his friend kissed him. How would you have reacted if Lainey planted one on you out of the blue?"

Shit. When she put it like that? I'd have run for the hills, worried I'd ruin their marriage. If Lainey had been single? Ugh. Can't say I wouldn't have avoided her a bit until I knew if she'd let up or not.

"Tell him you won't kiss him again, but that you're still his friend. I'm sure you both could use one."

"What if…what if he doesn't want to be friends with me now that he knows?"

"You need… No. You *deserve* a good friend. If Max is a good friend, he'll do his part to fix this."

"And if he doesn't want to fix it?"

She frowned and gave my arm a squeeze. "Then that's *his* loss, Jack. Not yours."

"So, what do I do after the whole swearing-not-to-kiss-him thing?"

Her brows pinched together like I couldn't have asked a dumber question. "Just be yourself."

My mouth tilted up on either side at my command. After all the melo-drama I'd unloaded on her, I wanted her to believe she'd inspired me. I didn't have the heart to tell her what I was thinking.

Just be myself? Sometimes, I didn't even know who that was.

CHAPTER 8
Max

The digital clock on the nightstand read eleven fifty-two p.m. Welcome to Tuesday night's episode of '*Restless Thoughts with Max.*'

Fuck. My. Life.

How could I be so exhausted and still be awake? This was getting to the point of delirium. I wanted to cry.

No. Scratch that. Already did enough of that Friday night. I still couldn't believe I'd bawled my eyes out.

Well, there had actually been plenty of days I wanted to cry in the last three years. I just... couldn't believe I cried and leaned on Jack. It wasn't the leaning part or even the crying part. He'd always been there for me. Men gave each other man hugs. I knew it happened. Those clap on the back ones. Jack and I had done them when he left for road games or when we celebrated holidays. But we'd never... held each other.

This had felt like being held, and I had participated in the holding. I couldn't put all the blame on Jack. I had a meltdown, and he reacted... with compassion. And since I was being honest, it felt good to be held. Really good. I missed being held. Was it wrong I felt better when he held me?

I didn't feel empty or like my life was fucking smashing me in a trash compactor for a few seconds. For the past three nights, I hadn't been able to get to sleep until I thought about that feeling. Those hands. Those big, strong, warm, manly arms and hands.

I was married to a woman, for Christ's sake. I wasn't supposed to think about how good it felt to be held by a man, but I didn't fucking care anymore. I was beyond exhausted. I had to allow myself this sedative, a Jack-hug sedative. I needed some goddamn sleep.

Wednesday morning, I was pretty sure every eye in the place was on me as I walked out of the reception area of the firm toward my office. It was like I was a character in some science fiction movie who had undergone a secret experiment and was failing miserably at concealing his body was transforming, growing scales and tentacles underneath his suit. Next thing, I'd be chewing on my stapler and chugging coffee straight from the pot as the authorities rushed in with a straight jacket and hauled me off to a government lab. A hundred bucks said Jennifer, our receptionist, probably thought I was a pervert.

"Nice sweater," I had told her. "It really brings out your eyes. Your legs look great in that skirt."

What. The fuck. Was wrong with me?

I woke up this morning thinking about arms and hands on me—Jack's arms and hands. And lips.

It had been five days, and I could still feel his lips. Thinking about the more-than-a-man-hug was only supposed to have been a temporary mindfulness technique to get me to sleep. I wasn't supposed to wake up with a hard-on that'd put a porn star to shame, still thinking about said man hug. I wasn't supposed to think about what it would feel like if those hands drifted higher... and lower.

Ah!

I needed to get laid. I needed to think about women, and I needed to do it without creeping out my receptionist and getting a sexual harassment claim thrown at me. The poor thing looked at me like I'd lost my damn mind. Couldn't say I disagreed with her.

Her legs? Didn't do a damn thing for me. Her sweater *did not* bring out her eyes. I couldn't even tell you what color her eyes were. Blue? Green? Did she have two?

Jack's eyes were this unique pale brown with flecks of light and dark in the centers. They fucking pulled you in and made you look at him when he talked. They always had.

They were the kind of eyes that told you they understood… everything. They were the kind of eyes that seemed to have all the answers. They were the kind of eyes you wanted looking at you all damn day, making you feel like everything was okay. And damn it, I could still see the hurt I put in them every time I blinked. What did they look like after he read my bullshit replies to his texts?

Son of a bitch. I broke his eyes. I broke his beautiful eyes.

I was such a fucking bastard.

For the next three hours, I signed anything that required signing and accomplished any other task that didn't require me to focus. Except the Dodson case. I scribbled notes as best I could as Roger Dodson babbled about his woes, but didn't let my lack of attentiveness weigh on me. The dumb bastard was going to jail one way or the other. I mean, there was only so much you could do for a guy with three priors for disturbing the peace who'd bowled watermelons down the grocery store aisle while he was blasted out of his mind. It was actually the highlight of my morning, knowing someone was more screwed up than me.

By lunchtime, I thought it prudent to get out of the office, hoping a stroll down the street to the deli would keep me from chewing on my stapler. Just in case. Standing in line next to a woman who'd introduced herself, all I could think was that she was gorgeous.

Hands down, she was probably one of the most beautiful women I'd ever seen. I was out of practice, but those were definitely *sex-eyes* she was giving me as I stood in line for a sandwich I didn't even want. I missed home-made breakfasts. And dinners. And… maybe even the chef.

I didn't know how much longer I could hold this stupid smile on my face. Her hand trailed down my arm. The touch was foreign and small and cold. Maybe she was a doctor, and her hands just gave off that disconnected vibe.

Lainey would be envious of her manicure, but the way the woman's red nails scratched against the fabric of my suit jacket was making my skin crawl. I *wanted* to feel something, but there was nothing. Not a damn thing.

Jesus. Did I not like women anymore?

CHAPTER 9
Max

Thursday morning's revelation: It was official. I did not like men.

I had been staring at Dan for the last ten minutes, and I could assure you, I would never—even by threat of torture—want his disgusting mouth on mine. I did *not* find him attractive.

Okay, honestly, he was the kind of guy *some* women may find attractive... until he spoke. But even when he wasn't speaking, there wasn't a solitary thing about him that did a single thing for me.

And Trevor?

Why, good morning, Trevor. Don't mind me while I check you out like the creeper I've become.

Trevor was in decent shape, had good hygiene, flawless dark skin, a sincere smile.

But... nothing. I felt no zing. No heat. No trickle of electricity. No erratic pulse. I did *not* like Trevor. Any man would have been lucky to have Trevor's affection if Trevor was gay, no question about it. I just couldn't picture ever wanting it to be me.

Thank Christ, neither of them could read my thoughts. Dan already asked me if I ate bad food last night and said my face looked like I was constipated. That said it all. Right? I did not like men.

There were men at the coffee shop this morning, men in the lobby of my firm. Tall men, short men, fat men, athletic men, men with thick heads of hair, balding men, young men, middle-aged, old aged. Black hair, brown hair, Latino, African, Caucasian, Asian, and I distinctly heard a guy with a Russian accent. There were things I could appreciate. I could admit that much. Like, the way a guy walked.

I didn't know why. I mean, I had never really thought about it before, but some guys had this easy saunter. They walked with a calm stroll like they had their shit together, but weren't trying to prove something. Kind of like Jack.

Exactly like Jack.

Thursday night

If Patti Cullen hit on me one more time when I picked Emma up from her house after school, I was going to sit outside and honk the horn when it was time to get her from now on. Just because we were both single and our daughters were the same age did not a connection make.

Uh, sure, Patti. Spin class looks like it's really paying off for you. Yeah, I bet it'd be great to take the girls out together sometime, but I bring so much work home I just don't have the time. Hmm. No. I hadn't heard they're doing 'Mamma Mia!' at the playhouse. I don't really follow musicals. Yes. Please tell me more about how your horrible ex didn't give you enough attention. I'm bringing my mother to the Christmas concert, but thanks for offering to carpool.

Pretty sure it was wrong to be mad at someone for dying, but conversations like that one made me want to pick a bone with Lainey. *Jesus, baby.* The woman was relentless.

The thing was, though, Lainey probably would have found it hilarious, so I still would have no satisfaction even if she was here. She would have signed us up for a damn spin class just to piss me off, since she knew her pranks made me horny. It was like she tried to instigate a very mild anger bang, and then we would have had endless spin class jokes.

Grabbing a new scouring pad out of the box, I scrubbed mindlessly at the frying pan as I stared out the kitchen window. They just didn't make cookware like they used to. The freaking packaging said non-stick, but the charred crustaceous matter left over from the rib eyes looked fucking stuck to me.

"Dad? What are you looking at?"

I jumped at the unexpected intrusion. The scouring pad went sailing into the murky dishwater. Twisting around, Emma stood staring up at me with curiosity in her bright blue eyes.

"What? I'm...washing dishes."

"I know, but you've been staring out the window ever since we got home. What are you looking at?"

I glanced out the side window again—the one that faced Jack's darkened, *empty* house. The one that gave me a view of his *empty* driveway.

"Uh. I was...bird-watching."

Bird-watching for a six-foot-four Springfield Eagle. Not a complete lie.

"Bird-watching?"

"Yeah. That's what they call it when people look at birds."

A wrinkle formed between her brows, and she blinked. Then she blinked again. It never ceased to amaze me how idiotic my child could make me feel, almost like she was the adult at times instead of the other way around. How had I never noticed that before? Oh, because it hadn't happened until about three years ago. Damn it again, Lainey, and damn me for damning her. Damn it!

"I know what bird-watching is, Dad. Since when do you like bird-watching?"

Since I was a dick to Uncle Jack, and he left town?

"Since I..." Birds. Birds. What was the name of one fucking bird? Eagle? No! Not eagles! "Since I saw a cardinal in the yard."

"Are those the red ones?"

"Yeah. They're the state bird of Illinois."

Nice save, single functioning brain cell left in my head.

She cast a curious glance out the window. "I don't see any."

Scrub. Scrub. Scrub.

"Well, it was there a minute ago," I lied because all *good* parents lie.

"Is Uncle Jack coming over tonight?"

Damn it. "No. I told you he was busy."

"When is he going to pick me up from school again? Jessica can be kind of annoying."

And so could Jessica's mother.

"Uh. Not sure. He had to go out of town."

She turned a frown on me and something that looked like panic in her eyes, the same panic I was starting to experience, wondering if the giant bird I was searching for would ever migrate back here.

"For how long? Will he be back for my Christmas break? I don't want to spend all Christmas break at Jessica's."

"What's wrong with Jessica?" Other than she was a snobbier, ditzier version of Patti. "I thought you two were like best friends."

Emma heaved one of those you-know-nothing-about-anything sighs. "She can be so dramatic sometimes and her mom is like...way too happy?"

I let out a snort, but quickly cleared my throat. "Well, that's the arrangement for now, unless you've got another friend you think would let you stay after school until I can pick you up."

"But what about Christmas break? What about Uncle Jack? Is he going to be gone?"

"I...don't know, kiddo. He didn't say."

"Can't you call him?"

My mouth hung open a second too long. Emma frowned like I was being as obtuse as I was.

"Uh. No. I...I don't want to bug him."

"You won't bug him. He calls all the time during the season. He said he loves being here for Christmas. We were going to make Christmas cookies, and he..."

"Emma! Enough. Okay?"

Her expression went from confused to crumpled. I heaved out a breath and flung the scouring pad into the water.

"Look. I don't know when he'll be back. He's got his own life. You know? We can't go depending on him forever. It's not right to ask him to be over here all the time."

Her lower lip grew in size. The look in her eyes said the thought of him having his own life, one that didn't involve us, was as appealing to her as it was to me. I didn't know if I was projecting my thoughts onto her or she was onto me, but her face looked like I'd just given away her giant puppy. And fuck if I hadn't, more or less. Jesus. I was a puppy abuser.

"It'll be fine. If you don't like going to Jessica's, I'll think of something else. Now, I want you to go clean up your closet before bed. Okay?"

She gave me a stare down that lasted only seconds but made me shiver. Could nine-year-olds tell when their parents had done something awful?

She huffed and turned away without grace or protest. Her footsteps on the stairs told me how happy she was about Jack being MIA, and how it was somehow my fault. *I* knew it was my fault, but *she* didn't.

Of course, I wanted him to watch her over Christmas break. There was no one I trusted more with her welfare, but I couldn't chance being near him until I got the laundry room meltdown out of my head. To do that, I needed to stop thinking about him every five minutes, but how the fuck was I supposed to stop thinking about him when Emma wouldn't stop talking about him? How was I supposed to put what happened out of my mind when he was everywhere?

He wasn't, though. He hadn't come back yet. He was fucking gone, but I still had a mental image of him in every room in my house.

I used to feel that way after Lainey died, but it got better. Now I had a new ghost in my house, but this one wasn't dead. At this point, it would be less discombobulating to see him in person, even though I still didn't know how I'd start a conversation with him.

"Shit." I was looking out the damned window again.

He never went anywhere during the offseason. All his text had said was *out of town*. How far out of town? For how long?

Would he go to Maui with Montez? I didn't think Montez would appreciate that after hearing his plans for his girlfriend. Some of their teammates took group vacations in the offseason. Not Jack, though. He had never gone since I'd known him. He was a homebody. A *'my home'* body. His place was here... with us. But what was to stop him now?

We only had two months to patch things up before pitchers and catchers reported to spring training. My stomach dropped. What if he spent all that time away before he reported? I didn't want to have to break the awkwardness with a phone call or video chat after he left. I couldn't wait that long. What if he didn't answer?

Shit. He wouldn't ask for a trade, would he? Where the fuck was he?

Pacing around the kitchen, I chewed at my lip. I could text him.

Except what the hell did you text your friend of six years who just kissed you, who you shoved away, and then avoided all week while you thought about him touching you in places he hadn't even touched you?

Lots of places. Places I'd never even thought about being touched and certainly never by a guy. And what douchebag shoved their best friend, then broke the ice with a text?

A car slowed on the street and my breath caught. Its lights cast a dim glow through the neighbor's Christmas lights across the street, but it continued down the road—along with my hope. Damn it.

He could fucking text *me*.

Did he think I wouldn't worry about him now just because I knew he was gay? Jesus. I hoped not. He probably thought I was as big of a dick as Dan.

I didn't even want to try to remember all the shit Dan said in front of him over the years, his stupid fucking jokes. And all the while, Jack just sat there, taking it. Laughing with good humor, probably forced. Did it hurt him every time Dan or I or anyone else at my house made some crack about homosexuality? I needed to set Dan straight. No. Not *straight*. Fuck. This is why I was in no way prepared to talk to Jack.

I couldn't believe I contemplated if Jack's preference made him less of a man. The only one who had been less of a man this week was me. I didn't give a shit what size spoon either of us were. He needed to come back.

So...what?

So he could be nearby while I avoided him? Whatever. He just needed to come back. I mean, what was I supposed to tell Emma if he didn't?

An engine rumbled outside. I raced back over to the window, skittering to a halt in my stocking feet on the hardwood floor. The weight on my chest flew away at the sight of the shadowed figure in the cab of a black pickup truck next door.

I knew that figure—that signature Jack figure. The Eagle had landed.

He was home. Thank God!

Well, of course, he came home. He fucking lives there, you idiot.

Everything was going to be fine. He'd stop over like he always did, and things could get back to normal.

Three hours later, I flopped onto my back in bed, wondering when this became the world's most uncomfortable mattress.

Fuck it. He wasn't coming over.

I screwed this up. Hadn't I?

Friends were supposed to listen and be understanding. But... friends were supposed to tell you if they were queer. A few more beached walrus flops in bed led me to another conclusion—friends weren't supposed to shove you and tell you to get out of their house after you told them you were queer.

I could have said a hundred other things. Friends weren't supposed to keep their kid away from someone who'd been an "uncle" to them since they were three years old.

Fuck. Yeah, I had *so* fucked this up.

Why did it feel like he was in the room? Could you feel someone's presence through the walls of two houses? The heat and the storm current in my blood were back. The tent of my dick under the comforter stared at me like it was asking for more man-hugs. I glared at it, telling it we didn't deserve more man-hugs, and reminded it we'd never craved man-hugs before.

I missed Lainey. That was all this was.

I didn't want other women. I didn't want men. I wanted Lainey to tell me how to fix this. I wanted to not feel like I was betraying her. I wanted her back. And I wanted Jack back the way it was before... before, in the cocoon that made everything in the world feel all right, before he claimed one of my kisses, before he gave one of his kisses to me.

CHAPTER 10
Max

My idea of Friday night fun was apparently a self-torture tactic called silent *Monopoly*, where my child and I pretended to be a happy family, where neither of us spoke unless necessary.

Most. Excruciating. Game. Ever. If my life was a TV show, Emma would have voted me off Dad Island by now.

"Dad. You don't have to buy every space you land on."

"I know. I just haven't made my mind up yet. Maybe I'll sell them to you later."

She rolled her eyes. "Maybe I won't want to buy them. I've already got Park Place and Boardwalk."

The fluorescent glow of the light fixture above the dining room table glinted off my little silver boot token. It was fitting that I was the heel. Emma was the car, likely to align with her ambitions to make a getaway from my thrilling company.

"You ready for the macaroni yet?" I asked, searching for any reason to get out of my chair.

"Can we get carry-out instead?"

"We've had carry-out like three times this week."

"Four," she corrected.

"More to the point."

"What does that mean?"

"It means we're having macaroni. Now, don't think I didn't notice you trying to get out of paying me for landing on my railroad."

"I'm not, but can we talk about the macaroni?"

"What's there to talk about?"

"Can you try not to make it chewy or burn it this time?"

We locked into a Hartwell staring contest, and I blinked first when I realized how much she was like me. Stubborn. Determined. She looked like a mini-Lainey, but that frown and the intensity in her eyes were all me. Damn. I didn't know whether to be proud or sympathetic.

Holding my palm up, I declared, "I solemnly swear to make the perfect consistency of macaroni."

"What's consistency?"

"Texture."

She responded with a blink and a pucker in her brow.

"What are they teaching you at that school?"

We returned to our game and not-so-companionable silence, which allowed me to return to my dilemma. I needed to talk to Jack. Tonight.

I was going to. Just as soon as this tedious game was over, and I'd cooked the perfect consistency of macaroni, and sent Emma to bed.

See? I had a plan. I was going to call him after dinner and ask him to stop by.

To talk.

And that was where my plan ended.

Did I have any idea what I was going to say to him yet? Not a fucking clue, but the important thing was that he was home. I couldn't wait and chance him taking another unplanned trip. Someone needed to extend an olive branch. Being that I was the one who created the need for an olive branch, the extension needed to come from me.

I had no idea my kid breathed so heavily or the clocks in my house ticked so loudly. Anxiety was kicking my ass, heightening all my senses.

Being nervous about speaking to a man I'd had hundreds of conversations with over the years was strange. I half-expected Jack would be his cool, calm, and collected self, which meant I was overreacting. Sounded like my usual M.O.

Emma purchased a pair of houses for one of her properties. I watched her nudge them together side by side on her game tile. Neighbors.

Wonderful. Once again, Jack was literally everywhere.

I couldn't invite him over to talk and stand here like a mute, but only two questions came to mind. Unfortunately, neither was anything I would ever imagine vocalizing.

Can we still be friends after the way I reacted?

That question was mostly for me. I had no doubt Jack would still give his friendship freely. It was the kind of guy he was, but *could* we still be friends? Would a chat make all the weirdness go away? My second question was the reason for the first.

Will I ever stop thinking carnal thoughts about you?

Yeah. I wasn't going to open or close with that one. I did have one answer, though, from this past week of madness. It was me, not him. This entire clusterfuck was all on me, and I didn't mean the kiss.

Either I hadn't listened enough or asked enough questions to get him to tell me sooner, or my behavior made him think he couldn't tell me. If some-one was bawling their eyes out, man or woman, I probably would have hugged them, too. Hell, I'd hugged clients before when they broke down.

I didn't have any *good* friends. I had a hell of a lot of acquaintances, but die-hard friends for life that you clicked with? Jack was it. You didn't throw that away just because life tossed you a curve ball. Jesus, even my meta-phors reminded me of him.

My heart skipped a beat as a figure passed by the front window. My first thought was '*intruder*,' and like an idiot, I plotted how I could flip the Mo-nopoly board at them because *Monopoly saves lives*, but it wasn't just any figure. It was a wide-shouldered, brown-haired, makes-my-confused-dick-stand-up figure.

"I'll be right back. Can you go fill the pot with water for the macaroni?" I asked Emma.

"Sure."

I got to the front door right as he knocked. Taking a breath, I counted to five, so I wouldn't look like I was ready to pounce on the Schwan's man. My hand was shaking. Fucking shaking.

Get it together. This is your friend, I told myself, and concentrated on opening the door at the speed of a calm, normal human.

A rush of cold air flooded the entryway, but as soon as my eyes locked with his, there was nothing but raw heat. I could have charbroiled steaks on the air between us, or Jack could have. I fucking burned everything, but maybe that was appropriate. I was scorched from head to toe under his caramel-eyed gaze. He looked good. Really good. Or maybe it was just good to see him. Could those all-seeing eyes read every filthy thought I'd had this week?

He lifted his chin to me, his smooth voice low. "Hey."

"Hey," I parroted.

That was all I could manage, but a sense of relief washed through me. It was a miracle a word came out of my mouth and that he was here. I hadn't realized how much I needed confirmation of his proof of life after he disappeared all week. Just like when his truck pulled in yesterday, his presence was a balm on my soul, knowing he was home safe.

"How…how's it going?" I stammered, like I forgot how to talk.

"It's going." His quick half-smile looked so foreign on his face.

Fast and furious footsteps descended behind me. Emma barreled to a stop at my side, wide-eyed, smiling from ear to ear.

"Hey, Uncle Jack!"

"Hey, Snuggle Bug! How are you?"

God. That look on his face, all lit up like Christmas. I wanted to be one of the people putting it there again.

"Good. We're playing Monopoly," Emma replied. "Why didn't you use the back door?"

Jack's smile tripped and fell off. His gaze flashed to mine, his cheeks flushed. I looked away as heat crawled up my neck.

Leave it to my kid to use a gay sex reference at a time like this. Just kill me now.

"It, uh, looked icy back there," Jack supplied.

Ice. Right. Because… it's winter. I was a fucking pervert.

Now I really wanted to crawl in a hole and not pop out until Groundhog Day. My back patio wouldn't be icy for ten years. I put more salt on it than Emma puts sprinkles on cupcakes.

Why? So if a certain someone decided to stop by and forgive his dickhead friend, he wouldn't crack his head open on the steps.

A new rush of shame flashed through me. Did he think I would lock the patio door? Or did him using the front entrance, knocking like a stranger, represent how big a wedge I had driven between us, as though we had to start over at square one?

"Are you staying for dinner?" Emma asked.

It was then that I registered the foil pan in his hands. It was the disposable store-bought kind, not a baking pan your neighbor washed and returned to you. He handed it to me awkwardly.

"Uh, no, Bug. I just made this and wanted to drop it off for you guys."

"Aw, but it's been so boring! All he does is sit in his office or stare out the window, watching the birds."

Duct tape! She was getting duct tape for her mouth for Christmas. I pinned her with a glare.

"Thanks a lot! Did you forget about Monopoly?"

Luckily, Jack didn't appear intrigued by my newfound hobby of watching for "birds", but I didn't miss how he made sure not to invite himself in by way of Emma. He was doing me yet another favor, saving the both of us from an uncomfortable meal.

But now I had a new problem. I couldn't take his food and then invite him over later to talk after we ate without him. Maybe he really couldn't stay for dinner. Maybe he had plans. He could be going out with his team-mates that lived around here. He could have a date.

Shit. How many dates had he gone on that I didn't know about?

It was just the three of us, a frigid silence, and a bizarre wave of jealousy as I imagined Jack being charmed by some guy on a date. Two pairs of eyes took turns looking at each other and then at me. The foil pan crinkled in my grip.

I glanced down at Emma. She was looking up at me with her lower lip jutting out as if to say even she knew something was amiss by the brevity of our exchange. I needed to remember how to be a normal human.

"Hey, uh, what do you say we go to The Game Room tomorrow?"

It was an arcade with a restaurant and one of the few places she enjoyed that didn't make me want to bang my head against a wall. Her eyebrows lifted, and she rewarded me with the same look she gave Jack when she ran to the door.

"Yeah?"

"Yeah." I shrugged, only slightly offended she sounded surprised that I could come up with fun ideas.

"Can Uncle Jack come?"

For once, she said exactly what I wanted her to say. Yup. I was using my child to get what I wanted. I had no fucking shame. I shrugged like I was suddenly the most easygoing man in the world.

"Of course, but that's up to him." I braced myself for a glance at the man still patiently standing on my front step. "Jack, would you like to come?"

The words were out before I could stop them. Fuck! I just asked him if he wanted to *cum*! Was my fucking brain going through puberty again?

"*With us!*" I amended, but then realized that only made my poor choice of phrase more obvious. "I mean, do you...want to go with us? Tomorrow?"

Shut up, Max. Just shut. The fuck. Up.

"I...yeah. I'd love to. If you guys want me to."

"Yeees!" Emma cheered with a fist pump.

I let out all my air. He looked like a starving dog, ecstatic for the table scraps of my offer. The only awkward thing on this porch now was me.

"How's eleven sound?" I asked, reining in my sanity.

Hands in the pockets of his well-worn jeans, he nodded. "Sounds great. I'll be over then."

I nodded back, afraid to say anything else, but then remembered the warm pan I was holding. "Thanks, man," I said, hoisting it up.

"No problem." He flashed me a stilted smile and turned back toward his house.

I watched him walk away. His sweatshirt-clad shoulders resembled their usual broad posture, not the defeated hunch I put in them last weekend. It gave me hope that I'd finally taken a step in the right direction.

When his head started to turn back, I made quick work of closing the door. We could do this. We'd hang out tomorrow just like we always had. Emma would have a blast. Maybe I could squeak in an apology while she was distracted. Everything could go back to normal. I headed to the kitchen with Jack's offering, thankful a macaroni debate was no longer in my future.

"Dad? How come you didn't invite him in?"

"What?"

"It's cold out. He didn't have a coat on. How come you didn't invite him in?"

"Oh. Uh. I wasn't thinking. I was...thinking about work stuff."

And because I was a jerk. And because I fucking forgot how to talk. And because I was terrified I'd pop a boner if he got any closer. Did he want to come in? Was he cold? Was he going to get sick now? Did I give *him* boners?

Emma's brow wrinkled, her blue eyes little wells of concern. "Are you all right?"

Absolutely not.

I exhaled and ruffled her hair. "Yeah, kiddo. Come on. Let's see what he made you."

Brushing her mussed-up hair from her face, she scrunched up her nose. "*Me*? He made it for *you*."

"What?" I stopped in my tracks at the island counter. Had I missed something he said? Could she tell something had happened by the way we acted, and his gift of dinner was the equivalent of flowers?

Propping herself on a stool, she shrugged. Her knowing smile made my knees weak.

"It's lasagna," she said matter-of-factly. "I can smell it. He knows that's your favorite, and that mine is tater tot casserole."

I gaped at the foil-covered tin on the counter. I'd been so distracted by Jack that I hadn't given a thought to the mouth-watering aroma wafting out of the pan.

"That's still your favorite. Right?"

"Uh. Yeah. Yeah. It is."

I glanced out the front window of the dining room, wanting another glimpse of the thoughtful man I had left in the cold. I *did* love lasagna. It *was* my favorite. I had no idea he knew that. It meant the world to me that he made it with me in mind, even after what I did.

I'd always loved *his* lasagna, but for the first time, I couldn't eat it. I didn't deserve it.

CHAPTER 11
Max

When I drove, I was usually on autopilot. I tuned out everything and kept my eyes locked on the road. I could answer Emma's questions like an *Alexa* device and still be a sensible, responsible driver. After Lainey died, I grew more vigilant behind the wheel, more aware that getting from point A to point B was filled with risk.

Today though? I was only aware of the people and conversations in my vehicle. We could be driving to Mexico for all I knew, rather than the arcade.

"Uncle Jack? Where've you been? We didn't see you all week," Emma called from the back seat, making me realize that including her in the breaking-of-the-silence between Jack and me was a huge mistake. Genius that I was.

"Oh, I've been busy. A sponsor wants me to do an exercise machine commercial, and I went to visit my sister for a few days," Jack replied, canting his head to the back, but keeping his gaze fixed on the view out the window.

I snagged that tidbit of information and smuggled it to a secret compartment in my thoughts. He was close with Carrie. Did that mean she knew about his sexuality and was supportive?

It was Christmastime. He always spent Christmas with us. Sometimes Carrie even spent Christmas with us. Never once had he ever mentioned going to his parents' place. He rarely ever spoke about them. Did that mean they knew and weren't supportive?

I mentioned to Lainey once how little Jack spoke about his folks. She told me his father didn't approve of Jack playing baseball and sounded like a disapproving hard-ass. I figured one of us being nosey was enough, so I never brought it up to Jack, but I remembered thinking what parent in their right mind could frown at their child being the best pitcher in the country? Now I was dying to know what else failed to meet the man's approval.

Jack drummed his fingers anxiously on one of his blue jean-clad thighs. His other elbow rested on the window ledge, his fist propping up his head, idly rubbing his thumb under his jaw. He was clearly uncomfortable, and I was achingly aware I was the cause of it.

This was supposed to have been easier. We were supposed to get in the car and start shooting the shit like old times. Now I had to add *delusional* to my list of flaws.

My tongue was dry, lodged in the back of my throat. The air was thick and static-charged. For some reason, I was acutely cognizant of the masculinity rolling off him. I had never been more aware of someone's presence in my life. Every inhale filled me with his spicy body wash scent.

Had he gotten bigger since the last time I saw him? He reminded me of a kid who'd grown out of his clothes. It was… kind of fucking adorable. I swear his muscular thighs filled those jeans more than I'd ever noticed before. The definition of his pecs in that snug *Blackhawks* sweatshirt and the way his biceps hugged the sleeves was like a shiny object I couldn't un-see.

Shit. Even the way he leaned on the window frame was so incredibly masculine it gave me a sense of inadequacy… or was it longing? Like even though he was sitting right next to me, he wasn't close enough.

From my peripheral, his jaw ticked. Even the man's profile was a sight—the thick bridge of his nose, his high, defined cheekbones, the hollows of his face, the perfect structure of his jaw.

I gripped the steering wheel tighter as I eased into a turn. Why the fuck was I appreciating a man's jawline? Why was I wondering if men kissed each other's jaws the way men and women did?

It was Christmas. I was horny. I missed Lainey. This would go away. We could still be friends. We *needed* to be friends for my sake and Emma's.

The voice in my head shouted at me to say something. Emma's curious gaze bore into the back of my skull like laser beams. Jack and I had never been this silent for this long in front of her. If I didn't say something, I'd get an inquisition when we got home.

"So, you going to do this commercial?"

There. That was conversational. Not sexual. Not awkward.

He ran a hand through his thick chestnut hair. I shook away thoughts of how soft it might feel between my fingers.

"I don't know. I haven't decided yet."

"Where do they want to shoot it?"

"Los Angeles. Next month."

California. That was many, many states away... from me. I didn't like this commercial.

"Never been there," I said like a charming chump, but it ended up being the stimulus our conversation needed.

He started talking about places he'd been in Los Angeles—restaurants, clubs, beaches, awards dinners. His voice filled the car with imagery of him at these places until we pulled into The Game Room parking lot.

We got a table inside near the back of the restaurant, something I was used to doing when Jack went out with us. He wasn't an attention-seeker, and it was no secret in Springfield that he resided here. He took a seat that put his back to the door. Emma took the one across from him, and I claimed the one next to her.

It reminded me of the times I'd been out with him and some of his team-mates. None of them went out of their way to be noticed, but it was difficult not to recognize a group of insanely fit athletic men.

Each time, fans came up to us, seeking autographs and selfies. Each time, Jack had lingered in the background as though he was using his teammates as a buffer, only stepping forward if a fan singled him out.

I thought I knew so much about him. How had I so severely overlooked his vulnerable side? His stories in the car about Los Angeles painted a sad picture. I imagined him alone at those restaurants, clubs, and beaches—our humble Jack alone in a big city. It didn't suit the man I knew. It wasn't the happy picture he deserved. It sounded too... lonely.

We ordered and ate, the chaos of arcade machine noises and excited children buzzing around us. Jack and Emma talked about school, TV shows, music, her friends, food, random facts—their usual myriad of topics. I laughed and chimed in with responses here and there, but mostly just lis-tened. It felt like we were almost us again—the three of us. Jack's presence, his acceptance of this day, boded like forgiveness, but it was forgiveness I hadn't earned.

Emma asked to go hit up the games. Jack nodded at my plate, which still held my half-eaten burger.

"I can take her," he offered.

"Sure. Have at it." I nodded, trying to smile.

And I'm sorry, I wanted to add. *I didn't mean to hurt you. Thanks for making this easier. Thanks for always making everything easier.*

As Emma sprinted away, I watched the unfathomable sight of Jack strolling after her. There went the best pitcher in Major League Baseball, a sports god, casually dodging children like this was any other day. He could have been doing anything right now. He could have been on a beach on a tropical island. He could have been skiing at a fancy resort or making commercials people like me saw on TV every day. Instead, he was here with me and Emma, in a restaurant with grease-smell saturated carpeting and French fries on the floor.

Emma bounced up and down in front of the Skee-Ball machines. I chuckled at her barely checked excitement as she gestured to Jack. He took a place on the lane next to hers. They wore matching mischievous grins as they waited for the game lights to signal the start.

He was so natural with her, so sincere. Emma flubbed a few balls in the outer loop, looking discouraged. Jack clasped his hand over hers and guided her through a few mock throws, showing her the technique. Her next solo toss landed her ball in the ring second from the center. She jumped in celebration, a big smile on her face. Jack held up one of his big palms for a high-five. I had always appreciated the way he was with her, but it was one of the most endearing sights I'd ever witnessed.

The scene was obscured as a red-headed woman and her son made their way between the tables toward me. Her eyes locked with mine as I tried to reclaim a view of Jack and Emma. The woman's lips parted, and I wondered if it was recognition I was seeing on her face, if I knew her from somewhere.

She smiled and said in a thick voice, near a whisper, "Hi."

Oh. *Oh.*

It was that kind of *hi*—here in broad daylight with her son only a foot away from her. I nodded, returning my attention to my burger, and laid my left hand on the table, leaving my wedding band on full display like a protective force field.

I held my breath, praying she wouldn't engage me. She slowed as she passed, but then moved on. Relief washed over me.

I took another two bites before glancing over my shoulder to make sure she wasn't lingering. The coast was clear, but I was ruffled.

I shouldn't avoid meeting people. It had been three years. Even Lainey's folks had been subtly hinting that I needed to get back out there. What did that say when your dead wife's parents told you that you should date again? Fuck if I knew, but I sure as shit wasn't going to make the effort when a sultry greeting made me wish I was a turtle that could retract in on myself until I was invisible.

Gathering up the utensils and napkins from our table, I cast a glance over to Emma and Jack. I couldn't sit here like an absent curmudgeon. I needed to get over there and make sure they both had a good time.

What was I saying? They always had a good time together. I needed to go be a part of that good time.

Like he could sense my thoughts, Jack's head turned at the end of a laugh, and he looked at me. His smile settled a bit, but then transformed into what could only be described as heartfelt.

It was the kind of smile that was mostly in the eyes. The kind that said a thousand things but had one simple message—love. Not head over heels or passionate love, just love. It was the love of someone who knew you, who put up with your shit, and still cared. It was an 'I-appreciate-you' smile and a 'thanks-for-being-my-friend' smile. Unlike the smile from the red-head or the woman in the coffee shop the other day, this one rocketed a giddy wave all the way to my toes. My heart skipped a beat like it had when I first met and was trying to impress Lainey.

Jack flinched and looked away, shattering the moment. A brunette woman who only came up to his shoulder had a hand on his back, her fingers splayed. Jack turned around to face her, but her hand didn't leave him. Instead, it glided across the back of his shoulder and down his arm, where it stopped on his biceps and squeezed.

I couldn't tell what they were saying, but by the rapid movement of her lips, she was doing most of the talking. She beamed from ear to ear, gesturing animatedly with her other hand, where she was clutching her phone.

Great. A fucking fan. First, he had to put up with my weirdness, then I brought him to a place where he was recognized.

Jack's mouth was a tight line, quirking upward at the corners in polite little jerks. Shit. He was faking it. He was faking it, and he was still too handsome for words. The woman must have thought so too, because she grew more animated and more handsy. Her palm settled below his neck and slid down between his pecs until he captured it, as though to stop her travel plans. He nodded and shifted his weight, holding his arm out to the side.

Ah. The dreaded selfie.

I would never understand why people vied for selfies with celebrities.

Hey, look at this photo of me acting like I'm best friends with a complete fucking stranger who only touched me because I invaded their space.

Yeah. Hang that on your wall. Hashtag—total creeper.

How many pictures were out there of Jack with people who insinuated themselves into a photo with him? The poor guy looked like he wanted to crawl into a cave and hide.

Emma was still lobbing balls up her lane, oblivious that he was being molested three feet away. The woman slinked her arm around Jack's back and turned her body into his, sandwiching her breasts around his rib cage. She stretched out her leg, draping it over the front of his, and leaned her head against his chest.

Could she get any closer? She was wrapped around him like a damn *Snuggie*. Finally, she extended her phone in front of them. Jack still had a patient smile on his face, but looked like he wanted this over with as quickly as I did. I caught movement behind him at his side. Her hand cupped his ass, her fingers curling around the underside of it. My teeth clenched.

What. The fuck. Lady?

It was subtle, like he'd had years of practice stifling his emotions, but Jack tensed. His smile was all teeth and no joy. As much as I hated seeing his misery, I wanted to laugh. Pride swelled in my chest. It was the best I'd felt in a long time. A sense of victory over this enamored fan lit me up.

Ha! Joke's on you, lady. I've got what he wants.

I froze. What was I saying?

This was ridiculous. I couldn't honestly be jealous of a woman hanging on him. Seriously. What the hell did I care who touched him?

Even if, for some reason, I was miraculously attracted to men now, Jack was my friend. *Just* my friend.

One kiss. That was all it had been. One kiss because I was blubbering my eyes out. He wasn't staring at and ogling me, which I realized I'd been doing since he got in my car. He wasn't the one thinking randy thoughts.

I was no better than that pushy fan. The guy was entertaining my kid, and I was sitting here getting jealous over who groped his ass. I was a widower. I was supposed to be… widower-y.

I shoved back my chair and made my way through the dining area, determined to be the two things I was allowed to be: a dad and a friend. Luckily, the brunette slinked away as I approached, saving me from whatever insanity I might have said to her to get rid of her.

"Hey." Jack tilted his chin toward Emma with a chuckle. "She's getting pretty good."

"Dad, you want to play? This lane is open," Emma gestured to the one next to her.

I shot her a grave look. "The manager stopped by our table and told me you two are playing so bad he's worried you're going to break the machines."

"He did not! You're lying."

"Sure did. I figured I'd better show you how it's done, so they don't kick us out."

Jack grinned and nudged her shoulder with his elbow. "You ready to help me embarrass your dad?"

"Yeah," she agreed a bit too readily, lifting her chin and narrowing her eyes at me. "We're going to beat you so bad, you're going to cry."

Two things occurred to me at that moment. One—my kid was fucking brutal and would never be bullied, so I must have been doing something right as a parent. Two—I did not need her help embarrassing myself.

CHAPTER 12
Max

"Emms!" I called to the backseat as I popped the car into park in the driveway. From the rearview, I could see Emma's head slumped against the door, her arms clutching a giant bag of cotton candy that I would have to kill Jack some other day for buying her.

"Hey, kiddo!" I tried a little louder. "We're home."

She grunted in protest but didn't open her eyes. Jack cast a 'she's-so-cute' smile over his shoulder.

"Great." I sighed. "I open the door and she's going to fall out on the driveway." I drummed my fingers on the steering wheel in thought. "But...I guess that *would* wake her up."

"You wouldn't," he chided and reached an arm back to shake her knee.

The sleeve of his sweatshirt brushed against my elbow, making my pulse zing. Since when had my elbow become an erogenous zone? His face was inches from my neck. Jesus. Body heat was a powerful force.

"Hey, Bug. Wake up, sweetie," he murmured, his soothing voice close enough I could feel his breath. "We're home."

We're home. I liked too much how that sounded.

"You taking any more trips this winter?" I blurted.

From the rearview, I saw Emma stir and sit up like the undead coming to life. When Jack righted himself, his gaze met mine. I looked away, fiddling with my keys.

"Not planning on it."

I nodded. That was all. Just fucking nodded, giving no indication why I asked about his plans. It shouldn't have felt like an invasive question, but I didn't have the right to ask him anything anymore.

Emma popped her door open, so I got out. We all ended up standing at the back of my vehicle.

"Do you want to come in and watch a movie?" Emma asked Jack.

His gaze darted to mine as he stood with his hands stuffed in his jeans' pockets. *Hesitant Jack* was new to me. My house had always been free rein to him. Was he seeking my permission? Did he not want to come in and wanted me to be the one to let her down? Did *I* want him to come in?

Yes, unequivocally, but my nerves had been raked over an old washboard all day. I needed to recuperate.

"Uh, not tonight, kiddo. You still need to finish cleaning your closet. Remember?"

She let out a soul-crushing sigh, her shoulders sagging. I gave two shits if she'd amassed four more bags of garbage in her closet. I just didn't want to push my luck after today had gone so swimmingly, minus my secret dirty thoughts. Jack's posture relaxed, like maybe he was grateful for my excuse. His quick acceptance stung. He shot an apologetic smile at Emma.

"I've got some things to do, Bug, but it was great seeing you."

Things? What fucking things?

She hugged him as the wind whipped, a strong gust, peeling my coat open. The overcast in the gray winter sky aligned with this mood of sorrowful parting, especially when Jack turned to me and said softly, "Thanks, Max...for inviting me. I really appreciate it."

My throat closed up. It was such a blatant statement of groveling, a message of how he felt about what happened.

"Thanks for going with us."

He turned and headed out into the wind. When I realized I was watching him go, I glanced down to find Emma looking up at me. Her little bow-shaped lips were set in a frown, her innocent eyes studying me. She didn't need to say anything. I knew what she was thinking.

This isn't us, Dad. This isn't how we do things. What's going on?

Jack's arms hugged around himself, his head down, as he reached the edge of my driveway by his yard. My idiocy was hurting the two people I cared about most.

"Hey, Jack!" I called over the howl of the wind.

"Yeah?"

"You home next week?"

He shrugged, but it was barely noticeable the way his shoulders were hunched up by his ears. Once again, I was keeping him out in the cold.

"Yeah."

"Christmas break starts Monday. You, uh, want the blonde terrorist here to keep you company?"

Surprise lit up his face, twisting the screws of guilt in my gut, but then he smiled sheepishly. I glanced at Emma. Every one of her front teeth was showing. It was humbling how much power I had over these two. I shouldn't have been the one in charge of their happiness.

"I think I can handle that," Jack said.

Emma clapped her hands together. "Yay!"

I let go of a breath, realizing it meant I wouldn't have to face Patti Cullen next week. I nodded at the freezing man in my yard, more grateful to him than he could possibly imagine. "Alright. That's great. Thanks."

"Anytime."

He waved and hurried away. I closed the garage door and spirited Emma inside. A sense of rightness settled over me. There was still a niggling sensation that something was missing between Jack and me, likely the apology I had yet to give him, but it felt like we were getting back on track. We were still friends or friends again or perhaps on our way to becoming a new version of the friends we were. We could do this. Maybe I wouldn't even dream about him tonight.

CHAPTER 13
Jack

For the first time in a week, it didn't feel like someone was sitting on my chest. Aside from the anxiety the winter howler going on outside was giving me, all the tension I'd been carrying in my shoulders the last seven days had settled to a dull tightness. Max and I might be okay after all.

He was awfully damn quiet in the car earlier today, but he laughed and smiled at The Game Room. It was more subdued than our former exchanges, but a giant step up from no contact.

I still couldn't believe he invited me. Maybe Carrie was right about being myself. My lasagna must have worked its magic.

I snorted, taking a sip of my beer, and shifted on my couch as the Blackhawks game played on my big screen. Listen to me, putting karmic values on food.

We still had a long way to go, but I had hope now that we could get there. '*There*' probably wouldn't be where we were before I kissed his incredibly straight ass, but I'd take any kind of new *there* he was willing to offer, if it kept him and Emma in my life.

The windows rattled louder. I turned up the hockey game to drown out the noise of the sleet pelting against the glass. At this rate, I was surprised the power was still on.

As if the universe could read my thoughts, a thunderous boom cracked. The sound echoed all around me, and the lights flickered. My spine went rigid at the velocity of the noise. I involuntarily jerked my shoulders to my ears and cringed as though I expected something to smite me from the angry sky outside. Lightning flashed, sending a white-yellow glow through the window. A loud cracking sound resounded, almost like an explosion—this one more isolated.

It was an ear-piercing, rupturing noise coming from behind my house. I turned my head and glanced through the living room entryway to get a view out the window in my dining room that overlooked the backyard. My jaw came unhinged. My beer slipped from my hand. I was up off the couch, barreling over it in a single move.

The giant oak at the edge of Max's property split in two halfway up on the trunk. A sickening wail ripped out of my throat as I sped to the back patio door, never taking my eyes off the tree as it crashed down on Max's roof.

"Holy shit! No. No. No!"

I was out my patio door and down the steps in a flash, racing across my yard. Freezing slush oozed between my toes. I didn't even care that I'd forgotten my shoes. I ripped open the gate to Max's yard, squinting through the blinding sleet at the treetop piercing through the roof right over Emma's bedroom. Dear Lord, let her be okay.

Racing past a wayward hanging branch, I dashed up Max's patio steps. Rock salt stabbed the soles of my feet. My lungs seized, realizing the door might be locked. Wrenching on the handle, it slid open. I pounded through the sunroom, down the hall. Max was ahead of me in a T-shirt and flannel pants, running too. He spun around, wild-eyed, as my feet barreled down the hall. I could hear Emma screaming for him upstairs.

"What the hell was that noise?" he huffed, turning back toward the stairs.

"Emma! Your tree fell on her room!"

Our shoulders jarred into each other's as we bolted up the stairs like a herd of wild buffalo. It occurred to me maybe I should slow down and let Max take the lead. Emma was *his* daughter, not mine. My panic wouldn't let me, though. I was faster, a lifetime of grueling workouts letting me take the stairs two at a time, leaving him behind.

Emma's door was cracked open a few inches. I could hear her whimpering inside.

"Emma!" I called out. "Baby, are you okay?"

"Uncle Jack?"

I pushed the door, but it didn't budge. Max came up behind me, panting, taking in the scene.

"Emms? Are you hurt?" he called.

"No," she answered warily, "but there's a tree in my ceiling."

I rammed my shoulder into the door. The wood creaked and gave a few more inches, but there was no way I would fit through that narrow a gap.

"Something must be hitting the top of the door on the other side," I told Max, keeping my voice low so Emma wouldn't think she was trapped.

"Fuck." Max surveyed the gap and gestured for me to move. He slid his arm and head through the space, so he was looking inside Emma's room. "Hey, kiddo," his muffled voice was tender. It was amazing to me how he could act so rationally when it counted the most. "Can you come over here and squeeze out the doorway?"

I stood by helplessly, listening to their voices. Cold air wafted through the gap of the doorway, chilling my wet feet.

Max sidled back. A moment later, a flustered Emma appeared in the doorway. She had a chokehold on her glittery pink Sock Monkey she'd had since I'd known her. She eyeballed the narrow passage skeptically.

Max motioned for her to turn. "You're going to have to squeeze out sideways, kiddo. We can't get the door open."

She nodded, glancing up warily. "The ceiling's sinking in front of it."

Max let out a sigh, but replied with patience, "I know."

Her elbow bumped the door frame when she tried to squeeze through the opening. Max reached for her monkey.

"Here. Give me Mr. Sparkles."

She handed over the well-loved Sock Monkey Max had repeatedly dubbed *'fucking creepy.'* I may have thrown it at him a handful of times over the years and arranged for it to take a secret trip to his office inside his briefcase once.

Hearing him refer to it by name, as though he now cared for its well-being, was a ray of sunshine on my panic. His big hand reached back to me, Mr. Sparkles dangling from his fingers like a festering dead rat. I bit back a snicker as he waggled his hand for me to save him from the not-terrifying-at-all stuffed animal. He glanced over his shoulder and must have caught my smirk. He let out a puff of breath and whipped Mr. Sparkles at my face.

"Fucker," he muttered.

He might as well have called me *baby* for how the familiar exchange lit me up inside. When Emma emerged in front of him, we dropped to our knees. Max braced her arms, eyeing her up and down like he was checking if pieces were missing.

Raking a hand over her hair, he asked, "Are you all right? You're sure you're not hurt?"

"I'm fine. It was *loud* though," she said, her wide eyes betraying her stoicism. "I thought the ceiling was going to fall on my bed."

He pulled her into a hug and let out an agonizing gust of air. My breath caught, and my eyes started to burn, thinking what it would be like to lose Emma forever after losing Lainey.

When Max released her, she turned to me with her lower lip protruding and held out her arms like I had a unique brand of comfort she specifically needed. It crushed my heart so hard I had to suck in a breath as I pulled her to me.

Max stood and ran his hands through his hair. "You're going to have to sleep in the spare room until we get things repaired, kiddo." Shifting his gaze to me, he added, "I should go up and check the attic and cut the fuse to her room in case any wiring got damaged. I don't want there to be a fire."

"Will my room catch on fire?" Emma sounded alarmed.

"No, sweetie," I reassured her. "Your dad's taking care of it, so it won't. Okay?" I rose to my feet, hauling her up in my arms with me. "Why don't we go get you back to bed in the spare room? It'll be safe in there. The storm's almost over."

Over Emma's shoulder, Max gave me a look of gratitude. He was still gripping his hair by the roots, though. I could only imagine a smashed roof would go over as well as his moldy washing machine.

On that note, I spirited Emma and Mr. Sparkles away. If Max needed to cry tonight, I did not want to know about it, considering how I had reacted last time.

I got Emma settled in bed and pulled the easy chair over. My T-shirt and pajama pants were damp from my mad dash through our yards. I folded my arms over my chest, tucking my hands under my armpits for warmth as I tried to take Emma's mind off tonight's disaster.

"Can we fix my room, or will we have to build a new house?" she asked.

"We can fix it. We'll have somebody come and get the tree off the roof first, then your dad will call someone to come fix the ceiling and the hole in the roof."

She nodded, processing my answer. "It was raining inside my room. All my stuff is going to be wet."

"Well, you're with me all week, so we'll work on bagging it up together. I'll wash everything and throw it in the dryer. It'll be good as new."

"We got a new washer," she volunteered.

That news shouldn't make my blood thick or my stomach turn, but it did both. "Yeah? Cool. I'll have to figure out how to work it."

I pulled out my phone and brought up my reading app. It had been a while since Emma and I had read bedtime stories. She was getting too old to appreciate them the way she used to, but readily agreed tonight.

We decided on *Percy Jackson* from the stash of stories Lainey had after her shock at discovering it was a series of books before they were movies. I was grateful for the selection because, I'd seen the films with the guys and wasn't the best reader. Maybe she'd realize that one day, and the end of story time would be for the best. I hedged through the words, cherishing a moment that might be the last of its kind.

Two chapters in, Max appeared in the doorway, looking bedraggled. His T-shirt was damp and grimy from rummaging, I assumed, in the attic under the rain.

"You guys okay in here?"

"Yeah. We're reading Percy Jackson," Emma said cheerfully. "Did you know it was a book?"

"I did." His mouth quirked up, making him look all kinds of sexy with his finger-tousled hair. "I'm going to go get cleaned up," he said, looking at me while gesturing to the state of his clothes.

"Sure. We're good. Just getting to a good part." I indicated with my phone.

He nodded and returned his gaze to Emma. "Goodnight, kiddo. Love you."

"Love you. Goodnight."

My chest squeezed at the exchange. Even though it looked like Max and I might be able to maintain our friendship, I knew nights like this with the three of us all together were fleeting. They probably always had been.

How long could I be *Uncle Jack* to a family that wasn't and never would be mine? I needed to remember I had always been a visitor with a limited pass.

Emma was growing up. One day she'd be into boys or maybe girls—she'd be into someone, and my company wouldn't be as appealing. One day Max would be ready to remember he was into girls. I couldn't imagine any girlfriend he'd find being as cool as Lainey was about me being around all the time, like a squatter.

Before I could sink back to the self-pitying thoughts that got me in trouble the night of the card game, I returned to the story. I savored every word, every page, every moment of reading this little girl to sleep. She was the closest I'd probably ever come to having children. I wanted to remember every moment.

Two chapters later, her eyes were closed, and her breathing was deep and steady. I turned out the lamp but left the door open. New room, new surroundings—I didn't want her to get scared if she woke up and forgot where she was. I placed a kiss on her forehead and imprinted the image of her serene face to memory.

Making my way downstairs, the house was quiet. The light above the sink in the kitchen was on, casting a glow through the darkened house.

"Max?" I called softly, but only heard clocks ticking and the soft hum of the furnace. I turned into the kitchen. There was light coming from Max's room down the hall toward the back door. I stopped by his doorway on my way out and rapped on the frame.

"Max?"

"Yeah. In here." His rumbly voice had an edge of exhaustion I could relate to.

Hesitantly, I stepped inside. I'd been in his room before, but only to deposit baskets of folded clothes. We'd never been in here at the same time. His presence made it feel like forbidden territory.

A foot inside the room, I stopped in my tracks when I located him. He was sitting on the end of his bed, freshly showered, hair damp, in nothing but a white towel wrapped around his waist. I'd seen him shirtless before, in swim trunks, but a towel? A towel was not swim trunks.

He was hunched over, his forearms resting on his knees as though I caught him deep in thought. He looked at me in question, and I finally remembered why I was here.

"Uh. Emma's asleep. I left her door open in case she wakes up and gets scared."

His mouth ticked up at the corner. "Thanks, and thanks for coming over."

I hooked a finger into the elastic waistband of my sleep pants for something to do with my hands. "No problem. That was crazy. You guys had quite the night."

His response was a grunt. He dropped his head and stared at the floor, his hands fortunately clasped between his legs, dipping the towel to keep my view from being indecent.

I knew I should go. There was nothing more I could do for them tonight, but something about his defeated posture and silence tugged at me.

"How's the roof look?"

He heaved a sigh. "Fucked. And apparently, I have raccoons living in my attic. There's raccoon shit everywhere up there, and they freaking shredded the insulation. It's like that fucking *Allstate* Mayhem commercial where the guy says they've *'been eating all this fluffy stuff.'* One of the little fuckers even had the nerve to look at me like, what are *you* doing up here?"

I leaned against the wall and folded my arms over my chest to ward off the chill of my damp clothes. Suppressing a shiver, I quipped a line from the Mayhem commercial he referenced. "Did they already have '*like four babies*?'"

"Yeah." He snorted. "At least that. It's the fucking *Brady Bunch* up there."

My mouth quirked, glad he could find some humor in his newest dilemma. Except, he dropped his head into his hand and rubbed his eyes.

"I can't fucking do this anymore," he muttered.

My throat closed up. Nothing good ever came from someone saying they couldn't do something anymore. My mind scavenged for possibilities.

He couldn't be friends with me? Or was he talking about his stress? When he didn't elaborate, I pushed off the wall and took a step forward.

"Do what?"

"All of it." He gave me a preposterous look. "Be there for Emma, keep up at work, run a practice, make dinner, laundry, the house, get rid of a tree." He threw his hand up, shaking his head. "And fucking raccoons."

"Hey. It'll be fine. Don't worry about it. I'll help you."

"No." He shook his head adamantly.

"Really. I don't mind. I've got nothing to do all winter."

"No. I...can't let you."

Can't *let* me. That sounded like *couldn't allow* or *wouldn't permit*.

"You let me before."

Before you knew I was gay, hung in the space between us. He must have caught my meaning, because his gaze darted to mine.

"It's not about that," he said with so much conviction it baffled me.

"Then...what is it?"

"It's just...everything is harder. I mean, Lainey used to make me laugh about shit like this. It made everything easier."

"Okay. Uh, we could go round up the raccoons and throw them in Dan's car." I'd never expressed my dislike of Dan, but I took a chance to lighten the mood, knowing how much he aggravated Max at times.

He chuckled, and the sound made my insides glow. "You make me laugh, too. I guess I meant...I'm one person, living a life built for two people."

The confession was soaked in raw vulnerability without the tears from last week. I think I knew that was how he felt these last few years, but he had never come right out and said it. He kept it locked up, eating away at him like rust. His honesty after what happened last week felt like getting the keys to a city.

"And you're doing a hell of a job, Max."

"With my best friend doing my laundry and feeding and babysitting my kid half the time, like a damn nanny?"

"Hey. We've been over this. You know I don't mind. I love spending time with Emma and making things easier for you, so you have more time to spend with her. I don't get to play house all season, so laundry and cooking are like my chance at normal. And…I'm really glad you still call me a friend."

He dropped his gaze, and it sent a trickle of panic through me. Did I push the envelope too far by mentioning 'the unmentionable?'

His expression was pinched when he looked back up at me. "I'm sorry… about the other day. Really sorry."

Like that, we were back in the laundry room, and I remembered the sickening sensation as I walked out of his house. I was grateful for his apology, but this conversation was a china doll. One fumble and everything could shatter.

"No apology necessary."

"No. I shouldn't have shoved you or asked you to leave. That…was super shitty of me. You just…caught me off-guard."

I rubbed my palm over my face, but dropped it when I realized I was doing it to hide my offending lips. "I don't know what the hell I was thinking."

He stayed quiet. When I glanced back at him, he was staring at me, lips parted. His features sobered as though whatever thought he was chasing fled, and he shook his head.

"I shouldn't have reacted the way I did."

"Max, it's okay. Really."

"It's not, but why…why did you kiss me?"

Shit. Fucking *unmentionable* time.

"I…you looked so miserable. It was breaking my heart. I just…wanted to make you feel better, but I didn't think."

"Oh."

The flat tone of that single word made him sound unconvinced, and even a little disappointed. I couldn't think of a better excuse to give him that would help him reconcile being kissed by a man.

Feebly, I offered, "Sorry. I know it probably had the opposite effect."

"It's fine. Don't worry about it."

He swallowed like it took effort and stared at the carpeting again. I didn't know if I was making things better or worse.

I scrounged for more logic to present him, wondering why he sounded almost bitter. "I haven't touched or…been touched by anyone in a long time, so that didn't exactly help my emotions."

His head popped up at my embarrassing addition. "How long?"

"Almost two years."

"But you're…"

"What?"

If he said *gay*, I didn't know whether I'd laugh or be offended. Did he think gay men had weekly orgies?

"Famous."

Laughter won. I cut it off when I saw the cluelessness on his face. "What does being famous have to do with it?"

"Don't famous people get laid all the time?"

I suppressed a scoff. "Not when you're...*like me*, and the whole world is watching you."

"I'm sorry. I...just wish you'd told me."

Our exchange reminded me of pulling off a bandage, uncomfortable but necessary. "I wish I had too instead of just springing it on you like that."

"Well, for the record," he said, lifting a brow, looking off at the wall, "when I have warning, I'm actually a decent kisser."

I chuckled at his proud humor, warmed that he was making the effort for my benefit. "I know. Lainey told me."

His head snapped back to me, his eyes wide. I glanced behind me to check for an axe murderer, but then it clicked.

Oh, fuck. Oh, fuck. Oh, fuck.

"What? Why would... Wait. Did Lainey know...that you..."

For the love of tiny white towels on sexy men I wasn't supposed to think about, I couldn't even think straight. Shit.

I shrugged like it was no big deal, hoping the power of persuasion would get him to shrug off my slip up. "Yeah. She guessed actually."

"When?"

"About a year after I moved in."

He looked toward the corner of the room at nothing like he was process-ing. Almost as if he was talking to himself, he mumbled, "She never told me. How come she never told me?"

"I told her we should, but she asked me not to. She thought it was more important that you had a friend."

Max's eyes pinned me in a flash. I shifted in the silence, hoping he un-derstood Lainey didn't want to complicate our friendship by throwing my secret out there. I should have just told them both from day one, but lack of trust and self-doubt had been my companions for so long that I couldn't.

He said the last thing I expected. "Because she thought I'd judge you."

His diagnosis kicked me with guilt and pity. I couldn't look at him, couldn't let him think either me or Lainey doubted or judged him. "I...don't know."

"Jack..."

The way he implored me, I had to look up. His expression was resolute, braced for any truth I wanted to give him.

"Tell me what she said," he urged softly.

I'd spent my life hiding who and what I was from everyone but a handful of people. It was a survival skill, a way to keep me from getting hurt. Until this moment, I never considered that hiding could hurt other people.

With a shaky breath, I told him a conversation I never thought I would repeat. "She said...you'd probably freak out and that...it wasn't worth ruining our friendship. She said...you needed a good friend." They were Lainey's words, but coming from my mouth, they reeked of arrogance and made me queasy. It wasn't for me to determine if I was a good friend. "Sorry. That sounds really conceited."

Max pursed his lips and shook his head. "No. It sounds like the truth. You have been a good friend."

"Well, still. I'm sorry I ruined the secret." What I really meant was *the friendship.*

"No. I'm sorry if I made you both feel like you had to hide who you are."

I didn't hate myself for being gay. I hated that in order to do what I loved, I couldn't be. Entrusting someone with my truth seemed the equivalent of giving them a drop of poison. They had to be cognizant of the real me and when to pretend they didn't know the real me, so the world wouldn't find out. I didn't come with burdens. I was a walking burden. Knowing the real me was a burden, and now Max had a drop of my poison forever.

"You didn't need to add worrying your best friend was gay to your list of problems," I told him.

His brow furrowed, and he scowled at me; six degrees of intense. "Jack. You're not a problem."

I crashed into every branch on my way down the why-does-he-have-to-be-so-fucking-perfect tree. My heart spasmed in my chest, and I had to press the heel of my palm to my cheekbone to fight the pressure of traitorous tears.

I came out to my parents when I was nineteen. My father told me to *'get over it'* and hadn't I *'fucked up enough already'* by being shit at everything besides baseball. He said if I *'went through with this,'* like being gay was some asinine hobby I wanted to dabble in, he was *'done helping me.'*

I still couldn't think of a single thing he helped me with in life unless he considered all the put-downs about every misstep and failure since the day I was born as helpful. What hurt the most was he resented that I wasn't as smart as him, that I lacked the desire to find a profession he deemed *worthy.* Sports were not a worthy profession. I earned my baseball scholarship from my performance with no encouragement or congratulations from him. Baseball was *mine.* I never asked him for a thing, taking pains to be completely self-sufficient.

I'd like to say I stopped caring what my father thought of me years ago, but knowing he saw me as a problem rather than a son had burrowed deep in my marrow. Max couldn't possibly know what his words unlocked in my chest, but my gratitude nearly choked me.

I didn't know whether to laugh or cry. He just proved Jack Spears Sr. right with that kryptonite sentence—*you're not a problem.* If I thought I could talk myself out of falling in love with Max, I really *was* as dumb as my father thought.

CHAPTER 14
Max

It felt like I was playing volleyball with water balloons. My words sloshed out, shifting unevenly as they lobbed toward Jack. I didn't know if there were even any perfect words to mend the damage I'd done, but judging by how upset he looked, I'd chosen the wrong ones. Again.

When he shifted his weight, I noticed his dirty feet on the carpeting. Had he come over here barefoot? Through the snow? Jesus.

My eyes traveled up, inspecting. His sleep pants and T-shirt had darkened spots where the fabric was damp. He shivered, and my paternal instincts kicked in.

"You're going to get pneumonia, man," I scolded and moved to my dresser. "Let me get you a dry shirt."

Jack was a size larger than me, so it took me a minute to find my bigger shirts—the ones people gifted without asking what size I was, and I kept out of guilt. I gritted my teeth at how desperate I was to find a proper shirt for him. It was such a pittance in light of the jerk I'd been. I'd barely treated him like he was human this past week, so wrapped up in my bullshit thoughts.

And Lainey—she freaking knew, but thought she couldn't tell me. Who was I that the people in my life hadn't been able to talk to me?

When I turned around, I was greeted by a shirtless Jack. Shamelessly, curiously, I took him in from the dips above his collar bones to the smooth bare skin below his belly button.

The flesh on his sculpted torso was golden, flawless, and hairless. Put quite simply, he was perfection to my paler, wolverine-esque body with my smattering of black chest hair. The need to know if he was naturally smooth or if he shaved or waxed became a focal point of my thoughts. It made me realize there were other secrets this man probably had—secret conversations with Lainey, secrets about his love life, his desires, what made him sad, what he found attractive. I desperately wanted to know all of Jack Spears' secrets.

When I looked into his warm brown eyes, I caught a hint of self-consciousness at my bold perusal. His nipples were hard, his skin speckled with gooseflesh. Was it from my gaze or his chill? He folded his big arms across his chest, clutching his spent shirt in his hand.

The lawyer in me knew people didn't give up their secrets easily. You needed to barter with them. Ignoring the chiding voice in my head that told me I was denying him warmth, I kept my spare shirt clasped in my grasp like a greedy pervert, my elbow casually resting on the open dresser drawer.

"What else did you and Lainey talk about?"

He shrugged and mulled the question over for a second. "Emma. Cooking. Celebrities. Yard work."

"I knew that much, but I mean, if she knew about...*you*, it sounds like you talked about other things."

He nodded once, his gaze dancing around to the floor and other points in the room. "She was curious about that part of my past," he conceded.

Envy over Lainey knowing things about him that I didn't rippled through me. I wanted to give into the sensations of being slighted, but I blockaded them. This was my opportunity to remedy that envy.

"How many men have you—"

"—been with?" he ventured when I hesitated.

Fuck. What was I doing? I was going to say *dated*, but now I wanted to know the answer to '*been with.*'

My face flamed, and I shook my head. "No. Sorry, that was...intrusive. You don't have to tell me."

"Four," he blurted out in a rush, almost like he wanted me to know or wanted me to know I could ask him things.

"Oh."

"You thought it would be more?"

"I...maybe."

"I'm not a whore, Max." He chuckled, allowing me to get my foot out of my mouth.

"What...what else did you guys talk about?"

"Max," he uttered my name like a warning.

"No. You can tell me." When he hesitated longer than I could stand, I added, "Seriously. You can tell me anything. What else?"

"Sex." The word fell as subtly as a bowling ball on a hardwood floor.

"Sex?" I parroted. "Wha-what...what about sex?"

By the way his brows knitted together, you'd think I asked him if grass was green. "About...how it works."

It took me a second as I focused on the wave of his hand to realize he meant how sex worked between a man and a man. The temperature of my blood shot up a hundred degrees, imagining Lainey asking about and him explaining what went where and various positions.

"Oh. *Oh*," I fucking babbled. "And, uh, you...you told her?"

"I...yeah. A little." He nipped at the corner of his thumb. How had I never noticed before that he did that when he was nervous? "She kind of nagged it out of me."

I smirked, taking pity on him, picturing my ridiculously tenacious wife slyly brow-beating Jack until he divulged his sex life. "She could be fucking persistent," I conceded.

"Yeah." He chuckled. "But in a charming way."

Our laughter was fleeting, as a thought curled around my brain. If he talked about his sex life to Lainey, it stood to reason she talked about hers, or rather *ours*, to him. Tit for tat and all.

"She didn't talk about *me*, did she?"

"Not about your relationship. She never had anything but good to say. She was crazy about you."

Time stopped. *Not about our relationship* wasn't a *no*.

Last winter, I came home to Jack scrubbing a giant fuchsia stain out of my living room carpet. He tried to tell me it was red wine, but it was during a time when Emma was on a cherry Kool-Aid kick and wouldn't keep her drinks out of the living room. Jack doesn't fucking drink wine. He may have been good at pretending to be straight, but he was shit at lying.

"But she *did* talk about me...and her?" I clarified.

"Nothing important." He did this goofy thing where he looked like he was trying to shake his head and shrug at the same time.

"What? What did she tell you?"

"Max, you don't want to hear this," he practically whined, shifting in place.

"No. I do. Please."

"No. Really, you don't." He shook his head and the fact that he looked a shade paler than a moment ago made my stomach knot.

"Well, now you've got to fucking tell me."

I took the spare shirt hostage with me to the bed and sat down. I didn't care if he froze his sexy-ass nipples off. He wasn't getting this damn shirt until he spilled his guts. If Lainey talked about our sex life, I needed to know. It seemed imperative to know what Jack knew about me.

He hissed out a breath like a leaky balloon. "I think…she saw me as a confidant."

"About?"

"Just…experiences. I think sharing was her way of trying to make me comfortable talking about myself or letting me know she was comfortable with me…being the way I am."

My bitterness simmered. I could see Lainey doing that. She had a way of making everyone comfortable, and honestly, I was grateful to learn she tried to put Jack at ease. But… I still fucking wanted to know how much of my most private shit he'd been privy to.

"What do you mean 'experiences?'"

He scrubbed a hand down his face and let out a long breath. It was like pulling teeth. The more he hesitated, the more anxious I got.

Maybe it was nothing. Maybe he just didn't want to talk about Lainey or talk about straight sex. Did he think straight sex was repulsive?

"She said…she said you liked this one time she played with your ass."

My eyes legit bugged out. "What? She fucking told you that? What the fuck?"

His palms came up. "Sorry! I'm sorry. I told you that you wouldn't want to know."

"Fuck! I do, but from her!" I gripped my hair like I could pull the knowledge out of my brain. "I mean, why would she talk to you about that instead of me?"

"She said you were kind of uptight when it came to talking about sex. She said she liked surprising you by trying new things now and then to see if you liked them, rather than asking you."

How could I feel this warm in only a damn towel? Holy shit. Just… holy shit.

I always knew Lainey was more vocal and adventurous about sex than I was, but no one apart from her needed to know how I fell short. I was probably what you'd call more traditional—get in bed and reach over if we weren't exhausted. Lainey, on the other hand, would initiate anywhere. She'd waltz into the den after Emma was asleep, pretending to be a horny client until I gave up on concentrating on work and scatter my files all over the place while we went at it like rabbits on my desk or the floor. That fantasy made me wonder if she had others she never told me about. Jack said they talked about *experiences*. Is that what he meant?

"Did she tell you about her fantasies?"

"Uh. Which...which one?"

"She had *more* than one?" I snapped.

"Max, I think I should go."

He glanced at the door, ringing his shirt in his hands. I held out my index finger in warning.

"Oh, no! No, you don't! How many fantasies did she freaking have?"

He raised his hands like shields again. "*One*. She only told me one. You said fantasies, *plural*, so I didn't know how to respond."

"Well, which one did she tell you about?"

"I...does it matter?"

"Yes," I demanded, narrowing my eyes for effect. "Was it the one about the doctor's office?"

He licked his thick sexy lips and... there he went with that damn thumb biting again. He hitched a shoulder, and said, "Yeah."

"You're fucking lying. I just made that up."

His features sagged. He grumbled something that sounded like, "Fucking lawyers."

"What was the fantasy she told you about?"

"Max, let's have some respect for the dead before this gets out of hand."

"*Or*...let's have some respect for the living who are stuck here, not knowing all these secrets," I countered.

"Aren't married people allowed to keep some secrets from each other?"

Wow. He was really desperate if he was using that line. I wasn't so sure I wanted to know now. My mouth did what it does best when I'm agitated, spoke before I could think. "Yeah, but now it's just me."

He heaved a sigh and grimaced. Shit. That line even made me sad.

Finally, he grumbled, "You won't like it."

"I don't care."

"After I...admitted I was gay, she said...she said she had a dream about me going down on you."

A jolt skidded down my spine and through my belly. My cock jerked at the mental image at the same time my lungs seized up. It was the most bizarre combination of arousal and shame. "The fuck she did!"

"I told you that you wouldn't want to know!"

I gasped or scoffed. I didn't know which, but all that came out was a choked breath. "Well...why wouldn't she dream about me with another woman?"

Jack's guttural noise managed to do the impossible—it made me feel even more foolish. "Did you ever dream about *her* with another *man*?"

"Fuck no! Why the hell would I do that?"

"Exactly." He held out his hand as though that clarified everything. "It was non-threatening to her relationship to think of you with another man since it would never happen because you're straight. It was just her fantasy."

Tunnel vision took over. I was lost in a *Twilight Zone* version of my life where my best friend, who I thought was straight, was actually gay, had aroused me the last week, and understood my wife better than I had. I couldn't have even spelled my fucking name right now if I tried.

Jack took a knee on the floor at the end of the bed by my side. "Don't be mad at her, Max. She never cheated on you or even thought about looking sideways at anyone else. I got the impression she was very satisfied...with whatever you two did. It was just a fantasy." I could feel him picking nervously at the bedspread as I stared at the wall. "Everybody has fantasies. She was actually kind of embarrassed to admit it to me. I think she was worried she'd offend me."

I could tell the intent of his soothing tone was to reassure me of Lainey's feelings, but it was pointless. Lainey could do little wrong in my eyes then or now. This wasn't the first time I learned new things about her since she died.

The other tidbits came from stories from her parents, Morgan, my mom, and even Emma. Like how she told my mom she wanted two more kids after she told me she'd be happy with only one more. Or how she told Morgan she actually hated my favorite restaurant, Caputo's, but never said anything because she knew how much I loved it.

It was laughable Jack thought his admissions would make me mad at her. The way I saw it, the dead got a free pass because they weren't here to explain in their own words. That and I took a vow—for better or worse. Lainey was definitely the better. I was the worse. It wasn't the differences I discovered since she died that bothered me; it was the fact there were unknowns. Not just on her part.

I hated how she popped her gum. She clipped her nails on the end of the bed instead of over the trash can in the bathroom like a civilized person would, thank you very much. And I always let her control the radio, but disliked her selections. I loved dance and techno music, always had.

We used to go to dance clubs when we were dating, but after we stopped, I realized she favored rock and country. I didn't think she knew I still listened to pop on my mp3 player when I worked out. I never told her any of that. I had no reason to hide my love of a certain type of music. It was just something so unimportant you didn't talk about it, and yet ended up being something I regretted the love of my life not knowing. You didn't think about shit like that when you thought you had forever.

We didn't need to know everything about each other, but if I could go back, I'd be more open with her and myself. Maybe then I would have been more approachable, or even happier—happier for her and Emma, happier with myself.

I was happy, but sometimes I wondered what happened to the carefree kid I was years ago. My nose had been to the grind since my dad died. I had been checking boxes ever since, doing what I thought was right, what I thought was expected of me as a provider, a husband, a father, a son, a brother, a boss, a man in society. I didn't want to fucking check boxes anymore. I just wanted to do what I wanted, say what I felt and thought, whether it was right or wrong. Checking boxes was fucking exhausting.

I wanted to ask Lainey what else she was afraid to tell me. I wanted to ask Jack if he did find the thought of going down on me offensive, and if so, why? I wanted to start listening to dance music even if it would give Dan an ulcer, since he liked to blare Metallica in his office between meetings. I wanted to stop worrying about Emma so much that I overlooked the happy moments.

"I'm not mad," I managed to say. I could hear the defeat in my voice. "I just feel like an idiot. Did you know I was actually kind of jealous of you at first? I was worried you might be tempted to screw around with Lainey until I realized you never looked at her like that, and I saw some women at your house a few times when you had the guys over after you moved in. I figured you had enough other prospects."

"The guys don't know about me. I have to let the women at parties hang on me, so nobody finds out."

The way he sounded like a kid confessing he was scared of the dark made me sad. What kind of life was it to hold things back around the only people he spent more time with than me and Emma?

"So...you don't talk about this to anyone?"

Still picking and staring at my bedspread, he shook his head.

"But...you talked to Lainey?"

He lifted a shoulder and nodded. "Yeah. And Carrie, sometimes, but I try to avoid it with her."

"I'm glad you had someone you could talk to."

The surprise on his face rubbed salt in my wounds. I hated that he thought I'd be mad about whatever he and Lainey discussed. They were the two people I trusted most in the world, and I had pushed him for information. My voyeurism died. They could keep all their secrets.

"She'd probably be laughing her ass off at me right now," I commented, imagining her response to my reaction to the fantasy.

Jack gave a little smile. "Probably."

"She could laugh at anything. I don't know what she saw in me." I didn't even mean to say that last bit aloud, so I was surprised when Jack responded.

"The same things I do."

His honesty smacked me in the face. I wasn't fishing for compliments, but he answered my truth with a truth. Maybe it was that simple. Give and take. I took another stab at the openness I wanted.

"You...ever been with a woman?"

"Yeah." He shrugged like I just asked him if he'd ever eaten hamburgers.

"You didn't like it?"

His brows knitted together. "It was sex. Of course, I liked it."

A week ago, the thought of Jack being with a woman would have seemed as appropriate as milk and cereal to me. Now? Picturing Jack with a woman reminded me of bad Chinese food I once had that left me puking like a zombie on the couch for three days.

"Then...why?"

His fingers stilled on the comforter and his lips parted for a beat as he glanced up at me. "We...like who we like."

"How did you know—"

"—that I liked you more than a friend?"

Now it was my turn to gape. I was going to say, *how did you know you were gay?*

He liked me...*more* than a friend? My head nodded of its own accord, eager for this shiny new secret that was only for me.

He picked at the gray bedspread again. There was a thread coming loose now. I didn't dare stop him. He could dig a hole all the way through the mattress for all I cared. My lungs burned from holding my breath.

"I always thought...you were attractive and funny, but I didn't think about you like that, as *more*, until *after*..." His gaze shifted momentarily to mine before focusing back on his veritable worry stone. "When I hugged you that night after the funeral, it felt like...like you guys were my responsibility then, since Lainey was gone. I mean, it really hit me then that she was gone, and I thought, my God, what if they move away, and I realized there was something more... on my part...when I thought about how it would feel if you weren't in my life anymore. And I thought about it the night of the card game again—what things will be like when you and Emma don't need me anymore."

He took a big breath and turned his attention to the doorway. His shoulders hefted with a self-deprecating laugh.

"I tried to tell myself how ridiculous it was. I mean, I think we both know you come across as kind of temperamental, but I know it's only because you're impatient. You're not really the crabby, serious guy all the time." He shot me an apologetic smile and went back to his picking. "You're the most amazing father, a hard worker, the best kind of hilarious. You're kind and more sensitive than you let on. When you feel, you feel big and...you admit when you're wrong," he paused to give me another smile and added, "eventually. And you're not afraid to stand by your opinions or feelings. That's...I think that's really sexy."

Quiet settled over the room. When I was sure he was done, all my nerve endings disconnected. They were sentiments I didn't deserve and claims I didn't think were entirely true, but, at the same time, I'd never felt like someone knew me as much as he did, or at least knew the man I wanted to be. He had somehow stripped my soul naked, looking deep inside at parts I'd never shown anyone.

I needed to say something. "Oh."

He huffed in embarrassment and got up. "Yeah, but don't worry. I'll get over it. I mean, I knew from the beginning it was stupid to fall for a straight guy. I'd still like to be friends, if...if you can handle it."

He took two languid steps toward the wall, folding his arms over his chest with his back to me as though he needed to pace. That extra bit of distance between us after telling me he'd get over his crush on me might as well have been an ocean for how far away it felt like he was.

My heart was a hummingbird over the quick dismissal of his own feelings. He just out-poured gallons, and I was sitting on a bucket of something. His truth deserved more than a response of, *'Oh.'*

"I thought about Lainey's fantasy," I blurted to the floor. If I told the floor and not his face, it wasn't real, except as soon as the words were out, my fluttering heartbeat leveled out. I'd just dumped my baggage in our ocean, and it was... freeing.

His feet turned around. I looked up to his ruddy cheeks and a grimace. "You're still stuck on that, huh? I'm sorry. It's probably like seeing something that can't be unseen." He let out a sour laugh, running a hand through his hair. "I'm a shit friend, after all."

"No. I...dreamt about it...*before* you told me."

Where the fuck I had gotten the balls to look him in the eye when I said that I didn't know, but I couldn't look away. His shock was an elixir. I was suddenly a fucking dispensary of uncomfortable truths.

His Adam's apple bobbed in his throat. His voice came out as dry as chalk. "When?"

"All week."

The dumbstruck lines on his face smoothed, and he nodded like he'd just solved a puzzle. "Now I know why you avoided me."

I despised that nod. He was closing the window on the topic, writing off my confession. I needed to jam something in that window while this conversation still had a pulse. I wanted answers before I was left alone with only my thoughts again.

"Did *you* ever have that dream?" I asked.

He stared, his bare chest rising and falling under his folded arms. "Max—"

The way he said my name sounded like another warning. I didn't want to be protected, not from him or myself.

"You talked to Lainey. You can talk to me, too."

"Yeah, but...about *this*?"

"If we're going to be friends, we have to be honest with each other. No more secrets."

"I..." He hesitated. His anxiety was a live wire, connected to my own in this space. Taking an unsteady breath, he nodded. "Yeah. I did."

His answer was so potent, I had to look away. I was holding my breath, but it was like I was in a courtroom in the middle of my line of questioning. I couldn't stop. His words were a drug, and I needed another hit of them. I'd gone this far, held back all week. I couldn't turn back now.

"Did you like it?"

"Did I...like the dream?"

"Yeah."

I was afraid if I looked at him, he wouldn't answer. I was afraid if I didn't, he still wouldn't. I was suspended in an excruciating space between hope and disappointment, even though I didn't understand why.

"I did," he finally said.

I closed my eyes, swallowing the confession I had demanded. It was mine now to do with whatever I wanted.

Jack had dreamt about me and liked it. The boxes I would instinctively check said I was being naughty, too bold, and maybe even confused. A voice in my head said, *fuck those boxes; we never liked them anyway,* so I drew new ones.

"Did *I* like it?"

"It was just a dream, Max. It wasn't really you."

He was balking, taking away my pen and paper before I could finish adding boxes. I looked up, pinning him, maybe even pleading with my eyes. "But in your dream, did I like it?"

"Well, yeah. It was a dream, not a nightmare."

"And you didn't mind...that *I* liked it?"

Hands on his hips, he was wearing the kind of face a parent had when they informed their children the family pet had just died. My stomach turned, but then his voice came out tender.

"No. I didn't mind."

My pulse was a beat box. I was aware of every surge of blood as more words tumbled out of my mouth.

"Would you really want to do that?"

He blinked once. Twice. A third time. I'd gone too far for the both of us.

I didn't even know why I was asking, but my mouth clarified anyway. "*To me?*"

CHAPTER 15
Jack

Did he really just ask me that? Maybe I had slipped in the shower, cracked my head open, and was lying on the tile floor in dreamland.

Max on his bed in nothing but a towel, looking at me, asking me about my fantasies, telling me about his—the fucking universe designed this torture specifically for me. *Dear Universe, you're a cruel bitch.*

He thought about me—about me sucking his cock. No. Dreamt it *all week,* he'd said. I had been a rerun.

I was trying to play it cool and keep an understanding ear open, but the mental image of him lying in this bed, pumping his dick to thoughts of me, was more vivid than technicolor. His intense, determined gaze was still on me. The foolishly smitten part of me wanted so badly for that intensity to mean lust, but the sensible part of me knew it was more likely fear.

This smelled like a challenge. Like he was doing his lawyer thing where he got to the truth. I agreed we needed to be honest with each other if we wanted our friendship to stand a chance, but damn. I assumed certain topics, namely my feelings for him, could get shoved in the *unmentionable* category.

Had I dreamt about Lainey's dream becoming a reality? Fuck yes. I wasn't a monk. Man could not survive on porn alone, but what happened if

I shared that truth? What happened when you told a confused, sex-starved, grieving straight man you'd gladly dream-sucked his cock and had enjoyed every minute of it?

Max wasn't a violent person, but fear did things to people. Confusion did things to people. I'd seen it. I'd been here before.

Junior year of high school, I had about a dozen secret sessions in the back of the empty baseball team bus and locker room with a hot senior, Gordon Hill. The summer good old *Gordie* graduated, I saw him outside the movie theater one night with a group of his friends.

I said hello. He didn't answer. Assuming he hadn't heard me, I said hello again. He told me to get lost. I asked what his problem was because I was just being sociable. It wasn't like me saying hello would have outed either of us. Next thing I knew, I found myself knocked on my ass in the parking lot. He had failed to mention I should pretend he was invisible if I ever saw him again.

My pulse was flickering in my jugular right now, like my ass knew it was about to become a landing pad again. Physically, I could take Max, but there was the little problem that I'd never hurt a hair on his gorgeous body.

"Max, I think maybe I should go."

"Would you?" he prodded.

Leave before this gets more awkward? *Hell yes*, I wanted to say, but I knew that wasn't what he was asking. I decided to play dumb because it wasn't like I had to try too hard to pull it off.

"Would I what?"

"Want to do that...*to me*...or would any man do?"

A puff of breath burst from my lungs as I reassessed the expression on his face. It *was* fear, but I had read it wrong. It was the fear of rejection.

He probably didn't even realize that was what his face said. Fucking straight guys—they wouldn't touch any dick but their own, yet they'd get offended if anything with sexual organs didn't want them.

Unless... he was judging me. Maybe he needed to know what type of man had made an advance toward him in his laundry room. I was appalled he'd even consider it a possibility I'd go down on *any* man. What did he think of me? Well, I'd told him I'd been with a woman too, but not that it was a ridding-of-virginity-agreement on prom night between me and Sarah Banks. Christ, I could only imagine what he thought.

His jaw worked anxiously. He was hanging on a ledge, waiting for me to pull him up or push him over.

Would you want to do that to me, or would any man do?

I rolled the question around again. Whatever the reason for the self-doubt on his handsome face, it pulled on my insides. Hadn't I made it embarrassingly clear that I wanted him? Didn't he know how special he was? Or could he still not fathom that sexual attraction for me was with a man—*this* man? Maybe some truths were meant to be in the open.

"Just you, Max. Only you."

He straightened up, putting his full torso on display. His chest rose like he was inhaling my confession bit by bit. My curious eyes snuck down his chiseled chest and then lower because they didn't know what was good for me.

Hello, happy trail. Hello, towel I've been trying to ignore during fantasy talk. And hello...

Whoa. Just...hello.

There was a distinctive bulge in the white terry cloth of his towel. I choked, trying to swallow the lump in my throat. Tearing my eyes away, I looked right up into his because, of course, people always looked the one freaking place they shouldn't.

Okay. That wasn't true—the *two* places they shouldn't. Note to self—shouldn't have looked at his cock either.

His eyes rounded and darted to his towel. His hand clamped down on his bulge so quick and hard, I flinched in sympathy for *Max Junior*.

"Fuck," he muttered, pinching the bridge of his nose with his other hand. *Nice, Jack. Nice.*

As if I hadn't made him uncomfortable enough last week, now I had just gawked at his hard-on that *I* had caused with inappropriate conversation. I cleared my throat.

"Don't worry about it. You're just...confused because of what I did. We've been talking about sex, and it's been a long time for you."

Oh, hell no. Did I seriously just remind him of how long Lainey's been gone? Smooth, Spears. Real smooth!

And because I hadn't said enough already, and I was used to fixing the man's problems, I blurted, "Look. I'll help you deal with the tree tomorrow, and then why don't I watch Emma for you afterward, so you can go out and unwind?"

He made a guttural sound. "If you know the secret to that, you're going to have to let me know."

"It's no secret, Max. Go out. Get a drink. Meet a woman. Get laid. Blow off some steam."

There. *Vaginas*. Talk about vaginas and *not* our cocks. This was medicinal.

"I just told you I dreamt about my dick in your mouth, and you tell me to go out and get laid? No wonder you're single."

I laugh-snorted so loud it hurt my nose and wondered if that was what it was like for Carrie. Shit. Maybe Max *could* handle having a gay friend if he was cracking jokes at a time like this.

"See?" I teased. "Best kind of hilarious," I reminded him of my earlier assessment.

He scoffed, which I took as a laugh, but then a moment passed. And then another. Silence swelled between us again. We were back to the elephant in the room… and the freaking elephant under his towel.

Shit. I needed to get a grip.

No! Not a grip. There would be no gripping. Ah!

I let out a breath to steady my nerves. Max was straight. Hard-on or not. He'd lost his wife, hadn't been laid in three years, and we were talking about sex. Nobody deserved the right of an inopportune erection more than him. If I wanted to be his friend, I needed to help him make decisions that were right for *him*, not hoard him to myself and the unrealistic fairy-tales in my head.

"Have you thought about dating again?"

"Bob and Ellen, of all people, are trying to set me up with someone. They said I'm still young, and it's not healthy to not move on."

Lainey's parents were trying to fix him up? What the actual fuck? I saw red on Lainey's behalf. And Max's. The *still young and not healthy to not move on* part, though?

"You are and it's not," I agreed.

"Yeah, but who wants to go out with someone who their dead wife's parents pick out? That's just fucking weird. Isn't it?"

Super fucking weird. *Thank you, Max.*

"Well, I didn't want to say it, but yeah. That's kind of awkward."

"Totally awkward."

Forging ahead, I shrugged, spewing a bunch of helpful crap I didn't want to spew. "So, pick someone out yourself."

He shook his head. "Thinking about someone who either pretends Lainey didn't exist or wants to ask me and Emma trivia questions about her to fit in? No thanks."

"Well, she existed, and it's okay to have needs. You're only human. She'd want you to be happy."

It was the right response, the response a friend should say, but the sullen voice in my head echoed, *even if it's not with me.*

CHAPTER 16
Max

She'd want you to be happy.

The words were jarring—a square peg in a round hole. Lainey wanted so much for me to be happy, she kept a secret from me about my best friend. I knew I hadn't handled Jack's secret well, but I should have. I could have. I would. She and Jack both deserved for me to handle it well.

It was strange. For some reason, I had thought his confession of being gay made him different, but he was the same as he'd always been. Tonight, when I was racing up the stairs to Emma's room and looked over, we were just two guys scared out of their minds about a little girl we both love. He was right there beside me when I needed him most, like he's always been.

Jack wasn't different, but in a way, I was. I was seeing him with new eyes, the eyes I should have seen him with all along. There was a giant tree on my house and a fucking family of conniving little *trash pandas* in my attic, but right now, with him standing here, I didn't even care.

He shifted his weight and rubbed the back of his neck. "You...keep looking at me like that."

"Like what?" Something rebellious kept me from pulling my gaze away.

"Like you don't know what to think of me. Like I'm a stranger."

"That's not what I'm doing," I assured him, finding his misinterpretation endearing. If he only knew.

He motioned to me. "Can I get that shirt?"

My face burned when I realized I was still holding my offering hostage. I tossed it to him.

"Sure. Sorry."

I avoided any more gawking by heading back to the dresser to get clothes for myself. I pulled on a T-shirt, growing more embarrassed by the second that I was still in a towel. Did we really just have the conversation we had? Logical-me was shocked at myself. Post-kiss me was grateful we opened a can of worms.

Behind me, I could hear the rustle of fabric over skin, as Jack put on the shirt I gave him. Then he said, "I can put in a call tonight to that guy who took down the dead ash tree in my yard a couple years ago. Maybe that'll get you on the top of the list tomorrow, in case other people had storm damage."

And like that, we were back to reality. Post-kiss me was pouting in the corner. "Yeah. That'd be great. Thanks. I'll look up roofing contractors tomorrow."

"Good. Um, I can come over and make Emma breakfast to keep her occupied while you call and deal with them."

"Sounds like a plan." I turned around to find him dressed in my snug-fitting T-shirt. "But are you sure that's how you want to spend your weekend?"

"It's fine, as long as I get my workouts in. I don't have any other plans, and I can exercise any time."

"Right. Well, Emma will be happy to have you around."

And me.

He nodded. "See you tomorrow then?"

"See you tomorrow," I parroted like a fool. "Hey. Did you run over here barefoot?"

"Oh. Uh, yeah." He flushed, glancing at his feet. "I saw the tree going down and didn't even think. I was halfway here before I even noticed."

I nodded toward the sunroom, where I kept my yard shoes and flip-flops on a rack. "Take a pair of my shoes."

"Thanks."

I was fully aware of every noise—Jack walking down the hall, putting on a pair of my flip-flops, sliding the patio door open. When I heard it close, I was fully aware of the loss of him in the house. Something told me when he left for spring training in February, that sensation of loss would be a hundred times worse.

CHAPTER 17
Max

"Mm. Bacon," I murmured into my pillow.

I was half-awake, so it couldn't be a dream. It was more like sensory déjà vu. Rolling onto my back, I strained my ears and homed in on the sound of sizzling, laughter, and faint music.

My nose twitched at the savory aroma. I did fucking smell bacon—bacon I didn't have to cook. It was the best smell on the planet. And that laughter—Jack's and Emma's—I couldn't think of a better sound.

I fell asleep replaying last night's *bedroom confessional*, wondering if I imagined the entire thing. I had been so... unfiltered, and Jack had answered all my outlandish inquiries with patience and honesty.

Staring at my bedroom ceiling, I waited for regret over the things I asked him last night to slam into me, but it didn't. I felt lighter; the tension that was always in my chest was gone. The void between us felt smaller.

I grabbed some sleep pants and threw them on over my boxer briefs. Making my way into the master bath, I splashed some water on my face and brushed my teeth.

My reflection in the mirror showed a dark shadow of stubble, one of the curses of having thick black hair like my father had. Did Jack like stubble? My face was never smooth for long, even after I shaved. His response to my ridiculous question last night jumped up to greet me as I stared in the mirror.

You. Only you.

He said he thinks I'm *really sexy*. The memory of his words warmed my chest. I wanted to know if it was simply a reaction to being complimented or if it was because his acceptance of my questions put me at ease.

He hadn't judged me, hadn't made me feel like I had done anything wrong by having lurid thoughts. I was very un-Max-like, and he didn't seem to have as big of a problem with it as I'd had.

My reflection frowned at me, remembering something else he said. He dubbed me *confused*. The word stuck to me like a piece of chewed up gum.

For the first time in a week, I fell asleep without feeling confused. As I made my way down the hallway to the kitchen, I searched for better labels for my emotional state.

Wonder.

Awe.

Peace.

As I mulled the captions over in my mind, I couldn't find a reason to change them. The words took root.

The sight that greeted me in the kitchen had me pausing in the doorway. Emma was perched on one of the island barstools in her pajamas, shoveling a fork load of pancakes into her mouth. Jack's phone was propped against the utensil crock in the center of the island, as usual. Fleetwood Mac's *'Tusk'* streamed from it. Him and his classic rock obsession. One of Emma's stocking clad feet dangled from the stool, bouncing in time to the notes.

"Will the stuff in my room get smashed when they fix the ceiling if something falls from the attic?" she asked Jack.

"Well, I'm going to have to go in there and bag it all up and take it out of there before they can work on it," he called over his shoulder from the stovetop.

"I can help."

"Well, I sure hope so." He chuckled. "It's *your* stuff, but you can't go in there. It's not safe until they fix the roof. We don't want you getting squashed like a real bug. I'll have to hand your things out to you in the hallway, and you can carry them to the spare room for now."

He was in an old grey sweatshirt and faded jeans, his broad shoulders shifting as he flipped bacon in a frying pan. The domestic vibe of the moment seemed so natural, so right.

"Hey, Dad!" Emma called.

"Hey, kiddo. You found us a chef, huh?" I asked, coming forward to tousle her hair.

Jack spun around like a kid who just got caught in the cookie jar. His eyes did a quick scan of me, up and down, making every inch of my flesh go hot. There was apprehension in his eyes as he flashed me a hesitant smile, like he was seeking permission to be here.

"There he is," he declared. I liked how it sounded as though he had been awaiting my arrival. "How's it going?"

"Good." I took a seat next to Emma, and for the first time in three years, I felt no guilt over allowing him to wait on us. He looked too damn eager to take this joy away from him.

"Coffee?" he asked, arching a brow.

"Sure, if you've got some made."

He pulled a mug out of the cabinet. I'd seen him do this hundreds of times. He knew my kitchen as well as his own, but this morning the easy familiarity flattered me.

Jack Spears knew my kitchen. He chose *my* kitchen out of all the other kitchens in the world, chose my house, my family, and *me—only me*.

His warm smile spread over me like honey, coating every pore as he handed me the cup of coffee. *Confused* was the last word I would use for the way his golden eyes made my heart stutter, how the hint of mischief in them gave me a spark of excitement, how his presence brought me tranquility and a sense of belonging, and how the beautiful lines of his strong body warmed my blood.

I was suddenly annoyed with him for his poor word choice. I was the opposite of confused. I was two hundred and ten percent attracted to Jack Spears.

The realization unfurled inside me, and for the first time in nine days, I didn't question it. It was a truth unequivocally set free. I bit my cheek to suppress a laugh; I was so overcome with relief. Setting my truth free was far easier than denying it had been, which I realized was what I'd been doing.

"So, the tree contractor will be here in two hours. I hope that's okay," Jack said, looking at me as he returned to the stove.

He called a tree contractor? He was making breakfast, planned to help clean out Emma's room, and thinks I'm really sexy. I suppressed another laugh. How could I not be attracted to that?

"Max? You all right?"

I had to clear my throat to form words. "Yeah. That's great. Thanks. I'll, uh, call the insurance company after breakfast to start a claim and then look up contractors for the roof."

He nodded and moved the bacon from the pan to a plate. I didn't miss the way he dabbed the grease off with a paper towel—the way I liked it.

As his hands worked, I wondered what they would feel like in mine. I couldn't remember ever feeling such a powerful pull to anyone in my life. My daughter was sitting right here, but I still had the urge to go over there and lick the bacon grease from his long fingers. I didn't even like bacon grease. Fuck me.

I shifted uncomfortably in my chair. The serene resoluteness of acknowledging my attraction to Jack—my insanely heart-warming, cock-hardening attraction—was gone.

Now I had a new problem. I had absolutely no idea what I was supposed to do with this revelation.

CHAPTER 18
Max

I learned three things today. One—I'd been lax at weeding out old toys and clothing from Emma's room since Lainey died. It was like a freaking episode of *Hoarders* in that child's room.

Two—when a contractor tells you they should be finishing up soon, that meant they had lost all of their ambition, and it would be at least three more hours before they vacated your life.

Three—it was painfully uncomfortable to work side-by-side someone you find irresistible. I could still smell Jack—his spicy soap and the sweet male scent of his sweat. Yes. Apparently, now the smell of sweat did it for me.

I could still feel every brush of his hand from when we removed Emma's bedroom door and passed trash bags full of her things out of her room. All of that resulted in half a hard-on and having to concentrate on breathing normally. The only thing that kept me from having a full tent in my pants was the proximity of my child and four contractors who did nothing for my libido. Still, every time Jack was near, I couldn't draw myself away. It was like a fascinating science experiment, studying every reaction I had to being near to him.

The tree was gone. The hole in the roof had been tarped. Emma's room had been emptied, except for her bedframe and mattress, which we propped against the wall and covered with plastic. The building contractor was coming tomorrow for an estimate and could start work Tuesday, which was a miracle this close to Christmas.

Emma fared well throughout the day and was an invested helper, likely because I told her we could repaint her room during the repair. I was not above bribery, although I regretted it when she informed me her new room color would be creepy Sock Monkey pink. Yet, what should have been a miserable day was actually quite tolerable. Until Lainey's mom called.

Ellen phoned around lunch, and I had to relay the entire tree debacle to her. Her way of lightening the mood was to mention the woman in her bridge club she'd been trying to set me up with was free next Saturday.

This coming Wednesday was Christmas. Who the fuck went on a first date three days after Christmas, let alone a blind date? Didn't this woman have family or friends or vacations to occupy her holidays? Was she that desperate, or did Ellen think *I* was that desperate?

Her name is Renee—Renee Thomas. It was one of those names that sounded like it belonged to a nice, normal person, free of fetishes or issues. Translation—probably the kind of woman who wouldn't dream about me getting a blowjob from an MLB player. I hated her already.

I was sure my mother-in-law vetted her with plenty of questions. Still, I found it impossible to be enthusiastic. I didn't know if it was the whole awkwardness of my mother-in-law picking out my date or wondering what Lainey would think of the situation, but I couldn't imagine anything coming from the arrangement.

I knew I should be open to at least the possibility of a new relationship at some point, but something about this or the timing just felt wrong. There was too much going on right now to have to deal with dating. Rolling over in bed, I sighed as I locked eyes with Lainey's in her picture on my nightstand.

"So, your mother set me up on a date," I told her.

I chuckled, imagining her laughing, which wasn't difficult since she was laughing in the photo. When things got too frustrating or confusing, I talked to her. I knew I was really just talking to myself, but instead of making me feel crazy for talking to myself, it calmed me.

"Renee Thomas. She runs marathons, plays bridge with your mother, and works for some tech company."

I heaved a breath, finding myself at a loss for words or emotions on the topic. Instead, I proceeded to tell her about the roof and Emma's room, but then I got to the part where Jack helped and realized I wasn't saying what I really wanted to say.

"What if...what if I was *bi*, and you didn't know it?" I blurted out, but then I remembered the fantasy she confessed to Jack. "Shit. Maybe you did know."

Why did the thought of her suspecting I could swing the other way make me feel guilty? I knew with unconfirmed certainty she wouldn't have judged me, but like a petulant child I deflected and vented, "I can't believe you knew about Jack. Did you think it was funny that I didn't know?"

No. She wouldn't have.

I sunk my teeth into my lip and pulled the covers tighter. I was sure she had enjoyed needling Jack for details, and he had probably laughed at whatever insane questions she came up with, but I knew it had to have bothered her that she felt she had to hide his orientation from me.

The whole blow job fantasy, though? Yeah. She probably thought that was funny. My cock twitched in my boxers, imagining her request.

I shifted, but it did nothing to relieve the exhilarating discomfort. Reaching under the blanket, I squeezed my shaft absently, imagining Lainey lying here dreaming her dream. I let out a scoff, remembering how she often slept with a smile on her face. Had I witnessed the smile from that dream?

Was that why she laughed her ass off and gave me shit when I said Jack was the epitome of manliness? We were sitting right here in bed for that conversation. She was reading a fitness magazine called *The Circuit* where Jack was featured in a five-page spread as their Sexiest Man of the Year.

"Shit," I grumbled, squeezing my hand around the head of my inconvenient erection. That magazine shoot was about *two years* after Jack moved in next door. Jack said Lainey guessed his sexuality about *a year* after he moved in. She freaking knew about him when we had that manliness conversation!

"You damn minx," I gasped.

A beat passed as I recalled the bold images of Jack's flesh in the magazine I had avoided looking at, but then I remembered how little purging I'd done since Lainey died as evidenced by Emma's room clean out today.

Ellen and Morgan went through and took away most of Lainey's clothes, with the exception of a few outfits I saved for Emma to have when she's older. They hadn't touched her nightstand, though. I swallowed at the thickness in my throat and glanced at the piece of furniture next to Lainey's side of the bed. She always read magazines in bed. A provoking voice in my head whispered, *I bet it's still in there*.

I scrambled to her side and leaned over the edge of the mattress, opening the bottom door of her nightstand. Sure as shit, there was a heap of dusty magazines still piled inside and…a fucking vibrator! Just what my ego needed.

"I'm not going to judge you, so don't judge me," I grumbled, flinging it aside so I could flip through the stack of magazines.

"Fuck. I need to clean in here."

My breath caught when I locked eyes with an image of Jack on the cover of *The Circuit*. I pulled the magazine out, hand trembling as though a mousetrap might snap on my nosy fingers just for touching it.

That was stupid. Wasn't it? The whole world had seen whatever was in this magazine.

I dropped it on my pillow and took in the shirtless image of Jack, a few years younger, on the cover, arms folded over his pecs. He was laughing, looking down. His eyes were crinkled at the corners, nearly closed, as though the photographer just told him a joke and he was embarrassed.

Did everyone else who saw this notice the bashfulness of that look? Did Lainey realize like I had how sensitive he could be? Of course she did. That was why they were friends. That was why he trusted her with his secret.

"What the fuck did you two talk about?" I asked her, flipping open the magazine.

I found the highlight photo of the spread and sagged onto my haunches. A speech bubble near Jack's luscious mouth, surrounding what was clearly Lainey's handwriting in black Sharpie read, *Hey Maxi!*

"Fucking…hilarious," I told her, but I couldn't tear my eyes away from the two-page image of our best friend.

Jesus. I was actually jealous of my wife that she had been uninhibited enough to look at this when I couldn't.

My blood thickened and burned hot all at once. My dick sat up and ached so hard I had to drag my hand across the bulge in my boxer briefs to relieve the tension.

The black-and-white photo of Jack sprawled out on a chaise lounge was the most breath-taking thing I'd ever seen. One of his legs was propped up, bent at the knee. The other was stretched out languidly with his foot resting on the floor. He had one beefy arm extended above his head, relaxing on the armrest. The fingers on his other hand were draped over the washboard muscles above his navel as though he was about to touch himself or just had. He was wearing a piece of fabric. Part of a sheet, maybe? It was like a damned jockstrap with a flap covering his junk. That was all. Nothing else.

"Holy fuck," I gasped.

His agent sure knew how to sell him. Everything about the picture screamed spank bank. How many freaking people had seen this? Thousands? Millions?

The thought of people in their bedrooms ogling pictures of him clouded my vision with a haze of...of what? Irritation? Jealousy? Protectiveness?

A noise startled me—a low, deep rumble. Holy shit. My hand was in my briefs, slowly running up and down my thick erection. That noise? It was me. I had just groaned.

A sheen of sweat had formed above my lip. I was being...*bad*. I cussed like a sailor, but I never did anything *bad*.

Glancing at Lainey's photo, I expected the discomfort of an audience, but no daggers of judgement stabbed me. There was just her smile.

"You want your fantasy?" I rasped, freeing myself from my boxer briefs.

A drop of pre-cum beaded at my tip. I raked over it with my thumb, shuddering at the contact on my sensitized head, and spread the liquid over my shaft.

I was so damned hard I could fucking crack one of Jack's baseballs with this erection. There was so much of his smooth skin on display, but my greedy eyes focused on the shadows near the V of his hips, under the curve of his exposed ass cheek. He was practically naked, and I still craved to know his unknowns.

Licking my lips, the kiss came to the forefront of my memory as I stared at Jack's barely parted mouth. He looked sleepy, satisfied, deep in thought, and even a bit haunted. My heart panged with the urge to erase the shred of agony on his handsome face that I bet millions of strangers hadn't noticed.

A shiver ran down my spine, remembering I wasn't alone. Not entirely.

"There, baby. Is this your fantasy?"

It seemed so wrong to look at Lainey's photo right now, but she was the only one I should be looking at. Yet, she wasn't here, never would be again, and I didn't think I could stop if I wanted to.

Fuck. I didn't want to stop.

I wanted desperately to keep this body-drugging rush of goodness, this feeling of being alive again that died when Lainey did. Something told me I had to do this. I needed to do this. I needed to know how far this attraction went. How long it was going to last.

My chest filled with frustration and humility, lust, and longing, light and dark. I was a powder keg of every spectrum of emotions as I dropped a hand to my pillow and pumped feverishly into my grip, chasing, fighting, searching, yearning.

My gaze traced the curves of Jack's muscles. Hot need coiled around the base of my spine. My balls were as granite-like as my cock, drawing on the memory of our kiss to fuse with the pleasure I was eliciting with my hand.

Was I no better than anyone else who'd looked at his picture and done this? The thought of another man taking himself in hand to Jack pulled an angry growl from my lips and a hard thrust into my grip. Who was I shaming more with this wild debauchery—my wife? Jack? Myself?

"You like that? You like me getting off to a fucking baseball player?" I spared a glance at the picture on the nightstand that was granting me this erotic permission. "You think I'm uptight now? I'm looking at him. Do you see this hard-on?"

I sounded like I thought she should be proud of me. That was fucking crazy, but all I knew right now was crazy. Crazy and agonizing desire.

I pumped like my life depended on it, oddly comforted by the knowledge I was fulfilling Lainey's fantasy. My cock throbbed harder by the second. My moans and panting breaths filled the empty room, sounds I hadn't heard in forever and missed making.

I was done thinking. I only wanted to feel. Wrenching open my night-stand drawer, I grabbed an old bottle of lube and squeezed some into my palm. My toes curled at the slick glide of my tight grip over my erection.

Had Jack done this to a man? Had he thought about doing it to me? Did he talk during sex? Sweet or dirty?

Would his mouth be hot and tight and wet like my hand was right now? Did he like having a dick in his ass? Or putting himself in a man's ass?

Fuck. What did that feel like? What did his cock feel like? Was he long? Narrow? Wide? The information was more important than the answers to all of life's mysteries.

The visions reeled past my mind's eye. I imagined half of my frantic breaths were his, imagined his lips on mine again, his hands holding me to him. Heat snaked down my legs. My balls burst as white-hot pleasure shot down my shaft and into my hand. My hips twitched as my release came in waves and a cry ripped out of my lungs.

Panting and satiated, my vision came back into focus. I licked my lips. I was practically drooling from longing for more kisses and the hunger that just ravaged my dormant body. The need to be held by a pair of big strong arms made me ache deep inside. Never in my life had I had a release like that from an image alone.

I cleaned up in a daze, tossing the magazine into my nightstand. Catching a glimpse of Lainey's photo as I stood, I went still. A wave of nausea hit me.

Christ. I'd forgotten all about her.

I may have told myself I was giving Lainey her fantasy just now, but it sure as shit hadn't been her I was thinking about when my eyes had nearly rolled back into my head.

CHAPTER 19
Jack

Another message from Hooper popped up on the big screen mounted on the wall of my home gym as my sneakers pounded the belt of my treadmill. I laughed at the chat box overlaying the music video that Hooper had picked: '*Freaks*' by Timmy Trumpet and Savage.

HOOPER: You give up yet, old man?

Such a cocky little shit. I was only four years older than him. Twenty bucks said his face was purple, and he was even more drenched in sweat than I was. Swiping the damp hair from my forehead, I tapped out my reply from where my phone sat in the cradle on the treadmill console.

ME: Not a chance. Just getting warmed up.

HOOPER: You need eight miles to warm-up? That's a lot of prep, dude. Glad you're not a firefighter.

The chuckle that bubbled out of my throat gave me pause when it didn't release the catch on the spring trap that had taken up residence in my sternum. My muscles were pliant like a freshly tanned animal hide. My steps felt light despite the burn of fatigue, but that obnoxious bubble was still there deep in my chest, refusing to burst with each panting breath.

I'd watched Emma all week from sunup till sundown since she was off school for the holidays. It had been better than old times, getting to see her all day, every day. We did crafts, played board games, had snowball fights, painted her walls Mr. Sparkles pink, and today we'd moved all her stuff back into her bedroom now that the roof was repaired, and the paint had dried.

She'd been a trooper, working with me side by side as we got her room back in order. I even motivated her to take on more cleaning responsibilities around the house to help Max. She liked the idea of being Cinderella when I told her it would pay off someday. We were buddies again, tighter than we'd ever been.

Max, on the other hand? Well, I didn't know what to think about Max. When he wasn't eerily silent and staring at me, he was like a person who assured you everything was fine and then overcompensated with a crazy laugh that said they were anything but fine.

He went from avoiding me last week to being nearly on my ass every second this week. *Literally* on my ass. Like whenever I turned around, I had to watch out that I didn't bump into him. And that look in his eyes…

He'd been looking at me like he either wanted to mug me, fuck me, or murder me. God, that sounded like a line from *Stepbrothers*, except in this circumstance it wasn't funny. It left me a prisoner under his gaze all week, half-terrified, half-turned on. The two feelings should not co-exist.

It got my stomach so twisted up in knots, and I knew this wasn't going to end well. I mean, everyone who gets laid in horror movies dies. Right?

Since I definitely wasn't going to get laid, that left mugging or murdering. Shit. So many wonderful outcomes.

I made more money than him. I guess mugging was still a contender. That was almost comforting.

I assumed he was still sorting things out about that kiss and the confessions the night of the storm that had left me stripped bare. I just wished he'd hurry up and decide what he could and couldn't handle. Were we friends or not? Being stuck in limbo with crazy-eyes sucked balls.

I was worried there was an expiration date on our precarious friendship. To make matters worse, the part of my brain that was led by my neglected dick kept reminding me he had dreamt about it before I even told him about Lainey's fantasy.

I had been reminding my stupid dick that Max having dirty dreams was just curiosity. He was straight. He'd always be straight. I wasn't the cliché gay guy that got his straight friend to have a sexual awakening.

Wiping the sweat from my forehead with the back of my hand, I searched for a peppy song to keep our workout flowing as Hooper's selection wound down. Finger typing while running should be an Olympic sport.

Hmm. Now there was a blast from the past and a total guilty pleasure song. Swedish pop singer Günther's remix of Samantha Fox's '*Touch Me*,' featuring the lovely Samantha Fox. Grinning, I hit play, eager to throw Hooper for a loop. He prided himself on his vast musical knowledge, but I was betting he hadn't met Günther. There were a few benefits to being an *old man*.

The music video streamed across my big screen, and I snickered. I'm sure Europe loved him, but the singer's pencil-thin mustache and mullet-y haircut were sure to stand out to an American like Hooper. A dozen or so naked men and women were sprawled on the floor, each draped in red bedsheets covering their unmentionables like it was the aftermath of a giant orgy.

Hooper was going to shit himself. I wished we had the cameras on so I could see his reaction. When his message popped up, I barked out a laugh.

HOOPER: WHAT. THE FUCK. IS THIS?

ME: LOL. Günther, baby!

HOOPER: Is that Samantha Fox as in 80s singer Samantha Fox?

ME: It is! Good job, youngin'!

HOOPER: Dude. She aged well!

ME: Yes. She did.

I wasn't playing 'straight Jack.' It was the truth. Even gay men could appreciate a woman's beauty.

HOOPER: There is no way this guy gets laid by any of those chicks.

ME: Maybe it's the 'stache.

HOOPER: Are you saying if I grow a dick duster, I'll get laid more?

Picturing Hooper with a tiny, creepy mustache made my chest rumble. Knowing he was dumb enough to take a stupid dare made me chuckle harder. Shit. It felt good to laugh after the last two weeks.

ME: DO IT!

HOOPER: I would rock the shit out of that thing.

ME: Would be impossible not to.

HOOPER: You down for a dick duster challenge? It could be our catcher-pitcher signature.

ME: Pass. It would take me like six months to grow one.

HOOPER: You have the hair follicles of a twelve-year-old boy.

ME: No. Ed says I have smooth, highly marketable, underwear model skin.

HOOPER: Tomato. Potato.

HOOPER: Why the hell is everyone eating grapes?

ME: To keep up their strength to satisfy Günther's needs?

HOOPER: Man, you're banned from picking the next two songs.

ME: Don't hate on Günther. The beat is great for cardio.

HOOPER: That's the problem. This video is a straight up orgy that makes me want to beat it. How the F am I supposed to run if I trip over my hard-on?

ME: Didn't know you could run on your knees.

HOOPER: That was low.

HOOPER: Get it? Low?

I huffed out a laugh through my heavy breathing and rubbed at a tickle on the back of my neck. Hooper clearly was entertained, but an odd sensation of squirminess crawled up my spine like I was revealing too much...or being watched.

Glancing over my shoulder, I sucked in a sharp breath when my gaze locked with a pair of crystal blue eyes.

"Jesus H. Montero!" I yelped to the baseball gods.

My steps faltered. My arms flailed, and my elbow bashed into the treadmill console as I careened over the side of it, rolling my ankle in the process.

Max was gaping, his eyes darting from me to the TV screen with an expression that looked like I had dicks growing out of my ears. I tapped my finger on the mute button, holding a hand to my hip as my heart bucked like a bronco in my chest.

"Max," I panted, trying to sound all casual and not like his creepy murder-eyes had unsettled the shit out of me. "Hey! Didn't hear you come in."

"Is that...Samantha Fox?"

Who? What? I followed his gaze to the TV. Samantha was crawling on her knees in a bed shirt, looking all come hither. Oh, God. Kill me now.

"Uh. Yeah."

There was a new chat message from Hooper.

HOOPER: Spears? You still with me?

Just as I read it, a new one popped up.

HOOPER: Dude. Did you trip on your dick?

I stabbed the stop button on the treadmill and practically dove for my phone. Freaking Hooper.

ME: BRB.

"Sorry. *Heh. Heh.*" I turned to face Max again. "Uh. Me and Hooper were doing our cardio."

Max's entire face was a frown from the creases in his brow to the severe lines around his mouth. Shit. There went the tinglies in my belly. Why was he scowling?

"Is Hooper..."

"What?" I followed his gaze to the screen and squinted through my panting to read the newest message.

HOOPER: Not cool to leave a guy hanging!

Fuck my life. I pinched my eyes shut. Just what I needed, Max finding subtext that made him think Hooper and I were an item.

"Oh. No," I scoffed, but flashed his disbelieving expression a reassuring smile and added, "No. He's just…immature."

Max nodded once, still looking like a teenage boy who had just seen that video they used to show in health class about live childbirth, the one I blame for warning me off vaginas for life. Running my fingers through my hair, I tilted my chin and went for super nonchalant.

"So. What's up?"

"Uh. Dan keeps nagging me to go out for drinks tomorrow after work," he said, looking conflicted. "I was wondering if you'd mind watching Emma?"

I folded my arms and bit the inside of my lip to keep from growling. Another night with Emma was good. Max getting out of the house was good… to go to a bar with that dickhead? Not freaking good.

"Yeah. Sure." My sunny smile hurt my face.

"I…could ask my mom if you have plans." His gaze darted to the TV when he said it, like maybe he thought I had plans with Hooper or Günther or grapes.

"Uh. No. I was actually planning to make Christmas cookies with Emma this weekend, but we can do that tomorrow night now while you're out instead."

His mouth twitched at the corner. "Yeah. She'd love that."

The conversation felt over, but he stood there, eyeballing me. The little dent above his eyebrow reappeared, and even though he knew my biggest secret, his intense gaze made me feel like he could see more secrets. We'd smoothed things over. Why was this so awkward? Shifting my sore ankle, I fidgeted under his gaze, debating the probability of mugging or murdering.

His eyes scanned down my body as I moved, and he cleared his throat. "Okay. Well, thanks." He tilted his chin to the TV. "Um, have fun."

I nodded and my nervous laugh was the most terrifying sound I've ever heard. Lifting my palm, I waved, and he turned down the hallway to my patio door.

I snatched the hand towel off the treadmill and buried my face in it, along with a groan. Being weirded out by Max was even more uncomfortable than being turned on by Max. When I came up for air, movement on the TV screen caught my attention.

HOOPER: Seriously, if you're rubbing one out. I'm gonna go take care of some business myself.

Hooper apparently didn't know shit about horror movies. No way was I rubbing anything out. I didn't want to die.

Damn it, eyes! You had one job. Just watch freaking *90-day Fiancé*—stay open long enough for Max to come home.

It was eleven-thirty on a Friday night. How much longer could he possibly stay out? Dan wasn't *that* much fun.

Why Max ever became friends with the man was a mystery, but I was glad I met Max *after* he married Lainey. She said he was kind of a hard-ass when they started dating when he was rooming with Dan in college.

Can you say bad influence? Surprise, surprise.

The fact that he was currently out with a bigot and going to come home to a *fag* on his couch after giving me creepy murder-eyes all week was not comforting. I knew the name of this horror movie. It used to be a book called *Gay Man Dies Alone*.

I whimper-groaned into my hands. I'd been working my terrified, celibate ass off all week with Emma's room, Christmas prep, housework, and shenanigans to keep Snuggle Bug entertained. After the restless nights of wondering what was going on with Max, Uncle Jack was drained. The headlines tomorrow would read: *Another celebrity collapses from exhaustion.*

After I got Bug to bed, I texted Montez for a while, played my Scrabble app with Hooper—turns out there is someone whose vocabulary is more appalling than mine—and checked in with some of the other guys. This rerun of 90-Day Fiancé was making me want to eat broken glass. I thought mind-numbing television was supposed to be...mind-numbing.

I sunk deeper into the couch, also known as self-pity. Something sharp stabbed the side of my ass cheek. Wincing, I rolled to my side, because that's how little energy I had at the moment. Bravely and blindly, I reached in between the cushions and unearthed the perpetrator—one of Emma's *Barbie* dolls.

"Getting fresh there, Barbie," I snarled and tossed her onto the recliner.

Yeah. In my bitterness, I had stooped to bitching at a Barbie doll. The tiny plastic hand that just groped my ass was the closest to intimacy I'd be getting for a long time to come. The idea of being attracted to someone else a month or even a year from now seemed impossible. It was depressing how a freaking kid's toy had to remind me I still needed to figure out how to get over Max.

I didn't want to analyze anymore or worry. I'd been analyzing and worrying half my life. Every time I met someone I liked, it was the same thing—a world of secrets and holding my breath until the bottom dropped out. Gordie-knock-me-on-my-ass-Hill in high school. Chad, my tutor in college—unanimously broken off when I got called up to the minors and he wasn't out to his family. Jason from Manhattan—who got sick of me refusing to attend parties with him where there would be countless people with camera phones. And the last guy? Well, I didn't need to think about how that had played out.

Rinse and repeat.

There were queer people who lived openly in the world and didn't give a shit what anyone thought. I couldn't even imagine what that felt like. I wasn't afforded that luxury if I wanted to be seen as *a* ballplayer rather than *the gay ballplayer*. And it was starting to get a bit depressing that I was also not afforded to have a best friend if I kept longing for him.

Carrie said if the world knew what a pessimist I was about myself, it would destroy my image. I think it was her polite way of telling me I was insecure. The irony was that the older I got, the more I cared about my insecurity and the less about my image.

CHAPTER 21
Max

Well, that was a fucking mistake. Dan is the reason bars are so loud—everyone in them is trying to talk over people like him.

Not only did he lose his volume control, but as soon as we walked into the bar, he went all Italian on me, talking with his hands. He nearly poked me in the eye three times and knocked over one of my drinks.

I've never seen anyone flaunt their money clip so much either. Money clips. Who the fuck carries money clips? That tight ass carries a wallet Monday through Friday, just like me and Trevor. Safe to say the theme of the evening was big dick energy.

My *Uber* pulled away as I jabbed my house key into the doorknob. The white fog of my breath from the cold wafted up into my eyes with every curse I muttered as I relived my night from Hell on the town.

"Come out for a drink. We haven't been out in forever. I miss you. It'll be like old times!"

Missed me, my ass. The bastard used me as his wingman, talking me up to groups of women in the hopes one would take an interest in me so her friends would be left for his picking. I felt like an accessory to a predator. If thirty-four-year-old Max could go back in time and talk to twenty-something Max, I'd tell him to request a different college roommate stat.

After reeling in attention from the third gaggle of women he'd practically cat-called, the handsiest one in the group made me her target. The woman kept licking my earlobe—*licking* my earlobe. I don't know if she had a salivary gland problem or if she thought sloppy was sexy, but there was more drool than a Saint Bernard.

My arm was sore from Dan bro-punching it, declaring me a *lucky bastard* like he was actually jealous of my ear douching. All I wanted was to *not* smell beer or perfume, hear noise, have a woman I had no interest in fiddle with my shirt buttons, check out the men and women at the bar wondering if they did anything to my fucked-up dick, or have to pretend to smile.

And, God damn it...

I tried not thinking about the giant man currently sprawled out on my couch, but look at him! He was like a fucking Adonis that fell out of the sky and landed in my living room. And how after six years of catching him shaking his ass to classic rock, had I just recently discovered he listened to a pop god like Günther? My cock leapt to attention, begging me to transform into the masturbation monster I had become this week.

Down monster. Down!

Not one fucking man—not one—at the bar twisted me up the way Jack did. The bitch of it was that I tried. I actually freaking *tried* to think inappropriate things about men I didn't even know. I tried to imagine them kissing me, touching me, doing what Jack said he dreamt about, but it didn't feel like...like whatever I was feeling just looking at my freaking best friend right now.

There was no *want* on my part for any of the men or women I eyed at the bar. Not a single spark. Standing here in my living room, staring down at Jack's completely innocent pose, there weren't sparks—it was a full-on inferno. There was want, baby.

So. Much. Want.

The way he was sleeping shouldn't have been enticing, but with one arm draped above his head on the arm of my couch, he looked like a character in a Renaissance painting, waiting to be ravished. It resembled that pose he did for *The Circuit*—the one I *hadn't* talked dirty to every night this week.

Lainey jokingly asked me once if I only loved her because she was beautiful. I told her it was everything else and that her being beautiful was just the bonus. I still couldn't believe I was saying this about a man, but Jack was beyond beautiful—inside and out. God, he was so fucking beautiful, it hurt to take it all in.

I didn't know if it was the beer or my exhaustion after two weeks of sleepless nights, but I was sick of being terrified that my reaction to him had to do with more than just his beauty. I'd surrendered to the fact I was physically attracted to him—you can't jerk off to a guy's picture six nights in a row and deny you're attracted. I think maybe I always had been a little bit but didn't know it. It was the other part that scared me—the non-physical part.

Was I supposed to want someone again? This soon? Who made up those rules? I wished there were a guide to being a widower.

It was just that... he was so fucking good with my kid. His cooking made me make involuntary sex noises. Watching him on the mound was a thing of awe. And whenever he looked after Emma, my house was spotless. Only deprived housewives were supposed to get enamored over other people doing housework.

I liked shit clean, okay? And I especially liked it when *I* didn't have to do the cleaning.

Glancing through the living room doorway to the kitchen, I could see he had done the dishes. And I think...

Fuck. Yeah. He vacuumed in here.

Son of a bitch. He vacuumed!

That should *not* be a turn-on, but damn me, it was liquid erotica trickling through my veins. I swear to God. I wanted to drop to my knees and suck his dick for vacuuming my damn living room, and I didn't even know how to suck a dick, or if I'd like it, or if he'd like it, or if I could do it. It's just that... *I was home*.

I hadn't walked into a shell of a house that used to hold my life—four walls that represented responsibility I couldn't handle. I'd walked into a home. It was a home because *he* was here.

The man made me laugh even when I didn't want to. He gave good advice, even if I didn't always agree with or want to hear it. He was a good listener. He always knew how to keep me calm. And he was the most self-less person I'd ever met.

The guy sent flowers to Montez's girlfriend like they were from Montez before the couple was dating because Montez was convinced she wasn't in-terested. Look at the two of them now—headed to Hawaii for three months soon, likely working their way toward marriage. Jack always did little things like that in the background. He helped all the new teammates, making sure to invite them out with the guys, so they felt welcome. He visited sick kids at hospitals and donated money to anything to do with children and dogs without ever telling the press. He was just... good. He was all that was good.

Dropping my ass down onto the coffee table, I sat in the darkness and contemplated the handsome enigma on my couch. I had wondered if some-one else came into the picture and spent as much time at my house, if I'd feel the same attachment. I couldn't fathom that, and even if I could have, it didn't explain the times he was on the road.

When he called or I called him, our time on the phone had always made me feel like a missing piece of me had been returned. It was *him*. It wasn't because of a clean house or food I didn't have to cook. It was Jack.

I'd gotten that feeling when I walked in here and the place was a mess and I had more work to do than I knew how to handle. I got that feeling because Jack was here. He just… made it easy to breathe. He was so damn relaxed and positive all the time. So fucking mellow and silly. So kind. Everything was natural to him; nothing was gay or straight, a man's work or a woman's work, too emotional or too vulgar. He accepted everything without batting an eye.

I thought he broke me with that kiss, but I was starting to worry I broke him. He hadn't been the same since that night in the laundry room. His playfulness and quiet confidence had ebbed. I hadn't caught him dancing in the kitchen once since then. His easy joy was gone, extinguished by the irrational asshole that I was.

Fuck. Why had I asked him about his number of partners? Why had I interrogated him about private conversations he had with Lainey? How could I shove him and kick him out of my house and then ask him if he dreamt about sucking my cock? I was seriously a grade-A lunatic lately.

Ironically, as much as I regretted my choices these past two weeks, I still had no shame. In my dreams, that conversation in my bedroom hadn't ended. He crawled a foot closer to the bed and showed me what he dreamt. And just like he said, I liked it. I *more* than liked it.

All week, I told myself that it was *his* dream, but that was a lie. He wasn't in my head or my bed when I was playing it out, burning through my lube every night. The only one writing the storyboards had been me.

It was like I was going through a twelve-step program, and the next step was finding out if I'd like it in real life, but each time I'd gotten close to him this week like my body was a motivated apprentice asking him to show me what the next move was, he shifted away.

It made me want to find out that next step even more, to ask him if it was too late for me to find out. Did he not want that dream anymore? What was he dreaming right now?

Holy hell. He could be dreaming about me *right now*!

I was right here, and he was dreaming about me. I needed to know. I couldn't live like this anymore. I was sick of dreaming.

CHAPTER 22
Jack

"Jack, wake up."

"No, Barbie! No!" I flailed at the insistent voice and opened my eyes to a looming figure.

Huh. *Not* a looming figure of a giant Barbie doll. Oh. Thank Christ. Most terrifying dream ever.

A hand was shaking my leg—a real hand, Max's hand. I was on his couch with horrible reality TV playing in the background.

"Oh. Shit. What time is it?" I croaked.

"Almost midnight."

"Is something wrong with Emma?" I asked through my grogginess, my vigilant instincts kicking in.

"No. Still asleep, I'm guessing."

"Sorry. I nodded off." I sat up and rubbed the sleep from my eyes. Max moved a step back and sat on the coffee table a foot away. His hair was mussed, his eyes glassy. "You all right?" I asked.

"Yeah. How did it go?"

"Fine. I made tuna casserole. There's leftovers in the fridge. We watched *Elf* and *The Grinch* while we made cookies. The snickerdoodles you like are in a box on top of the fridge, so she doesn't eat them all on you. I kept her up till about ten, so hopefully she'll sleep in for you tomorrow."

He chuffed and clamped a hand on top of my knee. "Thanks."

It was a gesture I used to see fathers do to congratulate their sons after our Little League games—fathers that showed up and gave a shit, anyway. Except, skin was more responsive when you first woke up, Max wasn't my father, and it wasn't a simple good job pat on the knee. His hand lingered and gave a squeeze to the meat of my leg.

Ignoring the flutter in my stomach, I flashed him a small smile. "No problem."

As though he was reading my thoughts, he looked down at his hand. His thumb circled over my kneecap, causing the downy inside of my sweatpants to tickle my skin. A crease formed in his brow, like he was suddenly annoyed.

Was he mad he realized he was touching me? Had he told Dan about me? Was he going to say he couldn't handle being friends now?

"Everything okay, Max?"

He resumed drawing little circles over my knee. It was all I could do to not move.

"I keep having that dream."

My spine stiffened. Shit. Here it comes. "I'm sorry."

"Why do you keep apologizing?"

"I...because I shouldn't have told you about that."

"Does it bother you I have that dream?" His blue eyes looked into mine as though he was desperate to know, but there was anguish there, too.

"Max, are you drunk?"

"No."

He answered so fast and sure, I had to suppress a laugh. "That's what drunk people say."

His gaze dropped to my leg again. His calm, steady breathing made mine get more erratic. His hand inched higher up my thigh. I wanted to run away and melt at the same time.

"Four beers and a shot over six hours. I'm not drunk." He shook his head. "I just...need to know."

"Know what?"

"If you want me to have that dream." The look he gave me was as serious as the heart attack I was having.

My tongue was suddenly triple the size, and the muscles in my throat forgot how to work.

"You...can dream whatever you want."

"That's not what I asked you." He sounded a little growly, and fuck me—why was that so sexy?

"It doesn't matter what I want. You're straight."

"And if I wasn't? What would you do?"

My brain. Stopped. Working. I was trapped in a stare down, pinned by his determined gaze. Finally, my voice came out. "Why?"

"I feel like there's six years of a side of you I don't know, and I need to learn about it."

"And a hypothetical will bring you up to speed?"

He blinked like he was either considering my question or it was the dumbest thing he'd ever heard. A crease formed in his brow, and that unnerving stare, those probing eyes, questioned mine. It was a look that seemed to say, *why are you being so difficult?* He inhaled roughly, and his gaze shifted to the floor.

I let out the breath I was holding. His touch was searing me through the fabric of my pants. My leg felt like it was on fire. Did he freaking have *Icy Hot* on his hands?

"You vacuumed, didn't you?" he said as though it were an accusation.

My head reared back. How in the hell did we go from blow-jobs to vacuuming? I guess if you got technical, there was the whole sucking connotation.

Focus, Jack.

I surveyed the room, trying to recall what I did during the hours before this hand was on my leg.

"Uh. Yeah. It looked like it could use it."

The breath he let out sounded exasperated. He stood up so abruptly, I flinched.

"Come with me," he demanded, holding his hand out.

Did he want me to take it? I must have stared at it too long because he reached for my hand and tugged at it until I rose, but he didn't let go when I got to my feet. I had no choice but to follow when he started walking. He wasn't just holding my hand now. His fingers had interlaced with mine.

"Wh-where are we going?"

"Out of here."

I couldn't stop looking at our grasp through the shadows of the house. I'd never held Max's hand. It had been years since I'd held any man's hand. I've never wanted to let go and run away at the same time. His thumb rubbed across my knuckles, making my knees nearly buckle.

When I looked up, we were entering his bedroom. My heart leapt into my throat like a scared cat in a tree. My brain reconnected the signal to my legs, and I stopped just inside the room. Max released my hand and shut the door. The click shot a jolt of terror and arousal up my spine.

Who was this man, and what had he done to my best friend? And for the love of Mickey Mantle, why had he brought me to his bedroom? Was this where he was going to murder me?

"Max, what, uh...what's going on?"

He stalked to the end of his bed, turned around, and plopped down on the mattress. Lifting one foot to his knee, he pinned me with an intensity in his eyes so strong it made me shiver. Unlacing his shoe, he tossed it to the floor. I jumped as it landed with a soft thud on the carpeting. He lifted his other foot and repeated the action, all the while holding my gaze with an, 'I've-got-a-bone-to-pick-with-you' expression on his face.

"I need to know," he finally said, all low and gravelly.

"Need to know what?"

"What you'd do...if I wasn't straight." He said it so matter-of-factly that I had to blink several times as I watched him pull his sweater over his head.

My voice came out like a rusty hinge. "Why?"

"What would you do?" he repeated.

I imagined a fox cornering a rabbit, all too aware of the closed door behind me. Everything about this screamed *trap*.

If I lied, he'd know because I was shit at lying. If I ignored him, judging by the determined expression on his face, he wouldn't let up. If I told him the truth...

Mugged or murdered came to mind again. The stupid sappy voice in my head said, *but he just held your hand!* I scoffed at that voice. That voice wasn't reality. That voice got murdered in horror movies.

"Tell me," he prodded, dripping with sultry encouragement, his fingers locked together between his knees.

If there was one thing I knew about Max, it was when he couldn't let something go. He once argued with me every day for two weeks about whether global warming was real or not. Like him, I believe it is too, but denied it just to screw with him. He wasn't going to drop this.

I let out a shaky breath. I hated lying. Carrie was right. I had to be myself, at least to Max. I couldn't call him a true friend if I only gave him an altered version of who I was, no matter what it cost me.

"I guess I'd make a pass at you."

"How?"

Apparently, the reward for jumping one hurdle was to jump another. My tongue wet my dry lips in an effort to stall. As nervous as I was, though, his conviction was the sexiest thing I'd ever seen and made me reckless.

"I'd do what anyone would."

"And what's that?"

I shrugged like this was a perfectly mundane, in no way whatsoever epic conversation. "I'd say something sexy. Flirt."

His Adam's apple bobbed. The huskiness in his voice gave me gooseflesh. "Like what?"

Harry Caray. I didn't know whether to girl-scream like Hooper did when he saw a spider or come in my pants. Trembling was actually a thing. I folded my arms over my chest like they could protect me from his crazy inquisition.

"Max, I thought we were trying to be friends."

"*Tell me* what you'd say."

Girl scream. I definitely voted for Hooper's girl scream. I settled for stifling a pathetic whine.

"Max, you don't want to hear this."

"I do."

Shit. I just died. Roll the credits. Could he be more stubborn?

"Fine," I huffed and eyed him up and down like I was assessing his durability.

What could he handle? Better yet, I was finally getting my chance to hit on Max. What did I want to say? Biting my thumb, I took him in. I wanted it to be irresistible. I wanted it to knock him on his ass in case he decided to knock me on mine.

This felt like a new game, a scarier, more dangerous, more exhilarating game than the *fuck off* game. I let out *all* the air.

"You ready?" I asked with a nod, like I was daring him to back down even as my knees shook.

"Yeah."

"Is that cock you're hiding as sexy as the rest of your body?"

His eyes flared. His lips parted. Wildfire spread across my face.

Fuck. Fuckity. Fuck! What the hell was I thinking? *Fix this, Jack!*

"Max. I don't think this is a good way to salvage our friendship. I...I think I should go home." I spun around, mostly to tear my eyes away from the shock on his face, but also to flee like the coward that I was.

"I'm not uptight!"

His growly words were cold water on my back. Is that what this was about? My lungs deflated as I turned back around to do damage control for the crap I told him the last time I was in this bedroom.

I nearly tripped on my feet. He was standing now, bare-chested, whipping his T-shirt on the floor. My jaw came unhinged, watching him hastily work the button of his jeans.

"Wha-wha-what are you doing?"

"I don't want to jerk off tonight," he huffed.

The sound of his zipper made me shiver and my cock jump. He shoved his pants down his hips and kicked them off in an angry striptease.

I was now the number-one fan of angry stripteases, featuring Max. I wanted to be the president of that club, right after I survived this murder.

"Then...don't?" I suggested.

"I don't want to jerk off *thinking about you*," he clarified, planting his hands on his hips.

I swallowed, probably ingesting my tongue. Max was standing defiantly in nothing but a pair of *very* flattering black boxer briefs, leaving too much on display for my frazzled brain. His skin was a shade or two paler than mine, a thin smattering of dark hair across the definition of his chest with a tiny trail that disappeared into the waistband of his underwear. I suppressed a whimper at the bulge being restrained by the poor, innocent black fabric that I wanted to rescue like a knight in shining armor.

"I...I'm sorry?" I stammered, like I only knew how to speak in question marks.

"Would you quit fucking apologizing?"

I opened my mouth, but snapped it shut immediately when I realized I was about to... fucking apologize. Frustrated, I crossed my arms. "Max. What do you want?"

"I want *to know*," he said, sounding pained.

"Know what?"

I absolutely fucking knew what he was trying to say. My skin prickled as he eyed me up and down like he was starving, and I was a banquet. I must have done something awful in a past life to deserve this kind of torture.

"Max, if you can't talk about it, it means you don't really want to know," I conveyed sympathetically.

His chest heaved, never taking his eyes off me. "I want to know what your mouth really feels like."

Time stopped. My head actually reared back as his words hung between me and the panting man with the giant hard-on standing five feet away.

And then, as though he thought I needed clarification, he added, "—*on my dick*."

"It's...not all about sex, Max. That's not why I kissed you. There are lots of nice things besides...*that*."

He palmed his erection. His teeth sunk into his lower lip, still scanning me from head to toe like he was learning my body. I had to bite the inside of my cheek to keep from groaning. This was just a dream. A really fucked up, hot as fuck dream, where I hopefully didn't die.

"I know, but you were right," he said.

"About what?"

"That I need to get off. With another person."

Was this real? Real feelings or was he just horny and freaking out because I kissed him?

"Max—"

I didn't know what I was going to say, but I didn't get the chance. He made his super-sexy-scowly face, dipped his thumbs inside his waistband, and shoved his shorts down over his hips.

"That pass you made—does this answer your question?"

I didn't even try holding in my reaction. I'd held too much in already.

"*Fuuuck.*"

I smeared my palm hard down my jaw. Yeah. His cock *was* as sexy as the rest of his body.

When my bewildered eyes made it back up to his, we stared at each other. It was just us, the silence, his gorgeous cock, and a room full of heated tension. I knew whatever happened tonight, nothing would ever be the same between us. He shifted in place, dripping with insecurity that belied his confident posturing.

"Is *this*—" he gestured up and down at himself, "—sexy to you?"

The way he said it crippled my heart like he was expecting me to reject him. I didn't know why he was putting himself out there or if he even understood why, but all I wanted to do was reassure him. I nodded, speaking behind my hand. "Very."

His chest heaved. His whoosh of breath reached all the way to me.

"Don't hide your mouth." It was part heady request, part plea, and all sorts of make-my-dick-weep sexy.

I obeyed, helpless to his heady whisper. He gripped his shaft and slid up his length in a slow stroke as he sat on the bed. Running his eyes over me, his legs parted a fraction as he conducted another languid slide.

"Show me," he whispered, "what you dreamt about?"

The only thing I was certain of at the moment was there were no right answers or actions for his request. If he was struggling with his sexuality, I didn't want to hurt him. On shaky legs, I closed the distance and dropped to the floor at his side, trying to look anywhere but at his cock.

"Max, I know you're confused, but I don't think this is the way to go about figuring it out. Just give yourself time."

His hand grabbed mine and clamped it down over his knee. I looked up into a storm of desperation in his eyes.

"I don't need time. I can't fucking sleep. I can't concentrate. It's all I can think about. I need to know. I need...to know if I'll like what I've been thinking about." His tongue lapped across his lips. His gaze sent a tingle through my body as he eyed me up and down again. "You started this, Jack. I need you to finish it."

Finish it?

I didn't want anything with him to have a finish. And a start? Guilt squashed me like a bug. I *did* start this. This *was* my fault. Max hadn't kissed *me*. He probably would have gone the rest of his life never kissing a man if it hadn't been for me.

"Please," he added desperately.

His irises were burning holes into mine, imploring me. His grip tightened on my hand as though he was asking again. I closed my eyes, but it didn't block out a thing. Instead, it heightened the scent of him, the heat coming off his body.

"You're *sure* this is what you want?"

"That's what I need to find out."

I let my gaze fall to his engorged head, a drop of precum glistening there. It would have been easy for me to take it into my mouth and taste him. That wasn't why I hesitated.

If this wasn't well-received, it would probably be the last time I'd ever see or talk to Max and Emma. If he couldn't handle this, he wouldn't just kick me out for a week and act awkward; he'd reject me in every way—a complete shutout.

But what if his curiosity continued to grow? The thought of him seeking out another man to test the waters made me ill. If I rejected him now—because he *would* see it as a rejection with how fragile he seemed right now—he'd never look at me the same. Hell, I'd lost him already. I was damned if I did and damned if I didn't.

"Max?"

When he didn't answer, I looked up. His chest was rising and falling rapidly. Was it passion or nerves? A bit of both? I took a mental picture of his face—lust, wonder, determination, vulnerability. I wanted to remember that look forever in case it was the last one I got. I squeezed his knee.

"Max, you were the best friend I ever had. It meant more to me than you'll ever know. Thank you for that." My voice wavered, and I had to look away.

Tugging my sweaty hand from his, I shifted onto both knees and focused like I was hyping myself up before a game. A favor for a friend. That's all this was.

I hadn't imagined it being so unromantic and negotiated like a contract, but it was what Max needed right now. Maybe it was my pride or my possessiveness, but as I stared at his begging cock, I determined to make sure it would be the best pleasure he'd ever have in his life.

Gingerly, I eased my other hand onto his other leg, waiting for cues, any sign he'd changed his mind. The soft hair on his thighs brushed against my palms. His muscles relaxed under the slow, caressing circles of my palms.

I leaned in, deciding on the spot I wanted to kiss first, but stopped an inch away. I glanced up one last time to read him. He was trembling, watching me with bated breath. Once I started answering his demand, it would be difficult to stop. I had a demand of my own.

"Tell me if you don't like something. Tell me to stop whenever you want, and I will."

He set his jaw as though to say he had no intention of stopping anything, as though he could take whatever I gave him. It was so fucking sexy and stubborn, so Max.

I thought his request had bordered on an order, but realized in that moment he was putting me in charge. He was trusting me—me, out of all the men in the world. If I could only be his lover for one night, I was going to show him what kind of lover I could be.

Lowering my head, I drank in his scent and gently pressed my lips to the inside of his knee. He smelled like mountain air and his salty essence that I was dying to taste. His leg hair tickled my nose, and he shuddered when the tip of my tongue connected with his skin. I was trembling right along with him, diving into the most crucial performance of my life. I'd never been intimate with someone I loved, having never been in love.

Coaxing my hands over the muscles in his thighs, I alternated between sensual caresses and massage. My lips treated me to an inch-by-inch exploration of the silky flesh of his inner thigh. A brush of my chin here, my cheek, my nose, my neck—I touched him any way I could with what he'd allowed. This was just curiosity for him, I reminded myself, but I wanted to show him how intimate it could be.

Leaning further, my shirt brushed the front of his shins. The warmth of the silky skin at the juncture of his thigh greeted my lips. His shuddery breath ghosted down the back of my neck, peppering my skin with gooseflesh. My forehead brushed against the soft hair of his happy trail, the contact making me close my eyes. I wanted to let go, to lose myself in his heady scent. I wanted to devour his mouth with kisses and feel his hands on me, but I knew that might be too much for him. At least he was still here. He hadn't jumped up and run away.

Would we do this again? What would happen when we were done?

I couldn't ponder those questions. All there was right now was this moment for me to worship him the way I'd wanted, to show him how much I cared through the tenderness of the physical. Max Hartwell was my undoing, so I angled my mouth to the base of his bold, beautiful cock and let him undo me.

ing, so I angled my mouth to the base of his bold, beautiful cock and let him undo me.

CHAPTER 23
Max

My body was an electrical storm. The ghostly sensations of Jack's kisses and touches still brandished my legs, my belly, the V of my thigh—every place he touched me.

I couldn't believe I asked him. I couldn't believe he agreed. I was either an evil genius or just...well, evil and horny, I guess. I knew he said he dreamt of this, that he's gay, but I needed to see him do it, needed to feel him do it. I needed proof. And fuck. Message received.

Every kiss he pressed to my body was a seal of that proof, making my head lighter. Gazing down at him in awe, I knew it wasn't just *his* confirmation that I needed; it was my own. I needed to know if I only wanted to fantasize about this, or if the real thing was as maddening as my dreams.

As his palms slid over the curve of my ass and his warm breath tickled my skin, I knew without a doubt; the reality was better, so much better than any dream. I was afraid if I moved, he'd stop or my untamed thoughts would shift, and I'd stop this blissful torture.

His lips dusted against the base of my shaft, followed by a soft lap from the tip of his tongue. White-hot heat jolted through me. My cock twitched violently, grazing the curve of his ear, the smooth skin of his cheek. It was all I could do to fill my lungs with my next breath as my body quivered with unchecked arousal.

His hands stilled on my hips. He circled his thumbs over my pelvic bones, hesitating as though he was gauging my every response. And, oh, did that excite me even more that he was reading my signals like he did Hooper's when he was on the mound.

Don't stop, I wanted to scream, but I didn't dare speak. I didn't trust words not to shatter this moment that had just been born.

After what felt like an eternity, his lips grazed the veiny underside of my shaft. His fingertips trailed across my waistline and wrapped around my aching erection. I watched in a trance as he dragged his open lips up my length, artfully worshipping me in a slow, gentle tease. I suppressed a groan, watching another bead of precum leak from my tip.

Fuck. He was good at everything.

Was it a lifetime of thinking this was forbidden that was making me a witness to a plane of passion I didn't know existed, or was it us? Were Jack and I coming together the equivalent of a supernova?

His bottom lip brushed the underside of my head. He moved me in his hand and, oh my God, he basted his lips with my precum, making his mouth glisten with my arousal. A current rippled through me as his tongue darted out, tasting me on his lips. It was the most sensual thing I'd ever seen.

My cock disappeared into his mouth. His wet heat surrounded my sensitized flesh. I could feel his tongue swirl around me, sending erotic sparks to my balls. I felt like I was being peeled out of my body as he took me deep, the hold of his mouth tightening.

If I lived to be old and senile, drooling in my soup, having forgotten everything about my life, I would still remember this very moment. A moan ripped loose from my throat. I was floating or falling, desperate for something to hold on to. My fingers clutched his soft brown hair. It felt like more heaven, deepening our connection.

"Jesus," I gasped.

His mouth abandoned me, slamming me with loss. Those caramel eyes peered up at me.

"You okay?" he whispered.

Words. We couldn't have words. I just needed to understand the actions. The sight of his eyes looking at me and the sound of his voice terrified and consumed me all at once. His big hand circled over my ass as though he were comforting me. My heart tripped. Did I imagine he would be this tender?

"I...I don't want to talk," I rasped, when what I really meant was, *I don't know what to do.*

There was hurt and concern on his face, and maybe even understanding. I was glad he understood because I didn't understand anything right now other than I didn't want him to stop. He nodded and slowly lowered his head, taking me in faster this time, all the way to my base.

My eyes fell shut as his mouth tightened around me and moved up and down my length. There was lava in my veins and electricity spiraling around my spine. This wasn't oral sex, it was fucking delirium. I was letting Jack suck my cock, and it was a fucking out-of-body experience. Why was it so good? How could it feel like this if I'd never wanted a man?

I whispered in wonder, "I'm not gay."

Jack's mouth slid off me again, and he shifted on his knees. "I know," he whispered back and then dropped his head lower, away from where I needed it.

My mouth hung open, dumbstruck. His cheekbones pressed against the insides of my thighs. His tongue connected with my balls, and all the breath left in my lungs flooded out. He circled one delicately and then the other, exploding static electricity through my sack all the way to my toes. All my muscles turn to gel.

No one had ever done that to me. I felt cheated that it had never happened until now, and filled with something like gratitude that Jack was the one showing me the light of nirvana. I showed my appreciation with a hiss like a boiler letting off steam.

"*Fuuuck*. Holy shit."

The pad of his finger slipped between my cheeks and pressed to my taint. My entire body lit up. My hips arched, and I tightened my grip on his hair at yet another new sensation of ecstasy.

"Oh! My God!"

And then it was gone.

Everything was gone.

I lost every connection to his touch. My eyes fly open. Why had this heinous crime of stopping the world's best pleasure been committed? Jack was looking at me expectantly, sitting back on his haunches.

"What?" I panted frantically when what I really meant was, '*Why the fuck did you stop?*'

"Stand up."

"What?"

Dread that I had asked too much of him, that he hated this and wanted to stop poured over me. Why shouldn't he? What was he getting out of this? He glanced at my dick, licking his lips, and repeated, "Stand up."

A thought invaded my sex-hazed brain. He probably needed something, but I couldn't. I wasn't ready for that. I didn't even know what to do.

"You…you're not fucking me. And…and I'm not fucking you."

"I know, man. Just stand up." He grabbed my hand and tugged.

It was a miracle my legs still worked. I rose, unsteady as a newborn colt, following the orders I'd been given. Jack dropped onto his ass and turned so his back was against the end of my bed. Insecurity prickled my skin. I was fully naked, standing over him. He was fully clothed. My self-consciousness was a little late to the game.

This didn't seem to bother him. He looked focused, like a man with a plan. His hands wrapped around my thighs and pulled. I went with them as he turned me to face him. He slid one hand down the backside of my calf and tugged for me to straddle his outstretched legs. Legs apart, my hard-on pointing at his face, I had never been more exposed in my life.

"Come here," he whispered, reaching out and settling his hands around my hips.

His touch was as gentle as always. My toes curled into the carpet to find purchase. He wanted me to fuck his mouth, or he was telling me he'd let me fuck his mouth.

I watched, disconnected as my hips went toward him, back to the place I wanted to be—a place I knew I had no right to be, but he let me in again, anyway.

My knees wobbled. Jack's arms wrapped around my waist as I teetered forward. I braced a hand on the bed as he took me to the back of his throat, and I whimpered.

One of his big hands reached for mine and brought it to the back of his head. Did he want my touch? Did he want me to guide him? I suddenly regretted my request to not talk, but there was little he could say while he dragged my cock repeatedly to the back of his throat.

"Oh, God." Groans burst out of me, breaking my self-imposed rule of silence. It was a stupid fucking rule.

I followed the rhythm of his push and pull on my hips, grateful for the intoxicating connection of his hair between my fingers again. My balls tightened and tingled. His palm was grazing underneath them and…

"Fuuuck! Jack! Oh," I cried out, arching my ass toward the finger he'd slipped between my crease.

The tip of his finger circled my hole, eliciting a full body shudder. My hips took over, pistoning into the tight heat of his mouth and then chasing the delicious pressure that greeted me on the back end of my plunges.

"Oh, shit. That…that feels…" I didn't get to finish my sentence. He was reading me again, learning what I craved.

His mouth tightened. He pressed the tip of his finger inside me, adding the press of his thumb to…to my taint. I circled my hand over the back of his head, kneading his hair into a snarled mess, and moaned like I was slowly dying.

"Jack. Oh, God. It's...what the...that's... Fuck. So good!"

Movement caught my eye. I glanced at my mirrored closet doors and saw us. I saw me thrusting into Jack's mouth, him no longer pulling me. It was all me, wildly abandoned and seeking out the pleasure he could give. And, fuck, if it wasn't the hottest thing I'd ever seen—my gorgeous friend on my floor, draining my sanity, feeding my desire, sucking the tension from my cock, and kneading a handful of my ass like it belonged to him.

My voice leaked out high and needy. "Oh. Yeah. Yeah. Oh. Shit. I...I'm gonna come."

Jack's hand gripped harder on my ass as I tried to pull away, holding me in place. That magical finger pressed deeper into my entrance and crooked, while his thumb bore down on my taint, hitting a bundle of nerves deep inside. The coil inside me snapped. A wave of heated lightning coursed in my lower back, my belly, my balls. I was owned, totally given over, and that in itself was a sweet relief to not be in charge of anything for a few moments. It was like this was my job right now—just to feel lavished. The greatest relief of pressure burst out of me, and Jack took it, all of it.

I moaned, blinded by pleasure to the point my vision crackled. "Oh! Jack! *Jack*!"

My entire body tremored. Jack was swallowing, lapping, caressing—doing so much with only his mouth and hands. I'd done nothing, yet I was helpless, spent, so satiated all I could do was involuntarily pulse and twitch.

My knees wobbled, but I didn't fall. Hands cradled the backs of my thighs, holding me up. Jack was still sucking my spent dick in slow, lazy motions, like it fell off a bike and he was licking its wounds. The drawn-out arousal was so intense that I wanted to weep. Finally, he let me fall from his mouth. His ravished lips, swollen and wet, pressed a soft kiss to my stomach.

I did that to those lips. *Me*. In *my* bedroom.

Guilt, hard and heavy, T-boned me. I just made the fantasy real. I just turned dirty thoughts into flesh, moans, and hot breaths in my bedroom—in my and Lainey's bedroom. The bedroom I'd shared with my wife, only my wife, and no one since my wife.

I was a father. I was supposed to be responsible and miserable, not coming so hard it nearly blinded me, screaming a man's name, bare-ass naked, in the bedroom I'd shared with my wife. God, I just screamed a man's name, and I loved every second of it.

Lust nipped at me again. Jack was running his hands slowly up and down my thighs, staring up at me with questions in his eyes and more tenderness than I knew how to process. My fingers were still laced in his hair.

Fuck.

Staggering, my legs moved in protest over his. I collapsed to my knees on the floor, hanging onto my bed to keep myself from face-planting.

A warm touch rubbed my arm. Even that innocent gesture turned me on.

"Don't." A whisper was all I could manage. "Don't touch me."

His hand pulled away. I hated that I grieved for the loss of it, while hating that I couldn't let it come back.

"Max, it's okay."

My head rattled back and forth. "No. It's not."

"What...what can I do?"

Fix me, I wanted to say. *Make me not miserable without betraying the woman I loved and the man I'm supposed to be without her. And don't be so fucking irresistible and perfect.*

But that wasn't what I said to the man who'd held me together for three years, that I just asked to give me the wildest fantasy of my life.

"Just go."

"Max...I don't want to leave you like this."

"Just go. *Please.*"

It was quiet, only my raging breath and the heartbeat that wanted to jump out of my chest. I could feel his heat, his presence still behind me. I dared a glance from my pathetic fetal position.

His eyes, his beautiful Jack-eyes, were broken again. I watched the nano-second when the flicker went out of them as he looked at me. He turned away, aiming a thousand-yard stare at a spot on the floor. His big hand took a slow swipe over his swollen mouth and then he nodded.

I wanted to die because of that nod, but I didn't take back my request. He had to go away from the toxic, unstable thing I was.

Jack got to his feet. I stared at the indent of his back where the comfort-er hung over the bed and shivered at his broken voice.

"I...I'm here if you need anything."

I stayed slumped there for a while, long after the floor creaked behind me, long after I knew the second Jack had exited my house by the empty feeling that descended on me. The stab of the carpet fibers, indenting into my kneecaps, anchored me from going over to the land of insanity.

Crawling onto my bed like some creature from the bottom of the ocean, I found my pillow and burrowed under my blankets. I didn't even bother with clothes. I was too numb to feel naked. There was too much pleasant stinging in my ass to erase with clothing.

When I dared to look at Lainey's photo, I did feel something—guilt.

"I still love you. You know that, right?" I asked her, but it wasn't a question.

Hot tears spilled down my face, the kind that leaked out without sputtering. The kind when you're too defeated to sob. They were the kind from a guy who realized how incredibly stupid it is to talk to a photo for three years instead of facing things head-on like a normal human.

At least it was Jack. She wouldn't mind that I picked Jack. It hit me softly like a firefly, cutting through the darkness and growing brighter. I scoffed at my self-consolation, but I knew it was true. Someone had to be the first— the first after the one who was supposed to be my last.

If I had done what I just did with anyone else, man or woman, instead of Jack, it would have felt like I betrayed her tenfold. She approved of Jack.

I knew I didn't need my dead wife's approval, and that there was no way to get it. Knowing that, accepting that, was what hurt. I didn't lust after Jack because of some fantasy she had or he had. I didn't do it because I thought I had her permission. I did that on my own, all on my own.

Even though she was gone, I hadn't been deciding things without her until now. This was the first decision that had been all me.

I didn't know how long I'd let this happen—clinging to my grief like a thorny security blanket. Being miserable meant I was paying her sufficient tribute, that I was grieving enough, that I was loving her enough that she could feel it wherever she was. Feeling something else for someone else meant I'd let my grief slip through my hands. I'd dropped the torch I was supposed to carry and let burn me until the day I died. I think I thought if I was sad enough, it meant she wasn't completely gone. It meant I could hide from whatever I was supposed to be without her.

The picture frame was cold against my hot skin as I turned it face down on the nightstand. She'd been gone for a long time. I could admit that now. What I was without her though? I had no clue. I'd never thought about it without her shadow on my shoulder, but I knew it was time to start.

"I can't worry about what you'd think anymore, baby," I whispered. "I don't even know what *I* think."

CHAPTER 24
Jack

It was Sunday, also known as the day after the day I sucked Max's cock speechless, or rather sucked Max speechless, not his cock. Except, he wasn't speechless until it was over.

His throaty cries of pleasure, his moans, and his husky words were etched in my eardrums and maybe even my soul. I made him feel good, so good I wanted to tear my clothes off and crawl on the bed with him, skin to skin, and tell him we could be doing that every night. I made him feel good... until I made him feel like shit.

Now I was at the start of a dreaded rerun like the day after the kiss. The clock was ticking a countdown to my future, a future held entirely in someone else's hands. Sitting in front of my breakfast, all I could manage to swallow was my wild desperation.

The slam of car doors outside had me scrambling off my stool and running to the window. Max's car was backed out of the garage, sitting in his driveway. My future was dressed in their winter coats, loading Christmas presents and what looked like overnight bags into the back of his SUV. When I spotted Mr. Sparkles tucked in the crook of Emma's arm, my stomach dropped.

"No, Mr. Sparkles," I cried like the stuffed animal was betraying me.

Emma didn't take Mr. Sparkles on car rides. She only took him out of the house if she was spending the night somewhere. Where were they going? Why were they putting all the presents in the car?

It was Sunday. Christmas Eve was on Tuesday. Max always had his family over for Christmas Eve. He always had *me* over for Christmas Eve.

My brain whirled, even as I shoved on my shoes. It took effort to slow my movements as I stepped out my front door. I strolled over to their driveway, trying to act as casual as a person could after going down on their best friend and being asked to leave while he sat there looking traumatized.

"Hey." I nodded to Max.

"Hey," he called, giving me a ghost of a glance while he arranged gift boxes in the back of his car.

"You guys taking off for Christmas?"

"Uh, yeah. Going to stay with my mom for a few days and help her out at the shop."

"Oh."

I didn't miss the way his cheeks turned pink or the way he avoided looking at me. Christmas was a busy time for a florist shop, but Bev Hartwell had a full staff and always hired holiday help. Max loved his mother, but he'd never spent the night over there since I'd known him. Bev only lived twenty minutes away. This was an escape attempt if I'd ever seen one.

I was used to fans flocking to me. I was used to being ignored by my father. Watching one of the people I loved most in the world actually run away from me—well, that was a fatal blow.

Their front door opened. Emma started down the steps with a gift in her arms that I'd helped her wrap for Morgan. Her face lit up when she saw me as she sprinted over.

"Uncle Jack! You're here! Are you going to be here for Christmas?"

She sounded surprised. On instinct, I reassured her. "Yeah, Bug."

Her features crumpled, and she stopped in her tracks. "Dad said you were going out of town. If you don't have to go now, can we still have Christmas here?"

Max came around the back of his car and took the present from Emma. I could only imagine the look on my face.

I never said I was going anywhere. I knew it was a lie, an excuse to steal Emma away, so he could avoid me, but the set of his jaw and how he focused on Emma when I was only two feet away hammered it home.

"I already told you, Emma. We're having Christmas at Aunt Morgan's this year," he told her, sounding a little perturbed.

Emma's expression grew hopeful as she looked at me. "Are you coming to Aunt Morgan's?"

I looked to Max for direction, but he walked to the back of the car with the present. Suddenly, I was mad. He was going to make *me* be the one to break Emma's heart? If he didn't want me, fine. That I understood, but he didn't have to be a coward. Biting my tongue, I tried not to choke on my words.

"Um, I...I don't know if I can make it, Bug."

"Aw, but you always spend Christmas with us."

"Emma!" Max barked, making both of us flinch. "Leave Jack alone and get in the car. Grandma's waiting for us."

"But...I don't want to. We'll see her on Christmas Eve. Can't I stay with Uncle Jack until then? I promise I'll be good."

"No. We already talked about this. Grandma needs your help wrapping presents," he huffed, closing the trunk and walking to the driver's door.

"Grandma wraps all her presents the day after Thanksgiving," she argued.

Max ran a hand down his face, his shoulders sagging. "Just...get in the car. Please. I don't have time for this."

I blinked, my jaw unhinged in the breeze. Why was he doing this? It didn't have to be like this. In a way, I'd known it was coming. I just didn't expect it to be so harsh. It was over. I'd lost them, both of them. When I looked at Emma, her cheeks were pink, her bottom lip pressed firmly into her top one as she looked helplessly from Max to me.

Her nose twitched, and she sniffled as we stared into this cold reality manifesting before us. I had seconds, only seconds left. My heart cracked, and I dropped to a knee, holding out my arms. She ran into them, wrapping me in a hug. I squeezed her tighter than usual. Was this the last time I'd get to hug her?

"It's okay, little bug. I'll see you again. Be a good helper for your grandma, okay?"

Her head nodded against my shoulder. "I'm starving, and I miss you," her muffled voice pouted.

I sputtered a laugh through a sob at her dramatic dig at Max's cooking. "I miss you, too."

"Why is he so mad?" she asked quietly as she leaned back.

Great, I got to tell more lies for him.

"He...has a lot going on right now with work and worrying about you. It'll be fine."

"You don't get mad about work."

I forced a smile, dragging a strand of her unruly hair from her face. I could feel my eyes glistening. "Well, I get to play baseball. How could I be mad?"

"He needs a new job. He's always in a bad mood lately."

"It'll be okay," I reassured her, but my voice broke because I knew it wouldn't be okay, and it was my fault.

Her hand went to my cheek. Her eyes scanned my face. I wanted to break into a million pieces.

"Why do you look sad?"

I sucked in a breath and plastered another smile on my face. "Oh, because I'm going to miss you."

"Will we see you after Christmas when we get back?"

"I...I don't know. I think I should go see my family this year, but...I promise I'll drop your presents off sometime, okay?"

"Did you get me something good?" She grinned, relieving some of the pain in my chest.

"Don't I always?"

Max was sitting behind the steering wheel. His gaze darted down when our eyes met, as though something inside the car suddenly needed his concentration.

I gave Emma's arm a pat and stood up. "Alright, now. Be a good girl for your dad, okay? I love you."

"I love you, too." She threw her arms around my waist and murmured into my sweatshirt, "Merry Christmas."

"Merry Christmas."

As she walked away, I felt the pull of each bit of distance. My body trembled, but it wasn't from the cold. I ran hot, but the freezing temperature wouldn't have bothered me right now. My life was in that car—the life I wanted. The one I couldn't have.

I stepped to the edge of the driveway and stared, willing Max to look at me. I wanted him to see how sorry I was, how much I cared, how I'd never hurt him. If he'd just look, maybe he'd see that he didn't need to be embarrassed or scared. Maybe he'd see his friend, not a mistake.

As he backed out, his head tilted up and our gazes locked. His eyes were a mix of pain and vacancy. The message was clear—I was his shame.

My last shred of hope evaporated. Suddenly, I was aware of the chill. Love had left me, no longer protecting me from the frigid blast. My lungs burned, sucking in a sharp breath of the arctic air.

I couldn't look at them. I turned toward my house, foregoing a wave. My body rattled as I gasped for more air and pressed my palms to my cheekbones. All I had left now was baseball, and for the first time, I couldn't care less.

CHAPTER 25
Max

My five-year-old niece and four-year-old nephew zipped past me, shrieking at the top of their lungs. I squinted as the piercing sound stabbed my eardrums. They dashed under Morgan and Mike's dining table in a torrent of laughter and screams. Badger, my sister's cocker spaniel, darted out from under the table a second later, clearly being flushed out from his place of sanctuary.

I nearly tripped over him, a whir of brown fur skittering past my feet. My mother, my brother-in-law Mike, and his parents laughed from the living room at Randy Quaid's declaration of '*shitter's full*' as *National Lampoon's Christmas Vacation* played on the big screen TV

Mike's sister grabbed the last of the dirty plates off the table, giving me a polite smile, and carted them into the kitchen. I could hear Morgan chattering to her and the sound of Emma helping place dishes in the dishwasher.

I made my way through the glow of the Christmas tree lights to the enclosed front porch. The hardwood floor creaked beneath my feet, and I tensed at the noise that could give away my escape.

"Max?" my mother called from the armchair. "Are you going to come sit with us?"

"Yeah. Just have to make a phone call." I gestured with my beer to the porch.

"Alright. I'm serving the pies in about half an hour."

I nodded and did my best to return her warm smile. The cooler air of my sister's enclosed porch enveloped my skin, cleansing me from the suppressive heat of food smells, the happiness of my family, of Christmas.

I leaned against the wall and let out a breath I'd felt like I'd been holding since I left my house Sunday. Rubbing my neck, I burrowed my fingertips into the tight muscles, a gift from sleeping in my childhood bed at my mother's house the last two nights, or more accurately, a gift from my own stupidity.

All I could see was the devastation on Jack's face as I sat in my car, the way his shoulders sagged when he turned away. I realized at that moment that he was a happy crier. I don't know why I never acknowledged it before. His eyes used to glisten when Emma would do something endearing. He does this thing where he sniffs and brings the heel of his palm to his cheekbone like it helps hold the tears back. He did it when he walked back to his house like a wounded animal.

I made him cry. Merry fucking Christmas.

I knew now without a shadow of a doubt, and knew even at that moment, the only excuse for my behavior, for running away: I was a chickenshit.

I could have *not* called Morgan that morning and *not* asked her to have Christmas at her house instead of mine. I could have done anything other than avoid him again and drive away, but I didn't.

I wanted him.

I wanted him in a way I'd never wanted anything. I wanted to possess him and be possessed by him. I wanted to hold him, to feel his breath, smell his scent. I wanted to hear his stories, his secrets, his jokes, his joys, his sorrows, his laughter. I wanted to hold his hand, watch him cook, watch him sleep, watch him play ball, catch him dancing in my kitchen, take him to a spin class or the playhouse to see fucking *Mamma Mia!*

I wanted to know what he was doing and feeling every second he wasn't with us. I wanted to know what he had done and felt every second he hadn't been with us over the last six years. Every knot in the mystery I'd been trying to unravel was undone. I wanted Jack to be mine, and I wanted to be his.

How that happened, how or if it could ever be possible, I didn't know, but the giant kernel of truth brought me peace as I lay alone in a bed last night that was across town from this man, too far away from him to feel his presence through the walls. As much peace as it gave me to grasp that truth, to own it, it filled my bones with loss. How could we ever be?

I wasn't supposed to want him for so many reasons. He was my friend. He was my neighbor. He wasn't *out*, at least not publicly, anyway. I was a father. I was a widower. I had no idea how to be not straight even if I suddenly was. And recently, I was an asshole.

Jack deserved so much better than an asshole. There were so many labels wrapped around me, even considering breaking through them was daunting. How would it work?

When I shuffled Emma and all our gifts out of the house Sunday morning, I told myself distance would make everything better. I told myself distance would right this grievous error I had committed of falling hard for my best friend. The twenty-minute drive might as well be a continent away for how much I missed him. The more I thought about it, the more I realized if I called my feelings for him an error, I was calling Jack a mistake. Nothing about Jack was a mistake.

The door to the living room opened with a creak. A large round belly emerged, preceding my little sister. She waddled up to me, leaving the door ajar behind her.

"Happy birthday, sweet baby Jesus," she chirped, clinking her glass of sparkling cider against my beer.

I cracked a smile at her playful smirk. "Merry Christmas. Thanks for hosting this year."

Shrugging, she rubbed a circle over her baby boulder. "Fine by me. Then I don't have to waddle in and out of a car and can go pretend to pass out on my bed so everyone else can finish the clean-up."

"You are supremely evil," I deadpanned.

"Thank you."

We shared the silence for a moment, watching cars passing by the front windows, but then she tilted her chin to me. "What's with you?"

I bristled at her concern, but answered casually. "Nothing. Just getting a little warm in there. Thought I'd step out here for some cold air."

"No. I mean. Something seems...off. Emma said you've been moody lately." She lifted a shoulder and added, "Well, moodier than usual."

"Emma's nine. She thinks I'm moody when I tell her she can't have candy before bed."

"Oh. Shit. That's a rule?"

I cut her a dubious look, which earned me one of her devilish grins. She flipped her hair and sobered. "No. Seriously though. Emma said things between you and Jack have been tense, that you haven't been talking."

The reminder of my dickery made my skin crawl. I looked back out the window. "I'm busy. He's busy. It's Christmas."

"I thought you're off all this week?"

"Yeah, but I'm not his keeper. I don't keep track of his schedule."

Her dry laugh scraped my nerves. "Aren't you and Emma pretty much his schedule during offseason? I mean, he's spent like every Christmas with you guys since he moved in."

I shrugged, not trusting myself to keep the saltiness out of my tone. He *did* spend every Christmas with us, except this one… because of me.

"I invited him to come over here when you changed plans at the last minute," she added.

Her words both startled me and gave me hope. "You did? Is he coming?"

The space between her eyebrows wrinkled, and she took her time to answer. "He texted back that he'd *try* to and then wished me a Merry Christmas. In my experience, when people say they'll try, that's usually a polite way of declining."

"Oh."

"Yeah. I was disappointed, too," she volunteered.

I forced myself to take a swig of my now warm beer to avoid her inquiring gaze. Her response struck me as odd. I never told her I was disappointed. I was, but I had no right to be. It wasn't fair for me to avoid him and get pissy when he avoided me back. I knew why he declined—because I was a jerk.

Shrugging, I suggested, "Maybe he drove to Indiana to see his family."

It was a possibility, albeit a tiny one. Jack and his father didn't get along, which I now regretted not ever asking him more about. He talked more about his alcoholic, classic rock loving high school baseball coach that had eventually died of cirrhosis than he ever had about his father. Why hadn't I picked up on that red flag?

It was difficult to imagine the man who made Jack could be anything other than as compassionate as him, but what father went six years without seeing his son for Christmas? Who could throw a man like him away? I could, apparently.

A sharp pain stung the left side of my chest. I yelped, glancing down just in time to catch Morgan pinching my nipple through my sweater.

"Ouch! What the fuck was that for?"

"You're lying," she seethed, narrowing her eyes at me.

"What? I don't fucking know where he went. Maybe he flew to a beach with his teammates or had some celebrity event to attend. How the fuck am I supposed to know?"

"He's at your house *every* day. You know everything about him. What's up with you guys?"

I grit my teeth against the urge to say, *not everything*. "We had a disagreement. That's all. It's nothing."

Her fingers were quick, clamping down on my offended nipple again, but harder this time. I smacked her hand and reared back.

"Ouch! God damn it. What was that for now?"

Her eyes squinted as one hand went to her hip. "Did you hurt my Jack?"

"*Your* Jack?" I scoffed. "What the fuck?"

"Emma said you sat in the car and didn't even acknowledge him before you left the other day. And since when the hell do you have sleepovers at Mom's?"

"I thought she could use some help at the shop. Can't a guy be a good son and want to spend time with his mother?"

Her shoulders squared off. I took a step back to avoid being rammed by her giant belly.

"Oh, cut the crap. What's going on?"

"Nothing."

She leveled her index finger at me. "Bullshit. What did you do?"

"*Do*? Why do you assume *I* did something?"

I *so* did something, but what the fuck? Where was the loyalty? The faith?

Tossing her hand up, she gestured to me dismissively. "Because Jack is perfect and you...well, you're *you*. Whatever the disagreement was, it *had* to be your fault."

"Thanks a lot."

"What did you do, Max?"

My sister had always been a relentless pain in the ass, but this was crazy, even for Morgan. "Believe it or not, I didn't do anything."

Lies. All lies.

The back of her hand flew through the air and smacked me in the chest. What the actual fuck?

"Knock it off!"

My pleas went unanswered. She responded with another smack. "Tell me!"

"Fuck! Stop it. Just because you're pregnant doesn't mean you can get away with that bullshit."

I was holding my hands to my chest like a fucking squirrel or a woman who just dropped her bra, which left my shoulder exposed to her next backhand, this one wielding more force than the last.

"Yes. It does! Now tell me what you did to my future husband!"

"Fuck, Morgan!" I stepped away, rubbing my arm. "You're so fucking whack. You know that?"

"*Whack*?" Her eyes bugged out, and she snorted. "What are you, a nineties skateboarder? Tell me what you did?"

Sweet baby Jesus indeed. Why couldn't I have been an only child? Heaving a breath, I glanced through the doorway for eavesdroppers, but from the sound of it everyone was still balls deep in Christmas movies.

"Fine. I'll tell you, but you have to *swear to God* you won't say anything... to *anyone*, not even Mike."

"That bad, huh? Boy, when you fuck up, you fuck up good."

"I'm fucking serious, Morgan," I snarled, already wondering why I was even considering telling her other than wanting to stop her abuse.

"Fine. I swear. Do I have to pinky promise, too?"

I flipped her off and glared.

Her crazy ass smiled and returned the gesture. "Ooh. Okay, middle finger promise it is."

Talking to her could suck all the life out of a person. I swear. When I was done draining all the breath from my lungs to let her know my level of exasperation, I worked my jaw, trying to make the words come out. Maybe talking to someone might actually help at this point.

"He...he kissed me," I muttered.

She leaned forward like she didn't hear. "What?"

Fuck. Nothing like repeating something you didn't want to say the first time.

"He kissed me," I said out of only half my mouth like a fucking Smurf.

My ever-chatty sister just stared at me. My gut tightened, but not at her stupefied expression. Admitting the kiss to someone felt like a betrayal to Jack, like I'd taken something sacred and made it gaudy just by revealing it.

Either Morgan was having a stroke, or I'd finally discovered the thing I prayed for my entire life—how to render her speechless. I spread my hands expectantly.

"And?" she prompted.

"*And*? What do you mean, *and*?"

"And then what happened?"

Running a hand through my hair, I sputtered. "And then...I pushed him away and asked him what the fuck he was doing."

Her eyes rounded. "You *pushed* Jack?"

"Not hard or anything. Just enough to get him away. I was up against the fucking dryer in my damn underwear," I whispered sharply. I didn't need to make this the highlight of Christmas dinner. "Did you hear the part where I said he kissed me?"

"*Jack Spears kissed you* and you *shoved* him?" She said in full volume, her head bobbing with each word.

"Would you lower your voice? And yes. Apparently, *he's gay*, but keeps it a secret."

Her nostrils flared. I held my breath, watching as she set her glass down on an end table, waiting for her reaction to my big news. As soon as the glass rested on the table, her hands become a blur.

She pelted me with hissy fit slaps in rapid succession—on my chest, my ear, my arms, my lower jaw, my back. No matter which way I turned, she found somewhere else to connect.

"What the fuck, Morgan? What the hell is wrong with you?" I was sure I'd lost my mind. The one person I decided to tell, and I fucking picked my psychotic sister. She stopped slapping me and shoved me in the center of the chest with both her hands so hard I stumbled back a step, tripping on a snow shovel propped against the wall.

"That's for Jack. Asshole!"

Rubbing my calf where the shovel blade scraped me through my jeans, I snapped. "God damn it! What was I supposed to do? It shocked the hell out of me."

"Are you kids fighting out there?" my mother called.

"No!" we lied in unison.

Morgan's shoulders rose and fell on a huff. She folded her arms over her belly. "And then what?"

"And then what, *what*?"

"What happened next?" she asked with less heat.

And then a lot of things, but no way was I telling her that after her outburst. I always knew she adored Jack like a big brother—one she flirted with to annoy the fuck out of me. I wasn't even mad about it anymore, but I wasn't admitting to her I was grateful she adopted him. Her gaze was un-nerving, like if I looked at her too long, she'd discover all my sins. I shrugged and pretended to watch the traffic again.

"And then...nothing. It's just been weird."

I'd been weird.

"So...he's gay and...he likes you?"

Me. *Only me*. Was that even still true after how I'd handled everything?

"Did he tell you he liked you?" she asked.

Gripping my hair, I pinched my eyes closed. I couldn't believe I was doing this. "More or less."

"Really? What did he say?"

"What do you mean, '*what did he say*?'"

She arched one of her evil, tweezed eyebrows at me. "Are you just going to fucking repeat everything I ask you?"

"It's private," I gritted.

"Oh," she cooed on a gasp and covered her mouth like she thought it was adorable. "Just…give me an idea. I'm trying to help. I swear, but I can't do that unless I know what he said."

Her compassion was more unsettling than her hostility. I pursed my lips, still baffled that I was talking to her about any of this, but I wanted to set it free. I wanted a fucking lifeline to point me in any direction other than the one I'd been stumbling in.

"He said…he said he wants me—*only me.*" The bubble rising in my throat made it difficult to voice the sentiments. "And…he gave a list of all the things he likes about me."

Morgan made a weird whimper sound and cupped her mouth. "Oh, my God. That's so sweet."

"*Sweet*? He said I'm temperamental."

"You are." She laughed.

Like the mature man I am, I rolled my eyes.

"How was it?"

"How was what?"

"The kiss, dipshit." She beamed.

My face burned, knowing she now knew a man's lips had been on mine. I ran a hand over my mouth, remembering the breathtaking feel of it.

"I just told you."

"No, you didn't," she whined.

"It was…unexpected. What do you think?"

"And so…is that why you haven't been talking? Because he kissed you and you shoved him away?"

Because I asked him to suck my cock and came my brains out, and it would be nice if we could do that again. Nope. Not going there. I cleared my throat.

"We've talked. We're just…things are different, obviously."

"Oh. Poor Jack," she groaned and placed her hand over her heart.

At last, there was sympathy in her voice. She had sad puppy dog eyes, but they weren't for my struggles. I'd also thought '*Poor Jack,*' but I needed to hear what someone else who cared about him thought his perspective might be. Maybe that was why I told her.

"Why *poor Jack?*"

"You've been friends for how long and then just out of the blue one day he tells you all of this and kisses you? I mean…that's huge. Don't you see? He put himself out there for you, Max." Her eyes glistened, and she fanned a hand in front of her face. Her voice went all warbled. "Out of all the people in the world, he put himself out there for *my* big brother."

"Are you freaking crying?"

She shoved me again. "I can't believe you shoved him. How could you do that?"

Fuck. This again?

"I've never kissed a man. I was in shock. Okay? I fucking told you that. And I haven't kissed anyone since Lainey, Morgan. Did you ever think about that?"

She gasped and cupped her hands over her mouth. "Oh, shit. Oh, Max. I'm sorry. I didn't even think about that." Her touch was gentle as she laid a hand on my arm. I flinched, unsure whether to trust the comfort. "Were you worried she'd feel like you cheated on her?"

"No." The fact that I scoffed surprised me. My answer came so quickly, so sure. "Maybe. Not really. I mean, I knew I might move on someday. I just... didn't expect it to be...with a guy."

It was quiet, and I was grateful for the respite from the discussion, until I looked over to find her gaping at me. Her fingertips came slowly to her mouth as though I'd just shocked her.

"What?"

I swear her eyes watered some more. She gave me a serene smile and gently rubbed my arm. What the fuck now? Was she more hormonal than I thought?

I looked at her hand, petting me like I was a kitten, and stepped away. "Would you quit doing that? You're creeping me out. What's wrong with you?"

"You like him," she whispered.

Why the fuck would she think—and then it hit me, the way my response came out. I gaped at her for a second too long before answering with a snort.

"Oh, Max." She smiled, pressing her fist to her mouth to hide her sappy, creepy smile as my face flamed.

"What? We've been friends for years, of course I...I care about the guy's feelings."

"What are you going to do?"

"About what?"

She heaved a sigh. "About your man-feelings, moron."

"*Man-feelings,*" I grumbled. "I don't have *man-feelings.*" I *so* had man-feelings; giant baseball player-sized man-feelings. "I never should have fucking told you. And if you ever see him again, don't be fucking weird around him, okay? I don't want to embarrass him or have him know I told anyone his secret."

How did she react to my stern warning? She fucking grinned again, pressing her fingers to her *Cheshire Cat* smile.

"Would you quit doing that?" I snapped.

"What?"

"That serial killer smile you're covering up."

"I can't help it. You're being all protective of him. It's adorable. I'm so happy for you."

Oh. For the love of God.

"*Happy* for me? For what? That I don't know if I'm coming or going or how to talk to my best friend now?"

"Max." She shook her head. "Some people never find love. Some people go their whole life without ever getting even the chance to be in love."

"Who in the hell said anything about being in love?"

She chuckled and rubbed my fucking arm again. "You just a got a second chance if you want it. Don't you see that?"

"With…*a man*?" As I said it, I knew I didn't give a damn if he was a purple Boston Terrier. My heart fluttered with something resembling hope at her acceptance. I didn't need Morgan to tell me if I could do anything, but the way she made it sound so easy, set something free inside me.

"No," she scolded. "With the *best* man in the world."

Jack *was* the best man in the world. I didn't even know why I was arguing with my sister or why I snapped at her, but it might have had something to do with me wanting to cry about hurting the best man in the world. He'd shown me a possibility I didn't even know existed, and I'd destroyed it.

"Oh, I get it. You want me to say I'm attracted to a man so you can make shit out of me for the rest of our lives, is that it?"

"Look. I get that this was a surprise and out of your comfort zone. I get that it's probably really shocking and new, and confusing, but *look* at you. You're *different*. Something happened. I can tell. It's like…it's so obvious it left an impact on you. I mean, isn't that worth considering? Isn't that worth exploring what you and Jack think about it?"

Her words pulled the plug from a drain in my body. I was suddenly more exhausted than I'd been in years. I didn't want to fight anymore—with her or myself. I didn't want to lie. I rubbed my forehead, searching for a response. All I managed was nonsense laced with factoids.

"Morgan, I…I don't know what I'm doing. I don't…know how to do this, if I *should*, if I *could*…do *this*, if…I just… I was married to a *woman*. I have *a daughter*."

"You were married to a woman he loved and who loved him. And your daughter adores him as much as he adores her."

I folded my arms against the nakedness of my emotions. "Yeah, but how...how do you go from that to...to..."

She did the last thing I expected, pulling me into a hug. "Max, why are you so afraid to be happy again?"

I reciprocated with a lazy arm around her because we just didn't hug. My breath fanned her hair. I didn't think she required a response, but I knew what it would be. I *was* afraid to be happy, fucking terrified.

"I have a date Saturday," I blurted out because, apparently, now Morgan was my confessional booth for all the goofy shit in my life.

"With Jack?" she asked, sounding so damn hopeful I almost chuckled, while the word *date* in the same sentence as Jack did warm things to my insides.

"No. With some woman in Ellen's rotary club."

Her look of disappointment pleased me more than it probably should have. "Is it serious?"

"I've never even met her. Ellen set it up. It's a fucking blind date."

"*Ellen* is trying to set you up with someone?"

I nodded, trying not to appear grim. I'd already unloaded enough on her for a decade.

Her hands went to her hips. "Well, that's fucking awkward."

I snorted. "That's the consensus. I guess."

"Are you going to go?"

"I mean, I kind of have to. It's all Ellen could talk about the last few weeks. I brushed it off as long as I could, but now the plans are already made."

"*Have to*? Wow. Sounds like you can't contain yourself already."

I chuckled, shaking my head. For once, I actually appreciated my sister's lack of filter. Maybe that was why she was so happy. She always said what she meant.

"I better get back in there and check on Emma. Look. Please don't say anything about any of this."

"I won't. Just...promise me something."

"What?"

"Don't hurt him."

The warning cut me. Tugging at the cuff of my sweater grounded me under her stare. I wish I knew how much I had hurt him already.

She must have taken my silence as confusion because she added, "You guys had something special before. If you don't want to—" she trailed off, but the implication was big and tangible. "Just don't throw away what you had and don't lead him on. He's one of the good ones, Max."

That, without a doubt, was something I could agree with her on. I gave her shoulder a squeeze on my way through the door. "I'll, uh, tell him your security guard services are up for hire."

"I'm serious."

"Noted."

CHAPTER 26
Jack

As I prepped food with lackluster enthusiasm for my cookout tomorrow, my thoughts revisited the last few days to keep myself from glancing out the window at the house next door.

On Christmas Eve, I made the five-hour drive to my parents' house with the picture of the tears in Emma's eyes, blurred by my own, and the blatant avoidance on Max's face. Funny how being ignored could hurt more than disdain. I left one man who pretended I was invisible to drive across state lines to see another man who truly thought I was invisible. One I was just accepting, one I should have been used to by now.

The thing about being treated like you don't exist was that you started to believe it. I told myself to get in the car after Max made it clear he was cutting ties. I told myself it was time to go back to the old days of absorbing myself in any activity I could, to feed my restless energy—even if that meant driving to my childhood home I hadn't been to in eight years to see the man that made no pretense of his disappointment in not just my sexual orientation, but my existence. I told myself it was good for me to see him, like not hiding from him would somehow make up for keeping my secret from Max.

I told myself it was good for me to come to Mom and Carrie, so Mom didn't have to sneak phone calls and Carrie didn't have to put aside an entire day at Christmas just to visit me.

So, I willingly walked into my parents' house to stomach the man who couldn't stomach me. I thought I stopped letting his rejection bother me over the years. Little by little, it stung less. But after leaving Max and Emma, I guess I was too raw.

Sitting at the dinner table, with his silent, annoyed presence, was a stark reminder that I was not normal, that I was unwanted no matter what I did. He talked, but neither a word nor a glance was spared for me. Turns out, being invisible is easier from a distance.

Dinner lasted an hour. Unwrapping presents another. Dessert and coffee—a half an hour. The whispered pleas from my mother and Carrie in the foyer for me to stay as I said goodbye to them—fifteen minutes. Then, five more hours driving back to Springfield, feeling like a piece of chewed gum stuck to the driver's seat of my truck.

I met Montez, Hooper, and some of the guys for drinks and pool when I rolled back into town. I used to enjoy going out with the team, but I was starting to become the old guy. I don't care who you are—on a holiday, when you're alone and single, you never fit anywhere.

Holidays have a stigma that demands togetherness, couples, families. I smiled through the stories and rousing from the guys and played a few rounds of pool, even though everything inside me was more than dead. It was trampled, pummeled, incinerated, shredded. There were so many pieces they would never be able to be put back together. I'd officially lost the threading of my soul.

I host a cookout the day after Christmas every year for all the guys on the team that might not have anything planned or just want to get together as a team for the holidays. I had my thumb on the send button to cancel after Max and Emma left. It wasn't strength that stopped me. God knew there wasn't an ounce of fortitude left inside me. Long forgotten instinct kicked in and prevented me from hitting the button.

That instinct said, *this is the path*—the one I took when I first got drafted. The one when my first and last serious relationship ended because neither of us were ready for the spotlight or secrecy that would inevitably come. It is a path where I am alone and cannot love or allow myself to be loved, a path where the very thing my being craves is forbidden.

The path consists of answering the phone when a teammate calls, even if I don't want to talk. It's going out to eat, for drinks, to events, keeping up on social media, smiling, laughing—all while acting straight. It's being a man I am so good at pretending to be, I know him better than I know myself.

Maybe that was the problem. Max liked that version of me, not the real me. Maybe that was why it hurt so much. The number of people I'd shown the real me, I could count on both hands with fingers to spare. I wanted him to *like* the real me, even if he didn't *want* the real me.

And Emma—I couldn't even think about Emma right now. She was never mine, never belonged in my life. I was fucking kidding myself. I was never her uncle. I did this to myself. I opened myself up to get hurt like this. I forgot an important credo—don't get attached.

That was what I told myself after the first time I got my heart broken. That heartbreak was like a firecracker compared to the atomic bomb wasteland inside my chest. I didn't know how to get back on that path of smiling and pretending to be America's favorite pitcher, but I had to try.

I was afraid that this time the pretending would kill me inside, knowing it was another layer of bandages for what I just lost. I got too greedy, wanting something I was never meant to have. Not Max, not Emma, not even Lainey. I wasn't suburbia. I wasn't the friendly next-door neighbor. I wished I'd reminded myself of that six years ago.

CHAPTER 27
Max

Was it against the man's religion to wear a damn coat? From the view of my kitchen window, I watched as a gust of wind wafted a strand of Jack's hair while he stood on his deck, manning his grill.

"Too freaking cold to be grilling," I muttered into my coffee mug.

It was Friday, two days after Christmas. At least he was home. He was having his annual after-Christmas cookout and *yours truly* wasn't invited. Granted, I hadn't spoken to him since Sunday because I still had no clue what to say to him, but it didn't take away the sting of rejection.

"Dad? Can I take my new movies to Grandma and Grandpa's house with me?"

"Yeah, but you need to visit when you're there too, not just veg out on movies. Okay?"

"I know. Are we having lunch before we go?"

"Yeah. There's still some leftovers from Aunt Morgan's in the fridge." The relief on her face was evident. "Okay."

"Or I could cook you something," I teased.

She rolled her eyes. "No. Leftovers are fine."

At least I seemed to be back in her good graces. We had a nice chat about school, her friends, and her Christmas presents yesterday when we drove around to see the Christmas lights. She asked again why Jack hadn't been around, and I couldn't bear lying anymore. I told her I said something that hurt his feelings, which was an accurate enough description of recent events for a nine-year-old.

I meant for it to be a teaching moment for her, but I was the one who got schooled when, without hesitation, she informed me, "Then you should say you're sorry."

The kid's going places.

A few more guys spilled out of the back of Jack's house—third baseman, Ely McQuiston, shortstop, Martin Leland, and Hooper.

Ely dashed out into the yard, scooped up a handful of snow, and whipped it at Hooper. It pelted Hooper in the hand that was holding his beer. Hooper let out a hoot and barreled into the yard after him. Leland followed them, a snowball fight ensuing as Montez and Jack laughed from their place on the deck.

There was a squelch noise down the hallway. When I realize it was the patio door, my heart jumped into my throat, even though I could see Jack from where I was shamelessly spying on him.

Did he send someone over to invite me? Should I go?

A blonde head bounded across my snow-covered yard toward the fence. It was Emma in her boots, but no coat.

Shit. The sneaky kid really was going places. I swear her nose could probably smell Jack's cooking from a hundred miles away.

I shoved on my shoes and coat and headed out the patio door. Emma was leaning on one side of the gate that separated my yard from Jack's, telling him about Christmas at Morgan's—the one he didn't attend.
Just wonderful.

Standing next to the grill with an enraptured smile on his face as he soaked in Emma's story, Jack looked as good as ever. The sunlight in his hair gave it an almost auburn tint. Even as the view warmed my blood, I ached with wistfulness.

Hooper bounded up the steps to the deck and gave Jack's shoulder a squeeze, saying something that made Jack chuckle. A jealous grunt rumbled in my throat. I'd always liked Hooper, but every second his hand remained on Jack's shoulder made me want to punch him.

It was stupid. I know. I basically told Morgan we couldn't... *be*. Except something about her positivity during the conversation slowed my steps. She seemed so certain that Jack meant happiness for me. I wanted to believe that. I wanted to be happy, to have what I thought would make me happy. Could I picture myself over there with my arm around him instead of

Hooper's? A better question—if I thought he'd have me, would I walk over there and put my arm around him?

Yes. Absolutely yes.

These past few weeks, I had thought maybe that was my hang-up—how people would react to me being with a man—but if I was with Jack and someone didn't like it, I'm pretty sure I'd tell them to go fuck themselves.

I hated that he had to worry about what people thought, that we lived in a prejudiced world, but a part of me was grateful for it. If he didn't have to worry, if the world were a better place, he might be with someone. That was the most sickening thought I could imagine—him being someone else's. But what was the alternative?

Could I make him happy? If, by some miracle, he forgave all my childish bullshit from the last couple of weeks, I still didn't know the first thing about pleasing a man. I could dream about it all I wanted, but Jack had already proven to me dreams had nothing on reality. And why the hell would he want me, especially now? I'd kicked him out of my house twice.

Jack met my gaze. The smile on his face faded. He nodded. I threw him an awkward wave.

"Merry Christmas," I called, sidling up to Emma.

"Merry Christmas." He shoved his hands in his jeans, ambling over to the fence.

Emma called out to him. "Can I come over for a little bit and visit?"

"That's...up to your dad," he said, flashing me a wary glance.

"I've never had to ask before." She looked between us suspiciously. "Are you guys still fighting?"

From the mouths of babes. I rubbed a nervous hand over her hair to reassure her and maybe even myself. "No. Everything's fine. You just can't invite yourself to people's houses."

Her disappointment and Jack's avoidance were seventh-level-of-hell brutal. Instinct told me not to burden someone with my kid, but this was Jack. He loved her, and she loved him. Keeping them apart would deprive them both, so I made a show of checking my watch.

"Well, we've got about an hour and a half before we have to leave. How about you hang out until then?"

My heart flipped, watching Jack's face light up. Emma squealed. He opened the gate, and she burst through.

"Can't we wait to leave a little longer?" She asked once she was on the other side, pushing her luck. "I've barely seen Uncle Jack since the season ended."

"Emma, your grandparents are expecting us for dinner and it's a three-hour drive."

Jack looked like he'd been put on the spot. I had to give him credit—he had always had my back when I had to lay down the law with her. It was just one more thing that made me regret my idiocy these past few weeks.

"I bet they really miss you, Bug," he said. "You can see me when you get back. I was going to practice pitching tomorrow. If it's all right with your dad, maybe you can come over then."

She huffed. "I can't. I have to spend the whole weekend at Grandma and Grandpa's. Dad's going on a date."

Jack's head snapped to mine. I fucking flinched like I just saw a killer spider. Fuck. That was it. I was selling my child to gypsies on the drive to my in-laws.

It was bad enough she spilled the beans about my blind-*holidate*. She made it sound like I was shipping her off so I could get laid all weekend in my child-free house.

"It's not a date," I clarified quickly.

Emma tilted her head. "You're taking a woman out to dinner, aren't you?"

Of course, I looked at Jack first, and of course he was looking at me...with his soul-crushing sad puppy dog eyes.

"Uh. Yeah."

"Then it's a date," Emma confirmed, pleased she solved a riddle.

Fuck. Gypsies, gypsies, gypsies.

Jack rubbed the back of his neck, looking as uncomfortable as I felt. Didn't he know I didn't want to go? We'd talked about this.

"Uh, well, maybe some other time," he told Emma. "You want to head in so you don't catch cold? I'll be in there in a minute to get you your Christmas presents."

"Sure." Emma headed off toward his patio door.

The guys greeted her with hugs and high-fives. Ely held the door open for her. My kid walked inside like she owned the place and a bunch of famous ballplayers hadn't just acknowledged her.

It was just me and Jack. Trying not to think about how his hot mouth hugged my cock or how those hands deliciously kneaded my ass was an impossible task. He hooked a thumb toward his house—the thumb that had pressed on my prostate through my taint. It was all I could do not to whimper.

"Thanks...for letting her come over."

I opened my mouth, but nothing came out. I didn't deserve to be thanked. I managed a nod and quirked the corner of my mouth.

Chewing on his thumb, he added, "You're welcome to come over."

"Uh, thanks, but I've got to get a few things ready before we head to Lainey's folks."

He nodded. "Of course. Uh. Give them my best. I'll make sure to send Emma back over in time."

"Thanks."

We both turned away awkwardly. I took my time heading back to the house. It seemed vital to make sure he knew I wasn't in a hurry to get away from him. As grateful as I was that he didn't mention that night, I wondered what it meant that he hadn't. Did he resent me? *I* resented me. I practically demanded he suck me off, for Christ's sake.

With each step toward my house, the weight of how much I missed him pressed on me. I wanted him to hold me again, to touch me again, but I wanted so much more than that. I missed his voice, his laugh, his smile. I missed the way he danced in the kitchen when he thought no one was looking, the little smile he got on his face when he was cooking, the way his eyes filled with intrigue when he listened to Emma ramble, and the pucker in his brow when he read her stories like he really had to concentrate.

When I reached the door, I chanced a last look at his yard. The guys had all disappeared into his house. Jack was walking up his deck. And shit. The heel of his palm was pressed to his cheekbone.

Morgan's warning haunted me. Don't hurt him, she'd said.

All I'd done was hurt him. The hows and the whys I'd tripped over the last few weeks suddenly didn't matter. Lainey's approval didn't matter. I was no longer afraid to be happy, but I was fucking terrified my happiness wouldn't want me anymore.

CHAPTER 28
Max

It was Saturday. I finally got a weekend to myself, and what time did my body wake me up? Six o-freaking-clock. That whole worrying about your child instinct should shut off if they were safely in the care of other family members, but apparently my body was a sadistic asshole.

On the plus side, I got to read the entire newspaper and drink two cups of coffee without interruption for the first time in a decade. It was... weird.

Dinner with Bob and Ellen last night was painfully tolerable. They were great people, don't get me wrong, but when Lainey was alive, we talked about family. Now, it was this awkward mix of anything *but* family from Bob—complete reviews of restaurants from his business trips to places I'd never see about food I'd never eat. And when Ellen wasn't talking about houses her agency closed on, she was tossing out random opinions of what Lainey might have thought about something. I swore she did it to include or console me, but I'd rather get my chest waxed than hear it every fucking time.

I was studiously on the third load of laundry today in the new washer— there would be no more mold experiments under my watch, thank you very much. I hauled and put away the last of Emma's crap back in her room, sans hole in the roof, sans raccoons in the attic. I got all the bills paid, the floors swept, and it was only one in the afternoon. I'd accomplished enough that I wouldn't have to stress about the house when I went back to work Monday.

I should feel like Superman, but anxiety was kicking my dumb ass. The other topic of dinner last night—*the date*.

I was prepared to cancel, but Ellen looked like she was just offered her own *HGTV* show whenever she mentioned the infamous Renee Thomas. With every passing minute counting down to the moment I had to make small talk with a woman who was interested in the idea of me, I wanted to develop laryngitis.

At work, I talked to people I didn't know every day, but there was no expectation there to be copasetic. I didn't have to talk about myself. Come to think of it, I didn't talk about myself to Dan much either. I'd only known Trevor for four years, but I swore he knew more about me than Dan.

Trevor knew I loved Italian food, but hated garlic. He remembered Emma's birthday. When Dan and I went out last week, he ordered a garlic dip appetizer and told the *ear licker* that had hung on me that my daughter was twelve. My point is it was hit or miss, even with people you already knew. You couldn't force things. Everything about this date felt forced, and I hadn't even met her yet.

A repetitious smack noise outside caught my attention, making my nuts tingle like Pavlov's dog. Okay, maybe that was a bad analogy. It would imply Pavlov did something really strange with that dog. I hadn't heard the sound in a while, but I'd know it anywhere.

I skittered to the kitchen; slowly, like a dignified, grown-ass man. Leaning over the counter, I found the perfect view of Jack getting in some pitching practice in his backyard. He said he bought his house for the giant backyard to get his sixty feet, six inches in for pitching practice to mirror the distance from the mound to home plate. His pitcher's net rocked in the breeze from the last impact. It still amazed me a human being existed who could throw that hard, that far.

It didn't amaze me that he was only in sweatpants and a freaking hoodie. How had he not gotten pneumonia six times already this winter?

He leaned forward; the fabric going tight against the curve of his ass and wound up. Bringing his leg up only stretched the gray cotton more, accentuating his muscular thighs.

I was watching an apparition. It defied the laws of science for anyone to look that good in sweatpants. Mine always made me look like a frumpy mental patient. His fluid movements, his precision, and his power were such a thing of glory as I was treated to my own private show. Why was this magnificent man alone more often than not?

A cloud of vapor emitted from his mouth as he picked up another ball. He stared at it vacantly, like he was deep in thought. He looked so defeated.

My heart squeezed and every spare drop of blood raced to my cock at the thought of him mourning the loss of me, the coldness of me walking away twice.

Was Morgan right? Had he really picked me out of every other man in the world? He put himself out there, she said.

For me. *Only me.*

Me—who he thinks is *very sexy*. *Me*—who he knows is temperamental and implied there are other nice things besides blow jobs we could do to each other.

I'd never wanted to be sexy or not temperamental for someone so badly. I squeezed the ache inside my sleep pants from base to tip and shuddered when he fired another ball into the net. The velocity behind the *thwack* noise from the impact to the target shot a jolt of arousal through me.

Fuck. I had a date in three hours, and I was as hard as an ironwood tree for... not-my-date. Three things were clear to me as I reached inside my pants and pumped my dick.

One—I hadn't touched myself this much during puberty—I had a problem. Two—I needed to stop using Jack as my spank bank—he deserved so much better. And three—there was no fucking way number-two was getting accomplished right now. How had I resisted this man for six years?

His big hands gripped the ball tight, his fingers curving around the white leather. I remembered those fingers trailing up my legs, stroking the pucker of my hole.

A needy moan ripped from my throat. I was eternally thankful for the hindsight whoever built my house had to put two-way glass in the kitchen windows. The realtor said it was so the neighbor couldn't see inside from their adjacent kitchen. I doubted it would be a selling point that it was also preventing said neighbor from seeing how low I'd stooped this time, beating off to his smoking hot ass.

Would he want me to grab and knead his the way he had done to mine? Was it as smooth as the rest of him looked?

As he shifted and flexed, my body warmed and tingled from head to toe. Pressure built in my center and my balls, agonizing and yet still not enough. It wasn't just from the physical glory before me, maybe not even at all.

It was the way I could see his silent suffering, his hard work, his focus, his control—not just with baseball, but over his emotions. It was how gentle he had been with me when I knew the power he was capable of. He hadn't sucked me off. He'd made love to me with his mouth, with his hands. I didn't just want it again; I wanted to make love to him. I wanted him to feel so much bliss he moaned my name and forgot every way I had hurt him, and then I wanted to do it again and again until he was so satiated the only tears he'd ever cry again were happy ones.

The fever inside me was ready to burst. My hand was a blur, punishing my dick, begging for release. I let out a delirious, self-deprecating laugh. I was home alone, jerking off in my kitchen in the middle of the day. It was so far from uptight. I let loose a stream of filthy thoughts and got lost in the ride.

"You liked sucking my cock. Didn't you? You felt so fucking good. Uhn. Could I make you come, too? How do you want to come? Is your dick as perfect as the rest of you? What would you say when I made you come?"

It took all my effort to keep my eyes open. My naughty questions flooded my ears. They were bold, erotic lies. I didn't even know how to give this man the pleasure he deserved, but fuck, I wanted to.

"Look at me. Look at me," I pleaded, fucking begged, as a bead of sweat rolled down my spine.

He did, glancing right at the window for the briefest second. One glimpse of those brown eyes was all it took. I roared, painting the front of my cabinets with thick white spurts.

Panting, my hips jerked involuntarily with every *thwack* from outside, prolonging my orgasm. My moans echoed into the sink like a DJ was re-mixing my euphoria.

Eventually, I peeled myself off the counter, straightening on shaky legs. Grabbing the paper towels, I cleaned myself up and drew up my pants, then went to work on the cabinets. A tinny chirp disoriented me as I got my breathing back to normal. I located my phone on the counter and saw a reminder going off.

"Fuck!" I cursed, reading the alarm message I had programmed into my phone—*GET READY FOR DATE.*

There was no quicker way to come down from an orgasm high than going on a date with anyone but the only person you wanted. Why in the hell had I let my mother-in-law rope me into this?

One thing was for damn sure, this was the last box I was ever checking off because of something other people expected of me. Life was too short. I certainly knew enough about that.

CHAPTER 29
Jack

The sound of Max's garage closing next door was a window slamming shut on my heart. It was nine-thirty at night. He had left for his date around four. I hadn't had many actual dates in my life, but the shitty ones hadn't lasted anywhere near five and a half hours.

The Blackhawks were bombing tonight. The longer I tried to focus on the hockey game, the blurrier my TV appeared. Man, I really didn't want to cry anymore.

My biceps ached as I lifted my beer to my lips. I had overdone it today. First, two hours of cardio with Hooper over live stream this morning, then pitching for another two hours this afternoon, and finally weights after dinner. I had to do something with my nervous energy so I wouldn't tear a hole in the wall.

I told Max he should date. I had no reason to be bent out of shape over him actually going through with it.

He's straight. He's straight. He's straight. I clicked my heels together on the coffee table like Dorothy from *The Wizard of Oz.*

If I repeated it enough, maybe it wouldn't hurt so bad. I needed to think positively. I got to see Emma yesterday. That was huge. It gave me hope.

Until this freaking date.

Damn it. I didn't know I could hate a word so much—*date*. Ugh.

A bubble formed in the back of my throat, nearly choking me. I sniffed in a breath, making a nasally, snotty snort—one drawback of having a big nose that had been broken before. The damn thing was going to be dripping all night at the rate I was going.

Five and a half hours... That was certainly long enough to have sex. Wild, crazy sex. Sweaty, loud, straight sex. *Several* times.

Ah! This was torture, and it was only the beginning.

Once Max got a girlfriend and started having sex regularly, I'd be the last person he wanted to see. I'd be his shameful secret. A reminder of his one night of lapsed judgement.

That pretty much summed up my life. Didn't it? I was so sick of living like a secret. Baseball had always been enough to take the edge off the curse of my orientation, but this wasn't some novel where LGBTQ+ athletes were barreling out of every closet and the world shit rainbows—pun fucking intended. It was gritty, dirty, cold-hearted reality.

I was the fucking fool who, for a moment, thought I could have it all. I had actually considered the possibility that maybe a player could come out and not tank his career or not have his orientation outshine his work on the field, but there were no fairy tales where a player got the straight guy *and* kept his place on the team. Man, I knew how to shoot for the moon.

The squeak of the patio door sent my spine rigid against the couch. My skin prickled at the familiar scrape of shoes on the hallway tiles. Max.

Shit.

I quickly slathered my sweatshirt sleeve across my eyes and under my nose. I snagged my ball cap off the coffee table and shoved it on, pulling the bill low like I was a freaking cowboy, trying to keep the sun out of my eyes.

"Hey there." Max nodded, coming through the archway from the hall and heading around the couch toward the recliner. "How's the game going?"

Did he have to look that good? Dark jeans, a pale gray V-neck sweater with a white T-shirt underneath that hugged his pecs just enough. His date got to stare at all *that* for over five hours. And now I hated that lucky bitch.

I gave a casual shrug. "Shit. How was the date?"

"Shit," he parroted.

That shouldn't have been music to my ears, but I wanted to Tom Cruise-jump on this couch right now. I shifted my gaze to him just long enough to be considered eye contact. "She that bad?"

He sighed and plopped down in the chair. Seeing him make himself at home like he used to was an odd comfort.

"No. She was...nice."

The Tom Cruise bouncing in my head tripped and fell off the celebratory couch. My nose decided it wanted to drip, forcing me to sniffle and dab it with my sleeve. I took a sip of my beer because that was what people did when everything was hunky dory. Right?

She was *nice*? What did that mean if the date was shit?

"They fuck up your dinner or something?" I asked.

"No. Dinner was fine, way the hell out by Decatur. We had a drink beforehand and bullshitted about Bob and Ellen and work a bit. It just...isn't going to work for me."

I breathed easier hearing he spent half his time driving and had no intention of seeing her again. I told him what a friend was supposed to tell him. "Well, at least you got back out there, man. That's the important part."

From the corner of my eye, I saw him nod. Suddenly, I had the urge to fill the silence with chatter.

"You need a beer?" I asked, tilting mine, but keeping my eyes glued to the game from hell. Well, it *was* the game from hell. Now it was a freaking *Preparation-H* commercial.

"No. I'm good." He was quiet for a moment, and I pinched my eyes shut when he glanced at the TV. "*You* all right?" he asked.

"Yeah. Just...watching the game," I said casually and pointed my beer to the hemorrhoid cream commercial like an idiot.

"Jack? What's up? You don't look all right."

Shit. I couldn't do this. I couldn't do the silent, pretend-it-never-happened-thing he seemed to want to do. I scratched my temple to hide my watery eyes.

"Uh. I was just thinking, once you get a girlfriend, it'd probably be weird for you to have me around so...then I won't get to see Emma anymore."

Or you, I didn't say.

Picking at my beer label was a nice stress ball, but I added a jaw flex to help keep the tears at bay. I looked like I was pouting. I hated that I looked like I was pouting.

"I'll never keep Emma away from you. She'd be hell to live with. The last few weeks have taught me that."

His attempt at humor almost made me chuckle. At this point, it was more ridiculous to pretend I wasn't crying, so I wiped my nose and sucked in a needed breath. "Yeah. Well, all the same. I'll, uh, understand if...if that's not how it ends up working out."

Whatever end there had to be between us, I didn't want there to be hard feelings. I didn't want to regret Max, and I didn't want him to regret me.

He got up from the chair. I picked at my beer label again, so I didn't have to watch him leave. When the couch cushion dipped beside me, my entire body tensed.

Max was sitting next to me. Right next to me. Facing me with one leg bent in front of him, his knee brushing my thigh.

He said nothing, just studied me. I fixed my gaze on the game. Thank fuck it was back on, but it did little to help my nerves. Was this the part where he flipped out and beat my ass for making him feel gay?

He nodded, gesturing for the half-full bottle in my hand. His voice was low and smooth, giving it a sultry timbre that turned the back of my neck to gooseflesh. "Give me that beer."

It was such an odd request that I hesitated. Dudes didn't share beers. I handed it to him but offered, "There's more in the fridge."

"I want this one," he said, voice soft as raw cotton.

His fingers wrapped around mine, high on the bottle where I purposely held it so he could avoid having to touch me. As he pulled his hand away, his fingertips dragged across my knuckles, sending a shiver down my spine. He tilted the bottle to his lips, never taking his eyes off me the entire time.

I folded my arms over my chest now that my hands had nothing to keep them busy. My eyes darted from the TV to Max. He drained my beer and held my gaze, looking determined.

Finally, he leaned forward and set the bottle on my coffee table. When he sat back, he didn't move away. If anything, he settled in closer, draping his arm over the back of the couch behind me.

"I don't know how to be gay," he blurted matter-of-factly, his expression frustrated.

"I...don't know how to be straight."

He snorted and shook his head. It was enough to lower the red flags for me. He was trying to let me down gently. I could help him with that.

"I'm sorry. I shouldn't have told you that crap me and Lainey talked about. She told me that in confidence. I feel like I betrayed both of you. And I shouldn't have...done what I did last weekend. I told myself I was helping you figure things out, but really, I was just being selfish. I shouldn't have... said or done anything to ruin our friendship."

"You didn't ruin it. You just...broadened it. And you only did what I asked you to do. I was there, too."

"Yeah, well, it won't happen again. I promise. I don't want to lose you and Emma."

Max nodded. A truckload had been lifted off my chest, but as the silence bloomed and he watched me, still so close I could feel his body heat, my nerves ping-ponged all over the place. He said the last thing I expected.

"Does that mean you'd be cool watching Emma if I go on another date?"

"I thought...I thought it didn't work out."

"It didn't, but I've got someone else in mind."

"Oh." More like oh, fucking hell, just kill me now. I gripped the leg opening of my gym shorts. "Well, that's...that's great, Max."

About as great as getting my balls waxed.

He nodded again, still watching me. His arm was still draped over the back of the couch, inches from my shoulders. And here I thought it was miserable when he didn't want to come near me. This was freaking torture.

I cleared my throat and went for nonchalant. "Yeah. Of course. I'd be happy to watch Emma. Thanks...for asking me."

"You sure? You don't look too happy about it."

I scoffed, because was he that clueless after how I'd put myself out there? A traitorous tear spilled down my cheek. Wiping it with my sleeve, I heaved a breath. This was shaping up to be the epic low point of my life, so I might as well go for broke.

"I'd rather be jealous than not see Emma at all, so it's fine. I'll get over it. I won't make it weird between us. I swear."

His sharp inhale told me maybe he finally got how big my crush on him was. I could feel his gaze on the side of my face, like he was studying me.

"Good," he finally said. "When we get up tomorrow, come pick up Emma with me, and then we can have our date."

I turned my head to look at him because who the hell was we? Did he already have someone else lined up after tonight's failure? He gave me an eager smile, like he didn't realize this was killing me.

"You have another date tomorrow already?" I asked.

He swallowed and then nodded. "Only if you'll say yes."

Great. His love life depended on my babysitting availability. Nice to feel useful.

"Bob and Ellen pick this one out for you, too?"

"No. I did." He cleared his throat. "And I'm pretty crazy about him, but I've been a complete ass the last couple weeks, so I'm worried he won't want to have anything to do with me."

Wait. *Him?* Did he just say *him*, as in Ken, *not* Barbie?

The way he was looking at me... He couldn't mean...*me*.

Max and *me*...on a date?

What the actual fuck was wrong with him now? I was finally at my patience limit for confused straight men.

"Is this fuck with the queer neighbor? Because it's not funny."

He licked his lips and straightened up a bit. "No. I'm serious. Our date will have to include Emma because I don't have a sitter tomorrow. I promise

I'll make it up to you though some other time...just the two of us." His voice was soft and tender. No matter how hard I looked, I couldn't see any insincerity, any confusion. "So, do you think you could give me a chance, or have I screwed everything up too bad?"

Holy. Shit.

CHAPTER 30
Max

My heart was about to hammer out of my chest from equal parts excitement and fear of rejection. Jack's brow was furrowed, and his beautiful, reddened eyes were staring at me like I just asked him to make hamburger out of kitten meat.

"Max...you've never wanted a man. You'll probably change your mind by tomorrow when you freak out again."

Okay. Not the answer I wanted, but it wasn't a *no*. Thank fuck.

So, he needed convincing? Well, of course, he did. I only shoved him and avoided him like he had the plague.

My fingers trembled as I moved them to the back of his neck, touching for the first time a place I wanted to touch. I rubbed the soft warm flesh there, trying to reassure him as I searched for the response that held my fate with this man.

His body tensed under my fingertips. God, what had I done to him that he was reacting to me like that? What wouldn't I do to take it all back?

"I didn't freak out when I dreamt about you every night this week."

The line in his brow smoothed a fraction. I hadn't sold him yet, but at least he was listening. I made a gentle circle with my thumb, brushing the close shave of the hairline at his neck. His chest rose and fell, like maybe his heart rate was in overdrive, too. My thumb decided it belonged there. That simple contact felt so...right. He had to know this felt right to me.

"I didn't freak out when I jerked off while I was watching you practice this morning."

Jack's eyebrows lifted. He looked like he swallowed his tongue.

Ahem. Good. I'd say he got the point.

My embarrassment at admitting I was a tribute in the Masturbation Games died, knowing I'd shocked him instead of the other way around for once. It gave me the bravery I needed. I settled my other hand on the silky fabric of his gym shorts.

"And...I didn't freak out when I sat through an entire date tonight wondering if you were thinking about me, too."

Whoosh. My word vomit hung in the space between us. Jack stared... and stared.

Okay. Fuck. Now I was nervous.

Was he going to say something? Should I move my hands?

When I couldn't take it any longer, I grabbed his hand in desperation and blurted out the worst apology in history. "Alright. I know I freaked out a little bit at first, but I'm done freaking out. I swear. I want to do this, Jack. You and me. Am I too late? Can you forgive me?"

He looked away and rubbed his other palm up and down his thigh anxiously. I didn't miss how he squeezed my hand, though. That squeeze was everything.

"This isn't just a curiosity for me, Max. It took me more than a few weeks to be comfortable with it."

I knew *it* meant his sexuality. I thought my stupidity and inadvertent cruelty of late would be the thing to scare him away, but *shit*. I never considered he would doubt my commitment once I'd catapulted the elephant off my chest.

"It's not curiosity," I assured him.

He shot me with a doubtful frown, making me feel like Luke to his Yoda. It was a look that said he was protecting me from carnal delights he thought I couldn't handle, delights he thought I didn't want *with him*. How did I convince him he was wrong?

Damn. He was so sexy, I couldn't breathe right, which was *not* helping.

"Well, of course, there are things I'm curious about. I mean, I've never done this before, but it's more than a curiosity. It's...a want. I *want you*— the guy who understands me and makes me feel like I'm home whenever you're around. The guy who can put up with my shit and make me laugh harder than anyone else I've ever met. And if I sound uncertain about anything, it's only because I'm afraid you'll want no part of me after the horrible way I behaved the last couple weeks. I'm so sorry. I promise I'm going to make it up to you, no matter what you decide."

He sniffed and stared, processing. "Your friendship is important to me."

I know I said I'd be cool with friendship, but I wanted to scream, *fuck friendship*. There was so much more here.

"I've never been anybody's *first*," he continued. "I don't want to get hurt if you can't handle it because then I'll lose more than a friend."

The dam around my heart burst, spilling hope. I inched closer and cupped his jaw. He needed to see me, needed to see all the affection and good wishes in my eyes that I had for him.

"I'll tell you what I can't handle," I told him in a low, flirty voice I hadn't used in years. "Waiting any longer to get a redo on that kiss."

When his gaze darted from my eyes to my mouth, I grabbed the bill of his hat and tossed it aside. Gripping the back of his neck, I urged him closer. I dragged my nose against his, holding my breath, giving him a chance to tell me to stop. A rush of butterflies flapped in my stomach. If he said no, at this point, it might kill me.

When he licked his lips, I finally breathed again and brushed my mouth against his. It was a soft, sweet, two-person exchange that should have been our first, and for a second, I was floating outside of my body. His hand slid up the back of my arm. He was touching me. Touching me back. My throat made a grateful noise somewhere between a weak moan and a whimper.

Carefully, I captured one lip and then the other, trembling at the thought he'd hate it while it felt like all I ever needed. I'd never wanted to be better at anything than kissing Jack Spears.

Was he feeling the light-headed rapture I was? I had to know. If it wasn't good for him, I'd try until it was if he'd let me. My self-doubt got the better of me. I pulled back, ready to explain, ready to beg for time to make it better.

"I…"

"What?" he asked, searching my eyes as I searched his.

"I feel weird, but I…I don't care. I want you."

His fingers rubbed my arm. "It doesn't feel weird to me."

"No. Kissing you isn't weird *at all*, I just…it feels…"

"What?"

How embarrassing. First, I couldn't talk to him. Now, I couldn't shut my pie hole. I ran my hand down the heat on my face and shook my head. "It's stupid."

He reached for my hand and squeezed. "No. You can tell me."

Pursing my lips, I forced myself to look into his understanding gaze. "I don't know what you like. I want it to be good for you, but I feel like a fucking virgin."

He let out a scoff. "Max, I like *you*. There's no reason to feel like that. You've probably done more kissing and had more sex than I've ever had."

"Yeah, but... Wait. Yeah?"

He laughed at my surprise, and it was the best sound in the world, even though it was at my expense. "Yeah. Probably."

"Oh."

Shit. Now I felt like a slut. Great. Like I needed another reason to be unworthy of him.

"And...that was *really* nice," he added, his shy smile making my heart flip. "Lainey was right. You're a good kisser."

I gaped. My. Freaking. Wife. And. This. Man.

Maybe it would be bizarre to someone outside looking in, but I actually liked the fact we could talk about Lainey together since we both knew her better than anyone, and they both knew me better than anyone.

I gripped his neck and gave him a playful shake. "You *two*. If she was here, I'd sit the both of you down and chew your asses out about the rules of privacy."

Jack let out one of his sexy belly laughs, and I felt it to my toes. "Yeah, right. We'd fuck you up."

"Probably," I conceded because *that smile*. God, happy looked good on him.

His face went serious suddenly. "Max? Is that why you...because I knew Lainey?"

I blinked. Could he really think that's all this was for me—some kind of comfort in the familiar because of the connection we shared to her?

"Sorry. I have to ask," he added.

"No." I shook my head adamantly. "No. I mean, I like that you knew her, that you were friends, but that's got nothing to do with how I feel. You do. You're your own person, Jack. You're my best friend for a reason. Give yourself some credit."

"Oh." He gave me a half-smile, but I could tell the gears were still turning. "I don't mean to ruin the moment, but I've wondered if...it would bother her."

"I'm not going to."

His gaze snapped to mine, full of surprise.

"Haven't you learned anything from me? If you wonder that, you'll turn into what I've been the last three years." I licked my lips to take a pause.

"There was a time for that, and the time is done." I held out my left hand. "I...took my ring off tonight."

He frowned and traced his thumb over the indent on my ring finger. "Because you went on your first date tonight." He nodded, as though he thought he understood.

I weaved our fingers together. "No. After I got home, when I was coming over here to see you."

Watching the recognition dawn on his face made my heart overflow. We stared, mirror images of small smiles because it wasn't exactly something to smile about, while at the same time, it was. It had been a long road for both of us. I stroked his cheek with my thumb, feeding my need to touch and comfort him.

"I missed you, man. I really missed you...more than when you're on the road. And Emma's been so fucking pissed off at me."

"That's because she's got good taste."

And there was my smug-ass best friend. Thank God. I shook him again and chuckled. "Cocky fucker."

When our laughter died, the mood shifted. I imagined the tenderness in his eyes matched my own for him. I stroked his smooth cheek, reveling in the fact I could actually do that now.

"I'm so sorry. I acted like an insane person," I told him, kissing his temple. "I thought I lost my friend when you kissed me, then I thought I was losing my mind when I wanted you." He frowned, so I squeezed his arm and gave him a quick peck on the lips before I continued. "I *was*...losing my mind, but not because I want you. It was because I thought I couldn't be with you."

"Because you think men aren't supposed to be together?"

"No! No. Well, maybe at first, but I think I just used it as an excuse. I... felt like I needed permission from Lainey to be with someone else, which is stupid."

"No. It's not. That's what I was getting at just now."

I shook my head. "It was stupid. It is. And, honestly, it wasn't even that. I realized I needed my own permission. I was hiding behind her. Not just about this, about everything. I don't know how it happened, how I didn't see it sooner, but I think I thought if I wasn't miserable, it meant I didn't love her anymore. I thought...I wasn't allowed to be happy again, and deep down, not even deep, but right at the surface, I knew how happy you make me, and I guess I felt guilty about that. I was never mad at you. I was mad at myself, until I realized I didn't want to be, that I didn't need to be."

He traced my jaw. "Max. You don't ever have to stop loving her."

"I know, but it's past time I learn how to separate love from grief. For Emma's sake. For yours."

"For yours too, Max."

I leaned in, the need to be close to him overpowering. He sucked in a breath like he couldn't believe this was where we were at either. Our lips met softly again, and this time it was headier now that we'd cleared the air.

I shuddered when the tip of his tongue brushed my lip. His hand tensed on my jaw, and he started to pull back like he thought he scared me, but I followed him, licking the seam of his mouth. His full lips parted, welcoming me, and I accepted his welcome. Our mouths melded like two puzzle pieces, fitting together perfectly with each slant.

I could taste his beer and his natural sweetness as our tongues discovered each other. Jack was kissing me, really fucking kissing me, and I was kissing him. And it. Was. Perfect.

Liquid fire ran through my veins. I was overjoyed and sad all at once, connecting with him like this. It was like he'd been gone for years and if I stopped kissing him, he'd disappear. It was the power of both a hello and goodbye kiss, all wrapped up in one.

We were so close now that I was half on his lap. My chest brushed against the hardness of his. I weaved my fingers into his soft hair that I'd missed.

He snaked one of his big arms around my waist and traced my spine. I shivered underneath my clothes at his touch. His other hand did that caressing dance over my thigh like he did that night in my room.

Why had I denied us this? This man's hands *belonged on me.* I deepened the kiss and took what he gave back as our hunger spiraled. I felt like a runner, late to the starting line, desperate to up.

My hand traced down the curve of his pec muscle, exploring his chest. When I felt his nipple, I rubbed my thumb over it, and he moaned into my mouth.

Uhn. I wanted to make more of those moans and swallow them. We broke at the same time to breathe. I rested my forehead against his, panting in need and gratitude.

"I hated seeing the guys at your house yesterday," I confessed.

He made a noise, telling me I was being ludicrous, and rubbed my back. "They don't know about me."

The way he said it was quiet and broken. I drew back. I would never forget the haunted look in his eyes. It gutted me. I rubbed my thumb across his bottom lip, wishing I could curve it into a smile. I gaped, astounded by the torment on his face and what it said about his life.

"How do you fucking live like that?"

Jack swallowed, and his voice came out in a choked whisper. "I feel like I'm suffocating...every single day."

My heart. My aching heart.

I cupped his face in my hands, frantically scanning his face and shaking my head like it could make his pain go away. "Don't," I demanded. "You can breathe with me. Breathe, Jack."

His eyes closed, and his breath hitched like he was holding back a sob. The sound shattered me; seeing this big, strong, kind, beautiful man hurting so much. I had no idea the depth of what he was holding in and, all the while, he was helping me through temper tantrums about shit I should have handled with more dignity.

I pressed a kiss to his forehead like an emotional bandage and yanked him to me, wrapping my arms around him tight. He sighed and rested his head on my shoulder. I was grateful he trusted me enough to accept my comfort, but I hated seeing how much he needed it.

I stroked his hair and rubbed his back, wincing each time he sniffled. The front he'd had to put up around his team, at events, and even with me—how could I ever make up for anything I ever said or did to make him uncomfortable?

Words escaped me, so I offered him the only comfort I could. I cocooned him in my arms the way he did to me in the laundry room. We stayed like that for a long while. I peppered him with tender kisses on his neck, his cheek, his jaw. I must have been annoying the fuck out of him because he pulled back.

Shit. Was I like the ear licker?

He sniffled sharply and wiped away the moisture from his glossy eyes. His forlorn gaze darted to mine and then down, where he was picking at his gym shorts.

Note to self: Jack plucks at fabric when he's uncomfortable.

He grimaced and rubbed the underside of his nose. "I probably look like how a *Lifetime* movie feels."

I snorted and nudged his chin up, so he had to look at me. "No. If your sexy ass was in them, people would actually watch them."

That got a smirk out of him, so I stamped it with another kiss. The corner of his mouth ticked up, and he stared at me in wonder.

"I can't believe you're kissing me."

Well, well. I'd finally discovered the antidote for his sorrow. Leaning in, I murmured against his lips, "I can't believe you stopped."

He full-on beamed and cupped my face, rewarding me with a kiss so passionate I wanted to take notes. I never wanted to stop tasting him or stealing his breath.

I gripped his shoulder and felt the hard plane of his stomach through his shirt against mine. His mouth trailed away from mine. I tried to chase it, but he moved on to my jaw.

His hand slid high up my thigh, making my body say, *yes, please*. That single touch validated all the thoughts and feelings inside me I'd been bottling up for weeks.

I dusted my lips against the hot skin of his neck, down to where it met his shoulder. His taste and his spicy, clean scent were intoxicating. I wanted to dive into him like a pool and be fully immersed in Jack.

"Can I touch you?" I whispered, desperate to be closer, yet unsure of what he wanted.

His hands squeezed my shoulders. He pressed his forehead to mine, chuckling. "Baby, you can touch me anywhere you want."

I snorted at the endearment. I'd called him *fucker* as many times as he'd called me *man* in the past six years.

"What?" he asked.

"'*Baby*,'" I stated, scrunching my nose.

He rolled his eyes. "Fine. You can touch me wherever you want, *man*." He mock bro-punched me under my jaw.

"Fucking smartass." I swatted his hand away and gave him a hard kiss, but then the heat reignited.

My next kiss was softer, distracting him so I could be sneaky and explore more of him. Okay, I didn't need to be sneaky. He'd given me permission, but the whole virgin effect was real.

I wanted to make him feel good. Vaguely, I recalled there were bases for new relationships and some kind of order. You weren't supposed to round too many too soon, but fuck if I knew how they applied to men, and fuck if I cared after knowing this man for more than half a decade already.

He'd seen me cry. He'd seen me with kid vomit on my clothes, seen me with bedhead and in my pajamas. Covered in dirt and sweat, working in the yard. He'd seen me puking from food poisoning. And most recently, he'd seen me bare-ass naked and had my cock in his mouth. I was pretty sure that negated all other bases, and I'd be damned if I was having a conversation about sexual bases with a baseball player.

No more fucking boxes. Instinct was my guiding light now.

My fingers found the hem of his shirt. I slid under it to the silky ripples of Jack's stomach. It was the strangest and best sensation—touching him soothed my soul and made me weak all at once.

Our little moans, whimpers, and breaths filled his living room. I reveled in his sounds for *me* and more of his kisses. God, the man could kiss. The way he gently rubbed my thigh, my arms, and my back was like his hands were saying they wanted to touch the skin on those places.

I brought his shirt up to the point where he helped me tug it off, and then I gaped in awe. I'd seen him with his shirt off a few times, but never this close, never just for me, never as *mine*. It was a whole new view.

In a daze at the valleys and ridges of his six-pack and the mounded muscles on his chest, flat dark brown nipples on his bronzed skin, I trailed the back of my knuckles across one row of his abs. How the hell did he think *I* was sexy?

"Fuck. I need to work out more."

Jack scoffed and cupped my jaw. "No. You don't. You're perfect."

I cast him a disbelieving look and then returned to my shameless gawking. Flattening my palm against his warm skin, I ran it down his belly, feeling more relaxed and freer than I had in my entire life.

This was right. This was where I was supposed to be. It was what I was supposed to be doing, and who I was supposed to be doing it with.

I stopped at his navel, noticing the tent in his red gym shorts that reminded me of the discomfort locked away in my jeans. Jack lowered his hand from my jaw, allowing me to look. The hard proof of being wanted by him stoked a proud arousal in me.

His chest rose and fell, breathing passion. His tongue came out to wet his kiss-swollen lips. *I* did that. *We* did that. That was *us*.

I could tell he was waiting for me to make a move, to set the pace. It was nerve-wracking and exhilarating at the same time. Why was he trusting me? He should be as leery as I was when I let Emma paint.

I didn't know how to paint his canvas, didn't know what colors he liked. All I knew was what I'd dreamt and what I wanted him to do to me. I lowered my hand, cupping my palm around the outline of his cock.

His eyes slipped closed. His head fell back against the couch, and he sucked in a breath. Okay, he liked that color.

"Is *this* really for me?" I asked.

His hand took a wider sweep, venturing up to the V of my thigh and down to my knee, making all my nerve endings spark. "It's *because of* you, and it's *for* you."

The way he said it with patience and restraint when his arousal was so evident was humbling. He was a tender, patient lover, just like he'd always been in all things. It made me realize how brave he had been to fulfill my stupid request in my bedroom last week.

There was no one who could make my transition from grieving widower to sexually active again easier than how Jack was handling everything. The enormity of affection I wanted to shower on him was endless. I threw my man-virgin flag to the winds. I would probably paint outside the lines, but I was going to give him every color I could create.

man-virgin flag to the winds. I would probably paint outside the lines, but I was going to give him every color I could create.

CHAPTER 31
Jack

I was in a dream that I never wanted to end. Max was here, touching me, kissing me, and looking at me like I was the only person in the world he wanted.

His hand left the proof of my arousal, and he stood. I caught my breath, horrified that I was about to wake up, but he dropped to his knees in front of me. His hands slid onto my thighs. He leaned forward, pressing slow kisses to my chest and stomach. I closed my eyes and basked in the way he mapped every inch of my upper body for what felt like an eternity.

The arousal I was barely holding in check spiked when his fingers dipped into the waistband of my shorts, and he began tugging them down over my hips. My eyes flew open.

"What are you doing?"

He stopped, looking up at me like he'd been scolded. I wanted to smack myself for asking.

"Is this...okay?"

"Yes." I practically gasped. "Wait. No. Are you sure? I mean, you kind of got scared off the last time we...*touched*. I really don't want things to be weird between us again. Please don't feel like you have to do this."

"I'm not scared. I know I don't *have* to. I *want* to. I'm...ready." He cleared his throat and traced a circle over my pelvic bone with his fingertip. "Dying actually."

The heat in his eyes. It was surreal to witness what his passion looked like, since the only time I'd seen it before, I'd convinced myself it was something else. I lifted my ass to help him continue.

I must have still looked confused because he added, "I want to make you feel good."

"You already do."

"So, you don't...want me to..."

"Max, it's not that *at all*. It's just...you've been gay for like five minutes. I just meant that you don't have to prove anything to me."

Lord. Why the fuck was I talking? Let the poor man prove whatever he wanted to my poor hard-on!

"I'm not," he said adamantly.

I practically swallowed my tongue. "Not...*gay*?"

"No."

Oh, God. This was exactly what I was worried about. I dropped my ass and squeezed my hand on top of his so he couldn't drag my shorts any lower.

"Max," I started, but he cut me off.

"If I was gay, it would mean I'm attracted to men, *plural*...or I mean, at least open to the possibility of being attracted to men in general, which I'm not."

"I don't understand."

"I'm attracted to *you*. Not other men. Not any women. Only *you*. Whatever you call that, that's what I am."

And then he smiled. I sputtered, and a new wave of tears threatened me. Leaning down, I cupped his face and kissed him.

"I call that fine by me."

"Good," he said, urging me back against the couch and pressing a kiss to the center of my chest. "Now...why don't you sit back and let me show you how attracted I am to you? I have a lot of making up to do."

I laughed and answered him by lifting my hips. He slid my shorts down like a pro. His eyes glazed over and his lips parted as he stared at my erection. Maybe now that he'd seen it, this would be too much for him. I cleared my throat, unable to stand the silence while I was on display.

He glanced up at me and blushed. *Gah!* I made Max Hartwell blush. Then he did something even sexier. He looked down and scowled. Man, the man gave good scowl.

"What's wrong?"

"Of course, you had to have the perfect dick on top of everything else," he grumbled.

I snorted. "Not hardly, but I'm glad you approve. Compliments will get you everywhere with me."

"I'll remember that."

He grinned and lowered his mouth to the juncture of my thigh, the tip of his tongue drawing a stripe there. I shivered and closed my eyes. His hot breath ghosted my skin as he breathed me in like he was savoring me.

His palms stroked my thighs, my knees, my calves. He was generous with his fingertips, splaying them as he went like he couldn't touch enough of me, all the while licking little kisses around where I was dying.

He peered up at me and frowned. "Why do you look...wary? Is this okay?"

"Just too good to be true," I answered breathily.

He scowled at my dick again and muttered, "Well, you won't be saying that when I fuck this up."

Fucking Max.

I always wondered if he'd be as entertaining in bed as he was out of it. I ran my fingers through his thick, black hair.

"You won't fuck it up. Just do what you'd want me to do to you."

He arched a mischievous brow. I grinned and added, "Your problem is that you're a perfectionist, but it's kind of a huge turn-on right now."

He smirked and kissed my thigh, then let out a heavy breath. "Great. No pressure."

"No. There is no pressure."

When his gaze returned to mine, all the snark was replaced with deter-mination and vulnerability. "I want to make you feel the way you made me feel, better, if possible."

My chest heaved at the compliment and the intention. Max licked his lips, causing my cock to jump. He wrapped his hand around it, undeterred, like he was taming a wild animal. His fingers trailed over it like he was learn-ing the feel of me. I held my breath, watching his tongue dart out and lick my slit.

I gasped and gripped his hair. His gaze locked onto mine as his lips slid over the head of my cock, and I fucking whimpered. I had to fight to keep my eyes from sliding closed as his wet heat engulfed me. When he swirled his tongue around my tip with a little groan and took me deeper, my eyes rolled back, and I moaned because holy fuck, his mouth was actually on me.

I forced my eyes back open so I could watch him. There was something sexy about seeing him on his knees, fully clothed, while I was completely naked, like he just came home from work but didn't care that he was exhausted as long as he could strip and worship me.

My breath caught in concern for him when I saw how deep he went. My tip hit the back of his throat, sending sparks of heat to my balls. He gagged and came up fast, coughing, eyes watering.

I bit the inside of my cheek. "You okay?"

He gave my offending dick a venomous glare. "How the fuck do women do this?"

I bit back a laugh. He was so... *straight* it was hilarious. I tugged at his shoulders, taking pity on him.

"Max, you don't have to. Really. I'm just glad you're here at all."

He moved my hands away. "No. I...let me try. Please?"

Biting my lip, I watched in astonishment as he gripped me with his hand and took me in again. He was a bit awkward with his lack of skill, but the fact he was trying and touching me in any way was fuel for my fire. His slurping sounds were so freaking adorable, and soon he found a rhythm that had me gasping, kneading his hair, and fighting not to thrust my hips.

He reached up and circled one of my nipples. I groaned and sucked his fingertip into my mouth, swirling my tongue around it the way he did to my shaft. His other hand snaked around behind me and gripped my ass. He moaned, vibrating my dick. The sound and sensation set my body humming.

"Max," I panted. "Oh, that feels good."

Shit. This was really happening. I widened my legs and cupped my hand over his on my ass, threading my fingers through his. He squeezed my hand when I moaned again, linking himself to my pleasure as his head bobbed on my cock.

"God. You look so fucking sexy doing that."

He growled, I think, and it vibrated me in all the right places.

"Oh. Yes!"

Holy hell. He was better than I ever dreamed. His mouth tightened. His pace quickened. His hand broke away from mine, and a finger slid down the seam of my ass.

"Oh, shit. Max, I'm gonna come already."

I urged his head up, but he resisted and gripped my ass, intent on staying. I appreciated his dedication, but he had no idea what he was in for. He reached between my legs, palming my balls. I was lost from the touch and his sheer determination.

I warned him with a cry. My release went off. Blissful relief washed through me as my cock pulsed into his warm mouth. He swallowed me, and I shuddered, but a second later his shoulders jerked. He made a guttural sound and came up coughing.

I covered my cock, catching the rest of my release in my hand, as Max sputtered, holding his hand to his mouth. His face was red, his eyes watering. I reached for his shoulder, giving it a squeeze.

"Shit. Are you okay?"

Breathless, he grunted. "Yeah. Don't I sound okay?"

Chuckling, I leaned forward and kissed him, rewarding the mask of his insecurities. "That was freaking incredible. Thank you."

He handed me my shirt to clean up my hand. Rubbing my thighs, he stared up at me with a pleased smile and so much affection in his eyes, my heart leaped.

I couldn't believe this was real. I wanted everything with this man. It was all new for both of us. In a way, I had felt straight around Max since he had always been off-limits. Having him now heightened the sense of discovery from friends to lovers, making me understand his virginal comment earlier.

I stood, reaching for his hand. He took mine, getting up with curiosity in his eyes. The outline of his arousal through his jeans made my spent cock twitch to life in solidarity.

He settled his hands on my hips and kissed me. I brushed his nose with mine and trailed my palm down to cover his erection, delighting in his gasp.

"I could give this some attention if you want," I murmured against his lips.

He swallowed and pressed his hips into my touch. "Well, you're the one who gave me this hard-on. It seems only fair."

"I can be very fair," I whispered, sucking on his lower lip, and pressing him into me. "I think I'm going to like your dirty talk. I never would have guessed."

He chuckled. "Yeah. Not like the conversations we usually have. Is it?"

"No." I smiled. "I like our conversations, but this kind is...a little better?"

He kissed my jaw and slid his hand up my back. "A lot better. You can't get a hard-on from talking about global warming. I knew you were fucking with me about that, by the way," he said wryly. "Everything in your house is energy efficient, and you compost and recycle. You shithead."

I laughed, took his hand, and led him to my bedroom, glancing back to check if he was still on board. I smiled at the hungry, mesmerized look on his face as he stared at my ass. Max glanced briefly around my room, taking in the surroundings. He'd never been in here, and the sight was dreamlike. His gaze returned to mine as I pulled back the sheets.

He kicked off his shoes, and then, to my surprise, started on his sweater. I helped him with his T-shirt, wondering what he was expecting. I had to stop myself from getting familiar with the muscles on his torso and the feel of the soft curls on his chest as we stood facing each other, silently learning each other's bodies. When his breathing noticeably hitched, and he pressed his hips into mine, I turned to my nightstand, pulling out a bottle of lube.

Setting it on the bed, a smile spread on my face when Max sidled up behind me to caress my ass. I leaned into him, reaching my hand back to cup his head and kiss him. The sound of his moan in my mouth lit me up. Reaching between us, I explored his stomach and then circled the button of his jeans. He wasted no time answering my wish, and soon my hands were gliding over the skin of his hips as he shoved his pants and boxer briefs down.

His hard shaft pressed against the seam of my ass as he wrapped his arms around me and let out a shaky breath into the crook of my neck. I stood still, letting him get used to the sensation. Reaching back, I covered his ass, basking in the first feel of us, skin-to-skin.

He kissed the rim of my ear and whispered, "Does it hurt? Fucking like this?"

I could imagine the questions he probably had and wondered if he thought that was why I brought him in here. The fact he was trusting me to be his first everything with a man was not lost on me.

Turning around, I wrapped my arms around his waist and lowered my mouth, flicking my tongue across his nipple. His cock jerked against mine, and he sucked in a breath.

"It can at first if you're not opened up. It takes some...preparation," I told him, gliding my middle finger down between his cheeks, so he understood my meaning. "And it's..."

"What?" he rasped when I trailed off.

"It's kind of a myth made up by straight people that it's all men do to please each other. It's not the endgame for everybody. A lot of people don't even do it."

"Oh."

The way his gaze dropped from mine had me chuckling, so I tilted his chin up. "Why do you sound disappointed?"

"I, uh, I..."

"What?"

He winced and his face bloomed pink. "I dreamt about...being inside you."

My hole clenched at the thought. I had to fight back a groan. I hadn't done *that* since I'd briefly dated that guy in New York, but there was nothing more I would have loved right now than to feel Max filling me, to be connected to him in that intimate way. But this wasn't a race. I wanted to savor every first with Max and let him discover it at his own pace. I smiled and brushed his nose with mine.

"You're going to have to tell me about all those dreams you had some time."

And do them, hopefully.

I trailed kisses down his neck and ran my hand down his stomach, wrapping my fingers around his thick, velvety cock, as I whispered, "Would you like my mouth or my hand tonight?"

He shuddered and gripped the back of my shoulders hard, alerting me to the level of his need. "What...what do you like better?"

"I told you, it's your turn."

"Well, wh-what do you think I'd like better?"

"Did you like my mouth?" I asked, nipping his lower lip. I was pretty sure he had, but I wasn't taking any chances where his pleasure was concerned.

His thumb traced my lip. "I fucking loved every second of your mouth."

His deep, gravelly voice had always been my undoing, and the effect was tenfold in the glow of my bedside lamp. I crawled onto the bed, tugging him along with me so we were both on our knees. He watched me with bated breath as I shifted around behind him and wrapped my arms around him.

Running my hands leisurely over his chest and stomach, we shared kisses over his shoulder. I was quickly learning how much he loved my hair. His fingers threaded through it as I nestled my cock between his ass.

When I leaned back to grab the lube, my erection pressed deeper into his seam, and he sucked in a breath. The way his hips jerked toward the contact had my balls fluttering, knowing it was a sign he might want me there someday.

I warmed the liquid in my hand and slickened his shaft and then mine. When I pressed my chest to his back again and wrapped my hand around his cock, he groaned, leaning into me.

As I stroked him, he widened his legs, giving me room to tease his seam with my length. He was so inviting, it still astounded me.

Sliding his hand down my hip, he whispered, "You're hard again."

"That happens when I'm around you." I kissed his ear, still amazed I could tell him these things now.

He made a wistful sound. His soft hair tickled my shoulder when he tilted his head back to rest there. "How often...did it happen?" he panted.

I stalled for a moment, peppering his neck with kisses as my grip glided up and down his slick shaft. I'd trained my brain to keep my dirty thoughts about 'straight Max' locked up for so long, it was instinct to not confess them.

"Just one example," Max suggested. "I just told you about my fucked-up dream."

I nipped at his earlobe, reveling in the feel of being wrapped around each other. "It wasn't a fucked-up dream. I'd love to do that sometime."

"You're stalling," he grumbled, but I didn't miss how his body tremored at my invitation.

"After I moved in, you remember that day you came over and helped me mount the TV on the living room wall?"

His hips jerked into my hand. "Fuck. That long ago?"

"Sorry."

He squeezed my ass, pressing me tighter against him. "Don't be."

His words set me free. It was strange to have permission for my history of attraction to him after feeling ashamed about it for so long.

"You're shaking," he whispered breathily.

"So are you."

"That's because I'm so turned on."

"I'm nervous," I confessed.

"Why?"

"I...can't believe you're here."

"Why?"

"Because...you're *Max*. I'm not supposed to want you."

"Says who?"

"It was...a rule I made up."

Max reached back, pulling my head forward for a deep kiss. He wrapped his hand gently around mine on his cock, not like he intended to guide my movements, but rather to reassure me he wanted what I was doing by touching my hand. When the kiss broke, his half-lidded, heated gaze bored into mine.

"Can we change that rule?" he asked. All I could do was nod. "There's nowhere else I want to be."

It emboldened me that he welcomed the pleasure I was dying to give him. I drew my hips back, smiling when he grunted in protest. I'd never been an overly confident lover in bed, but Max's rapt approval gave me a sense of sexual freedom I'd never known.

Sliding my free hand down his lower back, I slipped a finger between the svelte skin of his cheeks, massaging his seam. Circling his pucker with my thumb, I slipped another finger along his taint to find his p-spot and applied a hint of pressure.

He tensed at first as though he was shocked, but then let out a satisfied sigh and settled his ass into my hand like he was begging for more. I alternated with circles around his entrance and gentle depressions toward the bundle of nerves inside his taint.

"Fuuuck. That feels good," he practically purred.

It spurred me on. I gripped him tighter, pumping him faster as his hips rocked.

He moaned into our kiss, and then suddenly pulled away. Concern clutched my chest. I watched, baffled, as he spun around to face me and snatched up the bottle of lube as he went.

"What are you doing?"

"I...I don't know," he stammered, squirting some liquid into his hand, his eyes scanning me up and down. "I just..."

He trailed off, scooting forward to wrap his hand around my shaft. Grabbing my slick hand, he brought it to his own cock again, showing me what he wanted.

My nerves died away as Max wrapped his free arm around my shoulders and stroked me in time with my own movements on him.

Shit. My man wanted to double-jerk us.

My man. God. I loved the sound of that and was oddly proud of his adventurous side and eagerness. I smiled, letting him know I approved. Cupping his head, I devoured his mouth as he worked to relieve me of a new wave of desire.

A few moments later, he pulled back from the kiss, teeth bared. "Ah, Jack. I'm gonna come."

Seeing and hearing him barely grasping control over his passion for *me* was just... *wow.*

"Yeah?" I teased, sucking on his lower lip. "I loved it when you said my name that night."

He whimpered, giving me a quick peck, then rested his forehead on mine and whispered, "Jack."

I moaned at the sound of my name on his lips like a desperate plea. He clenched my shoulder, dropping his head to rest on my chest.

His feral cry shot white heat to my navel. "Ah, Jack! Jack!"

Fuck. My name, agonizingly whimpered by him, was a trumpet blast of celebration as his hot seed spilled around our hands. I moved his slackening grip from my shaft and took both of us in my grasp, stroking us together, slickening us with his release. It was electric and heavenly, like we were claiming each other. My orgasm ripped through me, shredding me to pieces as I joined Max in going over the edge.

"Oh. Oh, God. Max," I cried, pumping our pulsing erections together as Max panted and moaned against my chest.

We hung onto each other in the aftermath, regaining our breath and exchanging soft kisses. I loved the way he let me nuzzle him, the way he nuzzled me back, and his sweet, satiated smile.

"Sure you haven't done this before?" I joked, sliding off the bed.

He gave my ass a crack before I saw it coming. "Smartass."

Hmm. Max was an ass-man—a *my* ass-man. My ass approved. Take that, Barbie.

CHAPTER 32
Max

I listened to the sound of Jack running water in his bathroom sink, as I stared at my toes where I sat on the edge of the bed. There was a smile on my face that a crowbar couldn't pry off. That was the most intimate experience of my life, so full of emotion my heart was still trying to remember its rhythm.

Why did I just now think of a man this far into my life? Maybe I just needed the right one. My sex-hazed mind wandered, reliving my favorite moments of what we just shared.

I chuckled, imagining what Morgan would have to say. Rubbing my chin, I realized I should consider what Emma would think. I'd need to. There was no way I was letting Jack go now that he was mine.

Mine. Damn. Another new wonder, but yet he shouldn't be anyone else's *mine.* He'd always been mine. Now he was just *more* mine.

A hand brushed my arm. Jack held out a damp cloth to me.

"Freaking out?" he asked, worry lines marring his forehead.

"Thanks." I took the washcloth from him and shook my head. "No. I said I wouldn't."

"I freaked out the first time, so I wouldn't hold it against you if you did," he said somberly, taking a seat beside me on the mattress.

The topic intrigued me. There was so little I knew about that aspect of his life. "How old were you?"

"Seventeen."

"And how long has it been since...since you last..."

He scooted back, showing off his flexibility by drawing his knees up to his chest. "Almost two years."

I lay down on my side, facing him. He didn't look like he was kicking me out, so I caressed the side of his ass with my fingers and propped my head in my hand.

Two years? What was I doing two years ago when it happened?

Wistfully, I wondered if he had been trying to give up on me, but still, I pitied him for being deprived of intimacy that long. Now that I knew he wanted me, I didn't think I could go two days without touching him.

"I know why it's been so long for me, but why'd you go so long?"

His jaw tensed. He was quiet for such a pause, I thought he might not answer.

"There's only been two MLB players in history to ever come out. One never made it a secret to his team back in the seventies, but that was before the media got too invasive. The other one came out only after he retired. Both of them had their struggles in the clubhouse because of their lifestyle. I don't exactly work in an atmosphere that's conducive to...my *preferences*. I'm owned by the team, under the microscope a hundred and sixty-two days a year, followed every minute by the press, who are just looking for signs of drama or weakness. Anything I do—if I make one wrong move or say the wrong thing—there's a chance either my team or the world could find out. And it wouldn't just affect me. It'd be a shit show for my team, for the entire league. All of that makes it kind of difficult to get close enough to anyone long enough to make something happen."

My jealousy faded, replaced by a troubled sensation after his speech. One—I suspected he had never felt he could trust someone. Two—Was I expendable? Was this temporary for him because of what he felt was at risk for him?

"Your last...why did it end?"

"End?" He scoffed. "It never started. I met him at a bar near the hotel I was staying at."

"You don't sound like it's a good memory. Was it a bad one-night stand?"

I didn't want to know about him with another guy, but I wanted to know what would make him end a relationship, or in this case, have a fling. He chewed on his lip. The frown on his face made me wonder if I'd gone too far. One night of jerking off together and I was acting like I had the right to read his diary. I was so out of practice. I smoothed my hand across his thigh.

"Hey. I'm sorry. I didn't mean to pry."

"No. It's… Uh. I had to pay him," he said, the pain in his eyes telling me he wasn't proud of it.

Pay him? Jack had to *pay someone* to sleep with him? In what world would that even be a possibility?

"You hired a prostitute?"

"No! God, no. We went back to his room and…and he must have figured out who I was even though I said I was just in town on business because afterward he said if I didn't want anyone to find out, I had to pay him."

A queasy surge stirred in my belly. I sat up, seeing red. Who the fuck would do such a thing, and to Jack, of all people?

"What? That's blackmail."

"No, Max." He grimaced. "That's life."

He got up, taking the damp rags from where we tossed them on the floor, and headed to the bathroom. My mind was reeling.

Jack had been muscled by some scumbag while I was wallowing in self-pity. The fact that he looked oddly resigned to it, as though this was just shit he had to accept, infuriated me on his behalf.

"How much did you pay him?"

I was sure he heard me as he disappeared into his bathroom, but he didn't respond. When he came back out, his gaze was focused on the bed, not me. It was clear he was avoiding the topic, but I couldn't let it go.

"How much, Jack?"

He sighed, crawling past me to the other side of the bed. "I paid him what he asked for."

He settled onto his side so his back was facing me. He pulled the blankets up over his hips and arm like he could protect himself from the conversation with them.

"How much?"

"Fifty grand," he mumbled.

"Fifty grand! What the fuck? Why didn't you come to me?"

Pulling the comforter tighter around his shoulder, he grumbled into his pillow. "Pretty sure I make more money than you do, Max."

"That's not what I meant. I'm a fucking lawyer. I eat scumbags like that for breakfast."

Jack let out a sigh and canted his face toward me. His voice was dry and so defeated it sounded foreign.

"If you'd threatened him with a lawsuit, it would have just given him a green light to run to the press and make even more money, then probably some bogus tell-all book. And my career would have been over. It's better this way, Max. Trust me."

"The fuck it is. You can't just let people take advantage of you for the rest of your life. And I doubt your sex life is a breach of contract."

"They'd have benched or traded me, and I'd never get another contract. I wouldn't be a baseball player anymore. I'd just be the gay guy. I'd be a joke."

I gave his shoulder a squeeze through the blanket, somehow having ended up sitting behind him. "You don't know that. We could have talked it over."

"Max, that's...really sweet, but you had your own problems at the time. You didn't need to find out your best friend was gay and potentially caught in a scandal on top of everything else you were dealing with."

Pulling back the blanket, I crawled in behind him. I was fucking fuming that someone had used him so callously, that he felt he had to pay to protect his career and privacy, and that I hadn't been there for him.

"I'm sorry if I made you feel like you couldn't tell me."

"Don't worry about it."

Laying down behind him, I wrapped my arm around him and pulled him close. It was as much to comfort him as it was to calm myself. Nestling my face against his neck, I pressed a kiss there and took a relaxing hit of his glorious scent. It was the scent of a beautiful man that no one should hurt.

"You spending the night?" he hedged.

Shit. I dove right into cuddling without giving a thought to whether he was down with that. He looked like he'd be a cuddler, and I sure as hell didn't want to leave him after that confession.

I drew my arm back and peered over his shoulder. "Why? You kicking me out?"

He chuckled and grabbed my hand, drawing it over his heart. "No. Never."

"Good." I settled back in, smiling against his back like I'd just won a prize and simultaneously obliterated the word temporary from the English language. There would be nothing temporary about this if I could help it. "You can wake me up in the morning to go get Emma," I added casually, nobly using my kid as bait to hook him into non-temporary things. Evil genius strikes again.

Jack ran his hand down my hip and drew my leg between his, eliminating the last of the space between us. *Giant cuddler*, I mused with a smirk as I reveled in being tangled together. Fuck. It was so good to share a bed and body heat with someone again, particularly this someone.

"I never would have expected this," he whispered.

Trailing my hand up and down his stomach, I stopped to interlink his fingers with mine and kiss his shoulder. "Yeah, well, maybe we don't know shit about our expectations. I know I didn't."

His back rumbled against my chest. "Well, whatever happens...tomorrow, I'm glad you came over. Goodnight, Max."

Whatever happens.

He could have meant any number of things, but I suspected it was primarily a warning of his disbelief about my intentions. I curled into him more and pressed one last kiss to his neck.

"Goodnight, Jack."

I'd already vowed to never hurt him again, but my attachment expanded in my chest like when the *Grinch's* heart grew three sizes. I was never going to let anyone else hurt him, either, and I was going to make him feel wanted and cared for—every day.

CHAPTER 33
Jack

The space in time when you're not sure if it's sunlight or moonlight casting a soft glow through the window was upon me. Max Hartwell was still in my bed. The peaceful rise and fall of his chest was a mesmerizing sight in the silence of the early morning hours.

I couldn't believe I fell for a straight man—and that he made love to me last night. Anything this wonderful had to be a fluke.

If, by some miracle, Max didn't question his supposed attraction or feelings, my schedule was sure to place enough strain on a relationship to kill it even before spring training ended. I sighed, resigning myself to cherish the moments for however long the beautiful thing we created last night could endure.

I could no longer resist and reached out, trailing my hand across the smooth skin of his stomach. The top of his happy trail tickled my palm as I watched my lover sleep. Max—*my lover*. The reality of the statement sent a chill down my spine as though I was in an alternate world.

His stomach clenched beneath my touch, making me flinch. He bolted upright in bed, his hair a fine sexy mess from sleep and my fingers. His eyes cracked open, and he scowled in the shadowy blue glow of the light like he was trying to figure out where he was.

Shit. Here we go.

I braced myself for the moment reality hit him, when he'd dash out of here and ignore me again.

Groggy-eyed, he looked down at me. "What time is it?"

"Five o'clock."

He let out a stream of air and collapsed onto the pillow like a felled tree. Tossing his forearm over his eyes, he groaned. "Why the fuck are you up so early?"

He wrapped his other arm around my back, pulling me into him. I blinked stupidly. He seemed to realize he was in *my* bed *with me.*

"Uh. You were snoring." I made a circle over his hip with my finger, resisting the urge to pinch him or myself awake from this dream. "Did you forget where you were?"

He let out a sleepy moan and rolled onto his side, burying his face in my neck. "No. I always wake up like that when Emma spends the night somewhere."

My lip quivered. I pressed a kiss to his forehead and stroked his hair.

Max tilted his head back. "You all right?"

Nodding, I smiled and rolled onto my back. Max really was still in my bed—*on purpose.*

Things that make me cry for five hundred, please, Mr. Trebek.

He propped up on his elbow and interlaced our fingers over my chest. "Hey. What's up?"

"You...actually stayed."

Max frowned, but then he leaned down and pressed a soft lingering kiss to my lips. "Of course, I did. Where else would I want to be?"

This man was going to kill me with sweetness. I smiled in disbelief.

He slid his hand under the blanket, down my stomach. He stilled when his palm glided over my morning erection.

"Shit," he rasped, his eyes looking at me hungrily. "You're hard already."

"I can't help it. You're in my bed."

He smirked and gave me the best morning kiss ever, gripping my shaft as his lips melted into my mouth. When he pulled away, he treated my neck and chest to kisses. My body came alive as he worked his way lower, down my stomach, to the juncture of my thigh.

And *good morning!*

Damn. I could get addicted to *this* Max.

Shit. What was I saying? I was already a Max-junkie, his lips around my cock or not.

When he circled his finger around my hole, I sighed and drew my knees up instinctively, opening myself for him. I had zero problems with letting my body be his wonderland into male pleasure. His finger pressed gently, penetrating me with just the tip. I groaned, pushing into it, craving more.

His hand froze, and he released me from his mouth. I found him looking at me in awe. I reached for the lube and handed it to him, probably looking half-hopeful, half-guilty.

"Here. Man's best friend."

He let out a snort, but took the bottle and made quick work of slickening my entrance and his fingers. The way his gaze ping ponged from mine to where he was touching me was such a turn-on, knowing he craved to see my reactions. He circled my rim, but his lips paused right above the head of my cock.

"Tell me if you don't like it."

I gave his shoulders a squeeze. "Anywhere you touch me, I'll love it."

He looked skeptical, but took me in his mouth again, his hot tongue spiraling around my shaft. My balls drew up tighter as he slowly pressed his finger inside me.

"Yes," I hissed, kneading his hair as I thrust my ass down on his finger, welcoming the stretch, and didn't stop until I felt his knuckle clear my entrance. He gasped around a mouthful of me. Knowing the sensation of me hugging his finger was new to him gave me another burst of hunger, and I let loose a needy whimper. I had never imagined being anyone's first, but I was honored to be his.

He slowly lavished me with his mouth while working his finger in and out. It didn't take him long to realize when he'd found my prostate because he became bolder with his thrusts, likely alerted by my throaty sounds and the way I writhed.

"Yeah, Max," I encouraged him as all my nerve endings bundled, bracing for explosion. My voice had upped its pitch so much, I'd gone all full-Mitchell from *Modern Family*, but I didn't care. "Oh. That's it. Right...there. Uh, huh, oh! Oh, yeah."

I burst. Waves of satiation rippled through me. Amid my euphoria, I heard Max coughing. His hand was to his mouth. I could see his eyes glistening in the dim light. He freaking choked himself again on my dick. I let loose a laugh, unable to help myself.

He swatted the side of my ass with a *crack*. The sting sent a delicious shiver up my spine as the last of my orgasm hung on.

"You keep fucking laughing at me, I'm not going to do it anymore," he warned all growly, but was smirking at me.

I chuckled and closed my eyes, shuddering again from the heady pleasure in my limbs. I moaned when I felt Max's hands glide up my thighs.

He whispered, "I want to feel what you're feeling."

I opened my eyes to him watching me, his gaze filled with wonder and hunger. I nodded and tilted my chin to the place beside me. "Lie down."

Once he was situated, I knelt between his legs. The sight of him licking his lips as he watched me coat my fingers in lube was a picture I'd put to memory.

I slid my finger through his seam and circled his rim. He let out a shuddery breath and widened his legs. Seeing him trust me with his body filled me with possessiveness. Rubbing the underside of his thigh, I relished in the feel of the soft hair that peppered his skin as I dipped my head and licked the precum from his tip.

Each of his sexy gasps was pure motivation, as I adored his cock with my mouth. When I pressed the tip of my finger just inside his entrance, he clenched around me.

Releasing him from my mouth, I lowered my lips to his sack and whispered, "Breathe."

I licked the circumference of one of his testicles, eliciting a groan from him, and felt him relax around me. When I took his length in my mouth again, he eased down onto my hand, taking me deep inside his tight heat with a feral sound. His fingers burrowed into my hair, and soon he was thrusting into my mouth and down on my finger. I peered up to find him watching me.

"God, baby. You're good at that," he whispered.

I snickered around my mouthful of him at the endearment he had grimaced over just last night. It's funny how sex can change a person's vocabulary.

"What?" he asked.

I drew off him and repeated, "*Baby.*"

"Fuck off." He laughed, but it broke off when I crooked my finger to hit his prostate.

A little too pleased with myself, I whispered just before taking him to the back of my throat, "Not until you come for me, *baby.*"

"Uh, Jack. Jesus Christ!"

I glanced up to check on him, stilling my mouth on his erection. Panting, he gripped my head, urging me to continue with a twitch of his hips. "No. Don't stop. Please, don't stop."

Happily, I obliged, enjoying the delirium in his expressions. He hardened even more in my mouth. I knew he was close when he showered me with a symphony of verbal delights.

"Oh, Jack. Baby, so good. So fucking good. Oh, holy... I'm there!"

His heady, salty taste filled my mouth. I drank him down, still grazing his prostate to draw out his pleasure.

When I came up to cover him with my chest some moments later, he was panting and quivering. I wrapped my arms around him and rolled us to our sides, kissing him to be a guest in the haze of his comedown.

"Jack. Holy hell," he panted, clinging to my chest as a tremor shook his body.

"Shit. I'm jealous," I whispered, kissing his cheek.

"Fuck. You should be," he croaked, pressing his lips to my chest as he shuddered again.

He let out a soft moan. I squeezed him tighter and murmured into his hair, "You okay?"

"No," he grumbled.

Alarm bells went off in my head. I snapped my head back to check on him. "Did I hurt you?"

"No, but you should have kissed me three years ago."

I chuckled, but it was short-lived when I recalled sensitive memories. "You wouldn't have been ready. *I* wouldn't have been ready either after losing Lainey. She was probably the best friend I ever had."

He screwed his neck back and scowled at me. "Hey. What about me?"

My tension dissipated, seeing him pout over something that could have darkened the mood. "*Second* best friend."

His hand came down hard on my ass cheek. I flinched, sending my hips crashing into his—the perfect cocktail of pleasure and pain.

"Ouch!" I laughed. "It's true! No contest. Lainey was way more easy-going. You're a fucking crab-ass."

"Oh, yeah?" He arched a brow. "Then why..." He indicated us being in bed.

"Because you're fucking hot when you're crabby."

CHAPTER 34
Max

The open cornfields, long empty of their harvest, now snow-covered, painted the landscape on either side of the road. The heat from my seat warmer
soothed the slight but welcome soreness in my ass, staving off the winter
chill. My belly was full of French toast and bacon that wouldn't have taken
as long to make if Jack hadn't cooked it while wearing nothing except his
underwear. Breakfast would never be the same now that I'd tattooed that
image in my mind.

Lazily, I ran my thumb over his knuckles, where our hands were joined
over the center console. I could smell his clean, soapy scent from our
shower this morning. If this was going to be my life now, I was eager to be
a participant.

Glancing over at the big sexy man in the passenger seat as I drove to
my in-laws to pick up Emma, I noticed like the good stalker that I was, he'd
been staring out the window for a while. There was nothing amiss about
that—even I enjoyed silence—but he was chewing on this thumb.

I gave his hand a squeeze. "Awful quiet over there."

Jack turned and smiled, but it looked a bit forced. "You're sure this is
okay? Showing up with me?"

"You've met Bob and Ellen plenty of times, and Emma talks about you to them every time she sees them. They know we're friends."

"Yeah, but...we've never showed up at their house *together*. What if... they can tell?" he hedged, squeezing my hand.

I gave him a wry smile. "I'm not going to hold your hand in front of them, if that's what you're worried about."

He rolled his eyes at me, and I got a twinge of offense at the thought of holding my hand being so easily dismissed.

"I meant what if they can tell from our body language or the way we look at each other?"

I fixed my eyes on the road, realizing I had a new milestone to tackle in my life, one I never had to consider before—coming out. I had to come out? That was what it was called, right? But the words...

The thought of having to announce that I was with a man was offensive—the *announcing* part, not the *man* part. That entire phrase—*coming out*—it was so...stigmatic.

I didn't have to make a production of telling my parents I liked girls when I hit puberty. Why did I owe anyone an explanation of who I liked now? Why did it have to be a production or even a conversation? I should just be able to walk into anywhere I wanted, holding Jack's hand. I'd found what was right for me, *who* was right for me—it defied every feeling inside me to conceal it.

I sighed, though, knowing Bob and Ellen didn't exactly fit into a don't-bat-an-eye-about-anything-new-Max-does box. I was married to their daughter. I didn't necessarily owe them an explanation that I was dating again, especially after they set me up. However, I did respect them as the parents of my dead wife and would like to delicately inform them someday that I was seeing someone—a *Jack Spears someone*.

"Well, we'll just have to make sure not to give each other sex-eyes while we're there," I finally said.

"*Sex*-eyes?" he asked, his brow furrowing.

I gave him my best smolder-y look, which wasn't difficult as I took him in. I threw in a playful eyebrow wriggle, and he cracked up, shaking his head.

"Stop! Whatever you're doing, just stop."

"What? You don't like my sex-eyes?" I laughed.

"First off, no one calls them *sex-eyes*. It's called *fuck-me* eyes, and second—your *sex-eyes* look like murder-eyes."

"What? How so?" I knew I was new in the land of man-love, but what the fuck?

"That's the way you were looking at me all last week. It was freaking me out. It reminded me of the movie *Hannibal* when Mason Verger asked his assistant the basis of Dr. Lecter's obsession with Clarice. *'Does he want to fuck her or eat her or what?'"*

"Wait. So...you thought I wanted to eat you?"

He chuckled. "It was a metaphor for murder."

"You thought I wanted to murder you?"

"Or...fuck me. I wasn't sure. You looked kind of scary."

"Oh, my God. I feel like we should pull over and have a serious discussion about this."

"No way! This is like the perfect spot for a murder."

"Oh, for the love of God. I did not have murder-eyes! Shit. For a guy whose job it is to read signals from a catcher all day, you're shit at reading signs."

Jack laughed. "Uh, or maybe next time something's on your mind, you should squat down and flash me hand signals in front of your junk, since you clearly have no control over your facial features."

The mental image I conjured wasn't a good one and had me cursing under my breath. "Shit."

"What is it?" Jack scanned the horizon like he thought I spotted a driving hazard.

"I just realized you spend literally hundreds of hours a year staring at Hooper's dick."

For some reason, that was hilarious to him, judging by the way he roared. "He wears a catcher's vest and the signals are just *below* his dick, though he'd probably argue about that."

I answered him with a glare. No wonder he was single. I had feelings. Damn it.

"Aw! Max. Are you jealous?"

"Why would I be if you're *not* staring at his dick?"

"Because you're giving me murder-eyes again."

"Oh, for fuck's sake! If there's no such thing as sex-eyes, then there's no such thing as murder-eyes. What the hell were we talking about, anyway?"

Jack chuckled and then sighed. "Bob and Ellen."

"Right. Well, if or when they notice, they notice." I shrugged. "We'll figure it out when it happens."

"Max, it's better if it doesn't happen."

My entire body tensed. "What are you saying? You don't want to do this?"

"That's not what I meant. I just think it's better to play it safe, otherwise the world will come crashing down on us because of who I am."

Seriously, I couldn't be the only one who knew. How could he live like this?

"Does your family know?"

He was back to staring out his window, chewing on his thumb. He nodded without looking at me.

"And are they cool with it?"

"My father hasn't talked to me in ten years. My mom has to sneak phone calls to me, so she doesn't remind him I exist. Carrie's been great about everything since day one, but it kills me she's stuck in the middle like her brother is a ghost."

I wanted to slam on the brakes and pull him into my arms, and then drive to Indiana to beat his father's ass. Instead, I snatched his hand and kissed his knuckles. "I'm sorry. That's his loss."

He shrugged, fucking shrugged like *eh, that's life*. Meanwhile, I was grinding my molars and trying not to squeeze his hand too hard. How could anyone hurt this man or make him feel like he didn't matter and couldn't make his own choices?

"You were dealing with all this shit and still showed up at my house with a smile on your face to take care of me and Emma," I said it more to myself.

"You two make it easy to smile."

I squeezed his hand because what else could I do? I knew most everyone learned at a young age that life isn't fair, but listening to Jack open up sure reinforced that lesson.

Jack took a knee in the entryway of Bob and Ellen's house, a signature move by any man who wanted to avoid getting dinged in the nuts by a child barreling toward them. Emma crashed into him, latching her arms around his shoulders, making me a puddle of mush at the sight.

"Uncle Jack! What are you doing here?"

"You said you missed me," he said matter-of-factly, chuckling at her enthusiasm.

Ellen leaned against the door frame, arms folded, an amused smile on her face. "Jack?" she cooed. "When are you going to have some kids of your own?"

It was a motherly request, the kind people who were settled in life made when they wanted to see others settled. It was an innocent enough remark, but I winced on his behalf.

Jack seemed unfazed, though, because he didn't hesitate. "When Emma gets sick of me. You sick of me yet, Emma?"

"No, but if you have kids, then I could be their aunt and babysit for you."

Now *that* sentiment I could smile at—Emma claiming him and offering him assistance. I imagined little Jacks throwing around baseballs. It was sad he wouldn't get that chance. I now better understood his attachment to Emma.

"No. I'm your uncle," he corrected her, "so my kids would be your cousins."

"Oh, yeah. I guess." She shrugged. "Well, I want three cousins. Two boys and a girl."

Jack belted out a laugh as he rose. I rolled my eyes because sentiment just got flushed down the toilet like a nail-polish-covered cotton ball and gurgled back up as awkward territory. I gestured to Emma.

"Okay, come on now, kiddo. Let's get you loaded up."

When she disappeared down the hall to fetch her things, I was completely blind-sided by Ellen's conspiratorial whisper. "So, Max? Tell me all about last night."

I nearly choked and swung a peek at Jack. "Last night?"

"Yes. How did it go? What did you think of Renee? Isn't she a doll?"

Last night.

All I could think about, all I *wanted* to think about from last night, was the look on Jack's face when I made him climax... twice, but I didn't want to think about *that* in front of my mother-in-law.

My cheeks heated, and a babbling sound came out of my mouth. I glanced at Jack for help, cues, or to be transported to another galaxy, maybe—anything other than having this conversation with Ellen. He folded his arms and gave me this saucy, '*yeah, how was the date, Max*?' look, which was not fucking helpful.

But shit. Yeah. I deserved it.

"It was...uh. She was nice," I managed.

"I know! Isn't she? She reminds me of Lainey so much."

Wow. Not really. Nothing about Renee Thomas reminded me of Lainey. I was suddenly deeply sad for Ellen. Was she clinging to Lainey and trying to replace her, or was she clinging to me and thought she needed to fix me out of some morbid sense of obligation?

Jesus. I didn't need fixing.

"Did you make plans to see each other again?" she added, looking anxious.

My skin wanted to crawl off my body and abandon me. When I realized I was rubbing the back of my neck and holding my breath, it hit me.

Why the hell was I trying to dance around this thing? I was caught in this awkward pocket of air between the person who was lighting the way to a shiny future, still so new and fragile I was terrified one wrong move would break it, and another who was making more boxes for me to check.

Jack's sassy posture had withered. He was now nibbling on the corner of his thumb, while Ellen stared at me, starry-eyed. Bob walked in, throwing me a nod, and slung his arm over Ellen's shoulders. All eyes were on Max. Wonderful.

Now was not the time to tell them I couldn't see anyone because I hoped I already was, but even if I knew without a doubt Jack was fully onboard, I wasn't about to make that announcement with Emma around. Nine-year-olds needed news delivered in a different way than fifty-something-ers.

"Look, Ellen," I started sagely. "Renee seemed...lovely, but I don't see it going anywhere for me."

"Oh, really? Are you sure? Maybe you just need to get to know her a little better."

"Ellen, let the man be," Bob said, slapping me on the shoulder. Thank Christ. "Can't you see he's not ready? Don't push him."

"I'm sorry, Max. I just don't want you to be alone."

Ellen's pout and sympathetic puppy eyes had me squirming. Fuck my life. It crossed my mind to spit it out that I wasn't alone. I hated how Jack was left standing here, like the conversation had nothing to do with him. Had he had to do this in the past? Pretend he wasn't with someone? I didn't want to do that to him.

"It's fine. I really appreciate your intentions, but I think I'd be more comfortable meeting someone on my own. No pressure that way. You know?"

She looked like a large-mouth bass, her mouth floundering open. "Oh, I didn't mean..."

Emma came skipping down the hallway with her bag slung on her shoulder. Between the chatter of asking if she had everything and the goodbyes, my dating status was forgotten.

Twenty minutes down the road, I finally stopped white-knuckling the steering wheel. Jack and I had done the whole no-talking thing already the last few weeks. It was supposed to be over. Where were we, though? Right back to not talking, at least not about things I wanted to talk about; not while Emma was in the car.

Was he okay after Ellen's questions? Was he okay with how I responded? Were we okay?

"Are you guys done fighting now?" Emma called from the backseat.

I freaking hoped so.

"I told you, kiddo, we weren't fighting."

"But did you apologize?"

I squeezed the steering wheel, contemplating the surprising lack of gypsies in Illinois. Jack gave me a sideways glance and asked neither of us in particular, "Apologize? For what?"

Emma was quicker. "He said he did something bad to hurt your feelings."

I couldn't really be mad at her for throwing me under the bus because, well, that summed it up. I bit the inside of my lip and sneaked a peek at the best friend I really wanted to get far away from my in-laws and child, preferably alone. Much to my relief, he smirked.

"Yeah, Bug. He apologized." Under his breath, he added, *"A lot."*

Speaking in innuendo in front of Emma with Jack—I could add that to the list of new things in my life. Let me say, it did not help my big-baseball-player-kidnapping desire.

"Good," Emma replied staunchly. "Because I was mad at him."

"*I* wasn't, so you don't need to be, either," Jack said, throwing me a wink I wanted to put in my pocket.

"Can you stay for dinner?" she asked.

"Yeah, Jack?" I parroted. "'*Can you stay for dinner?*'"

"Sure. I think I'd like that."

The smile he flashed me gave me the hope that taking him to my in-laws hadn't been a total failure. I had promised him a date, and so far, all I'd done was take him to an inquisition where I couldn't acknowledge him.

"Oh, hey! Dad? How was your date?"

Emma's curious eyes peered back at me through my rear-view mirror. Jack had his saucy eyebrow thing going on again, but looked like he was waiting to enjoy whatever asinine thing would come out of my mouth. Sadistic bastard.

I blew out a breath because who wants to talk to their kid about their dating life? At least she seemed open to the possibility of me dating. That was a good thing.

"Uh, it was okay."

"Just okay?"

This kid. Thank you for passing down the tenacious genes, Lainey!

"It was fine. We went to dinner."

"Can I meet her?"

"Uh, Emma, I don't think I'm going to see her again."

"Why not?" I could see the dimple in between her eyebrows through the mirror.

"She...just wasn't the right one for me."

"Was she ugly?"

I laughed out loud, and Jack made a noise, hiding his mouth with his hand. "No."

"Was she mean?"

"No."

"Did she smell bad?"

"What?" I turned my head to check if it was a nine-year-old or a gossip columnist in the backseat. "No," I clarified.

"Did she make you laugh like Mom did?"

Something bloomed in my chest that Emma was taking such an interest in my happiness. It felt wrong to not give her questions any thought.

Renee Thomas had been charming. We'd laughed over the kind of silly observations people make in restaurants and bars. They had been throw-away comments and jokes, though. There was only one other person who made me laugh the way Lainey had, so I gave her my answer, "No, kiddo. Not really."

"Oh. Well, you shouldn't go out with someone unless they make you happy."

I knew it would be one of those comments I would remember the rest of my life as a proud smile spread across my face over her wisdom. "That's good advice. I'll remember that."

I didn't have to speak in innuendo to get my point across. One look at Jack, and the smile he returned, told me he understood.

CHAPTER 35
Jack

I had sat on this couch hundreds of times before, watching this television with Emma and Max. It shouldn't have felt weirder now than when I was crushing on Max and had to play it cool, but it felt like a scarlet letter was sewn on my sweatshirt.

Emma was sitting between us, leaning against Max. The three of us had our feet kicked up on the coffee table like it was a movie marathon, and we had no plans to move for the next seventy-two hours. Comfortable, right?

Wrong! The man who wouldn't talk to me last week was drawing little circles on my shoulder every few minutes where his arm was outstretched over the back of the couch. Finger circles should not be sexual or naughty, but when there's a nine-year-old between you and you remember where those fingers circled the night before…

I might have to hurt him.

Correction. He was going to hurt my dick if he didn't stop touching me because there was only so much room in these blue jeans.

Glancing down at Bug, I was reminded of another dilemma. She smiled up at me with those wicked smart eyes of hers, and I swore her gaze just flicked from Max's fingers. Did she think it was funny her dad was touching me like that? Was she just glad I was back around? *What* was that look for?

Max gave my shoulder a squeeze and guided Emma off his side. "I'm going to get dinner started," he announced, getting up.

"You want some help?" I offered.

"Nope. I've got it. You two just relax."

I assumed his smile was meant to reassure me, but it did the opposite. I cast Emma a suspicious look. "Should we be afraid?"

"*Very* afraid."

Twenty minutes later, I was halfway through folding a basket of clothes and quizzing Emma on state capitals to keep her mind sharp over the break, when Max came back into the room.

"What are you doing?" he asked, sounding aghast.

"Studying."

"No, I mean, what's with the laundry?"

"It needed to get done. I can help her study and fold at the same time."

He stepped forward, toward my place on the couch, looking at me like I said bacon was outlawed and unceremoniously tossed the stack of Emma's folded clothes in the basket. I gaped, watching him snatch the basket up and start out of the room with it.

Emma and I exchanged befuddled looks. Her nose twitched, and she peered into the kitchen.

"Dad, are you burning something?"

Max stopped in his tracks, his face going slack. "No."

"You sure you don't want some help in there?" I asked when he dropped the basket and hurried into the kitchen.

"No. I've got it. You just...stay there and enjoy yourself."

A jangle of frying pans being shuffled around on the stovetop, followed by a stream of curses floated through the doorway. Emma met my skeptical thoughts with a look to match. Tilting my head toward the ruckus, she smirked at my suggestion.

We stopped in the doorway, surveying the scene. Max was trying to pry burnt steaks off a frying pan to flip them over. I cringed, hearing the scrape of the tongs against the pan's surface as he used the utensil like a snow shovel to free the underside of the charred meat. He glanced over, and I had to bite my lip when his pissed off expression turned more tender when he spotted us. The man was too damn cute.

"Hey, uh. It'll be a little longer."

Ignoring his delusions of saving those poor steaks, I glanced at Emma. "Quesadillas?"

"Yeah." She nodded and headed to the fridge.

Sidling up to the stove, I hip-checked Max so I could shut off the burner and remove the frying pan. Another one bites the dust. He better not find where I hide my good pans from him over here.

"Hey, what the hell? I'm still cooking that!"

"Uh, I think it's cooked enough."

Max spun around and fixed his gaze on Emma, who was pulling chicken breasts and tortilla shells out of the fridge. "And what are you doing? Put that back! I thought you liked steaks?"

"I do, but…"

"But what?"

I'd already started drizzling olive oil in a clean pan for the chicken when he turned back around and grabbed my wrist. "Hey. Knock it off. You're supposed to be relaxing."

I was? How interesting. The thought of Max wanting to coddle me made my stomach flip. Emma pulled out the cutting board and set it on the island, along with an onion and bag of tortilla chips she'd squirreled out of the pantry. Max looked so damn adorable, the way he glared at her.

"What is this? A mutiny?"

"Dad, you know Uncle Jack's a better cook."

I hid my smirk at one-upping him. He sighed and ran a hand through his hair. "I see how you are." He snagged the bag of tortilla chips from her and pretended to pout. "I'm never cooking for you again."

"Really?" Her face lit up like we just said we were going to *Disneyland*.

He head-locked her and growled. Undeterred, she tried to bite his chip, but he kept teasing her, keeping it just out of reach of her mouth. I laughed, watching him shove one in her mouth as he released her and ruffled her hair to let her get to dicing.

"You sure you know how to do that?" he asked when she picked up the paring knife.

"Yeah. Uncle Jack taught me."

I got a dubious look. "Fine, but don't chop your finger off."

His body heat hugged me when he sidled up beside me, peering over my shoulder with a pointed stare as I started grilling the chicken. He was closer than we'd ever stood in this kitchen while Emma was in the room. Maybe it was wishful thinking, but I could almost hear his dirty thoughts because that intense look certainly wasn't aimed at the chicken.

"Remember what I said about you looking crabby?" I asked, without taking my eyes off the seasoning I was sprinkling on the meat.

"Yeah?"

Conspicuously, I adjusted the front of my jeans. "Yeah. Well, I need to concentrate, so…" I shooed him with my hand.

He smirked and patted me on the back, but gave my arm a lingering squeeze before he walked away. I finished cooking and Max stayed out of the way—for the most part. When it came time to sit down at the table, Emma trotted back to the kitchen but then reappeared with one of the charred steaks on a plate and set it down in front of Max with an impish grin on her face.

"Very funny," he grumbled and poked her in the ribs.

"Can I go to Uncle Jack's after school again now?" she asked after we'd started to dig in.

Max looked at me for permission. I'd always felt like his equal, but now it seemed I'd been promoted, unless I was reading him wrong. I ticked up the corner of my mouth to give him my answer.

He must have understood because he told Emma, "Yeah, if you quit insulting my cooking."

She rolled her eyes. "Good, because Jessica can get annoying. Matt says she's mad because she didn't get to do a solo at the Christmas concert."

Max perked up. "Matt? Is that your boyfriend?"

"No. We're just friends. He's got all the Percy Jackson movies *and* has a dog." Max rolled his eyes at the d-word, but Emma wouldn't be deterred. "*And* the same karaoke game Uncle Jack has." She shifted her attention to me. "But Dad won't let me go over there because he's *a boy*."

"*No boys*," Max barked.

"Dad, gross. We're just friends."

Max's nostrils flared like his crystal ball was giving off toxic gas. I had missed this father-daughter bickering and being a part of it. Maybe I'd still get to keep being a part of it after all. It was still too serendipitous to believe.

After dinner, we gathered up the dishes and loaded the dishwasher. I gave Emma her goodnight hug, and Max followed her upstairs to tuck her in. This is where it became unfamiliar territory. In the past, I'd clean up, tell Emma goodnight, and then leave. Sometimes, if Max offered me a beer, I'd hang around and bullshit for a while. What was the protocol after your straight best friend goes down on you and spent the night spooning you in your bed?

The discarded laundry basket caught my attention like a lifeline. It was a good excuse to linger. I went to work folding and had just finished when I heard the floor creak.

Max stood in the doorway with his hands on his hips. Didn't he know that look didn't scare me anymore? I plopped the last stack of clothes in the basket and held up my palms in surrender.

"There. All done."

"This didn't go as I planned. You two are dangerous together."

"We've got to keep you on your toes." I stood up and tugged down the hem of my sweatshirt. "It was a nice time, Max. Thanks for dinner."

"Yeah, well, quesadillas are just one of my many specialties."

I let out an airy laugh, realizing I was nervous. Were we dating? I mean, he said he wanted to do *this*, me and him. My esophagus was choking me suddenly. I hadn't dated in a little over six years, and I wasn't as famous then. I had no idea how to navigate dating.

All I *did* know was that I wanted to hold him and kiss him and that my palms were ridiculously sweaty. How sexy was that? And how did one date his best friend and act in a house where he'd only acted as a friend? I might as well have been on Mars. I could not be the one to push this, so instead of us, I picked a safe topic.

"You, uh, want me to bring Emma over here after school or keep her at my place until you get home?"

"Whatever works best for you."

I glanced at the clock without even registering what time it was and headed around the couch. If Max didn't want to make a move, that was fine. This was all new to him. Fine can be translated to *this sucks*.

"Alright. Well, I know you've got to get up early, so I'll get out of your hair. Thanks for today. It was really...nice." Gah! I sounded like Max talking about his date. He was better than a Renée Thomas, I hoped he knew that.

"Next time, I'll get carryout," he said with a coy smile, knocking my arm with his elbow as we walked down the hall to the back door.

I snorted like Carrie. Seriously, was that a genetic thing?

Max stopped in the sunroom with his hands still stuffed in his pockets, staring like he didn't know what to say. Pockets were officially stupid.

I leaned in and kissed his cheek, wondering if it seemed as awkward to him as it did me. My face was on fire, but I wanted to let him know how much it meant that he'd spent the day with me.

"That was...the best date I've ever had. Thank you."

He let out a scoff and frowned. "Then whoever you dated was pretty bad at spoiling you."

Wow. Okay. I could live with that for tonight. "I'll see you tomorrow?"

"Yeah. Yeah, for sure."

We both stood there like we were constipated, lips parted, each of us holding our breath. I was being so freaking needy, but not knowing what tomorrow would bring was excruciating.

"Well, goodnight," I said when I couldn't take looking like a stalker any longer.

"Goodnight."

I walked to the patio door, grinding my teeth. Maybe the whole in-law visit had scared him off. Maybe it was too weird for him to see us as more than friends. Maybe he...

"Jack!"

I let go of the door handle at his urgent tone and spun around. His expression was conflicted, looking like he was about to tell me to get used to Barbie's hand. His hands came out of his pockets, and he flexed his fingers, scanning my face as he chewed his lip. When he took a step forward, I realized what I was really seeing, so I moved too. We met, nearly slamming into each other.

"Max," I whispered as his hands latched onto my waist because I was so desperate, I couldn't say more.

Our mouths crashed into each other, and all my worry evaporated in a red-hot inferno of lips and breaths and hands. We turned, trying to get at each other like starving hyenas. My back hit something solid. I heard the beer bottles in the spare fridge rattle behind me.

Breaking away from the kiss, I glanced at the ceiling, and panted out a warning. "Emma."

Max's finger traced my jaw, and he murmured in front of my lips. "She won't get up. Do you *need* to go?"

My head ricocheted back and forth. "No."

He dusted a soft kiss across my lips. I could still taste him and wanted more.

"Do you *want* to go?"

His blue eyes waited for my verdict with anticipation. Max wanted me. Still wanted me. I smiled like a fool, kissed him, and shook my head.

"No."

"Then don't."

He took my hand and started back down the hallway. When we reached his room, I didn't flinch this time when the door clicked shut, or when he locked it.

No. Seeing Max lean against his bedroom door with sex-eyes for me? Well, best date ever.

"I need to salvage this date."

Jack stepped forward and cupped my face. "It was a great date, Max."

"Can I still try to salvage it, anyway?" I countered, running my hands up his sides, getting him to chuckle.

"What did you have in mind?"

I swallowed against a giant lump in my throat. That was a good question. I hadn't planned farther than getting the object of my desire alone in my room.

"Well, I might need your help with that."

"How so?"

"Can you...show me something *you* have in mind?"

Jack peeled his shirt off because he was a cruel human being and tossed it on the floor. I grunted like a caveman.

"I have *you* in mind," he said, threading his fingers through my hair. "Anything with you in mind. Do whatever you want."

"Even if what I want is...severely limited to only what we've done?"

"Max?"

"Yeah?"

"Kiss me."

"Okay," I said like a hypnotized robot, and lost myself in his kiss.

When his hands drew my ass in closer, pressing me into him, I was a goner. I moaned into his mouth and broke away to tear off my sweater.

"I was dying to kiss you all day," I breathed into his ear.

"You drive me crazy just being in the same room," he whispered, cupping the front of my jeans.

I made something like a growling noise at the contact and treated myself to two big handfuls of his solid backside. "I love your ass."

"I noticed." He laughed.

I worked the button of his jeans free and slid my hand over the bulging soft cotton of his boxer briefs. "Love touching you," I murmured against his jaw, and caught a hint of his soapy scent at the base of his neck. "Love smelling you," I whispered there. "Fuck. Sorry. That sounded creepy."

His laughter rumbled against my chest. "I love your smell, too." He rubbed his nose just below my ear, making me shiver, and then darted his tongue along the sensitive skin there. "And your taste. *All* your tastes," he clarified, gripping the iron rod begging to be freed from my jeans, sending sparks to my balls.

"Fuuuck. Jack."

My hands became greedy thieves, tugging his pants and shorts down over his hips. We seemed to be on the same page because he helped me with mine at the same speed. His palm wrapped around me, hugging me in his grip. I'd anticipated that touch so much today, I gasped at the relief of finally having it.

Jack released me and stepped back. "I'm sorry. I'm trying to hold back for you. You'll tell me if anything's too much?"

Was he shitting me? I almost wanted to ask him if he was sure *he* was gay.

"Jack, my dick is pointing straight at you. Don't you fucking dare hold back on me. Just because I don't know what I'm doing doesn't mean I don't know what I want." But then an ugly thought occurred to me. "Unless…you don't want this."

He stared at me, and the confidence I had when I walked in here teetered, but then his jaw set. I swear it was like a transformation watching the tension lines in his face fade and his eyes fill with unbridled hunger as his chest rose. Like 'cautious Jack' had just turned to 'bold Jack' and, oh, was I eager to meet him, even if I did have dancing butterflies in my stomach.

He kicked his pants free from his feet, never taking his eyes off me. Sitting on my bed in all his naked glory, he scooted back and crooked his finger at me. "Get over here, handsome."

Damn. Sometimes venting frustrations paid off.

"Okay," I croaked, kicked my pants free, and crawled onto the mattress after him.

"Look at you," he whispered hypnotically, running a hand up his cock.

I shook my head, thinking, *'No way. I'm looking at you.'* "You look good in my bed," I told him.

"Stay there," he said, holding up his hand and getting to his knees.

I froze on all fours, shivering as he moved to my side and slid a hand down my hip. He shifted again, settling behind me. His hands ran up the back of my thighs to trace the curve of my ass. Arousal and anxiety bubbled inside me at the sensations and unknowns.

"What...what are you doing?"

"Seeing if I love your ass, too." He pressed his lips to the top of my ass, and I felt his palm circle gently over my balls.

I shuddered as he kissed and licked his way down my backside. I was so exposed. This gave new meaning to the word *trust*.

"Well, what's the verdict?" I rasped.

"Pretty sure I'd like to keep it." His warm breath ghosted the seam of my ass as he said it, and the tip of his hot, slippery tongue made a slow swipe between my cheeks, causing a jolt to rack through me.

"Okay?" he asked.

"Yes," I hissed, settling on my elbows because every muscle in my body had suddenly given up on life. The outline of his smile pressed against one of my cheeks. He *should* be proud of himself. All feelings of being exposed had left me. There was still a hint of self-consciousness because, *hello*, this was my ass. Everyone knows what happens back there.

Was it hairy? What if I passed gas? Did I stink? I decided that was Jack's freaking problem to figure out as my skin prickled when his teeth nipped at one cheek. I was no longer responsible for whatever happened back there right now and would plead the fifth.

His tongue lapped again, making me moan. It circled my hole and then he kissed it. I planted my cheek on the bedspread, groaning as I widened my legs, and jutted my ass higher in the air in case he had any terrible ideas like stopping.

The wet tip of his tongue swirled around my pucker once more. The next thing I knew, there was the slight pressure of an intrusion breaching me. I let out a carnal sound that probably meant *what-the-fuck* and *yes-more-please* in Klingon.

"Jack! Mother of God. Holy. Fuck!"

He nipped at my cheek again, making my entire body tremor. When he reached around under my waist and stroked me as he licked again, my eyes rolled back into my head. I was on a fast-track to *Climaxville*.

"Fuck. Stop. Stop!"

"Shit. I'm sorry," he said, laying a hand over my ass. "Sorry! Are you okay?"

Scrambling to my knees, I spun around and grabbed him, tackling him into the pillows. "I don't want to come yet, you bastard," I panted, scooting down between his legs. "I'm supposed to be salvaging this date, not losing my mind."

Jack widened his legs for me even as he laughed. "Max, I was enjoying myself. Don't worry about... Oh, yes!"

My tongue found his pucker and delivered some payback. After I made a sweep of his circumference, I pressed a kiss there. "Yeah?" I taunted him, delighted by his noises. "How do you like it?"

He snorted, but then gasped when I made another pass. "Fuck. What do you think?"

I ran my hands up the muscles in the backs of his thighs, over the smooth skin around his hips, to his stomach as he gripped my hair. My hand found what I was searching for and wrapped around him, giving his cock a tight slide as I explored the unknown, pressing the tip of my tongue inside him. His scent was so intoxicating, and I couldn't believe how high I was from tasting him.

He mewled and arched his hips, lifting his ass higher to chase my mouth. "Oh. Shit. You're a fast learner."

His words were a golden crown on my head. I delved faster, deeper, in awe as his body hugged around me. Giving him pleasure was as addictive as receiving it.

"Max! You're going to make me come. Get up here."

I ignored him with a grunt and pumped his cock harder. His palm wrapped over mine.

"Please, Max. I want to come *with* you," he begged.

"I thought you liked it?" I teased with the tip of my tongue.

"That's the problem."

"Then enjoy it and come for me," I said, burying my face again in his heady heat.

"Fuck. If you don't get up here, I'm going to hide Mr. Sparkles in your room every day for a week!"

That threw a giant barricade in the middle of the road to *Climaxville*. I popped up and glared at him. "Okay. You're going to have to pick a different safe word. Like *literally* anything other than *that*."

Jack smirked, leaned up, hooked his hands under my armpits, and hoisted me quickly and hard onto his chest. I landed gracelessly with an *oomph*. His hand came around and pressed my ass into his hips.

"I don't know," he purred. "Seems like that one was pretty effective."

"Fuck off." I chuckled because him and that damn creepy Sock Monkey. His legs spread and settled around my hips. I groaned when I realized what he was doing, grinding us together.

"That feels good," I whispered, kissing his jaw.

"Yes. It does." He sighed into my mouth and slid a lazy finger down my seam, not exploring, just holding it there like he was claiming me with his touch. The overpowering urge to be claimed by him lit me up. Writhing against him, I deepened our kiss. How could this man want *me*?

"I was such a jerk." I came up panting and peppered his neck with my lips. "I'm so sorry."

He turned my face and nipped at my lower lip. "No more of that. Please."

We shared an unspoken message in that look. The past was in the past. I kissed him with all my wishes for the future.

His hands clasped my hips and helped me rock against him. Our cocks, pressed between our bellies, slickened by our arousal, created a burst of euphoria with every trace of friction.

I hadn't known it was possible to be so overwhelmed by desire. Whimpering into our kiss, I was determined to give him all the pleasure he wanted for as long as he wanted. I broke free, needing to taste and touch him everywhere. I showered the underside of his jaw, his cheek, his neck, his earlobe with kisses, running my fingers through his hair.

"Jack. Jack," I breathed, practically drunk on him. "I missed you at Christmas. I miss you when you're on the road."

He pressed a long kiss to my shoulder, rocking up with more force into me. "Max," he practically wept.

It was baffling to see the way I affected him, not just his body, but his emotions. His expression was so raw. It was humbling how grateful he looked to have me. I stroked his face and looked him in those beautiful eyes.

"I'm going to take care of you now, not the other way around anymore."

Jack's face pinched up, and he sucked in a breath. He cupped my jaw in both hands and poured himself into a kiss, but then he pulled quickly away and buried his face in my neck where I heard him sniffle.

I wrapped my arms around him tight, choked by a wave of protectiveness as we rocked against each other. My climax hit me like a freight train.

"Uh, Jack! Coming!"

"Yes," Jack moaned, reaching between us, and wrapping his hand around the both of us. He pumped us together, drawing out my ravaging bliss. When I opened my eyes, I could tell the moment he followed me over the edge—his head thrown back, his mouth in the shape of an 'O.' He was so fucking handsome like that, all abandoned and swimming in the wash of passion.

"Baby, yeah," he keened, basking in his release.

After a few moments, I moved off him, and we lay tangled up, our breath spent. With my cheek on his shoulder, I watched the rise and fall of his chest, like it was a hypnotic pendulum.

"This is crazy," I whispered.

Jack lifted his head, furrowing his brows. "Are you having second thoughts?"

"No. I mean…six years and then this?" I circled my fingertip over his heart like it would somehow convey my meaning. "Was it there all along and I just didn't see it? I mean, how did I not see it?"

He traced my collarbone with his thumb. "You were happily married. I'd have turned you down if you'd tried to cheat on Lainey."

"That's not what I meant."

He ran his fingers through the back of my hair, watching me.

"I woke up happy this morning," I explained.

"Me too." He smiled.

I gave him a squeeze for the compliment. "No. I…Lainey and I were happy. Who couldn't be happy around her?" He flashed an understanding smile as I continued, "But I woke up happier than I've been in years."

"I know what you mean." The way he said it so appreciatively made me sad that his description of *years* was probably longer than mine, and that the 'happy Jack' I'd known hadn't been as happy as I had always assumed.

I gave him a reassuring kiss. "I don't know why I freaked out. You make this easy."

"It was new. That's why you freaked out, but what do you mean? I make *being gay* look easy? Because I hate to tell you, it's not."

They were loaded words, but I didn't want to upset him right now by diving into his reasons. "No. I meant you make being together easy. You make being happy easy. You make everything easier. I *was* uptight, but I was always more relaxed when you were around."

He settled deeper into the pillow, burrowing his face in the crook of my neck. I pulled him in and kissed the top of his head.

"I hope you're getting something similar out of this."

I heard a muffled sniffle as he nodded against my neck. "I am."

I wanted to hold him forever. It was partly self-serving and partly because I thought he needed it, but I was learning the hard way that sex between two men was messier than between a man and a woman. I pulled back reluctantly.

"I guess we'd better get cleaned up."

A husky laugh treated my ears when I staggered to the bathroom on rubbery, post-sex legs. If my bare ass and spent muscles were the thing to get him to laugh, so be it. He joined me, and when we walked back into the bedroom, he picked his clothes up off the floor like he was going to put them on.

"Hey. Stay?" I suggested, coming over and placing a hand over his.

Jack glanced up at the ceiling. "But...Emma."

"We can get up before she does, unless...you don't want to."

"Of course, I want to, but...what if she suspects something?"

I set his jeans on the bed and interlaced our fingers. It was time we cleared the air for good. "Before I answer that, just to be clear, what is this to you? *Us*?"

His gaze traced my face, and he answered softly. "Everything." My heart bloomed in my chest, but then he added, "But you know what my life is like for most of the year. I'd understand if you..."

"If I'd *what*?"

"Want someone who could be around more."

Was he serious? Man, put a guy's dick in your mouth and he still doesn't get the message. And people thought women were confusing. His inability to take or ask for what he wanted was starting to concern me.

"Jack. I'm going to kick your ass."

He chuckled. "I'm serious."

"So am I," I insisted. "For the last three years when you were on the road, the best part of my day, aside from coming home to Emma, were the times we talked while you were gone."

He grabbed my shoulder and moved in, resting his head there. "Mine too."

God, my big, fragile man, I thought as I stroked his hair. *My man*. Huh. It had a ring of *rightness* to it. "So...we're doing this? You and me?"

His puff of breath ghosted my neck, and he squeezed me. "Yeah. You and me."

I purred like a happy cat. No words had ever sounded better. "Then since you'll be on the road half the year...you should stay."

Jack pulled back, shaking his head and smirking. "You sound like a fucking lawyer."

And I was damn glad to be one at the moment. I grinned over getting my way.

"And Emma?" he asked.

I had no clue how to have that conversation with Emma because I still had no clue how to have most conversations with Emma, but I suspected I would need to in the near future. I'd gotten Jack to agree to *you and me*, but I didn't know if he realized I didn't foresee an expiration to my definition of you and me.

"Well, I'd like her to know *some*day," I reasoned, "but maybe we should wait a little while to see if you get sick of my shit."

"I *won't* get sick of you, but kids talk, and then people talk."

The benefit of getting to know Jack intimately apparently meant finding out the most positive man I knew was also a great big truckload of doubts. This would need fixing, but not tonight. I could see it was going to take baby steps to work through his years of living in fear.

"I know…you have a lot to lose, but…for now…just stay?"

He studied me, looking uncertain, but then resigned. He nodded and crawled back into my bed, pulling me in when I joined him.

"You have a lot to lose too, Max," he murmured into my chest. "What would Trevor and Dan think?"

"Trevor?" I shrugged.

Jack tilted his head back, arching a brow. "And Dan?"

"Fuck Dan."

He huffed, but quickly followed with, "Your mom and Morgan?"

"I think my mom would be okay with it. Morgan would be jealous as hell." The thought made me smirk, but then I realized I had a secret of my own. "I, uh, told her you kissed me."

"What?"

"I needed to talk to someone. God knows why I chose her, but don't worry. She won't say anything."

"Oh, my God. What did she think?"

Reliving that tale wasn't my idea of happy pillow talk. I scoffed, but when I saw the worry in his eyes, I gave him a smile. "She thought the same thing I do—that I'm the luckiest man alive."

He buried his face in my chest and squeezed me. I didn't miss the breath he blew out into my skin.

"And Bob and Ellen?" he ventured.

His list of worries was starting to get under my skin. After living under a black cloud for the last three years, I'd finally found the sunshine, and now I was supposed to worry about everyone else's opinion of the sunshine? Fuck. That.

This should be the fun, nervously exciting part of a relationship—the beginning. All I wanted to do was enjoy every second of it, not focus on how to justify my happiness to other people.

CHAPTER 37
Jack

Morgan knew about me. Wow.

I'd told so few people in my life, gotten so used to expecting rejection, I didn't expect to feel the comfort of her finding out gushing through me. I should have expected. Morgan had always had my back, but that still left everyone else in Max's life.

"And Bob and Ellen," I prodded because he needed to consider what he was in for.

"I don't know, but no one gets a say in this except you and me. I don't care what anyone thinks."

"You say that now, but I've been there, Max. It's not as easy as you think. Not everyone's like Morgan."

"Thank fuck for that. She hit me about a dozen times."

"She hit you?" I laughed even as I rubbed his arm, feeling protective.

He rolled his eyes and made air quotes. "For hurting '*her Jack*.'"

"Hmm. I'll have to buy her flowers."

"Flowers? She fucking pinched my nipples."

"What? No, she didn't!"

"The fuck she did! Hello? This is Morgan we're talking about here. I swear to you. She caused me *bodily harm*. What the fuck does she get flowers for?"

My chest rumbled at his pouting as I circled his nipple with my fingertip. "Aw. Poor Max." I kissed the flat brown plane, and added, "She gets flowers for getting me you."

"Alright. That's fair."

"Max, about telling people, though. I don't want you to think I'm ashamed of you or anything, but the more people that know, the more chance there is the world finds out about me."

"Would it really be so bad?"

I leveled him with a look I didn't want to make. He heaved a breath and burrowed deeper under the covers.

"I fucking hate this," he muttered.

"It'll be ok. We'll just have to play it safe."

"No. I mean, we shouldn't have to play it safe. It's no one's business who you or I care about—who we want to be with."

"People don't see it that way."

"Well, people are ignorant pricks."

"Uh, two weeks ago, you shoved me away and quit talking to me."

"I know." He pulled me in tighter, making me regret giving him the reminder. "And that was the worst reaction, no matter..."

"No. It's fine."

"It's *not* fine, Jack. That's the point I'm trying to make."

"I know, and I appreciate that, but I just meant to take that reaction and multiply it by millions. That's what it would be like because of who I am."

"Well, you know how to kill the mood."

I chuckled, still in awe that Max could be in a mood for me. "No. I think I'm done for the night. You dragged me out of my sex hibernation this weekend, and now I'm tired."

Max turned out the lamp and then wrapped his arms around me again. He gave me a tender kiss, a preview of all the mushy kindness inside of him that his gruff speech usually hid.

"Good," he said. "Get some sleep, and then you can see our morning chaos from the beginning tomorrow."

Two days in a row of seeing Max with bedhead in a bed I shared with him? Sign me up, please. I drifted off, savoring the words *'you and me,'* and trying not to think of all the possible ways Max and Emma could get hurt because of the *'me'* in that sentence.

CHAPTER 38
Jack

It is extremely difficult to concentrate when your boyfriend has his dick pressed up against your ass and his arms wrapped around your waist so his hands can wander underneath your sweatshirt. Max's cuddliness had gone off the charts over the last four weeks, so much so that I no longer questioned when the word *boyfriend* rolled through my thoughts.

"You keep doing that and I'm going to burn this," I warned him.

His lips pressed to my jugular and his palm slid higher underneath my sweatshirt until he grazed my nipple with his thumb. "Then we'll tell Emma *I* made it."

There was no way he was going to quit until he got what he wanted. Setting down the spatula, I reached back, grabbed his hip, and gave in. Dinner would survive long enough for one more kiss. Poor me and the new sacrifices I had to make.

Just as our lips connected, a melodic voice called from near the stairwell. "Can I have some chips before dinner?"

I wrenched away from Max, slamming my hip into the kitchen counter, but he went with me because his hand got snagged in my sweatshirt. When he got free, he jumped back toward the stove.

"Emma!" he yelped, picking up the meat tongs like he needed to pretend he'd been doing something else besides groping me. "I thought you were upstairs."

Emma shrugged and twirled a curl around her finger. "I'm hungry."

"Well, dinner's almost ready. Just wait a few more minutes."

She looked from me to the stovetop, and then to Max. "*You're* not cooking, are you?"

"Out!" He aimed the tongs in her direction and clacked them.

She sighed and did her best street-urchin, sunken posture pose. "Fine, but...can I start a puzzle in the sunroom, then?"

"Yeah. Sure. Whatever. Sunroom. Go," Max babbled.

Jesus. And I thought I was freaking out. When she disappeared down the hall, I finally let out the breath I was holding. Max leaned onto the counter and let out an exasperated stream, like their banter was the cause.

"Max? I'm pretty sure she saw."

"Shit." He pressed his palms to his eyes.

"It's fine. Just calm down. Act normal."

"I'm calm!" he snapped, eyes wild when he dropped his hands. "Are *you* calm?"

I thought about it and decided he needed me to be calm, or he'd never make it through dinner. "Yes."

"The fuck you are. You're doing that thumb-chewing thing you do."

What thumb... Oh. Ew! I had a thumb-chewing problem? How come he knew that, and I didn't? I stuffed my hands under my armpits because *that* wasn't gross either.

"Alright. I just...I hate lying to her."

"We haven't lied."

"Well, it feels like it."

For the past four weeks, a sense of betrayal had clung to me whenever I was around Emma. Like I wasn't being who I was supposed to be—a reliable adult who didn't change. Kids needed stability. Right?

Max waved a hand at me. "This was *your* idea."

"What was?"

"Not telling anyone," he groused, cranked up the burner, and manhandled the pork chops in the skillet with the tongs.

"You *want* to tell her?"

"Yes! No!" His eyes pinched shut, and he sighed. "I don't know."

"See?"

"See what?" he shot back.

"If you're not sure, then it's better we don't," I said diplomatically.

"Do *you* want to tell her?"

I'd never thought about it. I didn't even know it was an option. He'd said once that he'd like her to know, but I figured it was a heat of the moment sentimentality. For the past month, I'd spent every night in his bed, and every morning, I snuck out to go change at my house before coming back for breakfast. It had become our norm. It was safe. I was fine with safe.

Was Max really considering letting the cat out of the bag? It was surreal to think he'd do that for me.

"I... It's not my decision."

I thought that was a good answer—the right answer—but he gaped at me like I just tore his heart out.

"Well, fuck you too." He scowled and turned his attention back to torturing our dinner.

"Hey, what was that for?"

"Leave it all on me and then act like she's not yours at all to top it off!"

Was he serious? I inched closer, invading his angry bubble, and took the opportunity to turn the burner down when he folded his arms and stared at the backsplash.

"I'm *not* putting it all on you. And she's *not* mine, Max. I have no say in this."

"What?" He pinned me with accusing eyes. "You've been here every offseason since she was three. You video chatted every week you were on the road. You've been at every birthday, every Christmas. Well, almost every Christmas." He threw a hand up. "You helped teach her how to ride her freaking bike. You read her bedtime stories. You're *Uncle* Jack. Christ, she won't eat anything unless you cook it." He glanced at the stove where the meat was starting to smoke and flung the tongs down on the counter. "Fuck! I burned these."

When he turned away and pressed the heels of his hands to his eyes again, I shut off the burner and sidled up behind him. "Max, I love her like she's mine. No question." I rubbed his shoulders, hating how rock hard they'd gone and that we were in a tiff. "I appreciate you want me to have a say, but *you're* her dad."

"Don't give me that placating appreciate bullshit," he huffed over his shoulder.

"Well, I do..."

"No. You want *me*? You get *her* too. We're a package deal. I thought you knew that."

When he turned his head to stare at the wall like he was avoiding me, my hands stilled.

"What are you saying? You want me to help parent, or you want to know what I think about telling her?"

His shoulders rose and fell. "*Yes*," he said, all pissy, but then he heaved a breath and pinched the bridge of his nose. "Look. I get the whole not telling the world thing, but this is *home*, Jack. We already went through what hiding things at home does. I want to be *us* at home."

My eyes glistened, and I rested my chin on his shoulder, wrapping my arms across his chest. I was so grateful the man I wanted to be an *us* with wanted me to be an *us* with him. It made it all the more painful to not be able to give him the things he wanted. I knew then it would be the thing that broke us.

I'd doubted his interest at first, but here we were a month in. I'd been gay for years and telling people terrified me. Max had been into me for a month and wanted to erect a *fuck-everybody-and-the-horse-they-rode-in-on* monument. He never did anything halfway. It was why I loved him. I wished I had his courage because being a *real us* was my fairy tale.

"I know," I said to his cheek. "I'm just...scared. I already broke one home by unloading my baggage."

Max squeezed my hand and turned his face. "You're not baggage. Don't say that. Emma's not your father."

It gutted me how well this man had picked up on all my hurts and tried to bandage them. I closed my eyes to fight the sting in my heart and nuzzled my face in his neck. "It's reflex, you know?"

"Not anymore," Max warned, squeezing my hand again.

"And I didn't think I had the right to parent. That's why I didn't think I had a say in whether to tell her."

"You've *been* parenting, Jack. You earned the right a long time ago."

Damn it. He was going to make me cry. I tightened my arms across his chest and breathed in his scent. If you asked me, it was what love smelled like. Max sighed, and I felt the rest of the tension go out of him as he rubbed my forearm.

"Fuck," he muttered. "We sound like an old, gay married couple."

"Not yet." I snorted.

"Well, what do we do?"

"I don't know." I let him go, but he turned around and put his arms around my waist.

"Welcome to parenthood." He smirked.

"I can't reach the puzzles," Emma called, sounding close—*really* close.

We broke apart like something exploded between us. I moved around the island cabinet and scrambled for the napkins since they were the first object I could find.

"Jesus!" Max yelled, clutching his chest. "You used to make noise when you walked! What are you, a shape-shifter?"

Emma's eyebrows quirked together. "Uh. Nooo. Sorry."

"Christ!" Max panted, still catching his breath as he spared me a wary glance.

"Are you guys fighting?" Emma asked, folding her arms across her chest.

"No," we replied in unison.

"It sounded like you were fighting."

Max's expression was desperate when he peeked at me. I channeled the posture of a calm, confident adult, and looked at Emma.

"We were, but we're not anymore."

Her gaze telegraphed to each of us, and the corners of her mouth turned down. "Are you mad at me?"

Max's features softened. "No. Why would you think that?"

She kicked at the floor, staring at her toes. "Because I saw you kissing earlier."

Max and I shared *oh fuck* looks.

"Are you sure that's what you saw?" Max asked.

I shot him an *'are-you-an-idiot*?' look. He responded with a *'don't-give-me-that-look'* scowl. Emma scrunched her nose up adorably and chuckled.

"Uh, yeah. You were hugging Uncle Jack and kissing."

When the silence stretched, and it was clear Max had been rendered speechless, I supplied, "Well, we weren't mad at you."

"Okay. Is dinner ready?"

Max grabbed a plate and found his voice. "Uh, yeah."

Emma approached the stove and watched him plate a charred pork chop like it was a monster.

"Uh, Dad. I'm not eating that."

Quickly, I scooped several of the canapés Max had conned me into making again on a fresh plate and handed it to her. "Here, Bug."

"Traitors," Max grumbled.

Emma headed to the dining room as though nothing was amiss. Either her stomach was taking priority over being weirded out by us making out, or she didn't give a damn.

When she cleared the doorway, I turned back to Max. Eyes wide, he mouthed, *what the fuck!*

I don't know, I mouthed back, holding up helpless hands.

My stomach growled, so I went to the stove on instinct, but lost hope at what I saw in the pan. "Yeah, I'm not eating those either."

"Fuck off." He chuckled and tossed the tongs on the counter again.

He went to the fridge and pulled out a beer. Max never drank at dinner. Apparently, the night you were outed by your daughter was an exception. He swiped the tray of canapés off the counter and headed to the dining room. I stood dumbfounded for a moment, having assumed we'd come up with a game plan to further explain or not explain to Emma what she'd witnessed. However, 'diligent Max,' who tirelessly prepared for his cases, had clearly left the building, so I grabbed the bowl of mashed potatoes and followed him into the unknown.

My kid had been shifting her beady little eyes from me to Jack for the last ten minutes. Jack was acting like one of those creepy dolls with the eyelids that roll up whenever you tilt their head, sneaking panicked glances at me from across the table as he shoved food in his mouth like he was stress eating. All because of me and my stupid man-hands and man-hormones.

I take that back. This was Jack's fault. It had to be his pheromones or something.

"Why are you guys so quiet?" Emma asked.

"We're...eating," I supplied and shoved a mouthful of potatoes into my pie hole.

She looked at Jack. "Can we play your karaoke game after dinner?"

"If your dad says," he started, but cut himself off when I arched a brow.

What part of 'we were in this together' hadn't he understood? I wanted him to stop acting like a neighbor and embrace his boyfriend status. He must have caught on, because he pressed his lips together and returned his attention to Emma.

"Is all your homework done?"

"Yeah."

"Alright, then I'll go grab it when we're done with dinner, but just for a little bit. You've got school tomorrow," he said like a champ, and pride bloomed in my chest because 'parenting Jack' was sexy as hell.

"I know," Emma assured him, because nine-year-olds know everything.

My smug smirk would not be tamed, even when he silently told me what he thought of my parenting challenge with a saucy glare. I sighed when I remembered fair was fair. He'd just done something he hadn't wanted to do. Now it was my turn.

"Emma?"

"Hmm?"

"What... Uh. How do you feel about what you saw me and Uncle Jack doing in the kitchen earlier?"

"Cooking?" she asked, at which Jack snickered until I scowled at him.

"Uh. No. The hugging and...the...the..."

"Kissing?" she offered.

Fuck my life. Was it hot in here?

"Um. Yeah."

She took turns studying each of us like we were fine art. "Do you like each other?"

"Yes," we said at the same time, which helped my nerves. I took a sip of my beer. If I acted casual, maybe she'd take the news casually.

"Does that mean I'll have two dads now?"

I choked on *casual*, spraying a mist of beer into the air. Jack's jaw flapped open, probably finally realizing how terrifying being Emma's father was.

Maybe this wasn't so bad. Emma didn't seem to be freaking out the way we were. I wiped my mouth and cleared my throat.

"Would you be okay with having two dads?"

She shrugged and smiled. "Matt has two dads."

"Your boyfriend from school?"

"Ugh. He's *not* my boyfriend!"

Details. I was more worried about the topic of *my* boyfriend, so I pressed on. "He...told you he has two dads?"

"Yeah."

"You mean his parents divorced and got married to other people?"

Her face scrunched up like I was an idiot. "No. His dads are married, and they adopted him. I told you this."

She so had not. Had she?

"When?"

Her lips pursed, and she rolled her eyes. "Like in first grade."

I rolled my eyes, and now knew where she picked up the habit. Jack snickered—the unhelpful bastard.

"Well, does it bother you if Uncle Jack and I hug and...kiss?"

"Are you going to get married?"

Jesus. Was I that bad at this? How did we go from hugging to marriage? Jack choked on air and fell into a coughing fit. When he started rearranging his silverware, I knew he'd recovered enough that he could try to find his balls.

"Anytime here, pal!" I threw my hand in the air, leaning back in my chair like I'd just benched myself.

He grimaced, but then clasped his hands together and gave Emma a patient smile. "Sweetie, we were friends for a long time, and I was friends with your mom, too." Emma nodded, her face pinched in concentration. "And when your mom died, me and your dad spent a lot of time together, and recently we realized we like each other...as more than friends."

"Like boyfriends?"

Jack glanced at me like he was looking for cues. I smiled. I couldn't help it. I wanted that word like beavers wanted to chew on trees.

"Yeah," he told her.

Emma shrugged. "I know."

"*You know*?" I blurted because although nine-year-olds knew everything, how in the hell did she know Jack and I were dating?

Please don't say you heard us screwing around, I chanted silently.

She giggled. "Yeah. You're always smiling at each other, and touching each other, and Uncle Jack spends the night."

Oh, shit. Here it comes.

"How... Uh. Why do you think he spends the night?"

"Because I see him sneak out the back door in the morning to go home before he comes back over for breakfast." She relayed her intel so matter-of-factly.

"Did you...tell anyone this?"

"No."

"Not even your boyfr—" I caught myself when she narrowed her eyes. "Not even Matt?"

"No, but I told him Mom died, and I have an Uncle Jack who's always here, so it feels like I have two dads, too."

"Anything else?"

"No. Why?"

I didn't give a damn if the whole neighborhood knew, but it was Jack I was worried about. The only time he'd budged on admitting he was gay was when he first kissed me, and when he'd sent Morgan those damn flowers a few weeks ago, but we still hadn't told her we were dating.

Emma looked confused about the interrogation. I didn't know how to explain that the world was full of assholes. Luckily, Jack stepped in.

"Honey, people don't always like it when men like men or women like women. They tease those people or pick on them. We don't want you to get teased because me and your dad are...boyfriends."

My heart spasmed. Part of him keeping it a secret was to protect Emma? How did he not see he was parent material?

"Some kids make fun of Matt for having two dads, but they only do it when the teachers aren't around because otherwise, they'd get in trouble. Mostly Rick Morton and Jeremy Rhiner, but I don't like them, anyway."

I whipped out my phone and brought up my notes app, typing in the perpetrators under my *Shit List* entry. "Jeremy who?"

"Rhiner," Emma supplied.

Jack chuckled softly, like I was being ridiculous. We'd have to have a talk sometime about the seriousness of my Shit List. Nine-year-olds became teenagers one day, and neither of those little asswipes would be taking one Emma Hartwell to prom.

When I returned my attention to Emma, the confusion in her eyes had me gritting my teeth. People shouldn't have to warn their kids to be afraid of certain things in life, otherwise they grew up to be, for example, successful baseball players who lived in fear of their own shadow. It is no fun explaining the rights and wrongs of the world to children.

"Well, it's not just about being teased for...having two dads, kiddo," I started. "Uncle Jack is famous, and nobody knows he...nobody knows I'm his boyfriend. If anybody found out that he has a boyfriend instead of a girlfriend, it could be on the news, and he might get in trouble at work."

"What kind of trouble?"

"They might kick him off the team, and he wouldn't be able to play baseball anymore."

"But why?" she demanded. "That's not fair!"

"I know. It's not." I spared a glance at Jack. His hand covered his mouth, propping up his chin like it was a seal preventing him from talking or crying. "It's not fair at all," I stressed to both of them, "but people can be mean. People are used to just a boyfriend with a girlfriend and mom and a dad, so anything different seems weird to some people. People...people don't always understand if it's not just a mom and a dad or a boy and a girl."

My stomach churned, and I blew out a breath. Fuck. This was hard.

Her mouth sagged in a dejected little frown, all her brash spunkiness nowhere in sight. She turned her watery blue eyes to Jack.

"I won't tell anyone. I promise."

Jack placed his hand over the top of hers, his eyes glistening. "I know you won't. I'm sorry. I know it's not good to keep secrets. You're too little to have to keep secrets. I don't want you to lie, I just...I think it would be better if we only talk about it at home with me and your dad."

Emma sucked in her lower lip and nodded. She picked up her fork, poking at her mashed potatoes like she was searching for proof of life. My heart didn't know which one of them to hurt for the most.

Jack rubbed his reddened eyes and then rested his mouth against his palm again. When he sniffled, I flashed him a sympathetic smile.

"Dad?"

"Yeah, kiddo?"

"I don't really want a new mom."

"Uh. Well...you're not getting a new mom. Why would you say that?"

"Remember, you went on a date with a woman when I went to grandma and grandpa's?"

Could a guy ever live a damned thing down? I swallowed and refused to glance at Jack about that sore subject.

"Yeah."

"Well, I was happy that it might make you happy, but I was worried you'd marry another woman, and then I'd have to have a new mom."

"Oh." I had wondered where this was going.

"I'm sorry," she added dejectedly.

"I'm not mad."

She made a sound of relief, and added, "I already had a mom, and I know I don't remember her a lot, but I don't want a new mom."

"O-kay." Could awkward time be over now?

Emma's spine straightened. Her mouth ticked up at the corners, and she added solemnly, "I'd rather have two dads."

My head took a slow turn to gauge Jack's reaction to this episode of *'Shit That Comes Out of my Kid's Mouth.'* I could see the hint of a smile behind his hand. He closed his eyes and shook his head, his shoulders raising on what I assumed was an emotionally drained laugh.

Yeah. I was about done with heart-to-hearts for the night, too.

"Well, good," I told Emma. "Because that's what you've got."

"Good," she concurred and beamed like she won the kid lottery.

"Great. That's all settled," I declared, like I was notarizing a document. I picked up a cold canapé, but only made it halfway to my mouth.

"Do I have to call you both *Dad* now?"

Fuck my life.

"Well, you're always going to call me *Dad*," I huffed, getting hung up on the words *'have to.'*

"I know, Dad. That's not what I meant."

She *knew*. She *always* knew! Jack must have sensed my frustration because he chimed in.

"I've always been Uncle Jack. Is it okay if I stay Uncle Jack or Jack?"

"Yeah."

"Great!" I enthused, getting up from the table. "Any more questions?"

Emma shoveled a load of potatoes into her mouth and grinned around it like an imp, shaking her head.

"Good. Who wants frozen pizza?"

The two pork chop-less people I cared about most glanced at each other. Both shot up a hand. I had created an evil dynamic duo.

"You need help with the oven?" Jack called as I went to the kitchen.

"No!" I yelled back, but added low enough, I hoped Emma didn't hear, "Fucker."

I had single-handedly signed myself up for this abuse. I grinned into the freezer. Being a masochist wasn't all that terrible when your kid loved you the way you were, and you had the best partner in the world.

CHAPTER 40
Jack

I walked in a daze, carrying our empty plates to the kitchen. Emma went ahead of me with the bowl of potatoes, smiling up at me as she passed. What just happened?

She was the second person to discover my sexuality in a month, and the second one not to judge me. I guess she needed flowers, too.

Max was unwrapping the frozen pizza at the island, oblivious to my internal epiphany. He'd just stuck his neck out to his family for me again, but it felt like so much more than that.

I knew we'd made a pact of sorts—*you and me*—but part of me had still whispered it was probably just lust on his part. After tonight, I didn't think I could believe that anymore. We weren't physical every night. Half the time, we just fell asleep, curled into each other's arms. When we *were* physical, the way he looked at me made my heart skip twenty-seven swoony beats. There was so much more there than lust. I needed to stop dismissing his intentions, especially after the way he'd fully claimed me in front of Emma.

And the whole two dads thing... God, neither of them had batted an eye at promoting me to that honor. This was serious, so I decided I'd better start acting like a dad instead of just a fun uncle.

"Hey, Bug. Go set out your stuff for school tomorrow and take your shower, and then I'll meet you in the living room after I get the karaoke game. Okay?"

"Okay!" She zoomed toward the stairwell.

"Pizza in twenty minutes," Max called to her. "If you use more water than that, there won't be any food left!"

"Ha! Ha! Dad!" she yelled on her mad dash upstairs.

Max slid the pizza into the oven. When he turned around and looked at me, he sighed.

"Are you okay?" I asked.

"I don't know." He scratched his head. "I guess it could have gone a lot worse."

"Yeah." I nodded and stopped myself when I realized my thumb was on its way to my mouth. "You think *she'll* be okay?"

Max glanced at the stairs. "I think...she'll never be *not* okay. Thank God she takes after her mother." He shook his head and chuckled.

"Yeah," I agreed and went to load the dishwasher.

Max's hand rubbed my back a moment later. "Hey. Are *you* all right?"

"Yeah."

"I hope I didn't say anything you weren't okay with."

"No. You handled that...very well." I flashed him a smile over my shoulder, too overcome with all the emotions bubbling up inside me to face him. He didn't buy it, bracing my shoulders to turn me around.

"Then what's up?"

"I...it feels like you just made me part of your family."

He dismissed my statement with a guttural noise. "You've always been part of my family."

"But it feels like...you just made *the three of us* a family."

Max went all sheepish and pointed over his shoulder. "Well, Emma helped, in case you weren't listening."

I laughed. "Blame it on the kid, tough guy. I see how you are."

He smiled and braced my shoulders. "Jack Spears, will you be a family with me and my precocious child?"

My lip quivered at the gift he was giving me. This was really my life. I pulled him in tight. "I'd love to."

For the first time, we kissed without worrying about Emma coming in. This was us. Max was right. It was good to be us at home.

"Hey, when she's older, I can tease her that I got a boyfriend before she did," Max joked.

"Oh, my God. Leave it to you to be smug about this."

He chuckled. "She's going to kill one or both of us some day. You know that, right? Hormones, dating, the teen years, driving. There's a heart attack or two in there somewhere, for sure."

All I could do was smile at the longevity of how that sounded, and wonder if he really saw an us that far down the road. "Maybe you're underestimating the power of two dads."

He snapped his fingers, and his eyes widened. "Oh, my God. You're right!"

"What?"

"There's *two of me* now. That means I get a vacation."

"Oh, hell no. That's not how this is going to work. I already do most of the cooking and homework help."

He stared off like he was in a trance while I finished packing up the potatoes. "I'm going to take a fishing trip," he whispered, like he was talking to himself.

"When have you ever gone fishing?"

"Exactly! Maybe my true calling in life is to be a master angler."

"Yeah, you got a fucking angle going here, and it's not happening, bud."

"I can go golfing…"

I knew he was screwing with me, but that was pushing it. "You don't fucking golf." I laughed and gave his chest a playful shove.

Max raised his brows, looking way too devilish. "I do now!" He pumped his fist in the air. "Yes! Two dads!"

I cracked his ass so hard it moved him forward. He yelped, even though we both were laughing. "Keep dreaming, pal." I checked the clock and the oven temperature while Max chuckled and rubbed his ass. "I'm going to run next door. I'll be right back."

"Take your time," he said cheerfully. "I'll be working on my vacation list."

I shook my head and fought giving him the satisfaction of a grin. Grabbing the timer, I set it and slammed it down by the oven with a pointed look.

Max rolled his eyes. "Oh. Fuck off. It's frozen pizza."

CHAPTER 41
Max

All was right in the world. How many times do you get to think that in your life and have it be true? I was a lucky guy, considering the state of mind I was in a month ago.

I smiled, hearing Emma's excited voice in the living room as she and Jack searched for another song on his karaoke game. I had no idea what the future held for the three of us, but there had to be a starting point. To Emma, this seemed to have been just another night, and that was exactly the way it should feel. My kid was happy, healthy, safe, and loved. Maybe I wasn't doing too bad, after all.

I chuckled, remembering the looks on Jack's face as I'd called out more two-dads-vacation-ideas through the kitchen doorway while he'd set up the game. If he wanted to be a true part of this family, he had to expect a little heckling.

When I finished cutting up the pizza and brought it into the living room, I stopped in my tracks. Where the fuck did they get feather boas?

Emma was standing on the couch, mic in hand, belting out the opening lines to Stevie Nicks and Don Henley's "Leather and Lace". She was sporting a pink boa and an old Elton-John-style pair of Lainey's sunglasses. Jack had a purple boa draped around his neck, singing along into his own mic.

When he cast me a guilty smile, I swiped my palm across my mouth to hide my amusement and shook my head. I didn't want to know where those came from, what Emma's idea of gay people was, or how Jack still managed to look hot while swathed in purple feathers.

"Uh, oh. We're busted!" Jack's voice boomed out of his mic.

I made my way around the couch, schooling my features as I set the pizza on the coffee table. When I reached to shift the game console further out of the way, Emma stopped couch dancing.

"No! Don't change it, Dad!" she pleaded.

Straightening up, I made a show of looking displeased, hands on my hips. When they both looked worried that I was being the fun police, I walked over to Jack and took the mic from his hand. He stared as I clicked it off and tossed it on the couch.

"Aw! Dad," Emma whined.

Jack gave her a pitying look until I placed a hand on his waist, interlaced the fingers of his free hand with mine, and started moving us in time with the music.

Emma let out a high-pitched giggle. Jack looked at me like I'd lost my mind, but when his gaze darted back to Emma and saw she'd resumed her off-key serenade, he smiled at me and his posture relaxed. He wrapped his arm around my back and rested his head on my shoulder like it was all too much for him.

I had wondered how he was holding up. His boundless sentimentality always made my heart turn to mush. "Breathe," I whispered as we swayed.

He answered by squeezing me tighter. I wasn't a classic rock junkie like him, but that didn't mean I didn't know a thing or two. I crooned along quietly in his ear with a line from the lyrics that reminded me of us.

He sniffled and raised his head. "Did you just Stevie Nicks' me? Because it's working."

I wanted to kiss him so badly, but I'd never been big on PDA in front of Emma, and this was all new to her, so I settled for the dance.

"Actually, I think I just Don Henley-ed you."

Emma bounded off the couch with a shit-eating grin. We separated our arms on one side, and each placed a hand on her shoulder when it was clear she wanted to join in. And then they both treated me to a very painful session of karaoke. I grinned like a fool the whole time.

"Got room for one more in there?" I asked the steamy silhouette behind the shower door after I'd put Emma to bed.

Seeing Jack make himself at home in all parts of my house did exciting, possessive things to my insides. I didn't wait for a reply but took his smirk when I entered as an invitation. He reached for the bottle of his body wash he'd finally brought over last week, but I grabbed his hand.

"Let me?"

He smiled and handed it over. His surprise was evidence he hadn't believed me when I said I was going to take care of him now.

"We still need to go on a real date," I said, lathering up his chest and arms.

He held my waist and kissed my cheek. "Mm. I don't know. I think I really like home dates."

I nudged him to turn around. He placed his hands against the tiles. He chuckled when I washed his hair but let out a sated breath when I started working the muscles in his shoulders and back with my fingertips. I got a groan out of him when I worked my way down his ass and onto his thighs. When his muscles were relaxed, I wrapped my arms around his waist, enjoying the peace at the end of this long, interesting day.

"You're going to put me to sleep after that," he murmured.

I pressed a kiss to the back of his neck, my own eyes half-lidded with exhaustion. "That's fine with me."

His hand latched onto mine and drew it down, placing it over a very hard, hot, wet erection. Damn. Now I was awake again.

"First, I'd really love it if I could be in that dream you had," he whispered.

Double damn. My brain whirred, remembering two dreams I'd told him about when we first got together. One, we'd done many times to each other since then—which had taught me how to curb my gag reflex, thank you very much. But the other... I had to clear my throat to speak.

"Which...which one?"

"The one where you're inside me." He pressed his ass into my cock in case I hadn't gotten the message.

Uh. Message fucking received.

Holy shit.

Dreaming it and doing it were two entirely different things. I loved that he'd never pressured me with anything and let me experience things at my own pace, but sometimes it was nice to be encouraged. I had wanted this, wanted to explore any deeper connection available with him.

My hand squeezed a languid slide up his length, making his head fall back against mine.

"Are you sure?" I asked.

CHAPTER 42
Jack

Was I sure?

Um. Had Bob Ross been sure about all those happy little trees?

The man had just officially made me part of his family tonight, letting me be a dad to the little girl I'd always thought of as partly mine. If I thought I'd fallen in love with him before, I'd crashed into it and bottomed out tonight.

I nodded. "Only if you want to."

He reached out and shut off the water. My heartbeat skittered. Max Hartwell was going to make love to me.

We got out and toweled off in a silence as thick as molasses. When I walked into his room, the bed looked different from all the other nights we'd spent in it. Something sacred was about to happen on it, something that was a first for the both of us in one way, but not another.

I turned around and found him biting his lip, staring at me. The way he looked at me, I'd never felt so sexy in my life. I dropped my towel and reveled in his intake of breath.

Stepping forward, I kissed below his ear and traced the skin above his towel. I nibbled down his neck, feeling his pulse against my lips as his hands went to my waist. Kissing across his shoulder and down his chest, I tugged his towel free as I took one of his nipples in my mouth.

His hands dug into my hair, and his hips jerked forward when I palmed him, meeting his lips for a sweet kiss. He tasted like promises I intended to keep.

"You don't mind, if you don't…do it to me?" he asked, nervous guilt swimming in his beautiful eyes.

I leaned in to whisper in his ear, ignoring his silly worry over the gift he was about to give me. "I can't wait to feel you inside me."

My confession was well received. He gripped my ass and moaned into my mouth. I settled my hands on his chest and backed away slowly.

"How do you want me?" I asked, crawling onto the bed as sexy as I could.

Max swallowed and gave himself a slow stroke, like I was irresistible. "I…how…how do you want to?"

I flashed him a sultry smile, every inhibition I'd ever had about sex evaporating at the want in his eyes. "How did you have me in your dream?"

The way his cheeks burned said *every way* and did that ever do it for me. My smile spread across my face.

"I was…behind you."

"Were you laying down on top of me or on your side behind me? Or maybe you were kneeling behind me," I suggested, in case he wasn't sure what to do.

He chewed on his lower lip. It was clear his imagination hadn't fathomed all the ways men could please each other, so I made another suggestion— one that would be easy for him where we could look at each other. I wanted to see his face when we shared this experience.

"Unless you'd rather I lay on my back while you lean over me or…maybe you'd like me to sit on your lap and ride you?"

He sucked in a shuddery breath. "Yeah. *That*. Can…do you want to do *that?*"

Smiling, I scooted over and patted the place next to me on the mattress. Max nodded and scrambled for the lube and a condom out of the nightstand. He held up the foil packet, looking self-conscious.

"It's probably expired," he said.

"I get tested. I'm okay."

"I…should I…"

"Pretty sure you're fine," I assured him, getting to my knees.

"Right." He nodded, joining me.

I wrapped my arms around his shoulders and kissed him. When he snaked his arms around my waist, I could feel him trembling.

"If you're not comfortable with this, we don't have to," I whispered.

"I want to," he said, holding my gaze. "I just...I don't want to hurt you...or be bad at it."

Guiding him to sit back against the pillow, I swept my tongue across his in a savory kiss. "You won't," I assured and straddled him.

His eyes tracked the length of my body as he glided his palm up my chest like he was seeing me naked for the first time. "Wow," he whispered.

I had never been more turned on in my life. I trailed my fingers down his stomach, then up the slit of his erection. He jolted from the sensitivity and watched me bring a drop to my lips. I wanted him so aroused he'd forget to be anxious and could concentrate better on the pleasure. "It is *so sexy* seeing you leaking for me," I whispered boldly as I tasted him.

His hands braced my head and hauled me in for a hungry kiss. He reached down and stroked me, building more heat in my belly than I wanted right now.

Panting, I pulled back and grabbed his hand. I retrieved the lube off the mattress and coated his fingers, bringing them around behind me.

"Get me ready for you?" I asked and leaned forward to brace the headboard.

Max watched my face, his fingers circling my rim. I wanted to tell him how much I loved him, but it had already been an evening of firsts, so I kept it strapped down inside me. I brushed his nose with mine, returning all his smiles, teasing his lower lip.

When two of his fingers slipped inside me, I moaned into his mouth at the pressure I knew would soon be the hard rod brushing against my thigh. I rested my forehead against his, sinking down as his fingers danced inside me. "Yes," I hissed.

"Will it feel like when you finger me?" he whispered at my lips.

"Better." I took his mouth and thrust into his hand with a groan when sparks shot through me.

"Fuck. I love making you feel good."

I placed my hand over his where he was inside me. "Then give me more."

He captured my lips like he was starving and treated me to a third digit, stretching me carefully. A moan erupted from my throat. I had to close my eyes to fight off an orgasm.

Max squeezed my ass cheek and nipped at my shoulder. "You have the sexiest ass."

My breath stuttered at his praise. He froze and cupped my jaw.

"Are you okay?"

Rocking down into his hand, I mewled, no longer able to hold it in. "Yeah, baby."

He groaned and dove at my neck like a vampire as I wrapped my arms around him. His thrusts quickened, and I greedily met them.

"Yes," I gasped, even though I knew we should stop. I was already going up in flames.

"Fuck. I love watching you go crazy. Love hearing you breathe like that for me." His voice was a rumbly, encouraging song. I couldn't take it anymore.

"Now, Max."

"Are you sure?"

I cupped his face in wild desperation. "Get that gorgeous cock inside me right now."

He slid out hastily and scrambled for the condom. I was about to help him in my impatience, but seeing him suit up for me was a sight to be left undisturbed. Retrieving the lube, I slickened him and tossed the bottle like a drunk at a tailgate party.

Grabbing the headboard again, I lifted to give him access. When he pressed his head to my entrance, his eyes found mine, searching, witnessing.

"I've thought about this for weeks," he confessed.

I bit back the L-word again and whispered as I eased on to what he was offering me. "I've thought about it for years."

"*Fuuuck*," Max slurred, like he was drunk, his eyes hooded.

I swallowed a moan I knew would wake Emma and every other person in a five-block radius as he started to fill me. It had been years since I'd done this with a man, but it wasn't the sting of the stretch or the ungodly pressure that had me biting my lip. It was the man inside me and how overwhelmed I was with knowing he was the one who was there, uniting us in the closest physical way two people could be.

He gripped my hips, gritting his teeth, I assumed, against the tightness. "Does it hurt?"

I let out a deep breath and folded my arms around his neck, relaxing instantly as my fingers weaved into his hair. "Baby. You feel incredible. I want all of you."

"You're so...tight," he grit out, but eased my hips down to take him all.

I couldn't help who I woke now. "*Uh*, Max!"

He dug his fingertips deeper into my hips. His voice was strained. "Oh, shit! *Jack*!"

I whimpered at the sense of completeness spilling into every inch of my body. "Fuck. I love it when you say my name like that."

I took his mouth, needing an outlet for my cries and wanting to be connected in every way. He kissed me like a dying man who needed air. My initial pleasure turned to more pressure that needed relief, but his grip was holding me in place.

"Let me move, baby," I begged, breaking the kiss.

Max loosened his grip. I took a slide up and down, then rolled my hips, sparking a delicious throb throughout my entire lower half. Max gasped, his eyes darting from mine to our connection.

"Jack, wait." His grip tightened again after I'd buried him inside me once more, and I froze as my heart stuttered.

Please, God, don't say he wants to stop.

"What?" I panted.

He stared at where we were joined and then looked up at me with such wonder in his eyes that I'd never forget it. All he said was, "I'm inside you."

"Yeah."

"I'm inside you," he repeated reverently, stroking his thumb across my bottom lip.

Here I was, so out of my mind with arousal I wanted to ride him like a rodeo bull, and he had enough control to pause for a mental *Hallmark* card moment. I glanced down, appreciating what he was, and wanted to weep.

"Yes. You are," I agreed, all warbled like Judy Garland.

"You feel fucking amazing. You. *Are*. Fucking amazing."

"Oh. Don't stop, Max. Please."

He urged me to lift as he took my mouth. "No way am I fucking stopping." He grunted and reached to stroke my throbbing shaft. "No fucking way. You feel too perfect."

"Yes," I moaned, even as I wondered if it was possible to die from feeling so elated. My body took over, riding him as we peppered each other with kisses.

He stroked me faster, his hips coming up to meet me. It spurred me on, making me rock onto him over and over.

"Oh, yeah. Fuck me, Jack!" he called out like a sexy cheering section. "Look at *you*, fucking me."

The man's newfound bedroom boldness was going to kill me from delirium. I threw my head back, making sounds I didn't know I could make as a tickling tension coiled tight in my balls.

"Oh, Max! I've wanted you forever," I practically whimpered.

"You've got me. You've got me now, baby."

A laugh barked out of me through the tears in my eyes at his endearment. I held his head in place to kiss him through the erotic slide of fill, release, fill, release.

"Christ, that's so fucking tight I'll never get my dick back," he choked out.

"I'm not giving it or your hand back."

He nipped my earlobe and growled. "Love it. Love when you talk like that. Shit. I'm about to come. Do I...can I come inside you?"

"Fuck, you'd better."

"Thank God." He laughed and sped up his jerking on my cock, but stopped thrusting his hips. He nipped at my bottom lip, teasing me with a sultry tone. "Are you going to come for me, babe?"

I laughed at his naughty voice, wondering what had happened to 'uptight Max.' It earned me a nip to my shoulder and a tight, fast thrust of my cock.

Lesson learned. Groaning, I placed my hand over his as all the pressure trapped inside me burst.

"Yeah, baby," I slurred, dropping my forehead to his. "I'm coming. *Ungh.* Max! I'm coming!"

"Yeah, Jack! Yeah!" he growled, squeezing my ass with his big, warm hand as I spilled onto his stomach. "Come, babe! Come for me!"

"Yeah. Yeah," I bellowed, feeling like I was the star of the hottest porn film ever.

"You like my cock inside you?" he said, all strangled and dirty, thrusting his hips up jerkily.

"Fucking love it!"

"Fits so...good. Your ass—perfect," he choked, gritting his teeth as he looked at me.

"Yes!" I'd have said anything to keep seeing him looking that sex-drunk over me and talking like the Mayor of Filthy Town.

His hands tightened on my hips, and his legs jerked, shaking the bed. He pulsed inside me like a secret heartbeat, crying out, "Oh, Jack. I'm...uh!" He slapped my ass, sending an electric shiver all the way to my toes. "Fuck, babe! *Ungh*!"

I could have died right then, and it would have been fine by me, holding onto each other as we moaned and panted like depraved animals. Max rubbed my thigh, giving me sweet, spent kisses.

"Oh, my God. That was...that was," he stammered.

"What?"

"The best kind of insanity."

Easing away, I flopped onto my back. Max wobbled to the bathroom to clean up as I sank into the pillow. He brought back a towel to clean me up, and then slid back in bed, running his hand up my chest.

"Hey? You okay?" he asked, still sounding as breathless as me.

I placed my hand on top of his, where it had stopped over my heart. "Way better than okay."

He pulled me in and kissed me like he was sealing a promise. I wrapped myself around him like a wet blanket, and we just laid there for a while in a silent afterglow.

"Wow," he whispered at one point, stroking my hair.

"Yeah." I chuckled.

He gave me a soft peck on the lips. "You and me."

"Me and you," I echoed, my heart spiraling farther away into the land of surreal promises.

"You were...cool with that?" he hesitated. "Even though you didn't get to do it to me?"

"Uh. Did you hear the noises I was making?"

Max chuckled and squeezed me. "I like your noises. Loud-ass neighbor."

As much as I wanted to hear any teasing or afterthoughts he had to say about our lovemaking, I couldn't fight the weight of my eyelids. I kissed the heart-eyed smile on his face that wouldn't go away and then buried my face against his chest.

Yawning, I informed him, "I'm sorry. I'm falling asleep."

"Goodnight, *Big Daddy*," he whispered.

My eyes flew open. It took my foggy brain a second to make sure I heard what I heard. When I tilted my head back, Max was grinning. I brought my hand down, swatting his ass. It's difficult to sound annoyed when you're laughing, still on a high from amazing sex, and were just made part of a family, but I tried.

"You are NOT fucking calling me that!"

"Hell of a game, babe. Wish I'd been there," Max said over the video chat on my phone.

"Thanks, but we don't need to talk about the fifth inning."

"Okay." He chuckled, but his expression turned tender. "I miss you."

Adjusting my position on the hotel bed, I traced the outline of his face with my fingertip. "I miss you too."

It had been the longest spring training of my life, having someone to miss for the first time. We had talked every day via video chat since I'd left in February, but the screen wasn't his arms, his bed, or even hip-checking him to stay away from the stove when we were in the kitchen.

I'd played hard today at the final exhibition game, telling myself the more I put in, the sooner it would be over, and therefore one step closer to seeing Max again. It was all wishful thinking. I was tied to my schedule, chomping at the bit for the month of April to be on its way.

I dismissed another incoming call. This one was from Montez, likely seeing if I wanted to go out to dinner with him, Hooper, and McQuiston. I'd been declining more and more invitations, too worried I'd get a call from Max and have to decline it if I was out with some of the team. Max had offered to come to some of the exhibition games. He'd taken it well when I said it wasn't a good idea for us to be seen together often, especially away from home, but I could tell it was wearing on him. Truthfully, it was wearing on me. It was why I'd caved and took him up on his plan to attend the upcoming Kansas City games.

"You're all still coming to the game next week?" I asked.

"Yeah. Why? You can't handle all of us?"

"No. I just wish I'd been there when you told your mom and Morgan."

"Are you mad? They won't say anything to anyone. I swear."

He'd tempted me with a visit by offering to come with Morgan, their mom, and even Carrie. His logic was that he'd be surrounded by so many women that no one would put two and two together about me and him. It had been a surprise when he told me he'd let his mother know we were dating. I'd half-expected Morgan would've figured it out by now since she knew about our first kiss.

"No. It's not that. I just…I wish I could have been there with you, so we could have done it together," I assured him.

It had taken him only four months to tell his mother, whereas it had taken me five years to tell my parents. I was both proud and envious of him while drowning in a pit of inadequacy.

"Well, I figured it was better to tell them before we fly out to see you," he went on.

"You think they would have guessed?"

"Well, yeah, because I would have asked them to watch Emma so I could stay in the same room with you. I didn't have to explain why after I told them about us."

"Oh, my God! Max, you came out to your family so you could get a babysitter for a booty call?" Heat crept up my face even though I was alone in my room.

Max laughed. "Well, I wasn't expecting anything, but *okay*. And when you put it that way, it sounds dirty."

I dropped my face in my hands. "No! How am I going to face them now?"

"Same way you always have," he said, all casual.

"Max! You're terrible."

"No. I'm a good planner, and you love it." He beamed.

"Do I?" I tried to imagine what Bev Hartwell's reaction would have looked like to Max asking her to babysit so we could be alone. Coming out to her was one thing, talking about alone-time with her son was throwing an elephant in the room. She'd always been so sweet to me, treating me like another son. Max had said she was happy for us, but it was still surreal to believe it had happened.

"Yeah. You get me for two whole days," he bragged.

"You know I only get one day off, right?"

"Yeah, but I'll be there to massage your sore muscles for moral support. I'm not going to fuck with your game."

"I'll look forward to that." Resting my chin in my hand, I couldn't fight my smile or the bubbles of giddiness welling up inside. "God, I miss you."

He moved closer to the screen. "I can't wait for you to come home. I'll make it out later in the season, too. I promise. And for some home games when I don't have court."

My stomach flipped while my heart soared. It was two contrasting reactions: the thrill of Max wanting to be close and the fear of him being close to me anywhere other than at home. We'd beaten the topic to death, so there was no point in bringing it up again, but I knew he still had no clue that my apprehension wasn't solely for my career.

In fact, the longer we were together, the less I cared if my name was ruined, and the more terrified I grew of how it would ruin *us* if the world ever found out my heart belonged to him. I'd seen what 'overwhelmed Max' looked like. There was no way that version of him could handle the consequences of being in a public relationship with me. He had no idea what it was like to be in the spotlight, and every night I wished for miracles to keep it that way.

CHAPTER 44
Max

Emma's arm hung limp at her side as Jack carried her sleeping body down the hallway of our rental house. Poor little thing. The excitement of Jack's late-night game had finally caught up with her. She'd passed out on the couch before the team even left the clubhouse for the night.

I moseyed after Jack and found Carrie and Morgan laughing in the doorway of the room they were sharing across from Emma's. My mother lingered in the hall, watching with a fond smile as Jack tucked Emma in.

"He's a good one, Max," she whispered to me.

"I know."

I draped my arm across her back, giving her shoulder a squeeze. She'd accepted my news about my relationship a few weeks ago with an open mind and heart. I was blessed to have a mother who would love my choice of partner right along with me.

The day Jack left for spring training had felt like I was losing an appendage. I knew I loved him more than a friend, more than a friend I was sleeping with, more than the air I breathed. He had pulled me from the madness of sulking by just being himself, by making me open my eyes and really see him. I'd only gotten a fraction before, blind fool that I was.

When he emerged from Emma's room, Mom cornered him for a hug, reaching up on tiptoe. "If it had to be anyone on the planet, I'm glad it was you, Jack. My son's a lucky man."

Insta-tears glistened in Jack's eyes—and damn it—the woman who'd chased my punk ass around with a flyswatter as a kid was going to make me cry, too.

"Thanks, Bev," Jack said. "I'm the lucky one."

"Mom," I warned, half-turned on, half-embarrassed. She needed to let him go because I knew exactly how few hours I had him to myself.

She released Jack and batted a dismissive hand at me like my word meant nothing. Before I could grab him by the arm, Morgan swooped in and snaked her arms around him like this was a freaking Irish immigrant funeral and he'd be lost at sea.

"Make sure he takes good care of you. I know what a pain in the ass he can be. We'll see you at one of the home games."

The girls were all leaving first thing in the morning, but I wasn't due to fly out until evening, giving us time to enjoy his one day off this month together.

When Morgan's hands slid up his back, pressing her newly not-pregnant middle against his, I had enough. Now she was just being annoying on purpose. I gave her a Teenage-Hartwell-Special, pinching behind her elbow and yanking her away.

"Alright. That's enough. Get your own man."

Morgan sputter-laughed. "Whoa! I'm glad your room isn't next to ours. Jealous much?"

"Oh, fuck off."

"Shh!" Mom warned.

I bit my lip and gave Carrie a quick peck on the cheek as a reward for being an example of a normal sister. Turning, I snatched Jack's hand like a fat kid claiming the biggest cupcake and tugged him down the hall. "Goodnight, everyone!"

The damned women didn't even have the decency to stifle their giggles and *awws* as heat crept up my neck. Jack's hand slipped out of mine. When I glanced over, he was skirting close to the wall like he was keeping his distance.

"What's wrong?"

"I feel like I'm breaking the law not being at the hotel."

It wasn't common for team members to be allowed to stay anywhere other than the team's hotel while they were on the road. Exceptions could be made on occasion. That Jack had been allowed to accommodate his visiting family—*thank you, Carrie*—just went to show how much the management valued him by getting us this private rental home.

I snatched his hand again as we neared the master bedroom on the other side of the house. "Well, good thing you know an attorney," I teased.

He shut the door, and for a moment we just stood there, appreciating the sight of each other. The last two and a half months had been a test of fortitude, worrying for him being out in the world on his own, longing for him, but also being proud of him from afar since I couldn't be by his side to witness his successes firsthand.

He smiled and stepped forward, pulling me into his embrace. "I'm so glad you're here," he whispered.

I took a hit of the soapy scent at his neck. "God, I miss you. Can't you pull a muscle or something?"

He laughed and stroked my cheek. "I'll be home in a few days."

"For a week. Then you'll be gone again."

"I'm sorry."

Making him feel guilty was my furthest intent. I just had so many sentiments bottled up that I wanted to get out now that he was in front of me in the flesh again. "I'm glad you get to do what you love," I assured him.

"School will be out soon," he said enthusiastically. "I'll get to be home every morning for home games with you and Emma. Did you find someone else besides Patti to watch her?"

"Oh! I didn't tell you yet?"

"What?"

"She's going to go over to Matt Gardner's house after school, starting Monday."

"Matt? Her boyfriend?"

"He's *not* her boyfriend," I mimicked Emma. "But yeah. I met his parents, Ryan and Zeke. Nice guys—both of them. Ryan's a stay-at-home dad, so it worked out great. He said he could watch Emma after school and even during the summer. I can drop her off on my way to work and pick her up when I get off, so *goodbye Patti!*"

I thought this was excellent news. Emma was happier than a pig in shit about it, but Jack frowned.

"Should I be worried?" he asked.

"About her talking about us?"

"No. About you making friends with another '*Dad*,'" he said, making air quotes.

"Oh, fuck off."

He cracked up. Why the hell was it funny that the thought of flirting with someone other than him was distasteful to me?

"Why do you laugh every time I say that?"

"Because I tell myself you really mean, '*I love you, Jack.*'"

My breath caught in my throat. Now was as good a time as any. "Well, I do."

He went quiet. I waited for a reaction, but he just stared, looking a bit stunned. Stunned wasn't good. I swallowed at my constricting throat.

"Did you hear me?"

He smiled and nodded. His thumbs rubbed my arms where he was bracing them.

"Well?" I demanded, because way to leave a guy hanging.

"Well, what?" He laughed. The bastard actually laughed.

"Well, aren't you going to say anything? You've always got something to say."

He chuckled again and pressed the heel of his palm underneath his eye. Shit. Why was he crying? I stood frozen, wondering if I'd jumped the gun, wondering if he'd say something like he couldn't let anyone be in love with him while he was still playing ball. He rested his forehead against mine.

"I thought you could fuck off a long time ago."

I was so stunned as I registered his words that my head actually bobbed backward when he planted a quick peck on my lips. A *long time ago*? He loved me *a long time ago* and never told me? And then he laughed when I admitted my feelings? What the hell was that about?

"And you didn't say anything?" I demanded.

He cupped my face, giving me a stupid grin. I'd been duped into being the one to spill his guts first, which was fine, but when someone tells you they love you, isn't proper protocol to say *I love you too*? I swatted his hand away.

"Well, fuck off," I replied. The smug bastard laughed even harder, like he thought I was joking. I pushed away from his chest to give him my back. "No. For real—fuck off."

"Max, that pout is seriously cute, but I know you're not really mad."

"No. I am!" I whipped my shirt off and flung it on the floor. What a wonderful night's sleep this would be. "'*Cute.*'" I scoffed, kicking off my shoes.

Jack must have had a death wish, because he laughed again. His big arms wrapped around me from behind, squeezing me tight.

"Why are you mad?"

"Because you took away my one joy, my signature line for when I'm frustrated." Or because I was fucking embarrassed. It wasn't every day you told someone for the first time that you loved them.

He freaking chuckled *again*. "Telling people to *fuck off* is your *one* joy? Gee, thanks. Don't tell Emma that."

"You know what I mean."

"Yeah. That when you say it, you really mean, '*I don't want to admit you're right, but I love you.*'"

"Fuck off," I said, instinctively, but busted up as soon as the words were out because, yeah, no effing way was I admitting he was right, and I *did* love him—stupidly, hopelessly loved him.

Jack roared into my neck and squeezed me harder. "See!"

I tried growling out of spite. "I hate you."

His warm breath fanned my ear. "I love you."

Every ounce of tension in me drained away. I wrapped my hands over his forearms, leaning back into him to get closer to his words.

He loved me. Jack loved me. Maybe I knew that already and had just been afraid it wasn't true. I closed my eyes and let it wash over me, wind through me, and wrap around me as we just stood there, holding onto each other.

When I turned around to face him, he ran his fingers through my hair. His loving smile was like a magnet, drawing my lips toward his. Halfway there, I noticed his mouth was ticked up higher at one corner. It was just enough to make him look a little too pleased with himself.

"Fuck off," I murmured, capturing his lips. Turns out it's difficult to kiss when you're both chuckling.

When we got it out of our systems, I no longer tasted amusement on his lips, but rather the intoxicating flavor of being loved by the man I loved back. I helped him lose his T-shirt, and we rediscovered each other—him, running his hands down my chest; me, caressing his big arms. The muscles there looked larger now that he was back playing.

"You need to get to sleep?" I asked, pressing a kiss to the collarbone of his pitching arm.

He looked tired after the full day he'd had, but he shook his head. Leaning down to capture my lips, his fingers went to the snap on my jeans, popping it open. The sound of my zipper followed.

Glancing down, I sighed. "Fine, but if you lose Thursday, it's not my fault."

He snickered and shoved my pants down, taking my boxer briefs along with them. His teeth nipped my lower lip once, twice, and then he sucked on it. All the while, his hands glided across my belly. They detoured down to the front of my hips. I was being casually groped as I tried to kick out of my jeans and work at his button.

Jack bumped his pelvis into mine, nearly making me trip over my tangled feet and take a step back. His nails scratched little circles over the curve of my ass as he nudged me further backward with penetrating kisses. It was kind of difficult to get a guy's pants undone when he wouldn't quit kissing you or grinding against you. I felt like dessert, but damn if I minded. I loved his eager side.

"Mm," I purred as the back of my knees hit the edge of the mattress. "Quit teasing me."

"I'm not teasing. I'm enjoying." He leaned in, forcing me to flop back on the bed. Before I could even raise up onto my elbows, his bare chest pressed against mine, and he devoured my mouth with his.

I had missed his delicious weight on me. The reconnecting was driving me wild. His hand slid between my legs over the sensitive underside of my ass. When his fingertip traced the silky skin around my pucker, I shuddered.

I finally got his fucking jeans undone and groaned in both relief and victory. His touch sent a wave of heat through my abdomen, anticipation pulsing through me. I had plans for this visit, and letting him know my feelings were only half of them.

The elixir of his body heat disappeared when he suddenly pulled back and removed his hand. What the hell was that look for?

"Max?" He traced his finger up the outside of my seam, staring down at where all my business was on display. "Did you...get your ass crack waxed?"

Fuck. Well, of course, I knew he'd notice at some point, but I had hoped for just an *'mm, that's nice,'* not shock and an attentive exam. I pinched my eyes shut, remembering the horror I had gone through to prep for this special reunion.

I shook my head and reached out to pull him back to me. "We don't need to talk about it."

His fingers traced over the silky skin between my cheeks, and he chuckled. "Baby, did you do this for me?"

I cracked an eye open and gestured for him to come back to me. "Well, you...don't have any hair."

He braced an arm next to my shoulder, hovering over me. "Yeah, because I don't want to have to scratch my nuts in front of millions of people. You didn't have to do this, though. You're sexy the way you are."

I grunted and pulled his head down for a kiss. That was one way to end this mortifying conversation, but Jack came up with a curious expression and traced my seam again.

"Did you do it yourself?"

I groaned and shook my head, trying to distract him with kisses to his jaw. He gasped, looking even more amused.

"You actually went somewhere? Man, I can't see you walking into a public place asking to be waxed." He chuckled. "Oh, my God. I wish I'd been there. Were they gentle with you? How bad did it hurt?"

I leveled him with a look. *Gentle* was not a word I'd use to describe the torture I'd subjected myself to. It was more like I had let out a war cry and distinctly remembered hearing a giggle from the *evil-ass defiler* who called herself an esthetician.

Pinching my eyes shut, I warned, "Jack, the first rule of *Fight Club* is to never talk about Fight Club."

His laughing lips captured mine, and I sighed in relief. His fingertip trailed up the underside of my ass.

"So smooth," he murmured.

"Shh," I warned.

I managed to slide his jeans and briefs over his hips. He wiggled out of them, never interrupting his kisses as he kicked them off. Grabbing my hand from the side of his face, he interlaced our fingers and pressed our clasped hands to the mattress. When he did the same to the other and ground his erection against mine as he kissed my neck, I knew what it meant to feel ravaged. Damn. He really wanted me tonight.

"Mm. I should tell you to fuck off more often."

"Yes. You should." He smiled, sliding his fingers down my arms as his lips worked their way down my chest.

When his tongue lapped against the tip of my cock, the jolt of desire made me panic. This wasn't how my plan was supposed to go.

"Wait," I told him, tugging at his shoulders. "I put some things in the nightstand."

He flashed me a knowing smirk and returned with a bottle of lube and a condom. My heart rate kicked up, watching him tear the foil packet open. When he pulled out the condom and brought it toward my erection, I caught him by the wrist to redirect his hand toward his own.

"I was hoping maybe this time...you could top."

"'*Top?*'" He blinked like I was speaking in tongues.

Fuck. Had my research failed me?

"Uh. Yeah. I thought that meant that...that you'd be the one to..."

"I know what it means." He chuckled. "But...how do *you* know what it means?"

"I know how to Google search shit, Jack."

He cocked a brow. "Oh, yeah? And what else did you Google search?"

Jesus. Tell a guy you love him, and he starts getting all cocky on you.

"What a man Google searches is a man's business. Why? Are you not into that?"

"Google searching?"

I pressed my palms to my eyes. "Oh, for fuck's sake. Is this going to be another *murder-eyes* conversation? Way to take the romance out of it."

His laughter tickled my neck, and he pressed a kiss there. "I picked up on the romancing, and I'd love to do that with you, but are you sure?"

When I dropped my hands, his expression was so full of concern and tenderness that I didn't know whether to be nervous or more turned on. His thumb traced circles on my arm as he studied my face.

I nodded, indicating my lower half. "Yeah. I'm ready," I assured him.

His brows lifted, and he chuckled before giving me a kiss. "'*Ready*?' Do I want to know what you've been up to?"

"Probably, but I'm not telling."

About a hundred dollars' worth of dildos to experiment and prep with while we were apart was what I'd been up to, but fuck if he needed to know that. Let's just say there was a reason Goldilocks tried out all those beds.

He raised on one knee, straddling my leg, smirking, and shaking his head. "Sounds like you had more than one Fight Club while I was away."

"Shh," I warned.

When he brought the condom to his shaft, I sat up and took over. A wave of possessiveness washed through me, knowing he was about to be inside me. There was something sexy about getting him ready for me. By the sound of his quick inhale, he must have thought so, too. When I looked up, the humor in his expression was gone. It was just us and this moment. The excitement of giving him the same gift he'd given me sizzled in my blood. I wanted him to know I trusted him with my body the way he'd trusted me to do this to him.

He leaned down and kissed me in a way that said how special this was to him. I laid back as he dragged one of the pillows over to slide under my ass. My hands shook, depositing some lube in my palm to slicken him. I was worried he'd see my nerves and call it off, but he didn't say a word, just ran his fingers up and down my side, smiling this little patient, loving smile.

He slickened his fingers and massaged my seam as he kissed me. When he slipped one inside, I moaned. That reconnection felt like coming home— coming home to my man. I wanted more of it.

My legs were still hanging off the mattress as I tried to think of how this would work. I brought my feet up and scooted back. Jack followed me and treated me to more of his hand when I widened my legs and groaned into his mouth.

I felt the press of another finger and finally another. We'd never tried three on me, but I knew it was a necessity tonight. When I hissed at the burn, he stopped.

"We don't have to. You know that, right?" he said. "You don't need to do this to impress me."

I scoffed because it wasn't all about impressing him. "I'm not. I want to feel you—*all* of you. I want to be as close to you as I can."

His nose twitched. "I love you, Max."

Shit. He was going to make me cry. I cupped his face and pulled him to my lips. "I love you too. I want everything with you."

His fingers thrust with more vigor and crooked, hitting that bundle of nerves inside me that made my back arch. I was literally going to blow it from emotional overload.

"Jack. Now, please."

He withdrew and kissed the inside of my knee, running the tip of his cock through my seam as I clutched a handful of the sheets in anticipation. The view from my position was magnificent as my eyes traveled up his stomach to his chest.

"You're so damn sexy," I murmured as headiness weighed my limbs down. "I love watching you play."

Jack sighed the way people do when they take a bite of their favorite food. "I love playing when you're watching." The blunt head of his cock stopped at my entrance, and he gripped my thigh with his free hand, then pressed forward. "God, I miss you," he whispered.

I couldn't stand the foreplay or the fear of the unknown anymore. "Take me. Please. Need to feel you."

He shuddered at my words and pushed past the first ring of muscles. It was like we sucked in the same breath as the tip of his cock breached me. My nostrils flared and my jaw clenched because *holy shit*. Could someone break their asshole?

The sharp slicing sensation intruded on my pleasure like a kazoo in a symphony. That wasn't supposed to happen. My dick was yelling '*Let the man pass,*' while my ass was unloading concrete road barriers and over-sized load hazard tape. I was pissed, and panicked, and not on the road to the way he'd thrown his head back and moaned the few times I'd done this to him.

His jaw flapped open. His gaze locked on mine. "Baby, are you okay?"

Okay? Not if you considered the complaint email I was typing in my head to The Pleasure Emporium for their misleading product descriptions of the prep items I'd purchased.

Guaranteed to initiate dual pleasure.

Total fucking lies—signed, *my ass!*

When I got home, I was going to find a grenade for the hundred bucks' worth of useless dicks in my nightstand and file a civil case so there would be no more victims of false advertising.

My breath hitched as I tried not to groan at the tightness and twinge of the stretch. I grunted my frustrations out through clenched teeth, "Why is your dick so fucking big?"

Jack's mouth turned into an *O*. He started to ease back. "Baby, let's stop."

I dug my heels into the backs of his thighs and clutched his forearm. "No. I can do it! Just...kiss me," I pleaded, desperate for a distraction from the way my body was ruining my biggest fantasy.

Jack swept down, covering me as he dove into my mouth. When his hand wrapped around my shaft and began to stroke, my locked-up muscles got a reprieve. The way he worked me and possessed my mouth melted me like butter, straightening out the equilibrium of the pleasure-pain ratio until there was nothing left but rampant desire. I sighed in relief.

The construction workers in my head hopped out of their truck and scrambled to remove the barriers like they were getting holiday pay. This was... better. So much better. I hooked my legs around his waist, free-falling into the white-hot need as his thumb grazed circles around my head with each upstroke. Fuck, yes.

Every thought of the mechanics was gone. *Better* turned into *incredible*. I felt so expanded, but there was no pain, just a sense of all-consuming belonging as Jack teased my cock and breathed sexy little moans into our kisses.

"Max," he whispered. "I'm inside you."

I opened my eyes and glanced through the narrow space between us, showing our connection. Fuck. I'd done it. My body thrummed, making my cock jerk in his hand as I absorbed the sensation and sight of being completely filled by him. I was going to freaking cry. Looking into his eyes, the intimacy of it was the most overwhelming thing I'd ever experienced.

I tried to smile, but my body was trembling so much I didn't know if my facial muscles would comply. "Take me," I gasped, running my hand through his hair. "Take me, babe. Please."

Jack raised up and braced my legs. Then it began, the slow rocking of his hips. Each delve built a pitch of needy tension that burst, creating an even more desperate need inside me. I pawed at his hands, his forearms—wherever I could touch him.

"Oh, Jack," I warbled like someone blathering over a 'chick flick.'

"Baby, you feel incredible."

"Not...as good as you."

I lifted my feet to chase the leverage I was mad for. Jack hooked them over his shoulders like I weighed no more than a rag doll. Could he be any sexier right now?

He wrapped an arm around my thigh and pumped my cock as he dropped a hand to the mattress, nearly bending me in half so he could kiss me. The new angle made him nail my prostate perfectly on every thrust as I jerked my hips into him like an addict.

I knew it was sex and that lots of people felt great while doing it, but the way we moved together—the love that emanated from us was too beautiful to absorb. How had I gotten so damn lucky that this man picked me?

"Jack," I cried—literally—as a tear slipped down my cheek. I cupped his face. "Fuck. I love you so much."

He ravished my mouth to the point I couldn't breathe, working his hips faster. "I love you so much it hurts," he gasped when he finally came up for air.

"I'm so...filled. Love feeling you."

"I'm home inside you. Love it."

My head fell back on a whimper, absorbing his words and the sensations. I clutched the sheet. Jack gripped my hand, pressing it to the bed. His hair was in his eyes, his cheeks ruddy, as he let out little gusts of air. The way he was exerting himself for *us*, for *this*, more than he had for any game, was the final straw. I hadn't needed this to know how hopelessly crazy I was for him, but I fell over the edge and passed a piece of myself to him to keep forever.

"Oh! Jack!" I spilled onto his hand and my chest.

"Yeah, honey. Feel it," he keened. "I'm with you, baby. I'm with you!"

I blinked through my glistening eyes to witness his reaction. He turned his head and bared his teeth like the pleasure he was receiving from my body was too much for mere mortals to handle, causing pride to balloon in my chest that my body was doing that for him.

He collapsed on top of me. I wrapped him in my arms and pressed sloppy kisses of gratitude to his cheek. There was a myth that men were generally rough, but that discredited our entire sex. Jack carefully eased out of me and pulled me to him, holding a chaste kiss to my lips.

He got up and returned with a towel, cleaning me up tenderly, like a worshipped deity. When he crawled back into bed, he pulled me into his arms.

"How much longer are you going to play baseball?" I asked, grazing his cheek with my thumb.

"Why? So, I can retire and stay home and love you every night?"

"Well, *yeah*."

We shared a laugh, but then he sighed. "I don't know. I'm already getting old for a ballplayer. I was hoping for a few more years before you came along, but maybe just one more now...if you can handle that."

"Uh. You're not old because then I'm old. And if you want to play lon-ger than that, you should. I don't want you to quit because of me. I'm just being sentimental."

He stroked my hair, looking contemplative. "I want to be around more. I don't want to miss watching Emma grow up. I know the guys always say baseball is hard on families, but now I really know what they mean."

My heart buckled in my chest under the weight of his meaning, and so I met it with my own wish. "You could sell your house and have one less thing to worry about. I'd sell mine, but Emma grew up there. I don't really want to give her anymore change than she's already gone through with losing Lainey."

His smile warmed every inch of me. "You asking me to live with you?"

"Well, you pretty much do already."

Sadness flickered in his eyes, and his smile dimmed. "Sometimes the guys stop over unannounced. I'm sorry, but it wouldn't look good."

"*Good*," I repeated, directing my hate of the word at the ceiling.

"I'm sorry."

"No." I sighed and patted his hand. "I'm just getting really sick of what everyone's definition of *good* is."

"I know. I never meant for you to have to deal with all that comes with this."

Was he serious? I propped up on an elbow, so I was looking down at him. "All that comes with *this*?"

"*Us*...being together. I still can't believe your mom and Morgan know and are okay with it."

I tugged for him to sit up and wrapped him up tight in my arms. "They're okay with it because they love us, and I'm not sorry about all that comes with *this*." I gestured between us. "If I was, that'd mean I was sorry for all the good that comes with it. You're a good person, Jack, a good friend, a good partner, and a good father." When his mouth ticked up, I returned his smile. "I'm not sorry about any of that, and whatever comes with it is worth it."

He did that scary thing where he kissed me and stayed silent. I still hadn't figured out if it was to keep from getting choked up, or if it meant he didn't believe me and was placating me with acquiescence. I'd said my piece, though. It was all I could do for now. One day, Jack would have to learn to trust the future and that I'd be right there with him no matter what it brought.

We showered and made our way back to bed. Morning would come fast when we had to send the girls off to the airport. Tomorrow evening, when I had to leave him for home, would come just as fast, so I fought sleep, stroking lazy patterns on his stomach in the stillness of the rental house.

Jack turned his head, nuzzling his mouth near my ear. "Max?"

"Hm?"

"When I retire, do you think you could help me sell my house?"

My smile branded his warm chest. Maybe the future I saw was appealing enough to him he could shake his worries after all. "Gladly. I'll even let you bring the Fleetwood Mac."

"Definitely the Fleetwood Mac. I thought you knew that was a package deal when you got me." He squeezed my shoulder.

A laugh tore from my chest, and I kissed the smirk on his face. "Fuck off."

CHAPTER 45
Max

I peeled out of my suit jacket and hung it in my office closet. The door mirror showed two damp circles under the armpits of my dress shirt. Fantastic.

Dan needed to explain again how three-piece suits gave off a professional air. You were either freezing in the winter or sweating your balls off from late spring through summer, and I didn't want to know how much I'd spent on dry-cleaning over the years.

Pulling the chair out behind my desk, I stifled a moan when the tenderness in my ass brought on a rush of precious memories from two nights ago in Kansas City with Jack. My new perma-smile grew in size, knowing he'd be home tomorrow.

I was going to move more of his clothes into my closet tonight as a surprise to make things easier for him. Nothing says romance like kidnapping someone's possessions. Right? I couldn't wait to hear him tease me about the possessive act.

The door handle to my office hit the wall with a familiar *thunk*. I didn't even have to look up to know it was Dan. He was the only one on our floor who entered a room with the grace of someone storming a castle. I glanced past him and noted the slight increase of the indent in the drywall as the door swayed from the ricochet effect.

"Man, did you see this shit about Jack?" he called.

"What?" I immediately thought of *my Jack*, but dismissed it. Dan and I rarely had reason to discuss him, so my mind scrambled to remember clients or anyone else he could be talking about.

"It's all over the internet," he said, phone in hand as he approached my desk. "Some gay home porn."

"What?" My stomach dropped. "Jack who?"

"Spears. Your neighbor." He scrutinized my intelligence with an exasperated look and turned his phone, so the screen faced me. "Did you know?"

I sprang up from my chair, trying to focus on an image pulled up on his screen, but he was still moving. My throat closed up, seeing a blurry picture of two naked men on a bed—two naked men that I knew were me and Jack. The bed was the bed we'd made love on in the rental house.

My stomach curled in on itself and rolled over. I couldn't breathe. This wasn't happening. I snatched the phone from Dan's hand as soon as he got close enough.

There was a sideways triangle on the image. It wasn't just a photo. It was a fucking video. My hand shook as I pressed the button, wanting to know how much of our private evening the world had seen. How had this happened? There was no way Jack had done this, no way my family or Carrie had done this.

Fortunately, there was no audio, but I still covered my mouth in horror as the footage played. Jack and I were on the fucking internet, bare ass naked, him leaning over and thrusting into me.

"Oh, my God," I whispered and had to steady the phone with both hands to stop the video.

"I know, man. It's fucking sick."

The derision in Dan's tone raked over my nerves, but I ignored it. There was so much more to worry about.

"Is it on the news?"

He barked out a cynical sound. "It's fucking everywhere, man. He's fucked." He pointed at his phone and laughed, adding, "More than that guy."

All my blood rushed to my ears, my heartbeat pounding in my head as I leveled him with a glare. "*Shut up*, Dan."

He gawked at me, but I saw the moment when understanding registered. My face bloomed with heat, but I didn't care. He shook his head, his face going lax. "No. No, man. That's *not* you."

I knew I could take back snapping at him, knew I could say I was just defending my friend and neighbor, but that would have been a betrayal of the man I loved. I stared at Dan's face as it morphed into a mask of disapproving shock.

"No. Tell me that's not you," he said, covering his mouth. "Jesus, Max! I thought *maybe* it looked like you, but…no. Are you fucking kidding me?"

Grinding my teeth together, I sucked in a breath, trying to rein in my nerves. I'd never expected Dan would accept me being not straight, but I didn't have time to listen to his bullshit. I needed to get a hold of Jack.

Trevor walked through the door with his thick black eyebrows raised. "Hey. I could hear you down the hall. Everything all right in here?"

Tossing Dan's phone on my desk, I pinned Dan with a warning look. "I don't want to see this shit, and I'd appreciate it if you wouldn't look at it either."

I turned my back and braced my pounding head with my hands. The world was falling apart around me. Everything Jack had fretted about had happened in the worst way imaginable. I didn't even know where to start fixing it.

"Dude, that's *not* you! Is it?" Dan blathered behind me. I heard him retrieve his phone from my desk and got a mental picture of him watching it over and over later as he spat out curses and slurs. Because that's exactly what he would do, and I was helpless to stop him or anyone else who would.

"Get out, Dan," I ground between my teeth, pressing my palms to my eyes.

"Holy fuck! Are you fucking kidding me? Max? What the fuck? You're fucking gay?"

"Dan!" I warned, clenching my fingers into fists as I pinched my eyes shut. "Get the hell out."

"Dan," Trevor cautioned, sounding near my desk.

"No, Trevor! Are you hearing this?"

"I don't know what I'm hearing, but it sounds like it's none of our business."

"None of *our business*? Are you shitting me? We run a practice together, and he's all over the internet taking it in the ass from a celebrity! This is our fucking *business*! He's going to ruin us with…with his sick home sex tapes, fucking another guy!"

Something snapped inside me, and I spun around. My entire body was vibrating like I was having a seizure.

"That's enough, Dan," Trevor raised his voice louder than I'd ever heard him be.

"Get the fuck out!" I yelled, pointing to the door.

"No! You owe us an explanation. Why the fuck did you do this? Were you looking for money? Or what? Do...do you get off on people seeing how sick you are?"

This was ridiculous for even Dan. It was taking every fiber of my control to not jump over my desk and pound him into the floor. "You think I want the world to see my private life? I don't know how the fuck it got out there!"

He made a gagging noise and covered his mouth. "Oh, God. It's true? Fuck," he spat, bringing a hand to his stomach like being in my presence was making him ill. "Holy shit. How could you?"

My nostrils flared at the way his question reduced Jack to a devious act rather than a person worthy of being loved and cherished. "How could I *what?*" I snapped, no longer caring about de-escalating the situation.

"Dan," Trevor warned again, grabbing hold of his arm like he was encouraging him to leave, but Dan had none of it. He wrenched his arm away and flashed wild eyes on Trevor.

"No! Are you shitting me? You're okay with this? Are you fucking queer too?"

I was around my desk in a second and had two handfuls of Dan's suit lapels in my fists. "Shut your fucking mouth! You ignorant prick!"

Dan grabbed my wrist with one hand, and my neck with the other. Trevor squeezed his arm between us, trying to pry us apart.

"*Me?*" Dan fumed. "You were fucking *married*. You have *a daughter*," Dan raged as I backed him toward the doorway. "What did he do, Max? Take advantage of you because Lainey's gone?"

I bit the inside of my lip so I wouldn't let out a war cry and snap his neck. How ludicrous was he that he believed I couldn't think for myself? The hits just kept getting worse the more he spewed, as poor Trevor scrambled along beside us in an effort to break us up. My foot snagged on Trevor's, and it was enough that Dan got an arm's reach away. Trevor squeezed between us, holding his arms out wide.

"Guys! Enough! Everybody just calm down," Trevor panted.

"You let him in *your house*, let him watch *Emma*," Dan said, pointing an accusing finger at me as though he gave a shit about Emma. "What if he did something to her? Did you ever think about that?"

I didn't even think. I just acted, holding an arm out to urge Trevor back as I sidestepped him and planted my fist in the center of Dan's face. His head reared back and bashed into the wall, causing him to stagger.

"Don't you dare say another fucking word about Jack! You don't know what the hell you're talking about!" I yelled over Trevor's shoulder while he braced my arm and held a palm to my chest to keep me from advancing. He muttered words of calm, but I barely registered them.

Dan straightened up and surveyed the blood on his hand when he pulled it away from his nose. "You're going to defend him? He probably put that shit out there as a way to ensure he makes money after his career is over. He fucking used you for publicity."

I growled like a damn bear and charged at him, swinging. "You don't know what the fuck you're talking about!"

All I ended up accomplishing was grabbing his stupid suit and slamming him into the wall, while Trevor clung onto me like those fish that affix themselves to whales. Dan held his arms up, warding me off with the finesse of a teenage girl, getting in a few open-palmed smacks to my head.

"Get the fuck off me!" he snapped.

Trevor panted, finagling his way in between us with a grip on each of our mussed dress shirts. Through a glass section of the wall, I could see Jennifer, our paralegals, and even the janitor watching the show.

"Alright, enough!" Trevor demanded. "Everybody stop. We can fix this."

"Fix it?" Dan squawked. "He's getting fucked in the ass all over the internet, Trevor! There's no fixing this. We're fucking ruined!"

I clenched my fists at my side, locking my jaw in place in the hopes it would keep me from being further provoked. Physical violence was never the answer, but I wanted to hit something so badly as an outlet for my outrage over this entire ordeal.

"No," Trevor replied to Dan's claim. "He's *a victim,* and that's what we do: help victims."

Dan pressed his hands to his head. "I don't believe what I'm hearing."

Like a switch, all my adrenaline fizzled, watching Dan's baffled expression. I had so many other things to worry about; I wasn't going to waste another second on his failure to grasp reality or human decency. I turned away, and a dizzy sensation came over me as I tried to collect my thoughts.

"I've got to go get Emma. I need to call Jack," I murmured the list of things barraging my mind. "He's got a game. Shit. He's got to play today."

"Max, it's okay. Go on and go," Trevor said. "But let me know if you have any idea how this got out. Who might have released it without your permission?"

"We didn't make it," I told him, my knees feeling weak. "We were at a rental house in Kansas City for his game. Somebody must have had a camera in there."

"Oh, God," Trevor whispered, running his hand over his head. "I'm so sorry. Send me whatever information you have on where you guys stayed, and I'll get an emergency order started."

"Are you shitting me, Trevor?" Dan stepped forward. "You want to get mixed up in this?"

"Dan, we're *partners*. He's *our friend*." Trevor sounded as exasperated as I felt.

Dan's cold eyes pierced mine and then flashed back to Trevor. "The fuck we are." He sneered and stormed out.

I made it to my desk, wondering how much louder the pounding of my heart could get. My hands moved with the speed of a robot whose batteries were dying, but I managed to locate my phone. Dropping into my chair, I stared at the floor, not seeing my office, but rather images of Jack's and Emma's faces, and the faces of my family. We were on the fucking news. We were fucking on the fucking news.

"I've got to get Emma before she hears anything," I said. "Then...I'm sorry, Trevor, but I'll have to push my meetings for today...and probably tomorrow and..."

"Max, it's okay. We'll handle it."

When I glanced up, Trevor was on the other side of my desk, taking a seat. He wasn't cussing or fleeing the room. He was calm, incredibly calm. He was wearing the face we wore when our clients were upset, when we solved problems.

"What do you need right now?" he asked. "Is there someone who can pick up Emma in case the press is waiting at your house?"

"Shit. Fuck. Yeah." I gripped my hair at the roots as lightbulbs went off in my numb brain. "I can call... Crap. Who can I fucking call after they see this?"

"Do you want me to call Barb and ask her to pick up Emma and take her to our house until you get there?" he offered.

It was a great idea. Lord only knew how much news of this had spread. I felt so helpless. This was about my life, and I knew absolutely nothing about what was happening. When had it been posted? What were people saying about it? Did Jack know? His team?

"I...no," I stammered. "No. Trevor, I can't ask you guys to do that. I...Emma's got a friend whose parents are...I know someone I can call."

Trevor nodded his approval. "Alright. I'll call Judge Hirscher and get an emergency order started. We need to call the authorities and get the FBI involved. We'll need to have them search that house and maybe even yours and Jack's houses too, in case this was a stalking situation."

Jesus. Could Jack have a stalker? I needed to stop being affected and start thinking like the lawyer that I was. If I fell apart, I'd be no good to Emma or Jack. "I...right," I concurred. "No. I can call the police."

"Max," Trevor soothed, tapping the surface of my desk with his index finger. "You need to call Jack and see what's going on with his team. I've got this here. Don't worry about it. Just take care of you, Jack, and Emma. It's okay. Everything's going to be okay."

Christ. How frazzled did I look if Trevor kept telling me things were going to be okay? I blew out a breath, trying to balance the upset over Dan's reaction with the gratitude I felt toward Trevor at that moment. Dan hadn't been completely off base. This would draw unfavorable attention to our practice, the practice that was our livelihood. My life, no matter how much it wasn't anyone else's business, had just affected those of my two law partners.

"Trevor, how... I can't... Why are you..." My mouth scrambled for the right words as my emotions clogged my throat. "Dan was right. You don't want to get mixed up in this. I'm sorry."

"Max, we're partners. You'd help me."

"But this is... This... Trevor, it's too much." I rested my forehead in my hand. "This is a fucking nightmare. And he's right. It could ruin us. I should leave and get a lawyer from another firm."

Trevor stood up abruptly. For a moment I thought his sigh was one of relief, like maybe I'd given him the out he wanted.

"Max, I've been waiting a long time to say this. I'm grateful you guys took me on, but Dan's an asshole." A breath of surprise and maybe even amusement at his admission passed my lips. "I've got this," he assured. "You didn't do anything wrong. Look at this from a business standpoint. If this were someone else's case, would you take it?"

I would in a heartbeat, but it wasn't someone else and suddenly I felt very small, truly understanding what it was like to be a victim. "But it's not, Trevor. I can't ask you to associate your reputation with me after this."

"You didn't ask. And I'd be more than happy to have my reputation be known for helping a friend when some criminal exploits his private life without his permission."

"I..." My throat closed up. Jack and I would need help, and there was no one I trusted more to handle it than Trevor. I nodded, unable to look at him. "Thank you."

"Send me everything you have on that property," he said, heading for the door with a swiftness that told me he was making my problem his number-one priority.

The way he'd jumped to help and give his friendship was humbling, but Jack's warnings and my behavior from months ago brought caution to my mind. It made me sick to give credence to Jack's fears, but it had to be said.

"Trevor?"

He stopped at the doorway. "Yeah?"

"There'll be…prejudice all the way through this thing, even with some of the judges we know. I don't want it to come back on you," I warned, knowing he understood my meaning. Half of the judges we worked with were older than my mother, born at a time when same-sex relationships were not as accepted as they were now.

Trevor's expression was amused. "Max, I'm Black. Prejudice doesn't scare me."

However more embarrassed I could be than if the world just saw my boyfriend fucking me, that's what I was. *Way to warn a Black man about prejudice, genius.* I nodded, giving him a smile, and hoped it conveyed even a modicum of my gratitude before he breezed out of the room.

I spent the next three hours on the phone, experiencing the six-degrees of separation effect when I realized everyone I needed to call. The first was to Matt's fathers, Zeke and Ryan Gardner, who wholeheartedly agreed to keep Emma after school and even overnight, if needed. Having just heard the news themselves, they offered their sympathy and support, assuring me they'd keep the kids off the internet. Next, I called the school where the principal insisted that Emma would be safe. He promised to call if the media found out I had a daughter and showed up at the school. After that, I phoned Jack, who didn't answer.

His game started in half an hour. He was probably doing warm-ups, which meant his phone would be secured in his locker. If it was all over the internet, though, like Dan said, wouldn't the team's PR people have been alerted to it by now? Maybe management and his agent, Ed, were going over damage control with him. Not knowing what the person you loved was dealing with was torture.

I made it through three more phone calls—one to my mom, one to Morgan, and one to Carrie, all of whom hadn't yet heard what happened. Carrie promised to get me Ed's number, so I could get word to or about Jack. I had just hung up with Morgan when a detective walked in with Trevor.

It was a necessity, the myriad of benign questions he asked me about the rental house, but it was all I could do not to pace a hole in the carpeting as we mottled through my statement.

What was happening with Jack? Did he know? Was he safe? Was he playing? I had to get to a television.

Trevor collected the rental information from me, worked with the detective to contact the FBI, and said he put in a call to the team's PR department. I'd never felt so useless or trapped. When the detective asked me to meet at my house so the FBI could check for surveillance cameras, I was both relieved to escape the confines of my office and horrified at the possibility someone had spied on us in my home.

As I sped toward the house, I found Jack's game and streamed it on my phone, while trying not to die in traffic. He was playing. *How* was he playing? Hadn't anyone told him?

There was one more call I had to make; one I really didn't want to. I dialed Lainey's dad, and he picked up on the second ring.

I cut right to the chase after an awkward hello on my part. "Look, Bob. The reason I'm calling… You might see something on the news."

"One of your cases making waves?"

"No. No. It's…personal. I'm seeing somebody, and it looks like someone hid a camera in…a house we stayed at. Then they leaked the footage to the media."

"I don't understand. I mean, that's illegal. What would the media want with illegal footage of someone? Did they catch the person? Is that why?"

"No. I…it's intimate in nature…the content, and it's because of who I was with." I sucked in a breath. This was not the way I'd wanted to tell my in-laws. "The person I'm dating is Jack."

"Jack?"

"Jack Spears. My neighbor. We're…we've been dating for a few months now. I'm sorry. This isn't how I wanted to tell you, but I wanted to warn you guys so you didn't find out by some misconstrued media coverage."

It was quiet for so long, I wondered if the line had disconnected. My console screen showed the line was still open, though.

"Bob?"

"You can bring Emma here. She can stay with us," he finally said.

"Thanks, but she's staying at a friend's tonight and probably at my mom's tomorrow or until I get done with the FBI."

"The FBI?" he chirped.

"It's a federal offense to record people in a home setting and the crime happened in another state when we went to Jack's game in Kansas City earlier in the week," I explained.

It went silent again, but then it sounded like muffled cursing on the other end. "How could you do this, Max?"

I nearly swallowed my tongue. "Bob, we had no idea someone recorded us. I certainly would never share something so personal like…"

"No. That's not what I meant. Damn it!"

My entire body went rigid as I stopped at a light. A man I'd never heard get excited about anything in his life had just yelled at me at the top of his lungs.

"How in the hell could you do this to us, Max? To Emma? A *man*? You were married to my *daughter,* and you were with *a man*?"

I bit the inside of my cheek. "*Jack,*" I enunciated. "I was with Jack, my and Lainey's best friend."

"Don't you dare bring her into this. This has nothing to do with her! Don't make excuses. How could you?"

He was right. It had nothing to do with Lainey. It only had to do with my daughter's grandparents. I took a deep breath and hit the gas. "My excuse is that I'm in love with a good person who happens to love your grand-daughter very much."

"Oh, my God. I don't want to hear this. He's lost his mind," he said, more muffled, which meant Ellen was nearby. Wonderful. "You bring Emma over to our house, or no. We'll come get her."

Un-fucking believable. "Bob," I said evenly. "Emma is fine. She's staying here."

"Max! I'm not going to—"

I cut him off before I had to hear one more thing I was sure I wouldn't want to hear. "Bob, I love you guys both very much, but I don't have time to deal with this right now. I'll call you when things get sorted. Goodbye."

I ended the call before he could answer. My ass was on television, my boyfriend possibly had no clue what was going on, Dan was probably going to quit, and my in-laws wanted to kidnap my child because they thought being with another man made me an unfit parent. The last three hours had been like getting my nuts squeezed in a vise. I couldn't wait to see what was next.

As I approached my house, a sea of cars lined the usually sedate street. News vans, police cars, and people who appeared to be just nosey onlook-ers. They descended on me as soon as my front tire crested the end of my driveway.

Holy. Fucking. Hell.

Two officers did crowd control so I could pull my SUV into my garage. An agent in a blue jacket with yellow FBI lettering approached the driver's side window of my car and knocked on it.

"Max Hartwell?"

I held up my index finger, watching it as my hand shook. Palming my phone, I brought up Jack's game again, but he was no longer on the mound. They'd brought in the relief pitcher and it was only the second inning.

He knew. If he didn't know, he was about to find out. My heart broke into a million pieces, knowing I wouldn't be there for him. I'd sworn to myself that no one would ever hurt him, but by loving him, I'd inadvertently made that happen.

CHAPTER 46
Jack

The high I'd been riding since Max flew out yesterday evening was dissolving by the second. As the breeze blew faint aromas of stadium food and draft beer to the mound, I squinted in the midday sun to catch a glimpse of the crowd while I made a show of finding my stance to buy time. Something was off. The usual revelry of a ball crowd had been replaced by long periods of silence broken up by bursts of heckling.

It reminded me of when I was a kid and once snuck to the ice rink to try to learn how to skate against my father's wishes. It might sound like no big deal, but my dad loathed hockey, classing it among the most undignified sports, along with football and wrestling. It wasn't a gentleman's game like golf, but twelve-year-old Jack wanted to play fucking golf about as much as thirty-two-year-old Jack. Long story short, I twisted an ankle and took a blade to the back of my head, requiring five stitches.

The shouts and cackling coming from the stands were starting to give me that same sickening apprehension as when I waited for my dad to come pick me up from the rink to take me to the ER. I spotted a sign in the stands behind the home plate and my heart convulsed.

Who's pitching and who's catching?

Maybe I was being paranoid, thinking it was about me, but I couldn't shake the feeling that there was a joke and I was the punchline. People stared at ballplayers on the field all the time. It's what they literally paid to do when attending a game, but I'd never sensed more eyes on me than at that moment.

Hooper gestured to me impatiently, even as he glanced over his shoulder at the crowd. He looked antsier than usual. I wanted to know what he was hearing from his position closer to the stands, but didn't want to spread my anxious vibes by calling him to the mound. I let the ball fly and knew before it even left my hand that it was going to be a shit throw.

The opposing crowd erupted in a mixture of laughter and booing as Hooper stretched to catch it outside the strike zone. I swallowed the lump in my throat, shaking out my arms, but it did nothing to ease my nerves when I spotted Amelia, our head of PR, in the dugout, talking to Coach.

Amelia never came to the dugout. Something was definitely up. When Coach signaled for me to leave the field, I stood dumbstruck on the mound for a moment. It was only the second inning. I'd never been relieved that early in my life.

When I finally got my feet to move and started trotting off the field, I knew. I knew whatever was going on had to do with me.

"You sick son of a bitch!" someone yelled amidst a jarring mixture of cheers and booing.

"Fucking pervert!" another person shouted, and still another, "You don't belong in baseball!"

I'd never had tunnel vision, but I was pretty sure this was what it felt like. I could hear my breathing in my head, and the world was in slow motion around me.

Montez raised his arms out at his sides from first base as I neared the dugout. Even if I were close enough to say anything to him, I didn't have an answer for his what-the-hell-is-going-on gesture.

"Spears. Need you to go with Amelia," Coach said solemnly when I stepped into the dugout.

"What...what's this about?" I asked.

Amelia gave me a tight-lipped smile that looked too much like sympathy for my peace of mind. She grabbed my arm gently and turned me toward the door.

"Something's come up. We'll talk in the clubhouse."

I stared at the steel door with its chipped paint, sensing it was my gallows, but I nodded and followed her. I waited for her to fill me in, but she said nothing as the clip of her heels echoed down the hall toward the clubhouse door.

"Did something happen to my family?" I finally asked, desperate to be let in on this eerie mystery.

I thought of Max and Emma but realized the team might not see them as my family or even know to tell me if something happened to them. The things I'd heard on the way to the dugout didn't jibe with my fears, though. *Sick* and *pervert*, they'd called me. Had that guy from the hotel two years ago that had blackmailed me come out with a scandal?

"There's been…a press incident, but it has nothing to do with your family," Amelia said like she was trying to reassure me, but her expression was grave. "Terrie and Vance are waiting in the clubhouse, and we called Ed. He should be here soon. It…it'll be okay, Jack. We'll get everything sorted."

"The *old man?*" I asked without thinking after her mention of the seventy-something owner of the team, Vance Rindall.

She nodded with that same rueful smile. Usually bubbly and full of information, Amelia was a far cry from herself today as she focused on the floor while we walked. Whatever this was, I had a feeling it was so much worse than sneaking off to an ice rink.

Terrie, our GM, and Vance were standing around a dining table in the visiting team clubhouse when we walked in. The way they sized me up made me give myself a once over. I hedged toward them, questioning them with my eyes.

"This isn't how we'd have preferred to handle this, Jack," Terrie said, his hands stuffed deep in his khakis.

"What?" I practically pleaded.

He looked at Amelia like I hadn't even spoken. "Any word on Ed?"

"He said he was just pulling in when I went to get Jack."

"Can someone please tell me what's going on?" The break in my voice was humiliating, but I didn't care. My entire body was vibrating.

"We'd, uh, like to wait for Ed. No sense in repeating things. Should be just a few minutes," Terrie said.

Minutes felt like hellacious hours. I was caught in an awkward dance of being eyeballed and the three of them averting their gazes whenever I glanced at them. Old man Vance hadn't said a word. Terrie paced. Amelia's phone kept dinging while she typed out replies in a flurry.

When the door banged open, I jumped. Ed breezed through in all his five-foot-eight wiry glory.

"Christ, I'm sorry. I got here as quick as I could," he said to the room at large as he approached. He patted my arm. "How you doing?" he asked in a tone you use at a funeral.

I shook my head because I had no idea how to respond. Ed swept his gaze to the others. "So, where are we at with all of this?"

More foreboding silence loomed. Terrie cleared his throat. "We...were waiting for you."

I was ready to crawl out of my skin. There was a ballgame going on, and I wasn't playing ball. Somebody needed to explain.

"Can someone please tell me what the hell is going on?" I begged.

Ed's eyes went wide. He gaped at me and then at the others. "You didn't tell him?"

"Tell me what?"

Ed blew out a long breath and ran his hand over his close-cut sandy hair. He grabbed me by the arm and steered me toward the easy chairs where the team hung out before the game. Throwing his arm across the back of my shoulder, he spoke in a confidential tone.

"Jack, buddy, there's...there's a video going around on the internet of you...with a man."

I quit breathing. My body went rigid as my mind recalled every guy I'd dated. I'd never put myself in a situation where video footage of me being seen with anyone I had dated could be construed as me dating a man. I'd been so careful it had contributed to the ruination of every single relationship. There was no way I'd done anything in public that could be used to question my sexuality.

"Doing what?" I asked when I realized that was the most important question.

"We haven't even confirmed if it's you. I mean, I've never asked...and you don't have to tell me."

"What...what's in the video?" I really was a dumb ballplayer. Everyone here but me had a freaking phone. "Let me see your phone."

He hesitated, but pulled his phone from his back pocket. Sighing, he handed it over. "I guess it is best you see it so you can confirm or deny for us. It's probably doctored, or they found a look-alike just to stir up a shit."

I searched the internet for *Jack Spears MLB*, but the usual ball stats and biography didn't pop up at the top of the results. There were gossip news headlines, and they all read along the same lines—*MLB player sex tape leaked*. I found a still of some video in the results and my stomach collapsed in on itself.

It was me—me and the one person I had wanted to keep from ever being drawn into the circus that would erupt if I came out. Except, it wasn't a circus. It was a horror show. The man I loved was naked on the internet for the entire world to scrutinize.

"Oh, my God." My hand shook as I covered my mouth on instinct at the wave of nausea slamming into me. "Oh, God."

"Jack," Ed hesitated, clutching my shoulder. "*Is* that...you?" he whispered.

The room shifted like we were in an earthquake. I managed a nod.

"Shit," he muttered under his breath.

"Jack," Amelia soothed. "We need to know if there's any more of these, if this was an isolated incident, or if there are...other men...or women."

Ed's phone fell from my hand, and I gripped the back of a chair to keep my knees from buckling. My life was over. Max's life was over. Emma's.

My stomach convulsed. Hot acid shot up my throat. I gagged as my body rebelled like it wanted no part of my life and was trying to escape from the inside out. Whirling, I lunged toward a trash can as my legs gave out and vomited in a violent upheaval, clinging to the receptacle for something to save me.

"Oh, Jesus," someone muttered.

"Shit," Ed let out again, as I lurched unholy sounds and imagined Max discovering our night in Kansas City was now global news. "Alright," Ed's voice grew, and I felt his hand on my back. "Give him some room. Breathe, Jack. Come on, just breathe."

It reminded me of what Max had once said, but breathing had made me drop my guard and my entire world collapse around me. My lurching turned to dry heaving. Tears sprang from my eyes like I no longer had control over my body, which felt like the truth. When the gagging finally stopped, I felt Ed's hand pat my back.

"Max. Emma," I gasped.

"What?" he asked.

"I need to call Max. *Max*," I repeated.

"Your neighbor? He called."

It was enough to take my focus off the daze of my misery. "He did? What did he say?"

"I don't know. He just left a couple of voicemails asking me to call him. He said the press is already outside your house. You can't go back there for now."

Max knew. Oh, God. He knew, and I wasn't there to keep this away from him and Emma.

"Is he..." Ed hedged.

Is he? Ed had no way of knowing that in my mind that sentence should end with the word *everything*. I nodded. I needed to pull it together. Needed to find out what we were dealing with.

"What's...what's going to happen?" I asked, staggering to my feet and wiping my mouth with the back of my hand. "Does the team know?"

"Jack, how old is this?" Terrie stepped forward. "What...the clubhouse can't help you if we don't know what's going on."

"I…it was at the rental we got Tuesday. Someone must have record-ed us. Max is…he's my partner." My voice broke when I added, "We have a daughter."

It felt so good to say it out loud and also incredibly painful. Did I still have Emma? This was so much bigger than a moldy washing machine, and as much as it grieved me, I wouldn't blame Max for not being able to handle it. It was going to destroy us.

"Jesus," old man Rindall finally spoke. "Did you go through travel?"

I nodded. It was all I could manage as my pathetic options played out in my mind. Keep Max and Emma, but have all the joy blazoned from our lives by the fallout from this, or…let them go and maybe I'd be enough to give the world the fodder they wanted.

"Christ! How did this happen?" Rindall looked at Terrie and Amelia.

I turned away, knowing I was no longer part of the conversation. No lon-ger a human being, just a ballplayer who'd fucked up. Pacing, I pressed my hands hard to my hips, needing the support to hold me up. I felt like I was drunk, staggering in aimless circles.

Voices mumbled behind me. I lost track of who they belonged to as my head pounded.

Check all the lodging, all the buses.

Should we let him go back out?

We can't play him.

Fly the whole team home as soon as the game's over.

How long should we sit him out?

How do we tell the team?

Bile started welling up at the back of my throat again. I knew the topics were all things they needed to address. This didn't just affect me. It affected the team. It affected the entire sport. The weight of the reality bore down on me.

I wanted to go home. I wanted Max and Emma, but I'd be the car-rot leading a stampede of horses to bring down our house if I did that. I couldn't go back on the field. I couldn't return to the comfort of the arms I needed. I was in quicksand. There was only one way to go, and it wasn't up. Every word uttered about me choked my windpipe tighter. I didn't want to be talked about, didn't want to feel like the pariah I had become.

So, I ran.

My shoulder hit the door, rocketing it open so hard it slammed into the corridor wall. The piquant scent of cleaning products and sweat in the dark-ened hallway was a vise around my burning lungs, further constricting me. I needed to break free, needed to move. I needed to escape.

"Jack!" Ed yelled. "Jack, you all right?"

Nothing was all right. The world, management, my team, and everyone that Max knew, had found out my secret in the worst way possible. Max's life would be over, which meant so was mine, all because I'd kissed my straight best friend in a laundry room when he had just needed a shoulder to cry on.

I ran and ran down the corridor, through doors, through the maze of turns. It was a fruitless, desperate act. There was nowhere safe to hide anymore.

CHAPTER 47
Max

"Mr. Hartwell?" Agent Sanchez said from the doorway of my den where I paced, taking stock of every knickknack, book, and picture frame I'd have to right after they'd been left askew in the search for hidden cameras. "We're all done. Everything looks clear. It appears to be an isolated incident."

"Jack's house too?"

Sanchez nodded. "We didn't find a thing."

My breath came out long and hard. It was a small reprieve, hearing our homes hadn't been compromised.

"Thank you."

"We'll get packed up and get out of your hair. I'll be in touch with you and your attorney as things develop. We'll keep a car posted out front for at least a few days...just as a precaution."

My quiet suburban street had grown even more flooded with media and onlookers since I'd arrived. Many had been dispersed by the law enforcement officials, but the staunchest had set up camp out front, exercising their right of freedom of the press. No doubt they were waiting for the same thing I was—Jack to come home.

Stepping forward, I extended my hand. "Thank you for all you've done. I appreciate it."

He returned my handshake. His demeanor, like the rest of his team who'd descended upon my house, had warmed over the last few hours. Once they realized this wasn't a case of a kinky home sex tape being leaked, they'd turned much more affable and sympathetic.

I got it. I did. I wasn't a fan of all my clients, particularly the ones that made their own messes, but the initial coldness of the team had put a chip on my shoulder, so I'd retreated to my den after setting them straight. One by one, they'd come in to apologize or kiss my ass to make amends. If this was what I'd had to deal with in my own home, I couldn't imagine what Jack was dealing with out in the jungle.

Dropping into my chair, I let my head fall into my hands. I needed an aspirin. Bacon would be good too. I was starving. And Jack. Most of all, I needed Jack.

When my phone rang, I gave a start, scrambling to retrieve it from my pocket. "Jack? Jesus! I've been trying to get ahold of you all day."

"Max, I...I'm so sorry." His voice sounded downtrodden, but I still sighed in relief at hearing him.

"Where are you? Are you home yet?"

"No. I'm at the team hotel in Kansas City. Did you...did you see the video?"

"Yes. Babe, are you okay? When are you coming home?"

"I...I'm so sorry, Max. I never meant for this to happen."

"Jack quit apologizing. You didn't do anything wrong."

"Does Emma know?"

"No. No. I don't think so. She's spending the night at Zeke and Ryan's. They know not to let her on the internet or watch the news."

"Where are you at?"

"I'm at the house with the police and an FBI team. They checked everything here and at your house too, but didn't find any cameras. They think it was just at the rental. The old people who own it have a manager who runs it for them. They didn't know he had cameras all over the house."

"Oh, God," he wailed.

"Hey, it's all right."

"It's *not* all right. Did they record Emma? Or the girls?"

"They haven't found any footage of them. They're still looking for the guy. He must know how badly he fucked up because they can't find him. The FBI is trying to shut it down wherever they can."

"My God." His sniffle was a shard of glass to my heart.

"When will you be home? We can go stay at my mom's until this blows over. There're people all over the place outside. I don't want you coming to the house. They'll bombard you before you even get in the door."

"Oh, my God. Max," he practically wept my name. "Your mom knows?"

"Yeah. I had to warn her in case people came to her shop. She won't look, Jack. Don't worry about it."

He scoffed, like it was a moot point. "What about the firm and Lainey's folks?"

"Trevor's handling all the legal stuff for us. I warned Lainey's parents," I said casually, hoping to glaze over that issue.

"What did they say?"

"They're fine. Don't worry about them."

"Max, what did they say?" he demanded, sounding a little too frantic.

Gnawing on the inside of my lip, I squeezed the phone tighter, hating that I had to tell him one more black mark about this fucked up day. "I hung up on Bob. I didn't have time to deal with it."

"Jesus. Trevor...Trevor's helping you?"

"*Us*. He's helping us," I emphasized. I didn't like how he was treating me like I was the only victim in this. I wasn't going to let him be a martyr. We were in it together. "He got a court order for the footage. Any media outlet that has it has to take it—or any images of it—down."

"And Dan?"

I tried steadying my breath. Being reminded of the things Dan had said wasn't what I wanted to talk about right now.

"Max? What happened with Dan?"

"Fuck Dan. Dan's gone."

A broken sob cut through my phone. It was such a sickening sound, knowing it came from the man I loved, and I couldn't comfort him. "Oh, God," he wept. "I ruined your life. I'm so sorry."

"Jack! Stop! You didn't ruin anything."

"Max, this will never go away."

I wasn't about to debate the distant future with him, not with the frame of mind he was in. I needed him to focus on the present.

"When do you get in? Can you meet me at my mom's?"

"I don't know. They're trying to fly us all out tonight."

"Are you still playing? What did the team say?"

"No. I don't know. They pulled me out of the game. People were heckling me, and I choked. I didn't know what was going on. You need to stay away from me or the press will hound you and Emma."

"What?" I bolted out of my chair. He couldn't be serious. "No way am I leaving you alone right now."

"No, Max. It's better that way. They won't go away if they think I'm with you."

"Jack! Don't be ridiculous. Where are you staying when you get home?"

"Max, I have to go."

What the hell? This conversation was so far from over.

"Jack, wait."

"Kiss Emma for me. Okay?"

"Jack!"

The connection went dead, along with a piece of my heart the size of Russia. I stared at my phone stupidly for a second, clenching it in my hand, then dialed him back. It went to fucking voicemail. I texted him to call me back. Then I texted him to tell me when he got back to Springfield. Then I texted him a litany of frantic supportive messages about how none of this was his fault, that we'd get through it together, and how much I loved him.

And my phone was silent. So fucking silent, like a light had been snuffed out on the other end of the line. I was terrified out of my mind that it had. I'd gotten a glimpse of what he was like when his Jack-light went out. My heart couldn't handle seeing a repeat.

It felt like he was running. I had the awful, sickening feeling I was the one being pushed away this time, and that did not fit into my plan of *you and me*.

CHAPTER 48
Max

You know how in the movies when someone is tailing someone else's vehicle and the person getting tailed floors it and gets away? Well, try doing it in suburbia when there are a thousand freaking stop signs, school crossings, kids on bikes, and people walking dogs.

Each time I had to stop, I told my Alexa to add the names of the news crews following me to my *never-fucking-watching-your-show-again* list. After gunning it down the highway to lose them, I wound my way back through town on side streets that were well out of the way of my destination. When I saw Jack, I was going to kick his ass for what he'd put me through.

It was Friday afternoon, and he still wasn't answering his phone. I hadn't slept a wink, worrying over not knowing where he was or what was going on in that stubborn, sensitive head of his.

I'd called Carrie last night and this morning. She was just as frazzled as me. She hadn't heard from him other than a text yesterday explaining what happened. He'd gone full radio silent. What the hell did it mean if he wasn't even picking up for Carrie?

I needed to see him and make sure he was okay, then I needed to go pick up Emma and see if she was okay for my peace of mind. Mom had picked her up from Ryan and Zeke's a few hours ago, since we decided to keep her out of school for the day, and she put her on the phone for me.

I got a full report of how *awesome* Matt's dog was, how dogs weren't *that* difficult to take care of, and how Ryan and Zeke said they were great for stress relief, so *'you know, Dad, we should really get you one.'*

Ha!

I desperately needed that laugh. And if Jack wasn't where Ed said he was, I was going straight to the pound to buy a damn flock of K9s because, at this point, I'd do anything to hang on to the rest of my sanity.

When I pulled into the employee lot of the Marquis Hotel and spotted Ed's car parked next to a Dumpster, I narrowed my eyes at him through the afternoon sun. I knew he was doing his job by protecting Jack's privacy and following team protocols for the incident or some bullshit, but not answering my calls had earned him a spot on my shit list. He'd finally phoned an hour ago, asking me to meet him here to talk to Jack.

I fucking resented being *asked* to talk to Jack like I was doing Ed, the team, and even the fucking sport of baseball a favor by making sure their golden boy was emotionally stable. They saw him as a paycheck instead of a human being. I didn't need to be asked to talk to him, and I sure as shit wasn't going to do it for fucking Ed, baseball, or even the damn pope. I was going to talk to Jack because I was going to be sick if I didn't, then I was going to yell at him for scaring the shit out of me, and then I was going to kiss the hell out of him and drag him home. Okay, maybe not home. That was a fucking hornet's nest right now, but perhaps to my mom's house where we could be alone, and I could do more pouting and get more of the kisses he owed me for this silent treatment.

Shoving my keys into the pocket of my jeans, I closed the distance between my car and where Ed was approaching from his. He had sunglasses on and glanced around the lot. The ripe scent of decaying food from the Dumpster next to where he parked had me scrunching up my nose. This was ridiculous to meet back here like it was a drug deal.

"Hey, Max. Thanks for coming," he said, shaking my hand.

I gritted my teeth at being thanked for coming to see the man I loved. "Thanks for returning my *twelfth* phone call."

"Uh. Yeah. Sorry it took me so long to get back to you. The game just ended, and I had to be there for the press meeting with...all this going on."

"What room is he in?"

"Three sixty-two. I just got a key made so we can get in."

"Or he can just open the door."

Ed tugged at the collar of his polo shirt. "Well, he won't see anybody, but I figured he'd have called you or his family or whatever, so that's why

I didn't rush to call you back. I assumed you'd have connected with him by now."

The plastic key card Ed slipped into my hand felt like Pandora's box. "What do you mean *'he won't see anybody?'* *You've* seen him. Right?"

"Well, yeah, but not since we flew in last night when I got him to the hotel." He pointed over his shoulder. "When he wouldn't answer his phone this morning, I got worried and went to his room, but he wouldn't open the door."

"What?" Unchecked fear shot through every one of my neurons. Nobody'd seen Jack since last night? It was almost four p.m. "Why the hell didn't you call me sooner? He could be…" I choked on the word *hurt*, not wanting to consider if Jack could be so wrecked from this that he'd do something drastic.

"Max, it's fine. He talked to me through the door. Said he wanted to be left alone. I checked on him again at lunchtime, and he answered me."

I let out a breath. Jack's greatest fear had been that the world would find out his sexuality. I realized now my greatest fear was if he'd recover from that happening, and, selfishly, if *we'd* recover from it happening.

"Is he playing tomorrow?" I couldn't imagine how he'd stand in front of thousands of people if he'd gone all Howard Hughes and wouldn't even leave his hotel room.

Ed made a disbelieving noise. "I doubt it. They've got him on *'medical,'*" he said, making air quotes. "They're talking about keeping him on it for the rest of the season." He ran his hand down his face. "What a fucking mess. I told him if he just comes to a press conference… He doesn't even have to say anything. He can just sit there while PR says how it was a crime, a violation of privacy, not some video you guys made and put out there. You know? That'd help dispel all this…crap." He waved his hand.

"So, what? He's just…done? They don't want to play him anymore?" That would be the final blow for him. I couldn't even entertain the idea. I needed some good news to bring him.

"No. It's not that. They don't know what the hell to do. They've never handled anything like this. Nobody knows how the fans will react. We can't trade him. It'd be a publicity nightmare for whoever took him, and there's no point in it. I mean," he sighed. "He can't get away from this just by going to a new team. It's public opinion. It's everywhere. Fucking internet."

I couldn't believe my ears, hearing Jack talked about like cattle. I knew trades were part of the process for any ballplayer, but why should he have to uproot his life because some pervert hid a camera in a bedroom? Why should he be benched because he loved a man?

"He's, uh. Well, I've never seen him like this," Ed continued, running a hand over the top of his close-shaved hair. "Can't say I blame him, but…I mean. Well, it's Jack. You know? He's always…"

I nodded. I did know, or at least I remembered the effervescent version of himself he'd shown me for years up until Christmas last year. There were more sides to him than that, and that's what had made me desperate to get to him. Ed, the team—they didn't know about that other side, the fragile one. He didn't belong up there in that high castle all alone with no one but a paid agent who'd do whatever he wanted him to, like leave him the hell alone when the last thing Jack needed was to be left alone.

Jack wasn't Ed's or the team's. He was mine. It wasn't their job to protect him or know what was best for him.

Ed crossed his arms and started pacing. "I mean, he can't just hole up in his room and expect it to go away while people are out there stirring the pot. That's not going to help him. It's like he's giving up."

Watching his agitated movements, my nerves settled. Ed was a businessman, but I could see he genuinely cared about Jack's well-being. Jack wouldn't have stuck with him for so long if Ed didn't.

"So, he goes to a press conference, hopes it dies down, and then what? He sits on the bench?" I was trying to see both sides of this. If I wanted to be a good partner, I had to better understand Jack's world.

"Yeah, but at least the heat would be off the team, and they could get back in the right mindset. They're not happy about losing him, either."

I thought of all the times Jack's teammates had been over—Hooper, Montez, McQuiston. They looked at him as a leader. He probably didn't even see it.

"Or he could play," I suggested.

Ed considered me for a moment, and then his shoulders relaxed. "Yeah. Or he could play."

"Would the team be all right with that?"

He shoved his hands in his slacks. "I think they'd be better off with him than without him. The problem is, will Jack see it like that?"

"Jack?" I called out when my knock went unanswered. Heart pounding, I pulled out the card key Ed had given me and slipped it into the key reader.

The door opened into a spacious modern kitchen and living room suite. At least they'd gotten him top-notch lodging for his hideout from fame. Everything was spotless. No room service trays. No vending machine snacks lying on the dining table. Even the trash cans were empty. Hadn't he eaten?

I turned into the bedroom and my breath caught at the made-up bed that looked like it hadn't been slept in. I was about to storm out and chew Ed a new one for letting Jack run off when I spotted Jack's travel bags by the window. There was only one place left to look, and it was so deathly silent I thought I might vomit.

Splaying my fingers, I pushed open the bathroom door and flipped on the light. My heart jumped into my throat. He was sitting in the empty tub, fully dressed, eyes closed, with his head against the tile wall. Jesus. He was so still. A dark thought niggled around my head. Had he been so distraught he got hold of sleeping pills? Oh, God. My body started to vibrate, but then his eyes popped open, and he squinted, adjusting them to the light.

"Ed?" he called out before his puffy, reddened eyes spotted me.

Fear does crazy things to people. I don't know why I had thought I'd yell at him for scaring the shit out of me. My shaky legs took me to the side of the tub, and I collapsed to my knees. I'd never let out such a breath of relief.

"Jack?"

"Max? What are you doing here?"

I reached out to stroke his cheek or his hair. Something. I needed the reassurance of touching him. He looked at me with such despair in his eyes, as though he didn't have a friend in the world. When my finger grazed his hairline, his mouth went tight. He flinched and drew away. "Max, don't," he said like a warning, his voice hoarse.

"Babe, are you okay?"

He swallowed and stared at his bare feet, his arms wrapped around his knees, holding them to his chest. "Why did you come? You didn't bring Emma, did you?"

"No. She's at Mom's. What do you mean, *why* did I come? You wouldn't answer your phone."

He worked his jaw but didn't look at me. He looked so young, crouched in the tub in gym shorts and a T-shirt, like a kid who was scared of the dark. Shit. I realized the lights had been off. What was the deal with that?

"You shouldn't be here," he said sternly, angling his head toward the wall when I smoothed back his mussed hair.

Okay. Now I was pissed.

"What?" I scoffed, cupping the back of his neck. "Don't pull away from me."

He let out a huff and turned his head toward me, but still avoided my gaze. "Max, you're not gay. You'd never even looked at another guy before I kissed you, and it ruined your life. And it'll ruin Emma's unless you distance yourself from me."

"What the fuck are you talking about? And why are you in the bathtub?"

He bit the inside of his lip, tightening his hold on his knees. "I couldn't...I was afraid there'd be cameras in the room. I don't want anyone to see me." He covered his eyes with his hand, resting it on his forearm. "Please, Max. Just go. I'm so sorry I did this to you." His voice broke, breaking something inside me.

I got up and shoved the back of his shoulders forward, satisfying my urge to shake some sense into him for the stupid shit he was saying to me. "Move forward."

"What...what are you doing?"

"Getting in this fucking bathtub since you won't get out."

The sole of my shoe came down on the side of his ass cheek, forcing him to shift. I staggered back into the wall before sliding down, but managed to squeeze in behind him.

"Max, please just leave me alone," he whined, trying to scoot forward, but I latched my forearms over his chest.

"No! You selfish bastard, I'm not leaving you alone!" I barked at the back of his ear as he squirmed. "And guess what? *You* don't get to tell me if I'm attracted to men or not. That's up to me."

He finally stilled with a huff of breath. "Well, you weren't until I forced you to get a blow job."

"You didn't force me."

"Pretty much," he pouted. It was almost cute, the way he was trying to sound as pissed as me. Almost.

"It was *my* idea," I countered. "*I'm* the one who asked, *and I* supplied the hard-on. Thank you very much. I wouldn't have been able to do that unless I'd wanted you."

"You said it was only because you had to know if you'd like it," he grumbled.

I scoffed into the crook of his neck because, man, was he on a roll. "I was kidding myself. I knew I'd like it. That was my pride talking—my scared pride."

He muttered something that sounded like, "Straight pride."

God, this was worse than arguing with Emma. I sighed, my brain scrambling for ammunition to shoot through his impenetrable wall.

"Remember last Christmas when you wore those tight-ass jeans and were bent over, looking in my freezer?" I asked.

"No," he said immediately, like he wasn't even humoring me.

"Well, I do. I wondered at the time what your ass felt like."

His sniffle echoed off the shower walls. "You have image issues," he muttered. "It was probably just straight-man body envy."

I squeezed him. "Jesus, you're fucking conceited."

His back rocked against mine when he snorted. Good. Maybe I was finally getting somewhere.

I pressed a kiss to his cheek and whispered, "I told you to fuck off. Doesn't that mean anything?"

He quivered in my arms. I could feel his jaw tremble underneath my lips as he sucked in a breath.

"Yeah," he wept. "And they ruined it. It was the best night of my life, and they made a joke out of it and hurt you and Emma."

My heart unfolded in that stupid bathtub then and there. Now we were getting to it. As usual, there was nothing selfish about him.

"The only thing that's hurting me about this is seeing *you* hurt, and you know the same would be true for Emma if she knew."

"How can you ever touch me again without thinking about it or feeling like a pervert?"

I gave him as much of a shake as I could in my awkward child-birthing pose. "*Why* would I feel like *that*?"

"I loved what we did, Max, but I feel like a freak now. I was...I thought I was fine with...'*the way I am*' after all these years, but it's like they took away my right to even secretly enjoy who I am."

I grazed his arm with my thumb and pressed a kiss to his neck. "I know."

"You do?" he asked, finally turning his head a fraction toward mine.

"I thought that at first too, but then I watched it again after the cops left."

He rubbed his eyes with his fingertips. "God, I can't believe you had to have the police at your house."

"FBI, actually. You think Springfield PD handles cyber-crimes? This is Illinois we're talking about here," I joked.

"Jesus."

It took some finagling since my freaking legs were falling asleep from being squished between his hips and the sides of the tub, but I managed to extricate my phone from my back pocket. I reached around so he could see the screen as I pulled up the infamous video I'd downloaded.

As soon as Jack realized what I was playing, he covered my phone with his palm, pushing my hand away. "Max, I don't want to see it!"

"Wait a minute." I moved my arm out of his reach. "I want you to know what *I* see."

His head *thunked* against the wall as he braced his knees again and sulked. "Yeah. *Us fucking*."

"Nooo," I countered as the video played, seeming so much different now that the man I wanted was in my arms. "I see two good-looking guys in their prime that everyone can be jealous of with bodies like those."

He snorted and covered his eyes. "You would see that."

"*And*," I continued undeterred, "in twenty years, when I'm old and fat, I'm going to look at this and remember how *great* we looked, how *fucking sexy* you were, how *lucky* I was the most handsome ballplayer in the MLB wanted me, how my best friend made my first time bottoming incredibly *special* and *tender*, and..." I broke off when it got to the part where Jack had hooked my legs behind his neck. "And Jesus, how unbelievably flexible I didn't even know I was."

I caught his glance at the screen before he rested his chin on his forearms. "One thread on the internet said I look like a gay rapist."

Even as my nostrils flared from the rage inside me that someone would slander him like that, I nuzzled my face in his neck. "No. You're gentle and considerate. Anyone with a brain can see that."

He scoffed like I was being the delusional one, so I pressed on. "And if that doesn't convince you, watch this ridiculous look on my face right here as I have the best orgasm of my life," I said, bringing my phone closer.

He looked, but his tone was sullen. "That's my point, Max. No one should see this but us."

"I know, but they did, and they got to see two people in love, making love. I'll never be ashamed or embarrassed about that. I'm never apologizing for that, and neither should you."

"It won't get any easier," he warned, looking back at me.

I sighed dramatically when, really, I was covering up a breath of relief. I'd finally gotten to see those caramel eyes of his.

"I know," I assured him with a kiss. "There's arthritis to think about and maybe hip replacements a few decades from now, but we'll manage. We can get creative." I wriggled my brows.

He snickered and rolled his eyes. "I'm serious."

"So am I! You keep playing ball and you're probably going to need a new hip or knee before I will, but I'll take it easy on you and rub muscle relief on you wherever you need it." I pressed my smile to his cheek. "I promise."

He shook his head and let out a breath. "I can't see me ever picking up a baseball again. I'm probably done for the season. No one's going to want to trade for me, and nobody'll give me a contract once mine's up in the fall."

"Well, you'll just have to suck it up and keep playing where you're at."

"Max, that's not going to happen."

At the sound of a knock on the door, I felt him tense in my arms. "Don't answer it," he warned.

"What if it's about the team? You can't stay in here forever."

"Yes, I can," he said, like he actually meant it.

I rolled my eyes at the shower ceiling. Just when I had thought I was getting somewhere. "And what? Be a tub monster?"

Another knock came—this one from inside the room. Ed's poor timing was perfect. I'd asked him to give me an hour before coming up. I just hadn't expected to be sitting in a bathtub for that long or like... at all.

"Guys? It's Ed," he called out from the other room. "You here?"

"Yeah! We're...in here!" I yelled, grateful for the crisis intervention, as Jack tried to cover my mouth.

"Hey, I brought some...whoa!" Ed stopped short in the doorway, his eyebrows climbing his forehead. Jack groaned and buried his face in his elbow toward the wall like maybe he finally realized how fucking ridiculous it was to be in this damn tub.

"I, uh," Ed stammered. "I can come back later."

"No. It's fine." I waved, even as I tried to urge Jack up from underneath his armpits. "We're getting out," I declared, more like a warning to Jack, but he wouldn't budge.

"Uh. Good," Ed said. "Because, Jack, you've got some visitors."

"No. I don't want to see anyone." Jack shook his head, somehow managing to close his giant body like a turtle, so all my efforts accomplished were to jostle him.

When I got him out of this tub, woke my damn legs up, and got him back in a better frame of mind, he was so going to have some kissing up to do. I nodded to Ed, hoping he'd accomplished a suggestion I'd made earlier. The only way for Jack to stop acting like he was in this alone was to let him know he wasn't.

Ed stepped back from the doorway and gestured toward the bedroom. One by one, Montez, Hooper, and McQuiston filed into the bathroom.

"Hey, Jack—" Hooper's cheerful greeting cut off when he spotted us.

"Whoa," McQuiston said, slamming into Hooper.

"Um, is this a bad time?" Montez arched a brow.

"Oh, God," Jack moaned and twisted himself toward the shower wall.

As I sat sandwiched behind Jack, literally spooning him, I hoped this would be the only time in my life four men saw me in a bathtub. Hell, what was I saying? They'd already probably seen more than that. Case in point, the damn video was still playing on my phone.

"What's the matter?" I called to our audience. "You've never seen two grown men watching porn in a bathtub before?"

"Max!" Jack groused, smacking my leg, but the guys all grinned.

Hooper shrugged. "Yeah. Sure. We do it all the time."

"I watch mine on the toilet sometimes," McQuiston volunteered.

Montez's lip curled up. "Ew! That's fucking sick."

"Yeah, TMI," Hooper added.

"What?" McQuiston raised his hands. "I do."

"Good to know," I offered patiently. "Now, somebody turn that shower-head on for me so I can get his ass out of here."

"Max! No!" Jack straightened up.

It took less than two seconds for my plan to be registered and initiated. Hooper stepped forward, turning on the sprayer. McQuiston and Montez hurried over, trying to keep Jack in the tub as he thrashed against all of us.

"Ah! Shit, that's cold!" Jack yelled as the icy water beat down on us and the guys laughed. Jack managed to barrel roll onto his side, elbowing me in the nuts in the process.

We were a tangle of arms and legs, abandoning ship at the same time like two old walruses. I fell over the side of the tub, breaking my fall with my hands. Jack landed on his knees, bracing against the vanity with one hand and swinging at a cackling Hooper with the other while he cursed words I'd never heard him use before.

His shirt was soaked, and his hair was plastered to his face. Panting, I rolled over onto my ass, snickering as Jack wiped his eyes and glared at the guys.

"You bastard," he spat when he locked eyes with me. Just as I got to my knees, he snagged me in a headlock, pulling me under the spray. I knew he was having a life crisis, but I never laughed so fucking hard. I flailed for the faucet, trying to catch my breath as we grappled.

"You too, Hooper," he snarled, releasing my neck to wield the shower hose at the group of hyenas who were retreating to the door. "All of you!"

McQuiston slipped and braced the door. Montez backed into the toilet, tripping over it. Hooper screamed like a girl, climbing over top of them as though he were made of salt.

I got the water shut off and twisted my soaked T-shirt. Water droplets sailed through the air as Jack shook his arms and snagged a towel off the rack. I must have been on my way to forgiveness because even though I got the stink eye, he tossed me one too.

"Hey, we just came by to ask you to play tomorrow," Montez said, having decided to just sit on the toilet.

"Tomorrow? I'm on medical."

"Yeah, but the doc says your *cold* is gone," Hooper said coyly. "If...you want it to be gone."

Jack looked at Ed out in the bedroom hall, who had somehow managed to remain dry. "What did the front office say?"

"They said it's your call, Jack."

I felt a twinge in my chest, seeing the bafflement on his face. He still had no clue of his worth; as a man *and* a friend.

"You guys...*want* me to play?"

Montez leaned forward, looking surprisingly prophetic for a guy sitting on a toilet. "You're the best pitcher in the league, Jack, and we're a team. Of course, we want you to play."

Jack chewed his lip while I held my breath. I could care less if he never threw another ball, but I knew what it meant to him. I knew what it was like to have something snatched away while you still loved it.

"And the rest of the guys?" he ventured, plucking at the towel fibers.

"Well, yeah." McQuiston shrugged. "But you can only fit so many people in a bathroom. We're just the messengers."

"He'll play," I announced when I wasn't convinced he'd stop wavering.

Jack shot me a scowl. I'd never seen him make one until today, and it made me both proud and amused, even if it was directed at me.

"I never said I would," he huffed.

"Well, Emma and I will be there, and if you don't play, *you* can explain to her why you don't."

His shoulders sank, and he made a guttural noise. "That's low, Max."

Folding my arms over my soaked shirt, I smirked. "No. That's parenthood."

He very maturely rolled his eyes, but said nothing. We all waited as the tub faucet dripped in the background. Jack surveyed us warily. "They were already heckling me yesterday. It'll only be worse tomorrow. And what about the press?"

Hooper held out his index finger. "You let us worry about that. We've got a few ideas."

"Well, that fucking scares me," Jack mumbled.

I'm glad the guys laughed. I felt like a spouse on the shit list who wasn't allowed to crack jokes if they wanted to live.

Montez slapped his knees and stood up. "We'll see you at warm-up to-morrow?" he asked, but it wasn't a question.

McQuiston angled his chin at the puddles on the floor. "Water aerobics don't count."

Jack cracked his towel, connecting with the man's thigh, but then he nodded. "Alright."

Montez slapped Jack on the shoulder before they filed out. Ed stuck his head back in, patting the doorframe.

"Max, we'll pick you guys up and get you into the family booth tomorrow. I'll work it all out with the front office."

Well, well. Ed for the win. Only spouses, kids, and immediate family were allowed in the family booth. No girlfriends and, I assumed it was safe to guess no boyfriends, had ever graced it, either. I did an internal victory dance because it was the closest I'd get to being the first guy to walk on the moon.

"You got this, Jack," Ed told him. "We'll get you to the field tomorrow."

I let out a calming breath when I heard the room door close and surveyed my saturated jeans. When I looked up, a giant, soaking wet, angry baby was glaring back at me with his arms folded over his chest. Yeah, I may have cried over a washing machine, but he was still acting like a baby. I was here. I'd fixed everything. Where was my thank you hug?

"What?"

He just stared at me like he thought he was intimidating. He was, but in the way it made one worry about never getting fed bacon again.

"What? What's with the murder-eyes?"

He narrowed said murder-eyes at me. "Proud of yourself?"

"Uh. Yeah, actually."

Hello. He wasn't in a fucking bathtub anymore, and I was going to walk on the moon. I'd call that winning.

When his shoulders slumped, I abandoned my gloating. "I don't know if I can do it, Max. What if I choke again?"

I went to him and wrapped him in my arms. "You won't. You get nervous, just look at me."

"You're really going to bring Emma?"

"Yeah. She needs to see you." I swiped a piece of damp hair off his forehead. "She needs a normal life. Hiding isn't a normal life. She knows something's up. Mom said she caught her switching to the game, and she knows you didn't play yesterday."

"Shit." He ran his palm down his face and then fiddled with the hem of my sleeve. "What if she hears people talking?"

I drew my arm across his back and guided him out of the scene of the crime into the bedroom. "You can't worry about that on the field. I'll be with her. I'll worry about that if it happens."

"*If?* I don't like it, Max. I don't like the thought of leaving you two out there to fend for yourselves when I won't be able to do anything about it."

"Yes, you can." I turned him to face me and braced his shoulders, so he had to look me in the eye. "You can be Jack Spears—starting pitcher of the

Springfield Eagles, the best pitcher in the league. And I'd like to see anyone with balls enough to talk shit in front of a ten-year-old girl."

"It's not balls, so much as a lack of compassion. You're telling me you forgot about the shit people talk at ballgames?"

"No, but I think I may have underestimated Emma. She might surprise you. I mean, look at who her boyfriend is. She already took a stand before she knew about us," I said playfully, but with a heap of pride.

"He's *not* her boyfriend." He captured Emma's saltiness so perfectly that I had to laugh and kiss him.

"That's the spirit."

He sighed and hugged me, resting his chin on my shoulder. "How can the guy who was barely holding it together a few months ago be the same one to make all of this seem like it's going to be okay?"

"Because I'm awesome like that."

His chuckle was music to my ears. "Now who's conceited?"

"Nooo. I'm just right."

"Oh, fuck off." He laughed.

"Hey, that's my line."

Jack smiled and rested his forehead against mine. I didn't delude myself that things were going to be easy, but just that gesture—I was home again, and he'd come home to me. Whatever happened, I knew we'd be okay.

"Now," I glanced down at the towel in my hand. "Can the team comp one of these towels because I don't want to soak my car seat on my way to Mom's?"

He let out a puff of breath and turned toward his bag. "I'll get you some shorts."

"I should...go talk to Emma," I said seriously. "But I can come back after she goes to bed." I didn't want to leave him alone just yet or...ever.

"No. I'll come with you if that's okay."

"Yeah, of course." I was a bit baffled as I took the pair of shorts he handed me. Players weren't allowed to have anyone in the team-assigned hotel room, let alone sneak off at night to stay somewhere else without approval. "But I thought you were on mandatory lockdown or something."

"I think I can get away with whatever I want to today."

"Oh, yeah?" I wriggled my eyebrows, liking his new defiant side.

"What?" He laughed, pulling more clothes from his duffel.

"We could drive by Dan's house and throw a bunch of dildos in his yard."

He snorted and shot me a challenging look. "You've got a bunch of dildos lying around?"

Yes. Actually, I did. Well, not technically a bunch, but I lied to continue with my plan to get him to smile again. "No, but I could pull some strings."

"I'm not even going to humor you by asking."

I stripped my wet shirt off and tossed it on the floor. When I started on my pants, I noticed his eyes darting around the room in a panic. He tilted his chin toward me and waved a hand toward the bathroom, like he was suggesting I change in there. I furrowed my brows. What the hell had this camera incident done to him that he was afraid for us to get undressed now?

The way I saw it, the world had already seen everything, and the FBI was going to make an example out of the perv that had recorded us. I needed to set an example of not giving a shit for him.

Turning around, I dropped my pants and boxer briefs in one swift move. Bending down to tug my pant legs free, I shot him a defiant look over my shoulder. He scoffed and shook his head.

"Hey, Ed said they swept the room and there's a security guard at each end of the hallway," I assured him, donning the shorts he had given me. "Relax."

He sighed and slowly stripped out of his shirt. As I donned a T-shirt, I noticed he replaced one article of clothing at a time, facing the wall like someone who had body issues. It was progress from the bathtub, but I knew it would take time to get him where he needed to be.

Distracting him from his thoughts with humor had seemed to work, so I tried again. "So, now that I have permission to get in the family box, that means I'll get to hang out with all the wives. Right?"

He arched a brow, and his pout was too damn adorable. "I don't like the sound of that."

"Why?"

"*You* surrounded by a bunch of women…"

"Nooo." I held up a finger. "*Me*, surrounded by a bunch of *lonely* women whose husbands are on the road half the season."

"And *that's* supposed to make me feel better?"

I moseyed up to him, planting my hands on his hips. "Babe, think about it. Lonely women have dildos." I wiggled my eyebrows, growing more excited about '*Operation: Dicks for Dan.*'

Jack sputtered out a laugh. "What?"

"Where did you think I was going with that?"

"Oh, my God," he barked, resting his hands on my forearms.

"What?"

"You're actually enjoying this. Aren't you?"

"Making you smile?" I stole a kiss. "Of course I am."

The smile he gave me, close to the ones he usually made, warmed my heart. He stroked my cheek and pleaded softly, "Can we get out of here now?"

"I thought you'd never ask."

Stepping out into the hallway felt like freedom, like the first step in the direction of the rest of our lives. All my teasing to distract Jack had distracted me from my own concerns, and now that I knew he was in a better place emotionally and was by my side, my vulnerability crept up.

I slung one of his bags over my shoulder as he shut the room door. "I'm glad you're going with me," I let out. Hoisting his duffel higher on his shoulder, he gave me a curious look as we started walking. "I didn't want to have to talk to Emma without you," I confessed.

His features softened into that understanding look of his, and he wrapped an arm around me. As much as I wanted to be the strong one for him, I appreciated how he humored this crack in my armor. He leaned in and pressed a kiss to my temple. When he pulled back, I spotted a woman passing by us in the hallway. She looked like a guest, not one of the staff, but she just nodded and smiled.

My knee-jerk reaction was to look at Jack for his. We'd never once touched or kissed in public, even after months of dating. We'd barely gone out in public unless it was to the grocery store or the occasional dinner, but we'd always had Emma with us.

He just smiled back at me, this little content smile like he was letting me know he was happy to see me. He mustn't have realized what he'd just done. He was wearing an Eagles T-shirt and one of his team ball caps, so he wasn't easy to miss.

"What?" he asked as I continued to gape, wondering how he'd react when I pointed out his slip-up.

I tilted my head to indicate the guest that had passed us. "You realize what you just did?" I whispered.

Jack glanced back and then looked at me. His mouth went tight with what looked like remorse as he squeezed my shoulder.

"Yeah." He sighed in resignation and gave me a small smile. "I'm breathing."

CHAPTER 49
Jack

People say when you're nervous, you should imagine your audience is na-ked. When you've done magazine spreads nearly in the buff and the entire world has seen how you fornicate, that deflection tactic doesn't work.

The clubhouse was alive with its usual activity of guys playing games on their phones or talking shit to each other from across the room like unruly twelve-year-olds. Montez had taken residence in the easy chair next to mine like I was the weird uncle at a family gathering people were obligated to include.

He told me a story about a kid in his high school who got teased after coming out and then took his own life, after which Montez had felt guilty for not stepping in to stop the bullying. I think it was his way of letting me know he embraced my sexuality, but it had not been the kind of uplifting story my frazzled nerves needed.

My fingers itched to check my phone for the latest buzz over the state-ment Trevor had given on my and Max's behalf this morning at an FBI press conference, but I'd promised Max I wouldn't look before the game. We needed to have a serious talk about how far he could push promises.

To make matters worse, all his posturing over getting in the team's family box had been for show. The sneaky bastard had informed me over breakfast that he and Emma were going to sit behind home plate so, *'we can see you better and you can see us.'* Apparently, Ed had gotten them some of the coveted seats there. Ed was no longer getting a birthday gift from me each year, especially if my family got mauled by crazed fans while I was stuck on the pitcher's mound.

I needed a bucket to throw up in, a Blackhawks game, and a *Martha & Snoop's Potluck Dinner Party* marathon to take off the edge. That and I was going to kill Max for talking me into this. I didn't want to let him down. I didn't want him to worry about me, but seriously. Even if I pitched the perfect game, it wasn't going to change anything. So, what was the point? To make myself more of a spectacle?

Not a single one of the guys had said a word about the media fiasco. I'd gotten a few slaps on the back, and some *glad you're here* comments. That wasn't the cold shoulder, but something was off. The vibe in the clubhouse had shifted. It was clear everyone was keeping their distance, except Montez with his cheery stories. Even Hooper was all the way across the room, and he was usually up my ass until the second we hit the field.

The doors creaked open. Coach walked in, along with the batting coach and Amelia, each of them carrying a big cardboard box. And...shit. Terrie, the GM, was with them too. Terrie seldom stopped by the clubhouse before a game. The room hushed as they filed over to one of the dining tables and set their boxes down.

Coach took his hat off and ran a hand over his thick silver hair. He turned to face the room, his hands finding his hips under the curve of his belly.

"Alright. Listen up! The roster change vote came back."

Roster change? When the hell had they called for a roster change? Wasn't I starting? They only did last-minute roster changes for special or extenuating circumstances.

Shit. No doubt a sex tape could be considered extenuating. As much as I had been dreading taking the field, disappointment weighed me down in my chair at the thought of having my usual position taken away from me for something I hadn't been able to control.

Coach pulled a scrap of paper from the pocket of his warm-up jacket and read the results. "Twenty-five in favor with one abstention."

Cheers erupted all around me. Some of the guys clapped. Everyone beamed, looking at me. What the hell had I missed sitting in that stupid bathtub yesterday?

The assistant coach, Amelia, and Terrie opened the boxes on the table and started pulling out jerseys while Coach called out the players by name. McQuiston was the first at the table. When he shook out the white home team fabric Terrie handed him, my jaw fell. Number thirty-four was emblazoned on the back. My number.

One by one, my team filed up to the table. I stared at the jerseys being pulled out of the boxes the way cats transfix their eyes to laser pointers. Number thirty-four. Number thirty-four. On down the line they kept coming. The only time a team ever wore one man's number was in remembrance of a teammate like on Jackie Robinson Day. I was no Jackie Robinson.

My reserve crumbled, falling off my shoulders like a pile of bricks. I dropped my head into my hands and choked on a massive ball of emotions. No one had ever done anything even remotely that thoughtful for me in my entire life.

"Hey, Spears! We'll see who wore it best," I heard Hooper call.

I looked up to find him smirking and replacing his jersey with the one with my number. His promise yesterday of *'let us worry about that'* sank in. I sucked in a breath, holding back a giant sniffle, and chuckled. Montez slapped me on the shoulder with a grin that told me he'd been the lookout to keep me company for this unbelievable plan.

"Hey! No fucking peeking," our outfielder said to McQuiston as he unbuttoned his jersey. "My wife will kick my ass."

My eyes stung, watching the team of guys I had played with day in and day out the last six years hoot and holler as they stripped off their jerseys to wear one of mine. I rubbed my eyes, shaking my head in disbelief.

"Spears!" Coach yelled, giving me a start.

The room fell silent, all eyes on me. I was beyond trying to figure out what came next. My knees wobbled as I approached Coach, parting the stillness in the room with my movement. He reached into his pocket and tossed me something, luckily not at my face. How embarrassing it would have been to fumble in front of a bunch of guys I needed to not let down when we took the field in ten minutes. I caught the small white box and turned it over in my hand.

There was a tag affixed to a red ribbon wrapped around it. The script on the kraft paper was some I knew well with the words *To: Uncle Jack, From: Emma.*

Shit. Now I really was going to cry, and I didn't even know what was inside of it yet. Glancing around, there was no place to hide from my audience.

Inside was a long loop of dog tag chain. I pulled it out and watched as a trifecta of adornments dangled from the length. Rubbing my thumb over a small purple feather that looked to be from one of Emma's feather boas, I chuckled. There were two circular fabric pendants that she'd clearly made from the jewelry-making kit I'd gotten her for Christmas. Contrary to Max's grumblings, it had not contained *'five-thousand-fucking-pieces.'* One of the handmade pendants was a round of leather, the other—a circle of lace that had been laminated to preserve its form.

Leather and lace.

I sucked in my lower lip and nodded at it like that wonderful little girl could see me doing so right now. Remembering the night Max and I had been caught kissing in the kitchen months ago, I smiled at the fond memory of him shocking the hell out of us with a dance in the living room. I traced the feather again, which I assumed represented Emma. They'd found a way to be right here with me after all, and I suspected it was as much father's idea as it was daughter's.

Clearing my throat, I slung the necklace over my head and tucked the pendants underneath my jersey. Scanning the faces of the men I thought I'd known these last six years, a wave of guilt coursed through me.

I'd hidden, in part, because I thought they wouldn't understand or accept the real me. Their compassionate expressions now told me it was impossible to know that until you gave someone a chance. I didn't know what was waiting outside for us, but I was grateful they'd be walking out that door with me. A bubble of laughter rose in my throat. So, this is what it felt like to not be alone?

The eyes staring back at me looked like they were expecting some uplifting speech, but I had none. "Thank you. I hope I don't let you down."

There were some gruff and growly *aw shucks* sounds as they descended upon me. I backed up and bumped into the table, but soon found myself in the center of a group hug that smelled like twenty-five different scents of cologne. Something heavy in my chest that had been there since I was a teenager playing this game flew away, and I suspected it would never return.

Ten minutes later, I blew out a breath as I trotted toward the mound with a stomach full of butterflies. Before I even got a chance to search for Max and Emma, a cacophony of cheers erupted in the stands all around me. Slowing my pace, I took in the sight of people on their feet, clapping, whistling, and cheering wildly from both the home *and* visitor sections. It was so loud my eardrums reverberated.

I did a three-sixty, blinking as my head spun and the sounds went on and on. The stands were almost entirely a backdrop of white T-shirts or fan jerseys in every section, all with the golden Eagles' scrawl over a number thirty-four on the chest of everyone wearing them. Even in the freaking visitor sections. I could taste the dust from the field as my mouth hung open, wondering how my Lifetime movie had just turned into a Hallmark flick.

When my bewildered perusal brought me to the section behind home plate, I caught a flash of familiar arms waving. There behind home plate were my two favorite people with my number on their chests. I squinted and choked on a puff of air when I also spotted Morgan, Mike, Trevor, his wife, their kids, Carrie, and... holy shit. My parents.

I might have had a mini-stroke, standing there gaping. My father was here? He wasn't waving or jumping because no matter how insane this dream was, *that* would never happen in the realm of any universe. Looking right at me, he lifted a hand like a stop sign with a somber expression on his face.

It was the most acknowledgment he'd given me in almost a decade. I didn't know what to do, so I mirrored his gesture. No doubt someone had dragged him here against his will, but... Jesus. He was here. I shook my head, wondering if someone's brain could actually malfunction from too much bewilderment in one day.

When my gaze found Max again, he had one arm around Emma like he wanted to make sure she didn't fall off the seat she was standing on. His other hand was stuffed in his pocket. I couldn't see him well, but the smile on his face was clear enough. I felt his love all the way to my bones. I knew he hadn't pulled all this off on his own, that it had to be attributed to Trevor's statement, and a lot of behind-the-scenes actions on the part of Hooper, the team, Ed, management, and even America from the looks of it, but something swelled inside my chest for the man staring back at me.

Smiling back at him, I knew then that sometimes choosing happiness wasn't enough. Sometimes to whom you gave your happiness was just as important. And when you couldn't believe in yourself, the least you could do was believe in the people who believed in you.

My first pitch was a solid fastball. I was too relieved that I'd actually thrown inside the batter's box to enjoy the over-the-top sound of the crowd going wild. And then it was like time and all the air in the stadium stood still.

My heart skittered in an uneven rhythm in my chest. My vision blocked out everything but the batters and the ball from inning to inning. I didn't look at the crowd. They became a blurry backdrop. I didn't even look at Max and Emma, not that I needed to. I could feel them. I could sense their love with me on the field. It was difficult to ignore the ruckus of the stadium completely as the cheers grew louder and louder with every batter I struck out until the revelry started to hush in the fourth inning. Every second I was at the mound after that, my pulse skipping beats, the silence hugging my skin. Christ. Were they really thinking I was going to pitch a shutout after everything that had happened already?

When I stepped back on the mound at the top of the ninth, I had lost all ability for thought. It was nothing but mechanics, prayers, and luck. There was no way I should be throwing this well this late in a game, not with how my body had been trembling for the last hour. I'd never heard the dugout so quiet in my life as during the last four innings. Nobody needed to say it. I could practically taste the anticipation in the air from the guys, from the stands, everyone's hope of witnessing a baseball rarity of an entire game of perfect pitching.

Every neuron in my body felt charged. Every muscle, loose and springy. My stomach dipped when the ump called the second batter *out*. I wanted this to be over, so I could take a normal breath, so every pore in my body would stop sweating, so I could go home and hug Max and Emma.

After two strikes and a ball with the third batter, I pinched my eyes closed and exhaled slowly. We were going to win. I didn't need to clinch this pitch, but at that moment, now that it could be one throw away from reality, I wanted to pull it off. I wanted to pull it off for the man who'd given me the pep talk yesterday and many other days before. Newfound determination filled me, replaying whispered promises and smiles in my head. Winding up, I strained every anxious muscle in my body and threw as hard as the love I felt in my heart. And like that love, it was perfect.

The *whoosh* of the bat slicing empty air. The *smack* of the ball hitting Hooper's mitt. The umpire, rearing his arm back like he was pulling a lawn mower starter cord. All the air flooded back into my lungs as I watched Hooper scramble to his feet and jump with a victorious fist in the air.

The stands went wild, like we'd just won the damn World Series. All I'd wanted was to not get heckled, not pass out, and not puke on national television. Instead, I'd just managed to throw the best game of my life. I knew exactly why, as the guys started pouring onto the field.

I found Max and hoped he could feel everything I was sending into the stands to him. He reached around Emma's head, covering her eyes, and then flipped me off with a smile as big as the sun.

CHAPTER 50
Max

Tossing the pastry bag on the passenger seat of my car was a sad reminder that I'd had to say goodbye to Jack last night for another away-game stretch. I hated when he was on the road. Or, more accurately, I hated I wasn't with him.

It had been two months since the video, and Jack was on fire this season. I had no doubts his head was in the game. He'd somehow managed to separate work and his private life in a healthy way. People were supportive, for the most part. His following had grown exponentially, something I hadn't thought possible. Yet, I could still see the impact the entire ordeal had on him in little ways.

I'd only just gotten him to go out to dinner with me two weeks ago. He'd loosened up more and more at home, back to cracking his usual jokes and laughing with Emma, but I worried he'd lost a vital piece of himself forever. It was what bothered me most about the entire series of events. When, if ever, would I get him back—all of him—the way he was before?

As I drove down the street toward the firm, I decided some uplifting music was in order, and switched off my talk radio program for a pop station. The infectious melody of '*MMMBop*' poured out of my speakers. I laughed, recalling Hooper's threat to Montez months ago. I bopped my head and kept time with my fingers on the steering wheel as I waited at the stoplight.

Something made me turn my head. When I glanced out my open window, I nearly did a double-take. In the next lane, Dan gaped at me from behind his steering wheel. I hadn't seen him since that day he dropped the bomb about my love life being global knowledge. He'd up and left our practice, leaving Trevor and me to scramble to find someone to pick up his share.

Taking in the look of abject disgust on his face as the Hanson Brothers serenaded us, a twinge of pity for him crept up on me. It hadn't been the best friendship, but how sad was it that he was willing to throw it all away over blind hatred?

He shook his head, his gaze returning to his windshield like he couldn't stand the sight of me—*me* in khakis and a polo, looking happy and loved, rocking out to a boy band. What an awful human I was. My pity fizzled as I took in his ridiculously expensive, uncomfortable-looking suit, and the way his lips moved, as though cursing me under his breath.

Remembering the things he'd said about Jack, I cranked the radio. Dan's head whipped back to look at me, his expression appalled. As the light changed, I blew him a kiss with my middle finger and floored the gas.

Was it childish? Immature? Maybe, but I laughed for two blocks, and *MMMBopped* my ass all the way to the parking garage of the firm.

Humming and shimmying into the elevator, I embraced the moment, appreciating how much promise everything held now. Carla Chang, a wicked smart attorney we'd faced off with over the years, had started last week. Trevor and I agreed too much testosterone in one firm could be a bad thing.

When I entered the lobby, Jennifer smiled at me from behind the reception desk.

"Morning Mr. Hartwell," she called and took the bag of pastries I handed over to her. "Thanks. I'll set them out in the lounge."

I'd made the effort to get to know my staff better since Jack and I had gotten together. Funny how you notice the world around you more when you're not wallowing in self-pity.

"Where's Jack playing today?" Jennifer asked, snatching a raspberry strudel from the regular treat delivery that had become my new thing.

"Florida. He's going to cream them," I declared, daring her to refute me.

She laughed. "I'll bet he is."

Strolling into my office, I flopped my briefcase down on my desk and flipped through the stack of messages Jennifer had given me. Picking up my bagel, I frowned at its inability to compare with Jack and our bacon mornings.

Looking out the window over the vibrant sunlight shining down on the city, I wondered what kind of mindset Jack would be in when he got back next week for his round of home games. He'd promised to go to the theater with me, and I was going to hold him to it.

I didn't want him making promises just to appease me, though. I wanted him to be comfortable in his own skin because he was comfortable in it. I wanted him to know that no matter who was looking at him, no matter what they thought, all that mattered was what he thought of himself.

He assured me last night before he left he was fine, and I'd even caught a hint of his old mischievous smile. I had to hope it signified that he was finally at peace with everything that had happened and his outing to the world.

I had new plans for my man. Considering how my last big plan had been soiled by a secret camera and blasted all over the internet, I was more than a little paranoid that something would ruin this one. Jack's biggest fear the entire time we'd been together was that the bottom would drop out. When I realized that was because the only thing permanent he'd ever had in his life was baseball, I knew what to do.

I was permanent. *We* were permanent, but there was no way I was even going to contemplate how to secure that permanence until his head was fully back in the right place. I wanted it to be as perfect as the perfect man deserved.

Sighing, I resigned myself to get to work and to hold off my excitement over concreting a future with the man I wanted to spend it with. I set my bagel down and dusted the crumbs off my hands before popping open my briefcase. When the lid flipped up, my heart lurched into my throat. I yelled and stumbled back. An arm flopped out over the side of my briefcase—an arm belonging to the creepiest, sparkliest pink monkey on the planet. It stared up at me with its maniacal red smile and soulless eyes.

"Fuck!" I gasped, clutching my chest. God, I hated that thing.

Squinting, I spotted a handwritten note pinned to its belly in Jack's handwriting. I didn't even bother undoing the safety pin. The jackass had probably pinned it on there just so I'd have to touch the damn thing. Snagging the square of paper, I gave it a sharp tug, tearing it from the pin.

Love you, baby. I'll be thinking of you while I'm gone. And now I know you'll be thinking of me.

"You son of a bitch," I muttered, but heard the laughter in my voice.

No wonder he'd had that weird look in his eyes last night. For the first time in my life, I was happy at the sight of that stupid fiber-filled pink monstrosity.

He'd come back to me. Jack was back.

CHAPTER 51
Jack

Seven months later

Was it possible to die from happiness? I wriggled my toes underneath the bedsheets to burn off some of my excitement. Turning the page of the baby magazine, I looked lovingly at the platinum ring on my finger and then at the adorable little baby with its bright blue eyes on the next page. Gah! Seriously, my face was starting to hurt from smiling for so long.

The January wind rattled our bedroom window as the TV played on the far wall. I still couldn't believe this was my life in this big warm bed with my *husband* sitting next to me. And after our visit with Morgan today... Somebody pinch me.

"I can't tell you how disturbing it is that my sister put a bigger smile on your face than I ever have," Max said.

"That's not true." I chuckled but cut it off with a content sigh because all I could see, feel, and hear today were hearts. "Max, do you know how lucky we are?"

"I knew that before we even went over there today," he boasted, leaning over to kiss me.

I cupped his cheek before he could draw back and whispered the wonder that had been flooding my brain all day. "I get to have a baby with you."

He smiled at me like he was seeing something in my eyes for the first time.

"What?" I asked.

He shook his head as though to ward off my worry. "I get to be the guy who has one with you, the guy who makes you this happy."

The bubble in my chest expanded even more. Just when I thought the day couldn't get any better, and then he goes and says something like that.

The incoming message alert on my phone interrupted our kiss. Max went back to reviewing some work notes while I checked my phone. Another text from Morgan.

I chuckled when I saw what she sent. Max had scolded her for hugging me too long this morning when we went to do *the big ask* of her and Mike. She kept insinuating that she and I were going to make the baby by having sex rather than her surrogacy being done through insemination in a lab just to piss off Max. I loved Morgan, but…you know. No, thank you.

I flinched when Max's voice barked beside me. "Aw! Gross! What the fuck is that?"

Chuckling, I angled the photo of Morgan in some lingerie toward him, forcing him to have a better view. "She's been sending them all day."

"What? Give me that!" He snatched my phone out of my hand and started scrolling through the text thread. Gasping, he pressed his palm to his mouth. "Oh, God! That's disturbing. I don't care what she tries. She's *not* fucking you."

I rolled my eyes. "I know, Max. That goes without saying."

"Then why the fuck is she sending you this shit?"

"It's Morgan." I shrugged and stroked his forearm. "Come on. She's excited for us about the baby, and you know she likes messing with you."

"Uh, yeah! And she's wanted your cock since the day she met you." He scowled at me.

Picking up my magazine, I tilted a brow and murmured, "At least somebody did."

When I felt his glare boring into the side of my face, I snickered. The sound of keys typing drew my attention back though. His fingers flew over the screen of my phone.

His message read, 'This is Max. What the fuck is wrong with you? He's GAY! Not happening!'

A second later, my phone dinged, and an image popped up. Oh, shit. It was Morgan in a chemise, making a naughty O-face at the camera. I found it hilarious that she had a stock of these photos on hand. It painted a picture of the kind of texts my brother-in-law got regularly.

"Ew! Gross," Max yelled, covering his eyes. When I snickered, he scowled at me. "Oh, you think this is funny? Huh?"

He drew the waistband of his boxers away from his stomach, and for a second my pulse hitched, wondering if I was about to get some grumpy sex out of him because that would be the epic finish to this fantastic day of days, but he didn't take them off. He flipped on my camera application and snapped a picture of his wilted junk. When he attached the photo to the text thread, my jaw dropped.

"*What* are you doing?"

"Ending this shit right now."

I panicked when his thumb went for the send button. "No. Don't piss her off! I want a baby!"

I grabbed for his wrist, but he deflected. My breath caught when I heard the *whoosh* sound of the sent message. Oh, no. If he ruined this for us by starting some stupid fight with his sister, I was going to…

My phone dinged and a text box popped up. I leaned over into Max's bubble, fully invested in this conversation now.

MORGAN: Yeah. I definitely got the better genes.

"Oh. Fuck. Off!" Max barked at my phone and then whipped it against the wall.

"Hey! My phone!"

"I'll buy you a new one," he growled, tossing my magazine onto the floor and straddling my legs. When his lips crashed down onto mine, I forgot what I was supposed to be mad about.

Running my hands up his sides, I drank in the stormy look in his eyes. "You look like a possessive caveman right now."

He nipped at my lip. "You look like you need your ass spanked for flirting with my sister."

Ha! *Possessive Max* was probably my favorite one. "I wasn't flirting."

When he sat back and rubbed his crease over my erection, my laughter melted into a sigh.

"Yeah, but you didn't block her either," he scolded, like teasing my dick was supposed to be some sort of punishment.

He traced my lip with the tip of his tongue before tasting me. I was still high off the two weeks we'd spent on our honeymoon in Maui after Christmas. There had been a lot of sex as any proper honeymoon should have, but when he proposed, I knew I didn't just want forever with him. I wanted everything forever with him had to offer. So, I may have spent the entire honeymoon trying to convince him we were getting older and that if we wanted to have a bigger family, we'd better start ASAP. Sex is a very enjoyable negotiation tool.

"Mm," I groaned into his mouth. "So, you want me to cockblock your sister?"

He snickered, running his hands down my chest. I wondered if he'd ever realized this was how most of our disagreements ended, and why I went out of my way to provoke him. As he sucked at the tendon in my neck, I forgot about what we'd even been bickering about until I heard my phone ding across the room.

"Are you kidding me?" he raged and bolted off the bed. "I'm going to kill her!"

I watched in disbelief as he marched toward where my phone had landed by the wall, picked it up, and started unlocking the window. Pushing back the curtain, he opened the window, letting in a frigid blast of air.

"What are you doing? Hey!" I yelled as he tossed my phone outside.

"Saying goodnight to Morgan."

He slammed the window shut and marched back to bed. Holy temper tantrum, *Batman*.

"You could have just turned it off," I suggested.

"No. She's too evil. She'd find a way to make it ring."

Just as he got his knee on the bed, his phone chirped. Max's head whipped toward his nightstand.

"Crazy bitch," he grumbled, reading a message and then powered it down as he sat on the bed.

"Oh, I see how you are. My phone's expendable, but yours isn't?"

He turned around and prowled to the end of the bed between my feet. "Don't even try to act put out," he warned, tugging on my ankles until he'd pulled me so far that I was lying on the mattress. "You're still in trouble," he said, tugging my boxer briefs down.

I lifted my ass to show him how much I was resisting, and laughed at the scowl on his face. "For what? I didn't do anything."

"For pissing me off," he huffed, tossing my underwear over his shoulder.

"Like that's hard to do."

His eyes narrowed. It wasn't fair how sexy he was when he got like this. I wondered what all the people in the courtroom thought when he got intense during a hearing or a trial. When he lowered his head and drew a circle around the tip of my cock with his tongue, I let my eyes fall closed for a second.

Controlling my breathing, I casually rested my hands behind my head and cast him a bored look. "Wow. It is *really* terrible having you pissed off at me."

Max smirked, his bedroom voice floating over me. "Shut your mouth and take your punishment, Mr. Spears." He cupped my balls in his palm and drew his tongue slowly up my length.

"Mm, the prices I have to pay, *Mr. Spears*," I countered, still loving that he'd insisted on taking my name.

As I melted into my pillow from Max's blissful torture, an idea crept into my head. Watching him work with finesse and hunger was such a change from last year, when we were both nervous friends touching each other for the first time and then rattled by the scandal. So much had changed. I went for broke, deciding to push the limits.

"Hey." I nudged at the underside of his jaw.

"What?"

"When you're done down there, could you snap some shots of me in my boxers to send to Morgan?"

"What?" he clipped.

"...to help get her ovaries primed, of course."

His nostrils flared as the blue diamonds bore into my gaze. "That's not even a thing!"

"It couldn't hurt."

He prowled up the length of my body with murder-eyes and shoved at my hip like he was trying to roll me over.

"Oh, ho," he guffawed. "My handprints on your ass are going to be so red they'll still be there for spring training."

I roared with laughter as I resisted his valiant efforts to get me on my stomach. When he managed to tip me to my side, I bent my knees, bringing my feet up behind me, along with one of my hands to protect my ass. He got ahold of my wrist and pinned my forearm with his weight as his palm came down and cracked me a good one.

"Oh, no. I'm scared!" I tried to breathe through the laughter as we grappled.

Max arched a brow and gaped at me. "Jesus! She's made you as cocky as her already."

His hand connected with one of my cheeks again.

"Ow!" I laughed and scooted up toward the headboard, but he scrambled after me.

I got ahold of his wrists, but he wouldn't give up, still twisting this way and that. He got a few dull swats in on the side of my ass, but I still had the upper hand.

"Great. I'm going to be on TMZ with a bruised ass when they feature celebrities with deranged husbands."

He scoffed, panting as he leaned in to kiss me. "You will after how hard I'm going to fuck you."

I grabbed his face and met him on my knees. "Promises, promises."

He blinked for a moment, like my taunt had shocked him, but then his mouth tipped up at the corner. He shucked his briefs and flopped onto his ass against the headboard, pulling me down on his lap. Rubbing my ass with one hand, he reached inside his nightstand drawer with the other and let out a dramatic sigh.

"The things I have to go through to teach you a lesson."

I snatched the lube from his hand and slickened us up, while he changed his shit-talking to a smattering of kisses across my chest and arms. When I tossed the bottle, he slid his hands around my hips and smiled one of those anticipatory smiles we gave each other right before lovemaking.

I knew he liked it this way, as did I. It always reminded me of our first time. When his hand cracked my ass, though, I realized I'd misread his smile.

"Ow! Enough!" I gasped as sparks trickled all the way to my dick. Leaning in to kiss him, I reached behind me to grab his hand just in case, but he had other plans. He slid it down, slipping a finger inside me as he stroked my erection with his other hand.

"Nooo," he purred. "I don't think you've had enough."

"Not nearly enough," I concurred with a satisfied sound, rocking into his hand as I gripped the headboard and took his mouth.

"Always complaining," he teased, replacing his finger with the head of his cock.

This tit for tat game was getting better by the second. Since it was my turn to surprise him, I settled deftly onto the hot silky rod at my pucker, groaning over the best victory ever.

"Oh. Yeah, babe," Max moaned.

He wrapped a hand behind my neck and let me know how much he wanted me with his mouth as he stroked my aching shaft just the way he knew I liked it. God, I loved fighting with him.

"Shit. I think Morgan was right," I whispered.

My dick pulsed like it was demanding to know why he'd stopped stroking it. I found him cocking a brow at me. "Uh, could you please not talk about my sister while I'm inside you?"

My lips sputtered, and I gave him a quick peck. Morgan had gotten her husband on board with our surrogacy plan by reminding him how horny she got when she was pregnant. "I mean," I scolded, "she was right about pregnancy making people horny. We're both rock hard."

Max gave me a goofy grin and rubbed my probably red ass cheek. "You're going to make the cutest baby, Jack. And you're going to be the best father...again."

He earned a tender kiss for that remark. "I can't wait to raise a baby with you and give Emma a little brother or sister," I whispered, rocking my favorite rhythm on him.

"Me too. And I love how happy it makes you."

"It does," I gushed, now that he was done harassing me. The life this man had given me, had already built with me, and the life I knew we'd continue to build brought tears to my eyes. "I love you so much."

He groaned when I rolled my hips. His hands squeezed my ass. "Fuck. I'm supposed to be torturing you, not the other way around."

Nipping at his lips, I circled one of his nipples with my thumb as my arousal spurred on my rocking. How was it possible it got better every time?

"Are we supposed to be this happy?" I gasped, growing slightly terrified of just how fucking happy I was.

Max cupped my jaw, forcing me to meet his eyes. "*Yes*," he insisted. "I told you when I married you how happy I was going to make you."

"You're so damn bossy," I joked, to stop the tears that wanted to make an appearance.

"When it comes to you being happy? Yeah. I am."

The man knew how to make my heart crazy. I gave him everything I could with slow, deep, languid slides and determined kisses.

"Max, I'm going to make you happy, too."

"You do, babe. You do," he moaned as I peppered him with kisses. "How the fuck did I get so lucky?"

His hands tightened on my hips, holding himself deep inside me. He kissed me like it was our last.

"Max," I wept. "Shit. You always make me cry."

He wrapped me up tight in his arms and pressed his lips to my ear. "You can cry all you want, baby. You're still the sexiest man on the planet."

My heart burst like a firework. I knew my body wasn't far behind. All his silliness, his grumpy posturing, his dirty talking in bed—things I never knew I'd like in one package—were the wrapping paper of the deep love of a passionate man with a big heart that beat just for me.

He stroked me and licked at the sensitive spot below my ear, causing me to shiver. It was a heady feeling when he said sweet things and did little moves like that for my pleasure through the haze of his own desire. I undulated, reaching down to cup his ass for a deeper connection.

"Fuck, Jack," he gasped. "I want you inside me first thing tomorrow."

A laugh bubble burst in my throat and came out as a needy whimper. Everything below my waist tingled as euphoria swept over me. "Oh, Max. I love you," I panted, kissing every inch of his face. "I love you."

"Yeah, babe," he groaned, like he was in pain. I didn't realize my face was wet until he cupped my jaw and started kissing my tears. "My beautiful man. God, you wreck me."

When he pulsed inside me, I hung on and buried my face in his neck because the culmination was almost too much as I met his release with my own. Even back when I had a crush on him, I never would have imagined we would be this way. I understood why people had sex now. Sometimes there's just too much love to hold inside.

His chest rose and fell beneath mine as he held me. "Guess I showed you," he teased all breathy, giving me a peck on the cheek.

I made a noise halfway between a sniffle and a snicker as I sat up. His tender smile made my heart spasm as he wiped a tear from my face.

"We're going to be this happy forever," he whispered, "and I'll love you even longer."

I rested my forehead against his. "Okay, husband."

"Practically had to beg you to marry me, and now you gloat about it every chance you get."

I eased off him, delighting in the little grunt he made at the loss of me. "*You?* Beg for anything? I don't think so."

He gave my ass a light swat as I stood. "You took some convincing."

"Yeah, but lucky for me, you were very convincing."

When we crawled back into bed after our shower, I pulled him into my arms. An urgent tap of his finger on my chest drew me from my afterglow.

"Hey. Carla said she'd come to the first home game this season."

"Yeah?" I liked Max and Trevor's new law partner already, but hearing Max would have more company in the stands made me happy.

"Yeah. She's bringing her husband. He's a Red Sox fan."

"Tell her I forgive her."

Max chuckled. "Still...better than Dan."

Dan would always be a sore point for me, not just because of what he thought of gay people, which was downright shitty of him, but for how he'd treated Max. "I'm glad I didn't know you in college," I groused, still baffled the man in my arms could have been friends with Dan even when he considered himself to be straight.

"I'm not," he murmured and kissed me.

I squeezed him for the compliment and asked cautiously, "When did you get sick of him?"

"After Emma was born." He sighed. "He didn't get it, being domesticated and loving people more than yourself. Lainey only tolerated him. I don't think she ever liked him."

"Lainey was smart."

"I'll overlook the fact you're implying she was smarter than me."

"Thank you." I kissed his temple, making him snicker.

Damn him. I'd almost been asleep. Now the hamster wheel in my brain was turning.

"Do you need anything while I'm out tomorrow?" I asked, mentally reviewing my shopping list.

"Where are you going?"

"Shopping for Emma's science fair project, so probably the craft store."

"What does she need?"

"Pipe cleaners, spray glue, glitter."

"Glitter?" He craned his neck to look at me.

"Yeah."

"How does glitter have a place in a science project?"

"We're making DNA strands."

"O-kay. And how does glitter have a place in DNA?"

"In Emma's it does." I chuckled at his confused expression. "She said she wants it to sparkle."

"And you told her that was a good idea?"

I could see where this was going and tried to hold my amusement in check. Max let out an exasperated sound and closed his eyes.

"Ugh. That shit is going to be everywhere. I hope you're planning on doing it in the sunroom."

"Of course. It'll sparkle better in there. All that natural lighting."

He narrowed his eyes at me. "What else are you two up to?"

Nothing actually, but there was something we hadn't discussed in a while. And who could say no to anything after fantastic sex? I pressed a kiss to his neck as my introduction. "Well...about the dog..."

"Fuck!" He covered his eyes with his palm. His nostrils flared below his hand.

"So," I continued breezily, "we narrowed it down to a corgi or a Saint Bernard."

He dropped his hand and shot me a look like I'd just informed him Mr. Sparkles had triplets. "Half a dog that sheds or two times the dog that slobbers everywhere? Great. You're fucking fired from the dog committee."

I held up my index finger. "I veto that decision."

"Oh, yeah? Who's going to clean up after this thing? We're going to have a baby crawling around here next year."

The word *baby* had become my kryptonite. I grinned like a loon and squeezed a smile out of him. "I'll be retired by then if we do. I'll take care of it," I assured him.

"Yeah, right. I'll be the one vacuuming up hair while you're playing with the baby."

"Okay."

He gaped at me. "*Okay?*"

I shrugged. "You're a neat freak. I'm not going to be able to stop you."

"So, you're taking advantage of my weaknesses? Nice." He scoffed and rolled to his side, giving me his back. "I guess the honeymoon's over."

Laughing at his pout, I leaned in and kissed the back of his neck. His body was stiff as a board. I spooned in close behind him, running my hand up his chest as I peppered tiny little kisses across his shoulder. His back rose and fell against my chest, and I could feel some of the tension go out of him.

"It's not sleeping in here," he grumbled.

Pressing my hips into his ass, I nuzzled behind his ear without a word. He just had so many buttons. How was a guy supposed to resist pushing them?

"*No,*" he warned, but I knew he wasn't talking about my kisses.

"Even if it's fluffy and warm?" I whispered.

"No!"

"*Please?*"

"Oh, my God!" he growled, angling his head back. "Go to sleep. I only negotiate between eight and four."

I held onto him like a security blanket, undeterred. "What if you end up loving it, and it's your best friend?"

"Uh. Then it'll bring me beer, clean the house, and not manipulate me," he huffed, tugging the blanket around him.

"Hey, I do two out of the three."

His pillow muffled his snort. I waited like the Cheshire cat for a beat. "Just think about it."

"I'm *thinking about* fur on my work slacks and if dogs can get sick licking lube off bed sheets."

"Gross."

"*See?* Didn't think about that. Did you?"

"You're so mean to me." I let my grip slacken.

He grabbed my forearm and tugged it back against his chest with a sigh. "Fine. Win the series this year and you can get your damn lube-licking dog."

"Only if you're there to see my '*we're-getting-a-fucking-puppy*' face when I pull it off."

The way his back rumbled against my chest was better than getting ten puppies.

"Cocky bastard."

EPILOGUE
Max

Sixteen years later

It was funny how happiness could make a person look like they were glowing. I smiled down at Emma in her white dress. Maybe the shimmery fabric of her wedding gown had something to do with it.

"Did you enjoy your big day, kiddo?"

"I'm married now. Are you ever going to stop calling me that?" she challenged, as we swayed to the father-daughter dance.

"No."

"At least at the office?" she asked hopefully.

"Nope."

Her shoulders shook with a laugh. "Fine."

"You all set for tomorrow?"

"Yeah."

I arched a brow. "Where are your passports?"

"In the room safe."

"And your tickets? The travelers' checks?"

Her expression teetered on sympathetic. "Dad, no one uses travelers' checks anymore."

"I do."

I got an eye roll, but then her brows shot up. "Hey, if the Gregsons send over their statements, forward them to me so I can check them in case we…"

"No. You're not working on your honeymoon."

"It's fine. I just want to read them over so…"

"No."

"…I can make sure they got their…"

"No."

"Dad!" she huffed, giving her pale skin a flush of pink.

"No working on your honeymoon," I scolded, turning us in a spin across the dance floor under the twinkling lights. "I'm shutting down your work email first thing in the morning."

The guttural sound that came out of her throat and the way she narrowed her eyes kind of ruined the whole princess look she had going on. "You don't know how to do that."

I shrugged. "No, but I can pay someone who does."

"Whatever." She chuckled. "Just try to stop me, old man."

Digging my fingers into her side, I nabbed a spot under her ribs and gave it a little pinch. She flinched and let out a squeak.

"*Old man,* huh?" I made a show of glancing over at the wedding party table to find Matt. "Fine. I'm going to have a talk with your boyfriend and see how far you get when I tell him to take your phone."

Her glistened lips ticked up at the corners even as she imitated a perturbed voice, "He's *not* my boyfriend." Her smile was radiant as she added proudly, "He's my husband."

"Well, he'll always be your boyfriend to me."

Her laughter, like a happy hiccup, warmed my chest. For a moment, it reminded me of when she was a little mischievous girl who used to make me want to pull my hair out, and I missed the hell out of those moments.

"What?" she asked, sobering as I stared at her.

I shook my head, blinking away the thought of tears. "Nothing. Just… your mom would be so happy for you."

Her eyes went all hopeful puppy dog on me. "Yeah?"

"Yeah. You look just like she did when we got married."

"Yeah?" She smiled, clearly happy with the comparison.

"Yeah, but…" I trailed off.

"But what?"

"Meaner," I said gravely.

Her head reared back, and she swatted my arm. "That's because I got stuck with you longer than she did. It makes a person tough."

I smiled and pulled her in closer so I could talk into her ear. "I'm sorry. I had to make you tough."

Her arm tightened around me at the back of my beige suit jacket. "I know. Thank you," she whispered. When she looked up at me, her blue eyes were a little glassy, probably the same way mine were. "I love you, Dad."

There's something about when your grown children tell you they love you that's uniquely as special as every time they told you when they were kids. My heart cramped as I hugged her now that the song was coming to a close. "I love you too, kiddo," I practically choked.

Her whisper tickled my ear. "Spin me, so people think you know how to dance."

I snorted, any worry of tears now gone as I grabbed her hand and twirled her. "I could dance circles around you."

"Maybe if one of your pant legs got caught in something." She laughed.

Just for that little dig, I whipped her around again, faster this time. When she rotated back to me, I braced my hand on her spine and dipped her as far as I could manage until my knees started to shake and my back gave a twinge. I let out a grunt and the little imp chuckled like she knew I was paying for my bravado. I kissed her cheek for the photographer like a good father and made my exit off the floor.

Zeke, Ryan, and Jack all clapped and smiled as I walked back to the white linen-covered parents' table. Pressing my hand to my lower back, I gave the Gardners a nod and tried to walk like a man wearing a suit should, since I had barely worn one in years.

"Very nice, Max," Ryan commended.

"Thanks."

I sank into my seat next to Jack with a sigh of relief.

His warm breath hit my neck, and his hand rubbed the small of my back. "You okay there, old man?"

"Fuck off." I chuckled. "What is it with you two?"

And like the cocky bastard everyone in my family was, he laughed. Lane hurried over to our table, his brown hair flopping down at the sides of his forehead.

"Hey, Dad," he said excitedly to Jack. "Matt's boss' son has a full baseball scholarship to U of I. I bet him I make it to the minors before he does."

Jack scoffed before taking a sip of his beer. "Not the way you've been hitting."

"Oh, come on," Jack's spitting image whined. "I had one bad game."

"What the hell are you betting, anyway?" I cut in when my brain caught up to the conversation. "No. Wait." I held up a hand. "Don't even answer that. It's your sister's wedding. There will be no gambling of any sort happening tonight."

Why both of my children constantly scoffed at my sound advice, I will never know. "Dad," he leveled me with a look. "I didn't actually bet anything."

Jack pursed his lips and set his glass down. "Just go try not to get into trouble or raise your dad's blood pressure any more than it is."

"Which one?" our little shit-talker retorted with a snicker.

Jack was out of his chair and had Lane in a headlock before I could even think of a proper comeback. He dug his knuckles across the top of Lane's head in a noogie while Lane squirmed to free himself from the hold. Zeke and Ryan laughed the kinds of laughs of people who had seen the trenches.

"And just because you're a groomsman doesn't mean you get to drink with the bridal party," Jack added a warning near Lane's ear.

"I wasn't!" Lane squirmed free of his arm, but I was pretty sure only because Jack let up.

Jack lifted his brown dress shoe and planted the sole lightly on Lane's ass. "Oh, whatever. I saw you sneak a drink up there."

"Fine." Lane chuckled with way too much mischief in his brown eyes.

Jack let out a long sigh as he dropped back into his seat and took another drink of his beer like he needed it. I stroked the top of his thigh over the smooth fabric of his slacks and smirked. That I-told-you-so sensation I felt when I'd warned him about the fuckery of children back when he'd hinted desperately that he wanted us to have a baby never got old.

"Can we give him back to your sister now?" he asked, wiping his mouth.

Reaching over, I squeezed his hand. "Babe, we've been over this. Her hospitality only covered the minor inconveniences of carrying and birthing your child, *not* raising him."

He let out a long breath as his eyes found Morgan laughing at the bar. "Selfish bitch."

I roared so hard my side hurt. He grinned and slunk an arm around the back of my chair.

The DJ's voice echoed across the room. "And now our second father-daughter dance of the night! Let's get Jack and Emma out here!"

A peppy beat chimed out of the speakers. Jack jumped up with the excitement of a bingo winner. The familiar notes of Fleetwood Mac's '*Secondhand News*' filled the room as Emma sashayed out onto the dance floor with a huge grin on her face.

"What the hell?" I complained as Jack scrambled around behind my chair. "How come I got a slow song?"

He laughed over his shoulder at me as he jogged out onto the floor to meet Emma. Well, that was some bullshit. I'd have at least liked to have been asked to be the cool dad with the cool song.

Not at all, actually. Me and my stiff back were totally grateful to be sitting my ass in this chair, watching the entertainment.

Jack hiked up the sleeves of his dress shirt higher on his arms. He'd rolled them up an hour ago. The jacket had been the first thing to go after the ceremony, then his vest, but now I noticed his tie was missing too and the top three buttons of his shirt were undone. Christ, at this rate, he'd be naked by the end of the night if I didn't keep an eye on him.

"How much did he have to drink while I was out there?" I asked Ryan and Zeke without taking my eyes off him as he hoisted Emma up, spinning her around on his hip.

Zeke laughed as Jack dropped down onto his stomach and started doing the worm. How did he know how to do the worm and I didn't know this?

"Oh, my God. My dick hurts just watching." Ryan winced and looked like he was holding his hands over his lap.

Emma simulated a fishing pole to Jack's worm. The entire room was on their feet, bobbing in time to the catchy song. Across the room, Hooper cheered Jack on as he stood with his arm around Carrie. There were times when I thought I wanted to kill the man that first year after he'd bought Jack's house, but luckily Carrie did us a favor by marrying him. Word to the wise, though. Do *not* go over there without knocking first.

Jack flipped over onto his ass, and I had to admire his sprightliness. He popped up onto the soles of his feet and started doing that Cossack kick-dance thing I tried once in college and about burned out my thigh muscles.

"Geez, Max," Zeke smacked my arm. "Jack's still got moves."

I chuckled, pride filling my chest. That he still did. His forty-eight-year-old ass was slightly meatier than it had been at thirty-two, but no less admirable. And the way he cut his hair a bit shorter than when we were younger, along with the tiny strands of silver that were starting to sprout at the sides, were a badge of time that reminded me, I'd been there with him through it all. I rubbed the smooth platinum band on my finger as I did when I was at work, missing him.

When the song ended, Jack swallowed Emma up into a bear hug. The room cheered. I could see one table over that even Jack's dad had cracked a smile. Turns out giving your father a grandkid will chip away at the most frigid ice block, that and a good talking to from a certain someone's ornery husband many moons ago.

I stood to join in on the applause, watching the beautiful man walking back toward me. His chest rose and fell. He had that vivacious grin on his face that always took my breath away. I could hear him panting, and his skin glistened under the lights.

"Jesus, you're sweating," I scolded him, snagging a napkin off the table to wipe his brow.

His grin grew as his chest heaved while he let me fuss over him. With his hands on his hips, I could practically feel the energy pouring off him as his eyes scanned the room. When I'd patted his damp hairline and tossed the napkin aside, he looked at me and blew out a breath.

I shook my head at the sexiest high school baseball coach in the world. One of these days, he was going to have to realize his limits. "Told you she was going to kill us," I reminded him.

He chuckled and nodded to the far side of the room where Lane was talking with his cousins and some teenagers, definitely wearing his trouble-maker eyes. "No. I put my money on the other one."

I snorted. "Yeah. Probably."

Seeing our son laughing with young adults while Emma and Matt made rounds, thanking guests, hit me in the solar plexus. I sighed and wrapped my arm around Jack's waist, feeling the need to be close. "She's married, Jack," I let out wistfully.

He gave me an understanding smile and shifted, wrapping his arms around me from behind. "About time. How many times did they break up?"

I huffed. "Two? Three? I can't remember."

"No. There was the high school break up."

"Ugh. That one was ugly."

"You're telling me," he said, resting his chin on my shoulder. I patted his hand, remembering the night Emma had come home at two in the morning her junior year, smelling like alcohol after breaking up with Matt.

When Jack had taken his turn giving her the talking to, she proceeded to tell him she hated him, and that he wasn't her father. After I kicked her out, I held Jack while he cried. Our darling daughter crawled in the next morning offering remorse after sleeping in the garden shed, apparently. Jack forgave quickly, but I held out, giving her the silent treatment for two weeks for what she'd said to Jack.

"Then there were a couple of college breakups," I added.

"They still talked the entire time. Do those even really count?" Jack asked.

"I don't know, but if she gets divorced, she's getting her own lawyer."

"They won't." He chuckled into my neck.

"And," I held up a finger, "I'm not paying for a second wedding."

His chest heaved into my back with a put-out sigh. "I guess I could take this muscle rub endorsement deal I got offered yesterday."

I twisted my neck around. Deals didn't come in like they had in our thirties. "Seriously?"

The laugh lines by his eyes crinkled tighter, and he nodded.

"Does it come with a free lifetime supply? Because I could get on board with that."

His laughter made my ears ring. "Or we could just buy you some."

"Who said it's for me?"

He pressed a kiss to my lips that tasted like laughter and squeezed me.

"Fuck off." I chuckled.

The tinny sound of a utensil on glass pierced the air, and the room grew hushed. Emma stood at the head table with Matt seated beside her. She picked up a mic and settled her gaze on us.

"I've been so lucky to not have one, but two of the most amazing dads who put up with me and gave me an example of what love looks like. I want to thank you both for everything you've done for me. I wouldn't have been able to do it without either of you. I hope I have as strong of a marriage as the both of you. Dad, Uncle Jack, I love you guys."

Something got caught in my chest. Jack squeezed me tighter while my hold on his hand did the same. Emma's praise felt like we'd just reached a life goal and filled me with both sadness and joy.

The way too fucking perky DJ called into his mic as he queued up the music. "And this next song goes out to Max and Jack from Emma."

The harmonic melody of *Leather and Lace* floated through the speakers. I groaned and muttered under my breath, "No. She didn't."

"Hey, you love our song!" Jack took my hand, pulling me toward the dance floor.

I shot Emma a look as he tugged me along. She grinned her shit-eating grin at me as Jack threaded his fingers in mine.

He settled his hand on my waist and smiled down at me with so much love in his eyes, my heart clamped up. Fucking weddings. I was an emotional ball of goo tonight.

If you ask Jack what the best day of his life was, he'd tell you there were three. The night I walked into his house sixteen years ago after the weirdest date in history, the day Lane was born, and the night he pitched a shutout after the worst scandal to rock MLB history.

Ask him the best game of his life, and he'll say that one too because it was the first one he got to play the game he loved as Jack Spears. He played for one more season after the world saw us bare-ass naked. The Eagles won the World Series in game four when he pitched another shutout the day before Lane was born. Jack made it to the hospital in time for Morgan to cuss us out and nearly break our hands, in case you were wondering. Sportscasters are still waiting for him to slip up and say game four was the best game of his life because, from a baseball standpoint, it was. Maybe they never knew who in the hell Jack Spears really was at all.

And *my* best day?

Jesus. All of them.

All but one.

I thought it was the end of the world when Lainey died. A lot of it was because I missed her and didn't expect her to be taken away so soon. But mostly it was because I couldn't fathom the future could even be half as bright as the past.

I had two people to thank for proving me wrong—my beautiful, smart-ass wife, and my beautiful, smart-ass husband. The thing about being inspired, though, was it's addictive. I got now why Jack loved to play ball so much, why he was glad to end it on a good note. Where the hell did you go when you got to the top?

I was fifty years old, and my little girl just got married to a good man that I approved of. Trevor, Carla, and I had one of the most successful, respected law firms in the state, where Emma would probably become partner once I retired. I got to fall in love with and marry my two best friends. My son was a pain in the ass, but a good-hearted pain in the ass with promise. And let's face it—we worry more about our little girls than our little boys. If you couldn't call that being at the top, what the hell did you call it?

Looking around this room at all the faces that served as reminders of how great my life had been, I was scared as hell. I had little left to gain and everything to lose. Maybe I was losing that inspiration because the future was starting to not look half as bright as the past again, even though my past was as bright as the biggest sun in the galaxy.

"Hey." Jack canted his head. I looked up to concern in his sparkling brown eyes and his mouth ticked up at the corner. "Come on. You love our song. Are you worried about the people we don't know seeing us dancing?"

I forced a smile, not wanting to dampen one more of the memories I knew I'd add to my treasure chest of wonderful life moments with this man.

"No. Sorry. I just…" I glanced over at Matt and Emma, arms interlocked together at the bridal table, smiling, probably whispering husband and wife secrets to each other. "Our grown daughter is married, and our son will… hopefully be graduating high school in a few years."

"He'd better, or I'll kick his ass."

His half-feigned ire over Lane didn't bring me the usual amount of amusement. I forced a smile, though. The whole damn room was watching us, thanks to Emma.

"What?" Jack prompted. "Are you getting the empty-nester syndrome? You want to have more kids?"

"No! *Fuck* no! God, don't even joke about that."

"Good. Because I don't think Morgan would be up for round two. She's no spring chicken. You know?"

"I know, Jack. That's what I'm saying. We're *old*."

He snorted like he thought I was being sarcastic. "Speak for yourself."

"You just got offered an endorsement deal for muscle rub, Jack. You're fucking old, too."

Turning us, he grinned. "I've been using muscle rub since my twenties. All ballplayers do."

"Yeah, but the young ones don't make the commercials."

"Because they're selling cereal and video games," he countered.

"Exactly! *Young man* shit. They save the muscle rub commercials for the old guys."

His face scrunched up adorably, but I would not be wooed by his cuteness. This was serious.

"So, are you saying you *don't* want me to do the commercials?" he asked.

"No. If it's good money, do it." I shrugged, looking off over his shoulder and not at that damn face that just wrecked me when I got like this.

"Then what are you pissed off about? That I'm old?"

Fuck. I labored under a heavy breath and tugged at the back of his shirt sleeve for emphasis. "Yeah. I don't want us to be old."

"Well, what's the alternative? Being dead? Because we can't go backward, Max. That's not how it works," he said, sounding way too amused while I was having an emotional life crisis.

"I go backward every day when I look at you. That's the problem."

"I don't know what you mean, babe. Going to have to spit it out for the dumb athlete." He leaned in so we were eye to eye.

"You're not dumb. You know I hate it when you say that."

He canted his head, waiting patiently for me to gut myself in the middle of this stupid dance floor. Fuck it. The world had seen us fucking almost twenty years ago. What did I care if two hundred family and friends saw me get emotional?

"We've had a great life, Jack. Haven't we?"

He smiled and rested his forehead against mine. Bringing our joined hands up, he stroked my jaw, giving me a chaste kiss. "No. We've had the best life."

I was glad he was finally getting it. "Yeah. So, what am I going to do without you?"

He drew his head back. "What? Where am I going? Or...where are *you* going?"

"You're not going to live forever. How the hell am I supposed to live through my old age without you?"

There. I'd said it. Maybe he'd finally understand my dilemma. Maybe he'd...laugh his ass off at me?

"What the fuck is funny about that?" I demanded.

"Who the hell said I was dying?" he gasped.

"Well, you *will* someday."

"Why are you so convinced I'll die before you?"

It made no sense. The more serious I got, the more amused he looked. Something was wrong with this man.

"Everyone knows the miserable, crabby ones live forever and the good ones die young."

"Well, honey," he pulled me in closer, "I'm flattered you think I'm one of the good ones...."

"Of course, you're flattered, you conceited jackass," I pouted because he was so evading the point.

He brought our hands up and raised his index finger. "But...but I don't plan on dying anytime soon."

"It's not a fucking ball contract, Jack. Hate to tell you the whole thing about dying is that you don't get to negotiate it."

He leaned in and whispered, "You know you're one of the good ones, too."

I averted my eyes at the compliment. "No. I'm not."

"You have your moments."

And now my eyes were back on his, giving him the scowl he deserved. "So, I went from good to *momentarily* good. Thanks! See? I'm going to live to be ninety fucking years old."

"I hope so. Then I get forty more years of arguing over stupid shit like this with you."

"Now, you're just trying to piss me off," I growled as quietly as I could, so we'd look like we were, I don't know, actually fucking enjoying ourselves.

"Well, yeah." He laughed.

I shook my head, mentally counting to ten. "Too many fly balls to the head. You're starting to get dementia already. Next thing you know, the only endorsement deals you'll be getting are for *Life Alert* and those fucking walk-in bathtubs with the door on the side, and I'll have to spoon-feed you soup and change your man diapers."

My feet stuttered to a stop when his head rocked back, and a deep belly laugh tore from his chest. Heat crept up my neck. The daggers in my eyes waited to be unleashed.

"Well, I'm glad the thought of my heartache is *so hilarious!*"

"I can't help it." He leaned in to steal a kiss, but I deflected in time.

"Fuck off. And *not* the good fuck off."

I don't know when he started moving us again or when this had become the longest song on the planet. His warm lips dusted the shell of my ear, and I grit my teeth at the thrill it gave me. *We're mad at him*, I told myself. *Don't give in!*

"You look *so* crabby right now," he whispered.

I answered him with the murder-eyes he deserved, and the bastard smiled. His hand slid down the small of my back and pressed my ass, so our fronts were flush. I swallowed at the feel of the hard outline pressing into my belly.

His lips grazed the side of my cheek as he annunciated, "So. Unbelievably. Fucking crabby that we might have to sneak out of here."

The man was insane. I tried to scoff, but my amusement poked through. "You're fucking crazy."

"Crazy about you," he said in his bedroom voice, and kissed me.

"You don't worry about it at all?" I tried again.

His smile was adoring as he brushed my nose with his. "Every day."

All my tension left me and was replaced with guilt. I knew he meant it. "I'm sorry. I don't want to ruin the wedding for you."

"Max Spears, I love you even when you wear your heart on your sleeve. And I'll keep loving you whether you leave me first or if I have to go first."

My stomach knotted, and a lump ballooned in my throat. "Shut up, Jack."

I had to drop my face in the crook of his neck because now he really had made me cry. He wrapped his arm around me tight and rested his head against mine like he needed a moment too.

"Do you still have that old Circuit issue of Lainey's where I did that spread?" he asked.

What the hell kind of question was that at a time like this? My head popped up. "The one she wrote on?"

"Yeah." He chuckled.

"You fucking know I do. I wouldn't throw that away."

"Okay. Well, if I go first..."

"Quit saying that." I shivered.

"No. Just listen. If I go first, I want you to frame it and put it on your nightstand so I can still see you every morning when you wake up."

"What?"

He smiled and kissed the tip of my nose. "I love how you look in the morning."

I scoffed because that was just ridiculous...and completely fucking sweet. And damn it. I did *not* want to cry.

"And," he continued, "I'll make you a tape and put it in your nightstand as long as you promise not to listen to it unless I crappie off first."

Was this still a joke to him? I rolled my eyes.

"I don't need a fucking mixed tape to commemorate you."

"Nooo. I'll make you an audio tape of all the dirty and sweet and smart-ass things I like to say to you."

I waited for him to say the words I needed to hear, but...nothing. So, naturally, I exploded. "Well, thanks for fucking asking what I'd leave for you! See! You *are* going to leave me first."

"No." He chuckled. "I was waiting for you to ask me what I want you to leave me. It's what I want for my birthday this year."

Oh. Well, shit. I honestly had no idea.

"What?" I asked with bated breath, curious as to how he'd want to remember me.

"So, I still know that photographer who did *The Circuit* shoot for me."

"Yeah..."

"Well, it's only fair. If I go, you get my photo. If you go, I'll need one of you."

"I'm not posing nude for a photo shoot."

"I wasn't nude. There was a loincloth, if I remember correctly."

"Watch our old video when you miss me," I suggested.

"I don't want a video. I want a professional photo to frame."

I pursed my lips. "Then I'll frame a still of the video for you."

"I'm not putting a picture of us fucking on my nightstand."

"I'm too fucking old."

"*No.* You're not."

"*Yes. I am.*"

He lifted his chin and looked off across the room, giving a careless shrug. "Well, that's what I want."

After sixteen years with the man, I was an expert at picking up on the slight inflection of his voice that warned he had dug in his heels. He'd just turned the tables on me.

I sighed. "Jack, I'm almost twenty years older than you were in those photos, and I'm not a former pro athlete."

He shrugged again, his nose still tilted up. "Don't care. That's my death wish. Would you deprive a dying man?"

"Oh, for fuck's sake. Your birthday's only six weeks away. That doesn't give me much time to get in shape."

His pouty face turned into an evil mastermind smile in a heartbeat. "I like your shape...*all* your shapes."

"*No.*"

"I'll call her, and she can come do the shoot at the house, so you don't have to go anywhere."

"You're *not* serious. You're just screwing with me."

"I'm totally serious, and it's going to be great. I can't wait." He fucking beamed like a little kid getting a pony. It was...kind of terrifying.

"Nuh-uh." I shook my head, knowing I was already doomed. He'd made a love request, a sweet, sexy, romantic, remember-me-forever-gesture love request. He was my world, of course I'd do the ridiculous fucking old man photos.

God, damn it. The man knew how to play me.

Jack chuckled at my last refusal. I didn't understand how he could look so smug when I hadn't agreed yet.

"Why the fuck are you laughing?"

"Because you just said, '*yes.*'"

My chest expanded with an amused huff because he knew me so well. How could I be annoyed? "Well, you're not going to get your money's worth."

He squeezed the crap out of me and pressed a kiss to my neck. "Oh, I don't think so. You're going to be so crabby they'll be the hottest pictures ever taken."

"Fuck off." I laughed.

"You can show me the poses you're going to do later." He wriggled his brows.

"How much have you had to drink tonight?"

My grinning fool swept his nose across mine again and giggled. Oh, boy. That explained it all.

"Fine," I conceded. "Because you're not even going to remember this in the morning."

"Oh, I'll remember," he crooned at my lips, nipping one of them as he squeezed my ass.

"Hey," I snapped, drawing back to see how many people were actually watching us. "Would you quit that? I don't want a hard-on at our daughter's wedding."

He gave me a chaste kiss this time and grinned triumphantly. "I love you, baby. Thank you."

I shook my head, wondering how in the hell I was going to get his big sloppy ass home, and how his hangover was going to affect the quality of my breakfast. We leaned in on each other as the song wound down.

He started humming at the side of my neck. Man, he was way off-key, but then I heard him singing.

"Happy birthday to me...."

I cracked his ass hard, not giving a damn who was looking. He came up cackling with mischief, love, all my secrets, and our happy memories in his eyes.

With a full heart, I burst through my own laughter, "God, I hate you."

Dear Reader

Thank you for reading *The Shutout*. I hope you enjoyed Max and Jack's journey as much as I enjoyed writing it. I let it linger on epic love story length because I just couldn't part with cutting any of the moments.

I'm not huge on excessive f-bombs, but I let Max take over at some point—it seemed to fit his character. I'm afraid farming, the Army, and listening to too much Billy Connolly ruined any chance I had of writing like a lady.

The Fleetwood Mac and Stevie Nicks references could not be helped either as they became one of Jack's signatures, but I dare you to try listening to '*Secondhand News*' without shaking your hips.

Be good to each other.

Best wishes,
Dianna

About the author

Dianna Roman believes in laughter, happily-ever-afters, coffee, talking to yourself, hard work, and above all, love. She enjoys writing stories about characters who don't have this thing called life quite figured out yet.

Dianna lives with her daughter in the woods where sunsets and making happy memories are the reason her house may be a bit messy.

You can connect with Dianna at www.diannaroman.com